☑ S0-AQM-940

AGATHA CHRISTIE

The legendary author of eighty-five internationally bestselling mysteries, Dame Agatha has been delighting several hundred million readers for more than fifty years with her classic novels of deduction. Don't miss these other thrillers from the peerless creator of two of mystery fiction's greatest detectives: the incomparable Hercule Poirot and the dauntless Jane Marple.

Bantam Books by Agatha Christie
Ask your bookseller for the books you have missed

DEATH ON THE NILE
A HOLIDAY FOR MURDER
THE MOUSETRAP AND OTHER PLAYS
THE MYSTERIOUS AFFAIR AT STYLES
POIROT INVESTIGATES
POSTERN OF FATE
THE SECRET ADVERSARY
THE SEVEN DIALS MYSTERY
SLEEPING MURDER

AGATHA CHRISTIE

POIROT INVESTIGATES

BANTAM BOOKS

TORONTO • NEW YORK • LONDON • SYDNEY • AUCKLAND

*This edition contains the complete text
of the original hardcover edition.*
NOT ONE WORD HAS BEEN OMITTED.

RL 6, IL 14 and up

POIROT INVESTIGATES
*A Bantam Book / published by arrangement with
Dodd, Mead & Company, Inc.*

PRINTING HISTORY
Dodd, Mead edition published April 1925
American Mercury edition published September 1948
Bantam edition / November 1961
30 printings through February 1988

All rights reserved.
Copyright © 1923, 1924, 1925 by Dodd, Mead & Company, Inc.
Copyright © renewed 1953 by Agatha Christie Mallowan.
Cover art copyright © 1988 by John Alcorn.
No part of this book may be reproduced or transmitted
in any form or by any means, electronic or mechanical,
including photocopying, recording, or by any information
storage and retrieval system, without permission in writing from
the publisher.
For information address: Dodd, Mead & Company, Inc.,
71 Fifth Avenue, New York, N.Y. 10003.

ISBN 0-553-27001-X

Published simultaneously in the United States and Canada

*Bantam Books are published by Bantam Books, a division of
Bantam Doubleday Dell Publishing Group, Inc. Its trademark,
consisting of the words "Bantam Books" and the portrayal of
a rooster, is Registered in U.S. Patent and Trademark Office
and in other countries. Marca Registrada, Bantam Books,
666 Fifth Avenue, New York, New York 10103.*

PRINTED IN THE UNITED STATES OF AMERICA

KR   39 38 37 36 35 34 33 32 31

CONTENTS

POIROT
INVESTIGATES

I
THE ADVENTURE OF
"THE WESTERN STAR"

I was standing at the window of Poirot's rooms looking out idly on the street below.

"That's queer," I ejaculated suddenly beneath my breath.

"What is, *mon ami?*" asked Poirot placidly, from the depths of his comfortable chair.

"Deduce, Poirot, from the following facts! Here is a young lady, richly dressed—fashionable hat, magnificent furs. She is coming along slowly, looking up at the houses as she goes. Unknown to her, she is being shadowed by three men and a middle-aged woman. They have just been joined by an errand boy who points after the girl, gesticulating as he does so. What drama is this being played? Is the girl a crook, and are the shadowers detectives preparing to arrest her? Or are *they* the scoundrels, and are they plotting to attack an innocent victim? What does the great detective say?"

"The great detective, *mon ami,* chooses, as ever, the simplest course. He rises to see for himself." And my friend joined me at the window.

In a minute he gave vent to an amused chuckle.

"As usual, your facts are tinged with your incurable romanticism. That is Miss Mary Marvell, the film star. She is being followed by a bevy of admirers who have recognized her. And, *en passant,* my dear Hastings, she is quite aware of the fact!"

I laughed.

"So all is explained! But you get no marks for that, Poirot. It was a mere matter of recognition."

"*En vérité!* And how many times have you seen Mary Marvell on the screen, *mon cher?*"

1

I thought.

"About a dozen times perhaps."

"And I—once! Yet *I* recognize her, and *you* do not."

"She looks so different," I replied rather feebly.

"Ah! *Sacré!*" cried Poirot. "Is it that you expect her to promenade herself in the streets of London in a cowboy hat, or with bare feet, and a bunch of curls, as an Irish colleen? Always with you it is the non-essentials! Remember the case of the dancer, Valerie Saintclair."

I shrugged my shoulders, slightly annoyed.

"But console yourself, *mon ami,*" said Poirot, calming down. "All cannot be as Hercule Poirot! I know it well."

"You really have the best opinion of yourself of anyone I ever knew!" I cried, divided between amusement and annoyance.

"What will you? When one is unique, one knows it! And others share that opinion—even, if I mistake not, Miss Mary Marvell."

"What?"

"Without doubt. She is coming here."

"How do you make that out?"

"Very simply. This street, it is not aristocratic, *mon ami!* In it there is no fashionable doctor, no fashionable dentist—still less is there a fashionable milliner! But there *is* a fashionable detective. *Oui,* my friend, it is true—I am become the mode, the *dernier cri!* One says to another: *Comment?* You have lost your gold pencil-case? You must go to the little Belgian. He is too marvellous! Every one goes! *Courez!* And they arrive! In flocks, *mon ami!* With problems of the most foolish!" A bell rang below. "What did I tell you? That is Miss Marvell."

As usual, Poirot was right. After a short interval, the American film star was ushered in, and we rose to our feet.

Mary Marvell was undoubtedly one of the most popular actresses on the screen. She had only lately arrived in England in company with her husband, Gregory B. Rolf, also a film actor. Their marriage had taken place about a year ago in the States and this was their first visit to England. They had been given a great reception.

Every one was prepared to go mad over Mary Marvell, her wonderful clothes, her furs, her jewels, above all one jewel, the great diamond which had been nicknamed, to match its owner, "the Western Star." Much, true and untrue, had been written about this famous stone which was reported to be insured for the enormous sum of fifty thousand pounds.

All these details passed rapidly through my mind as I joined with Poirot in greeting our fair client.

Miss Marvell was small and slender, very fair and girl-ish-looking, with the wide innocent blue eyes of a child.

Poirot drew forward a chair for her, and she com-menced talking at once.

"You will probably think me very foolish, Monsieur Poirot, but Lord Cronshaw was telling me last night how wonderfully you cleared up the mystery of his neph-ew's death, and I felt that I just must have your advice. I dare say it's only a silly hoax—Gregory says so—but it's just worrying me to death."

She paused for breath. Poirot beamed encouragement.

"Proceed, Madame. You comprehend, I am still in the dark."

"It's these letters." Miss Marvell unclasped her hand-bag, and drew out three envelopes which she handed to Poirot.

The latter scrutinized them closely.

"Cheap paper—the name and address carefully printed. Let us see the inside." He drew out the enclosure.

I had joined him, and was leaning over his shoulder. The writing consisted of a single sentence, carefully printed like the envelope. It ran as follows:

"The great diamond which is the left eye of the god must return whence it came."

The second letter was couched in precisely the same terms, but the third was more explicit:

"You have been warned. You have not obeyed. Now the diamond will be taken from you. At the full of the moon, the two diamonds which are the left and right eye of the god shall return. So it is written."

"The first letter I treated as a joke," explained Miss Marvell. "When I got the second, I began to wonder.

The third one came yesterday, and it seemed to me that, after all, the matter might be more serious than I had imagined."

"I see they did not come by post, these letters."

"No; they were left by hand—by a *Chinaman*. That is what frightens me."

"Why?"

"Because it was from a Chink in San Francisco that Gregory bought the stone three years ago."

"I see, madame, that you believe the diamond referred to to be——"

" 'The Western Star,' " finished Miss Marvell. "That's so. At the same time, Gregory remembers that there was some story attached to the stone, but the Chink wasn't handing out any information. Gregory says he seemed just scared to death, and in a mortal hurry to get rid of the thing. He only asked about a tenth of its value. It was Greg's wedding present to me."

Poirot nodded thoughtfully.

"The story seems of an almost unbelievable romanticism. And yet—who knows? I pray of you, Hastings, hand me my little almanac."

I complied.

"*Voyons!*" said Poirot, turning the leaves. "When is the date of the full moon? Ah, Friday next. That is in three days' time. *Eh bien,* madame, you seek my advice —I give it to you. This *belle histoire* may be a hoax— but it may not! Therefore I counsel you to place the diamond in my keeping until after Friday next. Then we can take what steps we please."

A slight cloud passed over the actress's face, and she replied constrainedly:

"I'm afraid that's impossible."

"You have it with you—*hein?*" Poirot was watching her narrowly.

The girl hesitated a moment, then slipped her hand into the bosom of her gown, drawing out a long thin chain. She leaned forward, unclosing her hand. In the palm, a stone of fire, exquisitely set in platinum, lay and winked at us solemnly.

Poirot drew in his breath with a long hiss.

"*Épatant!*" he murmured. "You permit, madame?" He took the jewel in his own hand and scrutinized it keenly, then restored it to her with a little bow. "A magnificent stone—without a flaw. Ah, *cent tonnerres!* and you carry it about with you, *comme ça!*"

"No, no, I'm very careful really, Monsieur Poirot. As a rule it's locked up in my jewel-case, and left in the hotel safe deposit. We're staying at the *Magnificent,* you know. I just brought it along today for you to see."

"And you will leave it with me, *n'est-ce pas?* You will be advised by Papa Poirot?"

"Well, you see, it's this way, Monsieur Poirot. On Friday we're going down to Yardly Chase to spend a few days with Lord and Lady Yardly."

Her words awoke a vague echo of remembrance in my mind. Some gossip—what was it now? A few years ago Lord and Lady Yardly had paid a visit to the States, rumor had it that his lordship had rather gone the pace out there with the assistance of some lady friends—but surely there was something more, some gossip which coupled Lady Yardly's name with that of a "movie" star in California—why! it came to me in a flash! of course it was none other than Gregory B. Rolf.

"I'll let you into a little secret, Monsieur Poirot," Miss Marvell was continuing. "We've got a deal on with Lord Yardly. There's some chance of our arranging to film a play down there in his ancestral pile."

"At Yardly Chase?" I cried, interested. "Why, it's one of the show places of England."

Miss Marvell nodded.

"I guess it's the real old feudal stuff all right. But he wants a pretty stiff price, and of course I don't know yet whether the deal will go through, but Greg and I always like to combine business with pleasure."

"But—I demand pardon if I am dense, madame—surely it is possible to visit Yardly Chase without taking the diamond with you?"

A shrewd, hard look came into Miss Marvell's eyes which belied their childlike appearance. She looked suddenly a good deal older.

"I want to wear it down there."

"Surely," I said suddenly, "there are some very famous jewels in the Yardly collection, a large diamond amongst them?"

"That's so," said Miss Marvell briefly.

I heard Poirot murmur beneath his breath: "Ah, *c'est comme ça!*" Then he said aloud, with his usual uncanny luck in hitting the bull's-eye (he dignifies it by the name of psychology): "Then you are without doubt already acquainted with Lady Yardly, or perhaps your husband is?"

"Gregory knew her when she was out West three years ago," said Miss Marvell. She hesitated a moment, and then added abruptly: "Do either of you ever see *Society Gossip?*"

We both pleaded guilty rather shamefacedly.

"I asked because in this week's number there is an article on famous jewels, and it's really very curious——" She broke off.

I rose, went to the table at the other side of the room and returned with the paper in question in my hand. She took it from me, found the article, and began to read aloud:

"... Amongst other famous stones may be included the Star of the East, a diamond in the possession of the Yardly family. An ancestor of the present Lord Yardly brought it back with him from China, and a romantic story is said to attach to it. According to this, the stone was once the right eye of a temple god. Another diamond, exactly similar in form and size, formed the left eye, and the story goes that this jewel, too, would in course of time be stolen. 'One eye shall go West, the other East, till they shall meet once more. Then, in triumph shall they return to the god.' It is a curious coincidence that there is at the present time a stone corresponding closely in description with this one, and known as 'the Star of the West,' or 'the Western Star.' It is the property of the celebrated film actress, Miss Mary Marvell. A comparison of the two stones would be interesting."

I stopped.

"*Épatant!*" murmured Poirot. "Without doubt a ro-

mance of the first water." He turned to Mary Marvell.
"And you are not afraid, madame? You have no superstitious terrors? You do not fear to introduce these two
Siamese twins to each other lest a Chinaman should appear and, hey presto! whisk them both back to China?"

His tone was mocking, but I fancied that an undercur-
rent of seriousness lay beneath it.

"I don't believe that Lady Yardly's diamond is anything
like as good a stone as mine," said Miss Marvell. "Anyway, I'm going to see."

What more Poirot would have said I do not know, for
at that moment the door flew open, and a splendid-looking
man strode into the room. From his crisply curling black
head, to the tips of his patent-leather boots, he was a
hero fit for romance.

"I said I'd call round for you, Mary," said Gregory
Rolf, "and here I am. Well, what does Monsieur Poirot
say to our little problem? Just one big hoax, same as I
do?"

Poirot smiled up at the big actor. They made a ridiculous contrast.

"Hoax or no hoax, Mr. Rolf," he said dryly, "I have
advised madame your wife not to take the jewel with
her to Yardly Chase on Friday."

"I'm with you there, sir. I've already said so to Mary.
But there! She's a woman through and through, and I
guess she can't bear to think of another woman outshining
her in the jewel line."

"What nonsense, Gregory!" said Mary Marvell sharply.
But she flushed angrily.

Poirot shrugged his shoulders.

"Madame, I have advised. I can do no more. *C'est fini.*"
He bowed them both to the door.

"Ah! *la la,*" he observed, returning. "*Histoire de femmes!* The good husband, he hit the nail on the head—
tout de même, he was not tactful! Assuredly not."

I imparted to him my vague remembrances, and he
nodded vigorously.

"So I thought. All the same, there is something curious
underneath all this. With your permission, *mon ami,* I

will take the air. Await my return, I beg of you. I shall not be long."

I was half asleep in my chair when the landlady tapped on the door, and put her head in.

"It's another lady to see Mr. Poirot, sir. I've told her he was out, but she says as how she'll wait, seeing as she's come up from the country."

"Oh, show her in here, Mrs. Murchison. Perhaps I can do something for her."

In another moment the lady had been ushered in. My heart gave a leap as I recognized her. Lady Yardly's portrait had figured too often in the Society papers to allow her to remain unknown.

"Do sit down, Lady Yardly," I said, drawing forward a chair. "My friend Poirot is out, but I know for a fact that he'll be back very shortly."

She thanked me and sat down. A very different type, this, from Miss Mary Marvell. Tall, dark, with flashing eyes, and a pale proud face—yet something wistful in the curves of the mouth.

I felt a desire to rise to the occasion. Why not? In Poirot's presence I have frequently felt a difficulty—I do not appear at my best. And yet there is no doubt that I, too, possess the deductive sense in a marked degree. I leant forward on a sudden impulse.

"Lady Yardly," I said, "I know why you have come here. You have received blackmailing letters about the diamond."

There was no doubt as to my bolt having shot home. She stared at me open-mouthed, all color banished from her cheeks.

"You know?" she gasped. "How?"

I smiled.

"By a perfectly logical process. If Miss Marvell has had warning letters——"

"Miss Marvell? She has been here?"

"She has just left. As I was saying, if she, as the holder of one of the twin diamonds, has received a mysterious series of warnings, you, as the holder of the other stone, must necessarily have done the same. You see how simple it is? I am right, then, you have received these strange communications also?"

For a moment she hesitated, as though in doubt whether to trust me or not, then she bowed her head in assent with a little smile.

"That is so," she acknowledged.

"Were yours, too, left by hand—by a Chinaman?"

"No, they came by post; but, tell me, has Miss Marvell undergone the same experience, then?"

I recounted to her the events of the morning. She listened attentively.

"It all fits in. My letters are the duplicates of hers. It is true that they came by post, but there is a curious perfume impregnating them—something in the nature of joss-stick—that at once suggested the East to me. What does it all mean?"

I shook my head.

"That is what we must find out. You have the letters with you? We might learn something from the postmarks."

"Unfortunately I destroyed them. You understand, at the time I regarded it as some foolish joke. Can it be true that some Chinese gang are really trying to recover the diamonds? It seems too incredible."

We went over the facts again and again, but could get no further towards the elucidation of the mystery. At last Lady Yardly rose.

"I really don't think I need wait for Monsieur Poirot. You can tell him all this, can't you? Thank you so much, Mr.——"

She hesitated, her hand outstretched.

"Captain Hastings."

"Of course! How stupid of me. You're a friend of the Cavendishes, aren't you? It was Mary Cavendish who sent me to Monsieur Poirot."

When my friend returned, I enjoyed telling him the tale of what had occurred during his absence. He cross-questioned me rather sharply over the details of our conversation and I could read between the lines that he was not best pleased to have been absent. I also fancied that the dear old fellow was just the least inclined to be jealous.

It had become rather a pose with him to consistently be-
little my abilities, and I think he was chagrined at finding no loophole for criticism. I was secretly rather pleased
with myself, though I tried to conceal the fact for fear
of irritating him. In spite of his idiosyncrasies, I was
deeply attached to my quaint little friend.

"Bien!" he said at length, with a curious look on his
face. "The plot develops. Pass me, I pray you, that 'Peerage' on the top shelf there." He turned the leaves. "Ah,
here we are! 'Yardly . . . 10th viscount, served South
African War' . . . *tout ça n'a pas d'importance* . . . 'mar.
1907 Hon. Maude Stopperton, fourth daughter of 3rd
Baron Cotteril' . . . um, um, um, . . . 'has iss. two daugh-
ters, born 1908, 1910. . . . Clubs . . . residences.' . . .
Voilà, that does not tell us much. But to-morrow morning
we see him *milord!"*

"What?"

"Yes. I telegraphed him."

"I thought you had washed your hands of the case?"

"I am not acting for Miss Marvell since she refuses
to be guided by my advice. What I do now is for my
own satisfaction—the satisfaction of Hercule Poirot! Decidedly, I must have a finger in this pie."

"And you calmly wire Lord Yardly to dash up to
town just to suit your convenience. He won't be pleased."

"Au contraire, if I preserve for him his family diamond, he ought to be very grateful."

"Then you really think there is a chance of its being
stolen?" I asked eagerly.

"Almost a certainty," replied Poirot placidly. "Everything points that way."

"But how——"

Poirot stopped my eager questions with an airy gesture
of the hand.

"Not now, I pray you. Let us not confuse the mind.
And observe that 'Peerage'—how you have replaced him!
See you not that the tallest books go in the top shelf,
the next tallest in the row beneath, and so on. Thus
we have order, *method,* which, as I have often told you,
Hastings——"

"Exactly," I said hastily, and put the offending volume in its proper place.

Lord Yardly turned out to be a cheery, loud-voiced sportsman with a rather red face, but with a good-humored bonhomie about him that was distinctly attractive and made up for any lack of mentality.

"Extraordinary business this, Monsieur Poirot. Can't make head or tail of it. Seems my wife's been getting odd kinds of letters, and that this Miss Marvell's had 'em too. What does it all mean?"

Poirot handed him the copy of the *Society Gossip*.

"First, *milord,* I would ask if these facts are substantially correct?"

The peer took it. His face darkened with anger as he read.

"Damned nonsense!" he spluttered. "There's never been any romantic story attaching to the diamond. It came from India originally, I believe. I never heard of all this Chinese god stuff."

"Still, the stone *is* known as 'The Star of the East.' "

"Well what if it is?" he demanded wrathfully.

Poirot smiled a little, but made no direct reply.

"What I would ask you to do, *milord,* is to place yourself in my hands. If you do so unreservedly, I have great hopes of averting the catastrophe."

"Then you think there's actually something in these wildcat tales?"

"Will you do as I ask you?"

"Of course I will, but——"

"Bien! Then permit that I ask you a few questions. This affair of Yardly Chase, is it, as you say, all fixed up between you and Mr. Rolf?"

"Oh, he told you about it, did he? No, there's nothing settled." He hesitated, the brick-red color of his face deepening. "Might as well get the thing straight. I've made rather an ass of myself in many ways, Monsieur Poirot— and I'm head over ears in debt—but I want to pull up. I'm fond of the kids, and I want to straighten things up, and be able to live on at the old place. Gregory Rolf is offering me big money—enough to set me on my feet again. I don't want to do it—I hate the thought of all that crowd play-acting round the Chase—but I may have to, unless—" He broke off.

Poirot eyed him keenly. "You have, then, another string to your bow? Permit that I make a guess? It is to sell the Star of the East?"

Lord Yardly nodded. "That's it. It's been in the family for some generations, but it's not entailed. Still, it's not the easiest thing in the world to find a purchaser. Hoffberg, the Hatton Garden man, is on the look-out for a likely customer, but he'll have to find one soon, or it's a washout."

"One more question, *permettez*—Lady Yardly, which plan does she approve?"

"Oh, she's bitterly opposed to my selling the jewel. You know what women are. She's all for this film stunt."

"I comprehend," said Poirot. He remained a moment or so in thought, then rose briskly to his feet. "You return to Yardly Chase at once? *Bien!* Say no word to anyone—to *anyone*, mind—but expect us there this evening. We will arrive shortly after five."

"All right, but I don't see——"

"*Ça n'a pas d'importance*," said Poirot kindly. "You will find that I preserve for you your diamond, *n'est-ce pas?*"

"Yes, but——"

"Then do as I say."

A sadly bewildered nobleman left the room.

It was half-past five when we arrived at Yardly Chase, and followed the dignified butler to the old paneled hall with its fire of blazing logs. A pretty picture met our eyes: Lady Yardly and her two children, the mother's proud dark head bent down over the two fair ones. Lord Yardly stood near, smiling down on them.

"Monsieur Poirot and Captain Hastings," announced the butler.

Lady Yardly looked up with a start, her husband came forward uncertainly, his eyes seeking instruction from Poirot. The little man was equal to the occasion.

"All my excuses! It is that I investigate still this affair

of Miss Marvell's. She comes to you on Friday, does she not? I make a little tour first to make sure that all is secure. Also I wanted to ask of Lady Yardly if she recollected at all the postmarks on the letters she received?"

Lady Yardly shook her head regretfully. "I'm afraid I don't. It is stupid of me. But, you see, I never dreamt of taking them seriously."

"You'll stay the night?" said Lord Yardly.

"Oh, *milord*, I fear to incommode you. We have left our bags at the inn."

"That's all right." Lord Yardly had his cue. "We'll send down for them. No, no—no trouble, I assure you."

Poirot permitted himself to be persuaded, and sitting down by Lady Yardly, began to make friends with the children. In a short time they were all romping together, and had dragged me into the game.

"Vous êtes bonne mère," said Poirot, with a gallant little bow, as the children were removed reluctantly by a stern nurse.

Lady Yardly smoothed her ruffled hair.

"I adore them," she said with a little catch in her voice.

"And they you—with reason!" Poirot bowed again.

A dressing-gong sounded, and we rose to go up to our rooms. At that moment the butler entered with a telegram on a salver which he handed to Lord Yardly. The latter tore it open with a brief word of apology. As he read it he stiffened visibly.

With an ejaculation, he handed it to his wife. Then he glanced at my friend.

"Just a minute, Monsieur Poirot. I feel you ought to know about this. It's from Hoffberg. He thinks he's found a customer for the diamond—an American, sailing for the States to-morrow. They're sending down a chap to-night to vet the stone. By Jove, though, if this goes through—" Words failed him.

Lady Yardly had turned away. She still held the telegram in her hand.

"I wish you wouldn't sell it, George," she said, in a low voice. "It's been in the family so long." She waited, as though for a reply, but when none came her face hard-

ened. She shrugged her shoulders. "I must go and dress.
I suppose I had better display 'the goods.'" She turned
to Poirot with a slight grimace.

"It's one of the most hideous necklaces that was ever
designed! George has always promised to have the stones
reset for me, but it's never been done." She left the
room.

Half an hour later, we three were assembled in the
great drawing-room awaiting the lady. It was already a
few minutes past the dinner hour.

Suddenly there was a low rustle, and Lady Yardly appeared framed in the doorway, a radiant figure in a long
white shimmering dress. Round the column of her neck
was a rivulet of fire. She stood there with one hand just
touching the necklace.

"Behold the sacrifice," she said gaily. Her ill humor
seemed to have vanished. "Wait while I turn the big light
on and you shall feast your eyes on the ugliest necklace
in England."

The switches were just outside the door. As
she stretched out her hand to them, the incredible thing
happened. Suddenly without any warning, every light was
extinguished, the door banged, and from the other side
of it came a long-drawn piercing woman's scream.

"My God!" cried Lord Yardly. "That was Maude's
voice! What has happened?"

We rushed blindly for the door, cannoning into each
other in the darkness. It was some minutes before we
could find it. What a sight met our eyes! Lady Yardly
lay senseless on the marble floor, a crimson mark on her
white throat where the necklace had been wrenched from
her neck.

As we bent over her, uncertain for the moment whether
she were dead or alive, her eyelids opened.

"The Chinaman," she whispered painfully. "The Chinaman—the side door."

Lord Yardly sprang up with an oath. I accompanied
him, my heart beating wildly. The Chinaman again! The
side door in question was a small one in the angle of
the wall, not more than a dozen yards from the scene

of the tragedy. As we reached it, I gave a cry. There, just short of the threshold, lay the glittering necklace, evidently dropped by the thief in the panic of his flight. I swooped joyously down on it. Then I uttered another cry which Lord Yardly echoed. For in the middle of the necklace was a great gap. The Star of the East was missing!

"That settles it," I breathed. "These were no ordinary thieves. This one stone was all they wanted."

"But how did the fellow get in?"

"Through this door."

"But it's always locked."

I shook my head. "It's not locked now. See." I pulled it open as I spoke.

As I did so something fluttered to the ground. I picked it up. It was a piece of silk, and the embroidery was unmistakable. It had been torn from a Chinaman's robe.

"In his haste it caught in the door," I explained. "Come, hurry. He cannot have gone far as yet."

But in vain we hunted and searched. In the pitch darkness of the night, the thief had found it easy to make his getaway. We returned reluctantly, and Lord Yardly sent off one of the footmen post-haste to fetch the police.

Lady Yardly, aptly ministered to by Poirot, who is as good as a woman in these matters, was sufficiently recovered to be able to tell her story.

"I was just going to turn on the other light," she said, "when a man sprang on me from behind. He tore my necklace from my neck with such force that I fell headlong to the floor. As I fell I saw him disappearing through the side door. Then I realized by the pig-tail and the embroidered robe that he was a Chinaman." She stopped with a shudder.

The butler reappeared. He spoke in a low voice to Lord Yardly.

"A gentleman from Mr. Hoffberg's, m'lord. He says you expect him."

"Good heavens!" cried the distracted nobleman. "I must see him, I suppose. No, not here, Mullings, in the library."

I drew Poirot aside.

"Look here, my dear fellow, hadn't we better get back to London?"

"You think so, Hastings? Why?"

"Well,"—I coughed delicately—"things haven't gone very well, have they? I mean, you tell Lord Yardly to place himself in your hands and all will be well—and then the diamond vanishes from under your very nose!"

"True," said Poirot, rather crestfallen. "It was not one of my most striking triumphs."

This way of describing events almost caused me to smile, but I stuck to my guns.

"So, having—pardon the expression—rather made a mess of things, don't you think it would be more graceful to leave immediately?"

"And the dinner, the without doubt excellent dinner, that the *chef* of Lord Yardly has prepared?"

"Oh, what's dinner!" I said impatiently.

Poirot held up his hands in horror.

"Mon Dieu! It is that in this country you treat the affairs gastronomic with a criminal indifference."

"There's another reason why we should get back to London as soon as possible," I continued.

"What is that, my friend?"

"The other diamond," I said, lowering my voice. "Miss Marvell's."

"Eh bien, what of it?"

"Don't you see?" His unusual obtuseness annoyed me. What had happened to his usually keen wits? "They've got one, now they'll go for the other."

"Tiens!" cried Poirot, stepping back a pace and regarding me with admiration. "But your brain marches to a marvel, my friend! Figure to yourself that for the moment I had not thought of that! But there is plenty of time. The full of the moon, it is not until Friday."

I shook my head dubiously. The full of the moon theory left me entirely cold. I had my way with Poirot, however, and we departed immediately, leaving behind us a note of explanation and apology for Lord Yardly.

My idea was to go at once to the *Magnificent,* and relate to Miss Marvell what had occurred, but Poirot vetoed the plan, and insisted that the morning would be time enough. I gave in rather grudgingly.

In the morning Poirot seemed strangely disinclined to stir out. I began to suspect that, having made a mistake to start with, he was singularly loath to proceed with the case. In answer to my persuasions, he pointed out, with admirable common sense, that as the details of the affair at Yardly Chase were already in the morning papers the Rolfs would know quite as much as we could tell them. I gave way unwillingly.

Events proved my forebodings to be justified. About two o'clock, the telephone rang. Poirot answered it. He listened for some moments, then with a brief *"Bien, j'y serai"* he rang off, and turned to me.

"What do you think, *mon ami?*" He looked half ashamed, half excited. "The diamond of Miss Marvell, it has been stolen."

"What?" I cried, springing up. "And what about the 'full of the moon' now?" Poirot hung his head. "When did this happen?"

"This morning, I understand."

I shook my head sadly. "If only you had listened to me. You see I was right."

"It appears so, *mon ami,*" said Poirot cautiously. "Appearances are deceptive, they say, but it certainly appears so."

As we hurried in a taxi to the *Magnificent,* I puzzled out the true inwardness of the scheme.

"That 'full of the moon' idea was clever. The whole point of it was to get us to concentrate on the Friday, and so be off our guard beforehand. It is a pity you did not realize that."

"Ma foi!" said Poirot airily, his nonchalance quite restored after its brief eclipse. "One cannot think of everything!"

I felt sorry for him. He did so hate failure of any kind.

"Cheer up," I said consolingly. "Better luck next time."

At the *Magnificent,* we were ushered at once into the manager's office. Gregory Rolf was there with two men from Scotland Yard. A pale-faced clerk sat opposite them.

Rolf nodded as we entered.

"We're getting to the bottom of it," he said. "But it's almost unbelievable. How the guy had the nerve I can't think."

A very few minutes sufficed to give us the facts. Mr. Rolf had gone out of the hotel at 11.15. At 11.30, a gentleman, so like him in appearance as to pass muster, entered the hotel and demanded the jewel-case from the safe deposit. He duly signed the receipt, remarking carelessly as he did so: "Looks a bit different from my ordinary one, but I hurt my hand getting out of the taxi." The clerk merely smiled and remarked that he saw very little difference. Rolf laughed and said: "Well, don't run me in as a crook this time, anyway. I've been getting threatening letters from a Chinaman, and the worst of it is I look rather like a Chink myself—it's something about the eyes."

"I looked at him," said the clerk who was telling us this, "and I saw at once what he meant. The eyes slanted up at the corners like an Oriental's. I'd never noticed it before."

"Darn it all, man," roared Gregory Rolf, leaning forward, "do you notice it now?"

The man looked up at him and started.

"No, sir," he said. "I can't say that I do." And indeed there was nothing even remotely Oriental about the frank brown eyes that looked into ours.

The Scotland Yard man grunted. "Bold customer. Thought the eyes might be noticed, and took the bull by the horns to disarm suspicion. He must have watched you out of the hotel, sir, and nipped in as soon as you were well away."

"What about the jewel-case?" I asked.

"It was found in a corridor of the hotel. Only one thing had been taken—'the Western Star.'"

We stared at each other—the whole thing was so bizarre, so unreal.

Poirot hopped briskly to his feet. "I have not been of much use, I fear," he said regretfully. "Is it permitted to see Madame?"

"I guess she's prostrated with the shock," explained Rolf.

"Then perhaps I might have a few words alone with you, monsieur?"

"Certainly."

In about five minutes Poirot reappeared.

"Now, my friend," he said gaily. "To a post office. I have to send a telegram."

"Who to?"

"Lord Yardly." He discounted further inquiries by slipping his arm through mine. "Come, come, *mon ami*. I know all that you feel about this miserable business. I have not distinguished myself! You, in my place, might have distinguished yourself! *Bien!* All is admitted. Let us forget it and have lunch."

It was about four o'clock when we entered Poirot's rooms. A figure rose from a chair by the window. It was Lord Yardly. He looked haggard and distraught.

"I got your wire and came up at once. Look here, I've been round to Hoffberg, and they know nothing about that man of theirs last night, or the wire either. Do you think that——"

Poirot held up his hand.

"My excuses! I sent that wire, and hired the gentleman in question."

"*You*—but why? What?" The nobleman spluttered impotently.

"My little idea was to bring things to a head," explained Poirot placidly.

"Bring things to a head! Oh, my God!" cried Lord Yardly.

"And the ruse succeeded," said Poirot cheerfully. "Therefore, *milord*, I have much pleasure in returning you—this!" With a dramatic gesture he produced a glittering object. It was a great diamond.

"The Star of the East," gasped Lord Yardly. "But I don't understand——"

"No?" said Poirot. "It makes no matter. Believe me, it was necessary for the diamond to be stolen. I promised you that it should be preserved to you, and I have kept my word. You must permit me to keep my little secret. Convey, I beg of you, the assurances of my deepest respect to Lady Yardly, and tell her how pleased I am to be able to restore her jewel to her. What *beau temps,* is it not? Good day, *milord.*"

And smiling and talking, the amazing little man conducted the bewildered nobleman to the door. He returned gently rubbing his hands.

"Poirot," I said. "Am I quite demented?"

"No, *mon ami,* but you are, as always, in a mental fog."

"How did you get the diamond?"

"From Mr. Rolf."

"Rolf?"

"*Mais oui!* The warning letters, the Chinaman, the article in *Society Gossip,* all sprang from the ingenious brain of Mr. Rolf! The two diamonds, supposed to be so miraculously alike—bah! they did not exist. There was only *one* diamond, my friend! Originally in the Yardly collection, for three years it has been in the possession of Mr. Rolf. He stole it this morning with the assistance of a touch of grease paint at the corner of each eye! Ah, I must see him on the film, he is indeed an artist, *celui-là!*"

"But why did he steal his own diamond?" I asked, puzzled.

"For many reasons. To begin with, Lady Yardly was getting restive."

"Lady Yardly?"

"You comprehend she was left much alone in California. Her husband was amusing himself elsewhere. Mr. Rolf was handsome, he had an air about him of romance. But *au fond,* he is very business-like, *ce monsieur!* He made love to Lady Yardly, and then he blackmailed her. I taxed the lady with the truth the other night, and she admitted it. She swore that she had only been indiscreet, and I believe her. But, undoubtedly, Rolf had letters of hers that could be twisted to bear a different interpretation. Terrified by the threat of a divorce, and the prospect of being separated from her children, she agreed to all he wished. She had no money of her own, and she was forced to permit him to substitute a paste replica for the real stone. The coincidence of the date of the appearance of 'the Western Star' struck me at once. All goes well. Lord Yardly prepares to range himself—to settle down. And then comes the menace of the possible sale of the diamond. The substitution will be discovered. Without doubt she writes off frantically to Gregory Rolf who has just arrived in England. He soothes her by promising to arrange all—and prepares for a double robbery. In this way he will quiet the lady, who might conceivably tell all to her husband, an affair which would not suit our blackmailer at all, he will have £50,000 insurance money (aha, you had forgotten that!), and he will still have the diamond! At this point I put my finger in the pie. The arrival of a diamond expert is announced. Lady Yardly, as I felt sure she would, immediately arranges a robbery—and does it very well too! But Hercule Poirot, he sees nothing but facts. What happens in actuality? The lady switches off the light, bangs the door, throws the necklace down the passage, and screams. She has already wrenched out the diamond with pliers upstairs——"

"But we saw the necklace round her neck!" I objected.

"I demand pardon, my friend. Her hand concealed the part of it where the gap would have shown. To place a piece of silk in the door beforehand is child's play! Of course, as soon as Rolf read of the robbery, he arranged his own little comedy. And very well he played it!"

"What did you say to him?" I asked with lively curiosity.

"I said to him that Lady Yardly had told her husband all, that I was empowered to recover the jewel, and that if it were not immediately handed over proceedings would be taken. Also a few more little lies which occurred to me. He was as wax in my hands!"

I pondered the matter.

"It seems a little unfair on Mary Marvell. She has lost her diamond through no fault of her own."

"Bah!" said Poirot brutally. "She has a magnificent advertisement. That is all she cares for, that one! Now the other, she is different. *Bonne mère, très femme!*"

"Yes," I said doubtfully, hardly sharing Poirot's views on femininity. "I suppose it was Rolf who sent her the duplicate letters."

"Pas du tout," said Poirot briskly. "She came by the advice of Mary Cavendish to seek my aid in her dilemma. Then she heard that Mary Marvell, whom she knew to be her enemy, had been here, and she changed her mind, jumping at a pretext that *you,* my friend, offered her. A very few questions sufficed to show me that *you* told her of the letters, not she you! She jumped at the chance your words offered."

"I don't believe it," I cried, stung.

"Si, si, mon ami, it is a pity that you study not the psychology. She told you that the letters were destroyed? Oh, la la, *never* does a woman destroy a letter if she can avoid it! Not even if it would be more prudent to do so!"

"It's all very well," I said, my anger rising, "but you've made a perfect fool of me! From beginning to end! No, it's all very well to try to explain it away afterwards. There really is a limit!"

"But you were so enjoying yourself, my friend. I had not the heart to shatter your illusions."

"It's no good. You've gone a bit too far this time."

"Mon Dieu! but how you enrage yourself for nothing, *mon ami!"*

"I'm fed up!" I went out, banging the door. Poirot had made an absolute laughing-stock of me. I decided he needed a sharp lesson. I would let some time elapse before I forgave him. He had encouraged me to make a perfect fool of myself!

II
THE TRAGEDY AT
MARSDON MANOR

I had been called away from town for a few days, and on my return found Poirot in the act of strapping up his small valise.

"*A la bonne heure,* Hastings. I feared you would not have returned in time to accompany me."

"You are called away on a case, then?"

"Yes, though I am bound to admit that, on the face of it, the affair does not seem promising. The Northern Union Insurance Company have asked me to investigate the death of a Mr. Maltravers who a few weeks ago insured his life with them for the large sum of fifty thousand pounds."

"Yes?" I said, much interested.

"There was, of course, the usual suicide clause in the policy. In the event of his committing suicide within a year the premiums would be forfeited. Mr. Maltravers was duly examined by the Company's own doctor, and although he was a man slightly past the prime of life was passed as being in quite sound health. However, on Wednesday last—the day before yesterday—the body of Mr. Maltravers was found in the grounds of his house in Essex, Marsdon Manor, and the cause of his death is described as some kind of internal hemorrhage. That in itself would be nothing remarkable, but sinister rumors as to Mr. Maltravers' financial position have been in the air of late, and the Northern Union have ascertained beyond any possible doubt that the deceased gentleman stood upon the verge of bankruptcy. Now that alters matters considerably. Maltravers had a beautiful young wife, and it is suggested that he got together all the ready money he could for the purpose of paying the premiums on a life

23

insurance for his wife's benefit, and then committed suicide. Such a thing is not uncommon. In any case, my friend Alfred Wright, who is a director of the Northern Union, has asked me to investigate the facts of the case, but, as I told him, I am not very hopeful of success. If the cause of the death had been heart failure, I should have been more sanguine. Heart failure may always be translated as the inability of the local G. P. to discover what his patient really did die of, but a hemorrhage seems fairly definite. Still, we can but make some necessary inquiries. Five minutes to pack your bag, Hastings, and we will take a taxi to Liverpool Street."

About an hour later, we alighted from a Great Eastern train at the little station of Marsdon Leigh. Inquiries at the station yielded the information that Marsdon Manor was about a mile distant. Poirot decided to walk, and we betook ourselves along the main street.

"What is our plan of campaign?" I asked.

"First I will call upon the doctor. I have ascertained that there is only one doctor in Marsdon Leigh, Dr. Ralph Bernard. Ah, here we are at his house."

The house in question was a kind of superior cottage, standing back a little from the road. A brass plate on the gate bore the doctor's name. We passed up the path and rang the bell.

We proved to be fortunate in our call. It was the doctor's consulting hour, and for the moment there were no patients waiting for him. Dr. Bernard was an elderly man, high-shouldered and stooping, with a pleasant vagueness of manner.

Poirot introduced himself and explained the purpose of our visit, adding that Insurance Companies were bound to investigate fully in a case of this kind.

"Of course, of course," said Dr. Bernard vaguely. "I suppose, as he was such a rich man, his life was insured for a big sum?"

"You consider him a rich man, doctor?"

The doctor looked rather surprised.

"Was he not? He kept two cars, you know, and Marsdon Manor is a pretty big place to keep up, although I believe he bought it very cheap."

"I understand that he had had considerable losses of late," said Poirot, watching the doctor narrowly.

The latter, however, merely shook his head sadly.

"Is that so? Indeed. It is fortunate for his wife, then, that there is this life insurance. A very beautiful and charming young creature, but terribly unstrung by this sad catastrophe. A mass of nerves, poor thing. I have tried to spare her all I can, but of course the shock was bound to be considerable."

"You have been attending Mr. Maltravers recently?"

"My dear sir, I never attended him."

"What?"

"I understand Mr. Maltravers was a Christian Scientist —or something of that kind."

"But you examined the body?"

"Certainly. I was fetched by one of the under-gardeners."

"And the cause of death was clear?"

"Absolutely. There was blood on the lips, but most of the bleeding must have been internal."

"Was he still lying where he had been found?"

"Yes, the body had not been touched. He was lying on the edge of a small plantation. He had evidently been out shooting rooks, a small rook rifle lay beside him. The hemorrhage must have occurred quite suddenly. Gastric ulcer, without a doubt."

"No question of his having been shot, eh?"

"My dear sir!"

"I demand pardon," said Poirot humbly. "But, if my memory is not at fault, in the case of a recent murder, the doctor first gave a verdict of heart failure—altering it when the local constable pointed out that there was a bullet wound through the head!"

"You will not find any bullet wounds on the body of Mr. Maltravers," said Dr. Bernard dryly. "Now, gentlemen, if there is nothing further——"

We took the hint.

"Good morning, and many thanks to you, doctor, for so kindly answering our questions. By the way, you saw no need for an autopsy?"

"Certainly not." The doctor became quite apoplectic.

"The cause of death was clear, and in my profession we see no need to distress unduly the relatives of a dead patient."

And, turning, the doctor slammed the door sharply in our faces.

"And what do you think of Dr. Bernard, Hastings?" inquired Poirot, as we proceeded on our way to the Manor.

"Rather an old ass."

"Exactly. Your judgments of character are always profound, my friend."

I glanced at him uneasily, but he seemed perfectly serious. A twinkle, however, came into his eye, and he added slyly:

"That is to say, when there is no question of a beautiful woman!"

I looked at him coldly.

On our arrival at the Manor-house, the door was opened to us by a middle-aged parlormaid. Poirot handed her his card, and a letter from the Insurance Company for Mrs. Maltravers. She showed us into a small morning-room, and retired to tell her mistress. About ten minutes elapsed, and then the door opened, and a slender figure in widow's weeds stood upon the threshold.

"Monsieur Poirot?" she faltered.

"Madame!" Poirot sprang gallantly to his feet and hastened towards her. "I cannot tell you how I regret to derange you in this way. But what will you? *Les affaires* —they know no mercy."

Mrs. Maltravers permitted him to lead her to a chair. Her eyes were red with weeping, but the temporary disfigurement could not conceal her extraordinary beauty. She was about twenty-seven or -eight, and very fair, with large blue eyes and a pretty pouting mouth.

"It is something about my husband's insurance, is it? But must I be bothered *now*—so soon?"

"Courage, my dear madame. Courage! You see, your late husband insured his life for rather a large sum, and in such a case the Company always has to satisfy itself as to a few details. They have empowered me to act for them. You can rest assured that I will do all in my power to render the matter not too unpleasant for you. Will you re-count to me briefly the sad events of Wednesday?"

"I was changing for tea when my maid came up—one of the gardeners had just run to the house. He had found——"

Her voice trailed away. Poirot pressed her hand sympathetically.

"I comprehend. Enough! You had seen your husband earlier in the afternoon?"

"Not since lunch. I had walked down to the village for some stamps, and I believe he was out pottering round the grounds."

"Shooting rooks, eh?"

"Yes, he usually took his little rook rifle with him, and I heard one or two shots in the distance."

"Where is this little rook rifle now?"

"In the hall, I think."

She led the way out of the room and found and handed the little weapon to Poirot, who examined it cursorily.

"Two shots fired, I see," he observed, as he handed it back. "And now, madame, if I might see——"

He paused delicately.

"The servant shall take you," she murmured, averting her head.

The parlormaid, summoned, led Poirot upstairs. I remained with the lovely and unfortunate woman. It was hard to know whether to speak or remain silent. I essayed one or two general reflections to which she responded absently, and in a very few minutes Poirot rejoined us.

"I thank you for all your courtesy, madame. I do not think you need be troubled any further with this matter. By the way, do you know anything of your husband's financial position?"

She shook her head.

"Nothing whatever. I am very stupid over business things."

"I see. Then you can give us no clue as to why he suddenly decided to insure his life? He had not done so previously, I understand."

"Well, we had only been married a little over a year. But, as to why he insured his life, it was because he had absolutely made up his mind that he would not live long. He had a strong premonition of his own death. I gather that he had had one hemorrhage already, and that he knew that another one would prove fatal. I tried to dispel these gloomy fears of his, but without avail. Alas, he was only too right!"

Tears in her eyes, she bade us a dignified farewell. Poirot made a characteristic gesture as we walked down the drive together.

"*Eh bien,* that is that! Back to London, my friend, there appears to be no mouse in this mousehole. And yet——"

"Yet what?"

"A slight discrepancy, that is all! You noticed it? You did not? Still, life is full of discrepancies, and assuredly the man cannot have taken his own life—there is no poison that would fill his mouth with blood. No, no, I must resign myself to the fact that all here is clear and above-board—but who is this?"

A tall young man was striding up the drive towards us. He passed us without making any sign, but I noted that he was not ill-looking, with a lean, deeply bronzed face that spoke of life in a tropic clime. A gardener who was sweeping up leaves had paused for a minute in his task, and Poirot ran quickly up to him.

"Tell me, I pray you, who is that gentleman? Do you know him?"

"I don't remember his name, sir, though I did hear it. He was staying down here last week for a night. Tuesday, it was."

"Quick, *mon ami,* let us follow him."

We hastened up the drive after the retreating figure. A glimpse of a black-robed figure on the terrace at the side of the house, and our quarry swerved and we after him, so that we were witnesses of the meeting.

Mrs. Maltravers almost staggered where she stood, and her face blanched noticeably.

"You," she gasped. "I thought you were on the sea—on your way to East Africa?"

"I got some news from my lawyers that detained me," explained the young man. "My old uncle in Scotland died unexpectedly and left me some money. Under the circumstances I thought it better to cancel my passage. Then I saw this bad news in the paper and I came down to see if there was anything I could do. You'll want some one to look after things for you a bit perhaps."

At that moment they became aware of our presence. Poirot stepped forward, and with many apologies explained that he had left his stick in the hall. Rather reluctantly, it seemed to me, Mrs. Maltravers made the necessary introduction.

"Monsieur Poirot, Captain Black."

A few minutes' chat ensued, in the course of which Poirot elicited the fact that Captain Black was putting up at the Anchor Inn. The missing stick not having been discovered (which was not surprising), Poirot uttered more apologies and we withdrew.

We returned to the village at a great pace, and Poirot made a bee line for the Anchor Inn.

"Here we establish ourselves until our friend the Captain returns," he explained. "You notice that I emphasized the point that we were returning to London by the first train? Possibly you thought I meant it. But no—you observed Mrs. Maltravers' face when she caught sight of this young Black? She was clearly taken aback, and he— *eh bien,* he was very devoted, did you not think so? And he was here on Tuesday night—the day before Mr. Maltravers died. We must investigate the doings of Captain Black, Hastings."

In about half an hour we espied our quarry approaching the inn. Poirot went out and accosted him and presently brought him up to the room we had engaged.

"I have been telling Captain Black of the mission which brings us here," he explained. "You can understand, *monsieur le capitaine,* that I am anxious to arrive at Mr. Maltravers' state of mind immediately before his death, and that at the same time I do not wish to distress Mrs. Maltravers unduly by asking her painful questions. Now, you were here just before the occurrence, and can give us equally valuable information."

"I'll do anything I can to help you, I'm sure," replied the young soldier; "but I'm afraid I didn't notice any-

thing out of the ordinary. You see, although Maltravers
was an old friend of my people's, I didn't know him very
well myself."

"You came down—when?"

"Tuesday afternoon. I went up to town early Wednesday morning, as my boat sailed from Tilbury about
twelve o'clock. But some news I got made me alter my
plans, as I dare say you heard me explain to Mrs. Maltravers."

"You were returning to East Africa, I understand?"

"Yes. I've been out there ever since the War—a great
country."

"Exactly. Now what was the talk about at dinner on
Tuesday night?"

"Oh, I don't know. The usual odd topics. Maltravers
asked after my people, and then we discussed the question of German reparations, and then Mrs. Maltravers
asked a lot of questions about East Africa, and I told
them one or two yarns, that's about all, I think."

"Thank you."

Poirot was silent for a moment, then he said gently:
"With your permission, I should like to try a little experiment. You have told us all that your conscious self
knows, I want now to question your subconscious self."

"Psychoanalysis, what?" said Black, with visible alarm.

"Oh, no," said Poirot reassuringly. "You see, it is like
this, I give you a word, you answer with another, and so
on. Any word, the first one you think of. Shall we begin?"

"All right," said Black slowly, but he looked uneasy.

"Note down the words, please, Hastings," said Poirot.
Then he took from his pocket his big turnip-faced watch
and laid it on the table beside him. "We will commence.
Day."

There was a moment's pause, and then Black replied:
"Night."

As Poirot proceeded, his answers came quicker.

"Name," said Poirot.

"Place."

"Bernard."

"Shaw."

"Tuesday."
"Dinner."
"Journey."
"Ship."
"Country."
"Uganda."
"Story."
"Lions."
"Rook Rifle."
"Farm."
"Shot."
"Suicide."
"Elephant."
"Tusks."
"Money."
"Lawyers."

"Thank you, Captain Black. Perhaps you could spare me a few minutes in about half an hour's time?"

"Certainly." The young soldier looked at him curiously and wiped his brow as he got up.

"And now, Hastings," said Poirot, smiling at me as the door closed behind him. "You see it all, do you not?"

"I don't know what you mean."

"Does that list of words tell you nothing?"

I scrutinized it, but was forced to shake my head.

"I will assist you. To begin with, Black answered well within the normal time limit, with no pauses, so we can take it that he himself has no guilty knowledge to conceal. 'Day' to 'Night' and 'Place' to 'Name' are normal associations. I began work with 'Bernard' which might have suggested the local doctor had he come across him at all. Evidently he had not. After our recent conversation, he gave 'Dinner' to my 'Tuesday,' but 'Journey' and 'Country' were answered by 'Ship' and 'Uganda,' showing clearly that it was his journey abroad that was important to him and not the one which brought him down here. 'Story' recalls to him one of the 'Lion' stories he told at dinner. I proceed to 'Rook Rifle' and he answered with the totally unexpected word 'Farm.' When I say 'Shot,' he answers at once 'Suicide.' The association seems clear. A man he knows committed suicide with a rook rifle on a farm somewhere. Remember, too, that his mind is still on the stories he told at dinner, and I think you will agree that I shall not be far from the truth if I recall Captain Black and ask him to repeat the particular suicide story which he told at the dinner-table on Tuesday evening."

Black was straightforward enough over the matter.

"Yes, I did tell them that story now that I come to think of it. Chap shot himself on a farm out there. Did it with a rook rifle through the roof of the mouth, bullet lodged in the brain. Doctors were no end puzzled over it —there was nothing to show except a little blood on the lips. But what——"

"What has it got to do with Mr. Maltravers? You did not know, I see, that he was found with a rook rifle by his side."

"You mean my story suggested to him—oh, but that is awful!"

"Do not distress yourself—it would have been one way or another. Well, I must get on the telephone to London."

Poirot had a lengthy conversation over the wire, and came back thoughtful. He went off by himself in the afternoon, and it was not till seven o'clock that he announced that he could put it off no longer, but must break the news to the young widow. My sympathy had already gone out to her unreservedly. To be left penniless, and with the knowledge that her husband had killed himself to assure her future was a hard burden for any woman to bear. I cherished a secret hope, however, that young Black might prove capable of consoling her after her first grief had passed. He evidently admired her enormously.

Our interview with the lady was painful. She refused vehemently to believe the facts that Poirot advanced, and when she was at last convinced broke down into bitter weeping. An examination of the body turned our suspicions into certainty. Poirot was very sorry for the poor lady, but, after all, he was employed by the Insurance Company, and what could he do? As he was preparing to leave he said gently to Mrs. Maltravers:

"Madame, you of all people should know that there are no dead!"

"What do you mean?" she faltered, her eyes growing wide.

"Have you never taken part in any spiritualistic séances? You are mediumistic, you know."

"I have been told so. But you do not believe in Spiritualism, surely?"

"Madame, I have seen some strange things. You know that they say in the village that this house is haunted?"

She nodded, and at that moment the parlormaid announced that dinner was ready.

"Won't you just stay and have something to eat?"

We accepted gratefully, and I felt that our presence could not but help distract her a little from her own griefs.

We had just finished our soup, when there was a scream outside the door, and the sound of breaking crockery. We jumped up. The parlormaid appeared, her hand to her heart.

"It was a man—standing in the passage."

Poirot rushed out, returning quickly.

"There is no one there."

"Isn't there, sir?" said the parlormaid weakly. "Oh, it did give me a start!"

"But why?"

She dropped her voice to a whisper.

"I thought—I thought it was the master—it looked like 'im."

I saw Mrs. Maltravers give a terrified start, and my mind flew to the old superstition that a suicide cannot rest. She thought of it too, I am sure, for a minute later, she caught Poirot's arm with a scream.

"Didn't you hear that? Those three taps on the window? That's how *he* always used to tap when he passed round the house."

"The ivy," I cried. "It was the ivy against the pane."

But a sort of terror was gaining on us all. The parlormaid was obviously unstrung, and when the meal was over Mrs. Maltravers besought Poirot not to go at once. She was clearly terrified to be left alone. We sat in the little morning-room. The wind was getting up, and moaning round the house in an eerie fashion. Twice the door of the room came unlatched and the door slowly opened, and each time she clung to me with a terrified gasp.

"Ah, but this door, it is bewitched!" cried Poirot angrily at last. He got up and shut it once more, then turned the key in the lock. "I shall lock it, so!"

"Don't do that," she gasped, "if it should come open now——"

And even as she spoke the impossible happened. The locked door slowly swung open. I could not see into the passage from where I sat, but she and Poirot were facing it. She gave one long shriek as she turned to him.

"You saw him—there in the passage?" she cried.

He was staring down at her with a puzzled face, then shook his head.

"I saw him—my husband—you must have seen him too?"

"Madame, I saw nothing. You are not well—un-strung——"

"I am perfectly well, I— Oh, God!"

Suddenly, without any warning, the lights quivered and went out. Out of the darkness came three loud raps. I could hear Mrs. Maltravers moaning.

And then—I saw!

The man I had seen on the bed upstairs stood there facing us, gleaming with a faint ghostly light. There was blood on his lips, and he held his right hand out, pointing. Suddenly a brilliant light seemed to proceed from it. It passed over Poirot and me, and fell on Mrs. Maltravers. I saw her white terrified face, and something else!

"My God, Poirot!" I cried. "Look at her hand, her right hand. It's all red!"

Her own eyes fell on it, and she collapsed in a heap on the floor.

"Blood," she cried hysterically. "Yes, it's blood. I killed him. I did it. He was showing me, and then I put my hand on the trigger and pressed. Save me from him—save me! he's come back!"

Her voice died away in a gurgle.

"Lights," said Poirot briskly.

The lights went on as if by magic.

"That's it," he continued. "You heard, Hastings? And

you, Everett? Oh, by the way, this is Mr. Everett, rather a fine member of the theatrical profession. I phoned to him this afternoon. His make-up is good, isn't it? Quite like the dead man, and with a pocket torch and the necessary phosphorescence he made the proper impression. I shouldn't touch her right hand if I were you, Hastings. Red paint marks so. When the lights went out I clasped her hand, you see. By the way, we mustn't miss our train. Inspector Japp is outside the window. A bad night—but he has been able to while away the time by tapping on the window every now and then."

"You see," continued Poirot, as we walked briskly through the wind and rain, "there was a little discrepancy. The doctor seemed to think the deceased was a Christian Scientist, and who could have given him that impression but Mrs. Maltravers? But to us she represented him as being in a grave state of apprehension about his own health. Again, why was she so taken aback by the reappearance of young Black? And lastly, although I know that convention decrees that a woman must make a decent pretense of mourning for her husband, I do not care for such heavily-rouged eyelids! You did not observe them, Hastings? No? As I always tell you, you see nothing!

"Well, there it was. There were the two possibilities. Did Black's story suggest an ingenious method of committing suicide to Mr. Maltravers, or did his other listener, the wife, see an equally ingenious method of committing murder? I inclined to the latter view. To shoot himself in the way indicated, he would probably have had to pull the trigger with his toe—or at least so I imagine. Now if Maltravers had been found with one boot off, we should almost certainly have heard of it from some one. An odd detail like that would have been remembered.

"No, as I say, I inclined to the view that it was a case of murder, not suicide, but I realized that I had not a shadow of proof in support of my theory. Hence the elaborate little comedy you saw played to-night."

"Even now I don't quite see all the details of the crime," I said.

"Let us start from the beginning. Here is a shrewd
and scheming woman who, knowing of her husband's
financial *débâcle* and tired of the elderly mate she has
only married for his money, induces him to insure his life
for a large sum, and then seeks for the means to accomplish her purpose. An accident gives her that—the young
soldier's strange story. The next afternoon when *monsieur
le capitaine,* as she thinks, is on the high seas, she and
her husband are strolling round the grounds. 'What a
curious story that was last night!' she observes. 'Could a
man shoot himself in such a way? Do show me if it is
possible!' The poor fool—he shows her. He places the
end of the rifle in his mouth. She stoops down, and puts
her finger on the trigger, laughing up at him. 'And now,
sir,' she says saucily, 'supposing I pull the trigger?'

"And then—and then, Hastings—she pulls it!"

III
THE ADVENTURE OF
THE CHEAP FLAT

So far, in the cases which I have recorded, Poirot's investigations have started from the central fact, whether murder or robbery, and have proceeded from thence by a process of logical deduction to the final triumphant unravelling. In the events I am now about to chronicle, a remarkable chain of circumstances led from the apparently trivial incidents which first attracted Poirot's attention to the sinister happenings which completed a most unusual case.

I had been spending the evening with an old friend of mine, Gerald Parker. There had been, perhaps, about half a dozen people there beside my host and myself, and the talk fell, as it was bound to do sooner or later wherever Parker found himself, on the subject of house-hunting in London. Houses and flats were Parker's special hobby. Since the end of the War, he had occupied at least half a dozen different flats and maisonnettes. No sooner was he settled anywhere than he would light unexpectedly upon a new find, and would forthwith depart bag and baggage. His moves were nearly always accomplished at a slight pecuniary gain, for he had a shrewd business head, but it was sheer love of the sport that actuated him, and not a desire to make money at it. We listened to Parker for some time with the respect of the novice for the expert. Then it was our turn, and a perfect babel of tongues was let loose. Finally the floor was left to Mrs. Robinson, a charming little bride who was there with her husband. I had never met them before, as Robinson was only a recent acquaintance of Parker's.

"Talking of flats," she said, "have you heard of our

37

piece of luck, Mr. Parker? We've got a flat—at last! In Montagu Mansions."

"Well," said Parker, "I've always said there are plenty of flats—at a price!"

"Yes, but this isn't at a price. It's dirt cheap. Eighty pounds a year!"

"But—but Montagu Mansions is just off Knightsbridge, isn't it? Big handsome building. Or are you talking of a poor relation of the same name stuck in the slums somewhere?"

"No, it's the Knightsbridge one. That's what makes it so wonderful."

"Wonderful is the word! It's a blinking miracle. But there must be a catch somewhere. Big premium, I suppose?"

"No premium!"

"No prem—oh, hold my head, somebody!" groaned Parker.

"But we've got to buy the furniture," continued Mrs. Robinson.

"Ah!" Parker brisked up. "I knew there was a catch!"

"For fifty pounds. And it's beautifully furnished!"

"I give it up," said Parker. "The present occupants must be lunatics with a taste for philanthropy."

Mrs. Robinson was looking a little troubled. A little pucker appeared between her dainty brows.

"It *is* queer, isn't it? You don't think that—that—the place is *haunted?*"

"Never heard of a haunted flat," declared Parker decisively.

"N-o." Mrs. Robinson appeared far from convinced. "But there were several things about it all that struck me as—well, queer."

"For instance—" I suggested.

"Ah," said Parker, "our criminal expert's attention is aroused! Unburden yourself to him, Mrs. Robinson. Hastings is a great unraveler of mysteries."

I laughed, embarrassed but not wholly displeased with the rôle thrust upon me.

"Oh, not really queer, Captain Hastings, but when we went to the agents, Stosser and Paul—we hadn't tried

them before because they only have the expensive May-
fair flats, but we thought at any rate it would do no
harm—everything they offered us was four and five hundred a year, or else huge premiums, and then, just as we
were going, they mentioned that they had a flat at eighty,
but that they doubted if it would be any good our going
there, because it had been on their books some time and
they had sent so many people to see it that it was almost
sure to be taken—'snapped up' as the clerk put it—only
people were so tiresome in not letting them know, and
then they went on sending, and people get annoyed at
being sent to a place that had, perhaps, been let some
time."

Mrs. Robinson paused for some much needed breath,
and then continued:

"We thanked him, and said that we quite understood it
would probably be no good, but that we should like an
order all the same—just in case. And we went there
straightaway in a taxi, for, after all, you never know. No.
4 was on the second floor, and just as we were waiting
for the lift, Elsie Ferguson—she's a friend of mine, Captain Hastings, and they are looking for a flat too—came
hurrying down the stairs. 'Ahead of you for once, my
dear,' she said. 'But it's no good. It's already let.' That
seemed to finish it, but—well, as John said, the place
was very cheap, we could afford to give more, and perhaps if we offered a premium— A horrid thing to do, of
course, and I feel quite ashamed of telling you, but you
know what flat-hunting is."

I assured her that I was well aware that in the struggle
for house-room the baser side of human nature frequently
triumphed over the higher, and that the well-known rule
of dog eat dog always applied.

"So we went up and, would you believe it, the flat
wasn't let at all. We were shown over it by the maid, and
then we saw the mistress, and the thing was settled then
and there. Immediate possession and fifty pounds for the
furniture. We signed the agreement next day, and we are
to move in to-morrow!" Mrs. Robinson paused trium-
phantly.

"And what about Mrs. Ferguson?" asked Parker. "Let's have your deductions, Hastings."

" 'Obvious, my dear Watson,' " I quoted lightly. "She went to the wrong flat."

"Oh, Captain Hastings, how clever of you!" cried Mrs. Robinson admiringly.

I rather wished Poirot had been there. Some times I have the feeling that he rather underestimates my capabilities.

The whole thing was rather amusing, and I propounded the thing as a mock problem to Poirot on the following morning. He seemed interested, and questioned me rather narrowly as to the rents of flats in various localities.

"A curious story," he said thoughtfully. "Excuse me, Hastings, I must take a short stroll."

When he returned, about an hour later, his eyes were gleaming with a peculiar excitement. He laid his stick on the table, and brushed the nap of his hat with his usual tender care before he spoke.

"It is as well, *mon ami,* that we have no affairs of moment on hand. We can devote ourselves wholly to the present investigation."

"What investigation are you talking about?"

"The remarkable cheapness of your friend's, Mrs. Robinson's, new flat."

"Poirot, you are not serious!"

"I am most serious. Figure to yourself, my friend, that the real rent of those flats is £350. I have just ascertained that from the landlord's agents. And yet this particular flat is being sublet at eighty pounds! Why?"

"There must be something wrong with it. Perhaps it is haunted, as Mrs. Robinson suggested."

Poirot shook his head in a dissatisfied manner.

"Then again how curious it is that her friend tells her the flat is let, and, when she goes up, behold, it is not so at all!"

"But surely you agree with me that the other woman must have gone to the wrong flat. That is the only possible solution."

"You may or may not be right on that point, Hastings. The fact still remains that numerous other applicants were sent to see it, and yet, in spite of its remarkable cheapness, it was still in the market when Mrs. Robinson arrived."

"That shows that there *must* be something wrong about it."

"Mrs. Robinson did not seem to notice anything amiss. Very curious, is it not? Did she impress you as being a truthful woman, Hastings?"

"She was a delightful creature!"

"*Évidemment!* since she renders you incapable of replying to my question. Describe her to me, then."

"Well, she's tall and fair; her hair's really a beautiful shade of auburn——"

"Always you have had a penchant for auburn hair!" murmured Poirot. "But continue."

"Blue eyes and a very nice complexion and—well, that's all, I think," I concluded lamely.

"And her husband?"

"Oh, he's quite a nice fellow—nothing startling."

"Dark or fair?"

"I don't know—betwixt and between, and just an ordinary sort of face."

Poirot nodded.

"Yes, there are hundreds of these average men—and, anyway, you bring more sympathy and appreciation to your description of women. Do you know anything about these people? Does Parker know them well?"

"They are just recent acquaintances, I believe. But surely, Poirot, you don't think for an instant——"

Poirot raised his hand.

"*Tout doucement, mon ami.* Have I said that I think anything? All I say is—it is a curious story. And there is nothing to throw light upon it; except perhaps the lady's name, eh, Hastings?"

"Her name is Stella," I said stiffly, "but I don't see——"

Poirot interrupted me with a tremendous chuckle. Something seemed to be amusing him vastly.

"And Stella means a star, does it not? Famous!"

"What on earth——"

"And stars give light! *Voilà!* Calm yourself, Hastings. Do not put on that air of injured dignity. Come, we will go to Montagu Mansions and make a few inquiries."

I accompanied him, nothing loath. The Mansions were a handsome block of buildings in excellent repair. A uniformed porter was sunning himself on the threshold, and it was to him that Poirot addressed himself:

"Pardon, but could you tell me if a Mr. and Mrs. Robinson reside here?"

The porter was a man of few words and apparently of a sour or suspicious disposition. He hardly looked at us and grunted out:

"No. 4. Second floor."

"I thank you. Can you tell me how long they have been here?"

"Six months."

I started forward in amazement, conscious as I did so of Poirot's malicious grin.

"Impossible," I cried. "You must be making a mistake."

"Six months."

"Are you sure? The lady I mean is tall and fair with reddish gold hair and——"

"That's 'er," said the porter. "Come in the Michaelmas quarter, they did. Just six months ago."

He appeared to lose interest in us and retreated slowly up the hall. I followed Poirot outside.

"*Eh bien,* Hastings?" my friend demanded slyly. "Are you so sure now that delightful women always speak the truth?"

I did not reply.

Poirot had steered his way into Brompton Road before I asked him what he was going to do and where we were going.

"To the house agents, Hastings. I have a great desire to have a flat in Montagu Mansions. If I am not mistaken, several interesting things will take place there before long."

We were fortunate in our quest. No. 8, on the fourth floor, was to be let furnished at ten guineas a week.

Poirot promptly took it for a month. Outside in the street again, he silenced my protests:

"But I make money nowadays! Why should I not indulge a whim? By the way, Hastings, have you a revolver?"

"Yes—somewhere," I answered, slightly thrilled. "Do you think——"

"That you will need it? It is quite possible. The idea pleases you, I see. Always the spectacular and romantic appeal to you."

The following day saw us installed in our temporary home. The flat was pleasantly furnished. It occupied the same position in the building as that of the Robinsons, but was two floors higher.

The day after our installation was a Sunday. In the afternoon, Poirot left the front door ajar, and summoned me hastily as a bang reverberated from somewhere below.

"Look over the banisters. Are those your friends? Do not let them see you."

I craned my neck over the staircase.

"That's them," I declared in an ungrammatical whisper.

"Good. Wait awhile."

About half an hour later, a young woman emerged in brilliant and varied clothing. With a sigh of satisfaction, Poirot tiptoed back into the flat.

"*Cest ça.* After the master and mistress, the maid. The flat should now be empty."

"What are we going to do?" I asked uneasily.

Poirot had trotted briskly into the scullery and was hauling at the rope of the coal-lift.

"We are about to descend after the method of the dustbins," he explained cheerfully. "No one will observe us. The Sunday concert, the Sunday 'afternoon out,' and finally the Sunday nap after the Sunday dinner of England—*le rosbif*—all these will distract attention from the doings of Hercule Poirot. Come, my friend."

He stepped into the rough wooden contrivance and I followed him gingerly.

"Are we going to break into the flat?" I asked dubiously.

Poirot's answer was not too reassuring:

"Not precisely to-day," he replied.

Pulling on the rope, we descended slowly till we reached the second floor. Poirot uttered an exclamation of satisfaction as he perceived that the wooden door into the scullery was open.

"You observe? Never do they bolt these doors in the daytime. And yet anyone could mount or descend as we have done. At night yes—though not always then—and it is against that that we are going to make provision."

He had drawn some tools from his pocket as he spoke, and at once set deftly to work, his object being to arrange the bolt so that it could be pulled back from the lift. The operation only occupied about three minutes. Then Poirot returned the tools to his pocket, and we reascended once more to our own domain.

On Monday Poirot was out all day, but when he returned in the evening he flung himself into his chair with a sigh of satisfaction.

"Hastings, shall I recount to you a little history? A story after your own heart and which will remind you of your favorite cinema?"

"Go ahead," I laughed. "I presume that it is a true story, not one of your efforts of fancy."

"It is true enough. Inspector Japp of Scotland Yard will vouch for its accuracy, since it was through his kind offices that it came to my ears. Listen, Hastings. A little over six months ago some important Naval plans were stolen from an American Government department. They showed the position of some of the most important Harbor defenses, and would be worth a considerable sum to any foreign Government—that of Japan, for example. Suspicion fell upon a young man named Luigi Valdarno, an Italian by birth, who was employed in a minor capacity in the Department and who was missing at the same time as the papers. Whether Luigi Valdarno was the thief or not, he was found two days later on the East Side in New York, shot dead. The papers were not on him. Now for some time past Luigi Valdarno had been going about with a Miss Elsa Hardt, a young concert singer who had recently appeared and who lived with a brother in an apartment in Washington. Nothing was known of the antecedents of Miss Elsa Hardt, and she disappeared suddenly about the time of Valdarno's death. There are reasons for believing that she was in reality an accomplished international spy who has done much nefarious work under various *aliases*. The American Secret Service, whilst doing their best to trace her, also kept an eye upon certain insignificant Japanese gentlemen living in Washington. They felt pretty certain that, when Elsa Hardt had covered her tracks sufficiently, she would approach the gentlemen in question. One of them left suddenly for England a fortnight ago. On the face of it, therefore, it would seem that Elsa Hardt is in England." Poirot paused, and then added softly: "The official description of Elsa Hardt is: Height 5 ft. 7, eyes blue, hair auburn, fair complexion, nose straight, no special distinguishing marks."

"Mrs. Robinson!" I gasped.

"Well, there is a chance of it, anyhow," amended Poirot. "Also, I learn that a swarthy man, a foreigner of some kind, was inquiring about the occupants of No. 4 only this morning. Therefore, *mon ami,* I fear that you must forswear your beauty sleep to-night, and join me in my all-night vigil in the flat below—armed with that excellent revolver of yours, *bien entendu!*"

"Rather," I cried with enthusiasm. "When shall we start?"

"The hour of midnight is both solemn and suitable, I fancy. Nothing is likely to occur before then."

At twelve o'clock precisely, we crept cautiously into the coal-lift and lowered ourselves to the second floor. Under Poirot's manipulation, the wooden door quickly swung inwards, and we climbed into the flat. From the scullery we passed into the kitchen where we established ourselves comfortably in two chairs with the door into the hall ajar.

"Now we have but to wait," said Poirot contentedly, closing his eyes.

To me, the waiting appeared endless. I was terrified of

going to sleep. Just when it seemed to me that I had been there about eight hours—and had, as I found out afterwards, in reality been exactly one hour and twenty minutes—a faint scratching sound came to my ears. Poirot's hand touched mine. I rose, and together we moved carefully in the direction of the hall. The noise came from there. Poirot placed his lips to my ear.

"Outside the front door. They are cutting out the lock. When I give the word, not before, fall upon him from behind and hold him fast. Be careful, he will have a knife."

Presently there was a rending sound, and a little circle of light appeared through the door. It was extinguished immediately and then the door was slowly opened. Poirot and I flattened ourselves against the wall. I heard a man's breathing as he passed us. Then he flashed on his torch, and as he did so, Poirot hissed in my ear:

"*Allez.*"

We sprang together, Poirot with a quick movement enveloped the intruder's head with a light woolen scarf whilst I pinioned his arms. The whole affair was quick and noiseless. I twisted a dagger from his hand, and as Poirot brought down the scarf from his eyes, whilst keeping it wound tightly round his mouth, I jerked up my revolver where he could see it and understand that resistance was useless. As he ceased to struggle Poirot put his mouth close to his ear and began to whisper rapidly. After a minute the man nodded. Then enjoining silence with a movement of the hand, Poirot led the way out of the flat and down the stairs. Our captive followed, and I brought up the rear with the revolver. When we were out in the street, Poirot turned to me.

"There is a taxi waiting just round the corner. Give me the revolver. We shall not need it now."

"But if this fellow tries to escape?"

Poirot smiled.

"He will not."

I returned in a minute with the waiting taxi. The scarf had been unwound from the stranger's face, and I gave a start of surprise.

"He's not a Jap," I ejaculated in a whisper to Poirot.

"Observation was always your strong point, Hastings! Nothing escapes you. No, the man is not a Jap. He is an Italian."

We got into the taxi, and Poirot gave the driver an address in St. John's Wood. I was by now completely fogged. I did not like to ask Poirot where we were going in front of our captive, and strove in vain to obtain some light upon the proceedings.

We alighted at the door of a small house standing back from the road. A returning wayfarer, slightly drunk, was lurching along the pavement and almost collided with Poirot, who said something sharply to him which I did not catch. All three of us went up the steps of the house. Poirot rang the bell and motioned us to stand a little aside. There was no answer and he rang again and then seized the knocker which he plied for some minutes vigorously.

A light appeared suddenly above the fanlight, and the door was opened cautiously a little way.

"What the devil do you want?" a man's voice demanded harshly.

"I want the doctor. My wife is taken ill."

"There's no doctor here."

The man prepared to shut the door, but Poirot thrust his foot in adroitly. He became suddenly a perfect caricature of an infuriated Frenchman.

"What you say, there is no doctor? I will have the law on you. You must come! I will stay here and ring and knock all night."

"My dear sir—" The door was opened again, the man, clad in a dressing-gown and slippers, stepped forward to pacify Poirot with an uneasy glance round.

"I will call the police."

Poirot prepared to descend the steps.

"No, don't do that for Heaven's sake!" The man dashed after him.

With a neat push Poirot sent him staggering down the steps. In another minute all three of us were inside the door and it was pushed to and bolted.

"Quick—in here." Poirot led the way into the nearest room switching on the light as he did so. "And you—behind the curtain."

"Si, signor," said the Italian and slid rapidly behind the full folds of rose-colored velvet which draped the embrasure of the window.

Not a minute too soon. Just as he disappeared from view a woman rushed into the room. She was tall with reddish hair and held a scarlet kimono round her slender form.

"Where is my husband?" she cried, with a quick frightened glance. "Who are you?"

Poirot stepped forward with a bow.

"It is to be hoped your husband will not suffer from a chill. I observed that he had slippers on his feet, and that his dressing-gown was a warm one."

"Who are you? What are you doing in my house?"

"It is true that none of us have the pleasure of your acquaintance, madame. It is especially to be regretted as one of our number has come specially from New York in order to meet you."

The curtains parted and the Italian stepped out. To my horror I observed that he was brandishing my revolver, which Poirot must doubtless have put down through inadvertence in the cab.

The woman gave a piercing scream and turned to fly, but Poirot was standing in front of the closed door.

"Let me by," she shrieked. "He will murder me."

"Who was it dat croaked Luigi Valdarno?" asked the Italian hoarsely, brandishing the weapon, and sweeping each one of us with it. We dared not move.

"My God, Poirot, this is awful. What shall we do?" I cried.

"You will oblige me by refraining from talking so much, Hastings. I can assure you that our friend will not shoot until I give the word."

"Youse sure o' dat, eh?" said the Italian leering unpleasantly.

It was more than I was, but the woman turned to Poirot like a flash.

"What is it you want?"

Poirot bowed.

"I do not think it is necessary to insult Miss Elsa Hardt's intelligence by telling her."

With a swift movement, the woman snatched up a big black velvet cat which served as a cover for the telephone.

"They are stitched in the lining of that."

"Clever," murmured Poirot appreciatively. He stood aside from the door. "Good evening, madame. I will detain your friend from New York whilst you make your getaway."

"Whatta fool!" roared the big Italian, and raising the revolver he fired point-blank at the woman's retreating figure just as I flung myself upon him.

But the weapon merely clicked harmlessly and Poirot's voice rose in mild reproof.

"Never will you trust your old friend, Hastings. I do not care for my friends to carry loaded pistols about with them and never would I permit a mere acquaintance to do so. No, no, *mon ami.*" This to the Italian who was swearing hoarsely. Poirot continued to address him in a tone of mild reproof: "See now, what I have done for you. I have saved you from being hanged. And do not think that our beautiful lady will escape. No, no, the house is watched, back and front. Straight into the arms of the police they will go. Is not that a beautiful and consoling thought? Yes, you may leave the room now. But be careful—be very careful. I— Ah, he is gone! And my friend Hastings looks at me with eyes of reproach. But it was all so simple! It was clear, from the first, that out of several hundred, probably, applicants for No. 4, Montagu Mansions only the Robinsons were considered suitable. Why? What was there that singled them out from the rest—at practically a glance? Their appearance? Possibly, but it was not so unusual. Their name, then!"

"But there's nothing unusual about the name of Robinson," I cried. "It's quite a common name."

"Ah! *Sapristi,* but exactly! That was the point. Elsa Hardt and her husband, or brother or whatever he really is, come from New York, and take a flat in the name of Mr. and Mrs. Robinson. Suddenly they learn that one of these secret societies, the Mafia, or the Camorra, to which doubtless Luigi Valdarno belonged, is on their track. What do they do? They hit on a scheme of transparent simplicity. Evidently they knew that their pursuers were not personally acquainted with either of them. What then can be simpler? They offer the flat at an absurdly low rental. Of the thousands of young couples in London looking for flats, there cannot fail to be several Robinsons. It is only a matter of waiting. If you will look at the name of Robinson in the telephone directory, you will realize that a fair-haired Mrs. Robinson was pretty sure to come along sooner or later. Then what will happen? The avenger arrives. He knows the name, he knows the address. He strikes! All is over, vengeance is satisfied, and Miss Elsa Hardt has escaped by the skin of her teeth once more. By the way, Hastings, you must present me to the real Mrs. Robinson—that delightful and truthful creature! What will they think when they find their flat has been broken into! We must hurry back. Ah, that sounds like Japp and his friends arriving."

A mighty tattoo sounded on the knocker.

"How did you know this address?" I asked as I followed Poirot out into the hall. "Oh, of course, you had the first Mrs. Robinson followed when she left the other flat."

"*A la bonne heure,* Hastings. You use your gray cells at last. Now for a little surprise for Japp."

Softly unbolting the door, he stuck the cat's head round the edge and ejaculated a piercing "Miaow."

The Scotland Yard inspector, who was standing outside with another man, jumped in spite of himself.

"Oh, it's only Monsieur Poirot at one of his little jokes!" he exclaimed, as Poirot's head followed that of the cat. "Let us in, moosior."

"You have our friends safe and sound?"

"Yes, we've got the birds all right. But they hadn't got the goods with them."

"I see. So you come to search. Well, I am about to depart with Hastings, but I should like to give you a little lecture upon the history and habits of the domestic cat."

"For the Lord's sake, have you gone completely balmy?"

"The cat," declaimed Poirot, "was worshiped by the ancient Egyptians. It is still regarded as a symbol of good luck if a black cat crosses your path. This cat crossed your path to-night, Japp. To speak of the interior of any animal or any person is not, I know, considered polite in England. But the interior of this cat is perfectly delicate. I refer to the lining."

With a sudden grunt, the second man seized the cat from Poirot's hand.

"Oh, I forgot to introduce you," said Japp. "Mr. Poirot, this is Mr. Burt of the United States Secret Service."

The American's trained fingers had felt what he was looking for. He held out his hand, and for a moment speech failed him. Then he rose to the occasion.

"Pleased to meet you," said Mr. Burt.

IV
THE MYSTERY OF
HUNTER'S LODGE

"After all," murmured Poirot, "it is possible that I shall not die this time."

Coming from a convalescent influenza patient, I hailed the remark as showing a beneficial optimism. I myself had been the first sufferer from the disease. Poirot in his turn had gone down. He was now sitting up in bed, propped up with pillows, his head muffled in a woolen shawl, and was slowly sipping a particularly noxious *tisane* which I had prepared according to his directions. His eye rested with pleasure upon a neatly graduated row of medicine bottles which adorned the mantelpiece.

"Yes, yes," my little friend continued. "Once more shall I be myself again, the great Hercule Poirot, the terror of evil-doers! Figure to yourself, *mon ami*, that I have a little paragraph to myself in *Society Gossip*. But yes! Here it is! 'Go it—criminals—all out! Hercule Poirot —and believe me, girls, he's some Hercules!—our own pet society detective can't get a grip on you. 'Cause why? 'Cause he's got *la grippe* himself'!"

I laughed.

"Good for you, Poirot. You are becoming quite a public character. And fortunately you haven't missed anything of particular interest during this time."

"That is true. The few cases I have had to decline did not fill me with any regret."

Our landlady stuck her head in at the door.

"There's a gentleman downstairs. Says he must see Monsieur Poirot or you, Captain. Seeing as he was in a great to-do—and with all that quite the gentleman—I brought up 'is card."

52

She handed me the bit of pasteboard. "Mr. Roger Havering," I read.

Poirot motioned with his head towards the bookcase, and I obediently pulled forth "Who's Who." Poirot took it from me and scanned the pages rapidly.

"Second son of fifth Baron Windsor. Married 1913 Zoe, fourth daughter of William Crabb."

"H'm!" I said. "I rather fancy that's the girl who used to act at the Frivolity—only she called herself Zoe Carrisbrook. I remember she married some young man about town just before the War."

"Would it interest you, Hastings, to go down and hear what our visitor's particular little trouble is? Make him all my excuses."

Roger Havering was a man of about forty, well set up and of smart appearance. His face, however, was haggard, and he was evidently laboring under great agitation.

"Captain Hastings? You are Monsieur Poirot's partner, I understand. It is imperative that he should come with me to Derbyshire to-day."

"I'm afraid that's impossible," I responded. "Poirot is ill in bed—influenza."

His face fell.

"Dear me, that is a great blow to me."

"The matter on which you want to consult him is serious?"

"My God, yes! My uncle, the best friend I have in the world, was foully murdered last night."

"Here in London?"

"No, in Derbyshire. I was in town and received a telegram from my wife this morning. Immediately upon its receipt I determined to come round and beg Monsieur Poirot to undertake the case."

"If you will excuse me a minute," I said, struck by a sudden idea.

I rushed upstairs, and in a few brief words acquainted Poirot with the situation. He took any further words out of my mouth.

"I see. I see. You want to go yourself, is it not so? Well, why not? You should know my methods by now.

All I ask is that you should report to me fully every day, and follow implicitly any instructions I may wire you."

To this I willingly agreed.

An hour later I was sitting opposite Mr. Havering in a first-class carriage on the Midland Railway, speeding rapidly away from London.

"To begin with, Captain Hastings, you must understand that Hunter's Lodge, where we are going, and where the tragedy took place, is only a small shooting-box in the heart of the Derbyshire moors. Our real home is near Newmarket, and we usually rent a flat in town for the season. Hunter's Lodge is looked after by a housekeeper who is quite capable of doing all we need when we run down for an occasional week-end. Of course, during the shooting season, we take down some of our own servants from Newmarket. My uncle, Mr. Harrington Pace (as you may know, my mother was a Miss Pace of New York), has, for the last three years, made his home with us. He never got on well with my father, or my elder brother, and I suspect that my being somewhat of a prodigal son myself rather increased than diminished his affection towards me. Of course I am a poor man, and my uncle was a rich one—in other words, he paid the piper! But, though exacting in many ways, he was not really hard to get on with, and we all three lived very harmoniously together. Two days ago my uncle, rather wearied with some recent gayeties of ours in town, suggested that we should run down to Derbyshire for a day or two. My wife telegraphed to Mrs. Middleton, the housekeeper, and we went down that same afternoon. Yesterday evening I was forced to return to town, but my wife and my uncle remained on. This morning I received this telegram." He handed it over to me:

"Come at once uncle Harrington murdered last night bring good detective if you can but do come—Zoe."

"Then, as yet you know no details?"

"No, I suppose it will be in the evening papers. Without doubt the police are in charge."

It was about three o'clock when we arrived at the little station of Elmer's Dale. From there a five-mile drive brought us to a small gray stone building in the midst of the rugged moors.

"A lonely place," I observed with a shiver.

Havering nodded.

"I shall try and get rid of it. I could never live here again."

We unlatched the gate and were walking up the narrow path to the oak door when a familiar figure emerged and came to meet us.

"Japp!" I ejaculated.

The Scotland Yard inspector grinned at me in a friendly fashion before addressing my companion.

"Mr. Havering, I think? I've been sent down from London to take charge of this case, and I'd like a word with you, if I may, sir."

"My wife——"

"I've seen your good lady, sir—and the housekeeper. I won't keep you a moment, but I'm anxious to get back to the village now that I've seen all there is to see here."

"I know nothing as yet as to what——"

"Ex-actly," said Japp soothingly. "But there are just one or two little points I'd like your opinion about all the same. Captain Hastings here, he knows me, and he'll go on up to the house and tell them you're coming. What have you done with the little man, by the way, Captain Hastings?"

"He's ill in bed with influenza."

"Is he now? I'm sorry to hear that. Rather the case of the cart without the horse, your being here without him, isn't it?"

And on his rather ill-timed jest I went on to the house. I rang the bell, as Japp had closed the door behind him. After some moments it was opened to me by a middle-aged woman in black.

"Mr. Havering will be here in a moment," I explained. "He has been detained by the inspector. I have come down with him from London to look into the case. Perhaps you can tell me briefly what occurred last night."

"Come inside, sir." She closed the door behind me, and

we stood in the dimly-lighted hall. "It was after dinner last night, sir, that the man came. He asked to see Mr. Pace, sir, and, seeing that he spoke the same way, I thought it was an American gentleman friend of Mr. Pace's and I showed him into the gun-room, and then went to tell Mr. Pace. He wouldn't give any name, which, of course, was a bit odd, now I come to think of it. I told Mr. Pace, and he seemed puzzled like, but he said to the mistress: 'Excuse me, Zoe, while I just see what this fellow wants.' He went off to the gun-room, and I went back to the kitchen, but after a while I heard loud voices, as if they were quarrelling, and I came out into the hall. At the same time, the mistress she comes out too, and just then there was a shot and then a dreadful silence. We both ran to the gun-room door, but it was locked and we had to go round to the window. It was open, and there inside was Mr. Pace, all shot and bleeding."

"What became of the man?"

"He must have got away through the window, sir, before we got to it."

"And then?"

"Mrs. Havering sent me to fetch the police. Five miles to walk it was. They came back with me, and the constable he stayed all night, and this morning the police gentleman from London arrived."

"What was this man like who called to see Mr. Pace?"

The housekeeper reflected.

"He had a black beard, sir, and was about middle-aged, and had on a light overcoat. Beyond the fact that he spoke like an American I didn't notice much about him."

"I see. Now I wonder if I can see Mrs. Havering?"

"She's upstairs, sir. Shall I tell her?"

"If you please. Tell her that Mr. Havering is outside with Inspector Japp, and that the gentleman he has brought back with him from London is anxious to speak to her as soon as possible."

"Very good, sir."

I was in a fever of impatience to get at all the facts. Japp had two or three hours' start of me, and his anxiety to be gone made me keen to be close at his heels.

Mrs. Havering did not keep me waiting long. In a few

minutes I heard a light step descending the stairs, and looked up to see a very handsome young woman coming towards me. She wore a flame-colored jumper, that set off the slender boyishness of her figure. On her dark head was a little hat of flame-colored leather. Even the present tragedy could not dim the vitality of her personality.

I introduced myself, and she nodded in quick comprehension.

"Of course I have often heard of you and your colleague, Monsieur Poirot. You have done some wonderful things together, haven't you? It was very clever of my husband to get you so promptly. Now will you ask me questions? That is the easiest way, isn't it, of getting to know all you want to about this dreadful affair?"

"Thank you, Mrs. Havering. Now what time was it that this man arrived?"

"It must have been just before nine o'clock. We had finished dinner, and were sitting over our coffee and cigarettes."

"Your husband had already left for London?"

"Yes, he went up by the 6.15."

"Did he go by car to the station, or did he walk?"

"Our own car isn't down here. One came out from the garage in Elmer's Dale to fetch him in time for the train."

"Was Mr. Pace quite his usual self?"

"Absolutely. Most normal in every way."

"Now, can you describe this visitor at all?"

"I'm afraid not. I didn't see him. Mrs. Middleton showed him straight into the gun-room and then came to tell my uncle."

"What did your uncle say?"

"He seemed rather annoyed, but went off at once. It was about five minutes later that I heard the sound of raised voices. I ran out into the hall and almost collided with Mrs. Middleton. Then we heard the shot. The gun-room door was locked on the inside, and we had to go right round the house to the window. Of course that took some time, and the murderer had been able to get well away. My poor uncle"—her voice faltered—"had been shot through the head. I saw at once that he was dead. I

sent Mrs. Middleton for the police. I was careful to touch
nothing in the room but to leave it exactly as I found it."

I nodded approval.

"Now, as to the weapon?"

"Well, I can make a guess at it, Captain Hastings. A
pair of revolvers of my husband's were mounted upon
the wall. One of them is missing. I pointed this out to the
police, and they took the other one away with them.
When they have extracted the bullet, I suppose they will
know for certain."

"May I go to the gun-room?"

"Certainly. The police have finished with it. But the
body has been removed."

She accompanied me to the scene of the crime. At that
moment Havering entered the hall, and with a quick
apology his wife ran to him. I was left to undertake my
investigations alone.

I may as well confess at once that they were rather
disappointing. In detective novels clues abound, but here
I could find nothing that struck me as out of the ordinary
except a large bloodstain on the carpet where I judged
the dead man had fallen. I examined everything with
painstaking care and took a couple of pictures of the
room with my little camera which I had brought with me.
I also examined the ground outside the window, but it
appeared to have been so heavily trampled underfoot that
I judged it was useless to waste time over it. No, I had
seen all that Hunter's Lodge had to show me. I must go
back to Elmer's Dale and get into touch with Japp. Ac-
cordingly I took leave of the Haverings, and was driven
off in the car that had brought us up from the station.

I found Japp at the Matlock Arms and he took me
forthwith to see the body. Harrington Pace was a small,
spare clean-shaven man, typically American in appearance. He had been shot through the back of the head,
and the revolver had been discharged at close quarters.

"Turned away for a moment," remarked Japp, "and
the other fellow snatched up a revolver and shot him.
The one Mrs. Havering handed over to us was fully
loaded and I suppose the other one was also. Curious

what darn fool things people do. Fancy keeping two
loaded revolvers hanging up on your wall."

"What do you think of the case?" I asked, as we left
the gruesome chamber behind us.

"Well, I'd got my eye on Havering to begin with. Oh,
yes!" noting my exclamation of astonishment. "Havering
has one or two shady incidents in his past. When he was
a boy at Oxford there was some funny business about the
signature on one of his father's checks. All hushed up of
course. Then, he's pretty heavily in debt now, and they're
the kind of debts he wouldn't like to go to his uncle
about, whereas you may be sure the uncle's will would be
in his favor. Yes, I'd got my eye on him, and that's why
I wanted to speak to him before he saw his wife, but
their statements dovetail all right, and I've been to the
station and there's no doubt whatever that he left by the
6.15. That gets up to London about 10.30. He went
straight to his club, he says, and if that's confirmed all
right—why, he couldn't have been shooting his uncle
here at nine o'clock in a black beard!"

"Ah, yes, I was going to ask you what you thought
about that beard?"

Japp winked.

"I think it grew pretty fast—grew in the five miles
from Elmer's Dale to Hunter's Lodge. Americans that
I've met are mostly clean-shaven. Yes, it's amongst Mr.
Pace's American associates that we'll have to look for the
murderer. I questioned the housekeeper first, and then
her mistress, and their stories agree all right, but I'm
sorry Mrs. Havering didn't get a look at the fellow. She's a
smart woman, and she might have noticed something
that would set us on the track."

I sat down and wrote a minute and lengthy account to
Poirot. I was able to add various further items of information before I posted the letter.

The bullet had been extracted and was proved to have
been fired from a revolver identical with the one held by
the police. Furthermore, Mr. Havering's movements on
the night in question had been checked and verified, and
it was proved beyond doubt that he had actually arrived

in London by the train in question. And, thirdly, a sensational development had occurred. A city gentleman, living at Ealing, on crossing Haven Green to get to the District Railway Station that morning, had observed a brown-paper parcel stuck between the railings. Opening it, he found that it contained a revolver. He handed the parcel over to the local police station, and before night it was proved to be the one we were in search of, the fellow to that given us by Mrs. Havering. One bullet had been fired from it.

All this I added to my report. A wire from Poirot arrived whilst I was at breakfast the following morning:

"Of course black bearded man was not Havering only you or Japp would have such an idea wire me description of housekeeper and what clothes she wore this morning same of Mrs. Havering do not waste time taking photographs of interiors they are underexposed and not in the least artistic."

It seemed to me that Poirot's style was unnecessarily facetious. I also fancied he was a shade jealous of my position on the spot with full facilities for handling the case. His request for a description of the clothes worn by the two women appeared to me to be simply ridiculous, but I complied as well as I, a mere man, was able to.

At eleven a reply wire came from Poirot:

"Advise Japp arrest housekeeper before it is too late."

Dumfounded, I took the wire to Japp. He swore softly under his breath.

"He's the goods, Monsieur Poirot! If he says so, there's something in it. And I hardly noticed the woman. I don't know that I can go so far as arresting her, but I'll have her watched. We'll go up right away, and take another look at her."

But it was too late. Mrs. Middleton, that quiet middle-aged woman, who had appeared so normal and respectable, had vanished into thin air. Her box had been left behind. It contained only ordinary wearing apparel.

There was no clue in it to her identity or as to her whereabouts.

From Mrs. Havering we elicited all the facts we could: "I engaged her about three weeks ago when Mrs. Emery, our former housekeeper, left. She came to me from Mrs. Selbourne's Agency in Mount Street—a very well-known place. I get all my servants from there. They sent several women to see me, but this Mrs. Middleton seemed much the nicest, and had splendid references. I engaged her on the spot, and notified the Agency of the fact. I can't believe that there was anything wrong with her. She was such a nice quiet woman."

The thing was certainly a mystery. Whilst it was clear that the woman herself could not have committed the crime, since at the moment the shot was fired Mrs. Havering was with her in the hall, nevertheless she must have some connection with the murder, or why should she suddenly take to her heels and bolt?

I wired the latest development to Poirot and suggested returning to London and making inquiries at Selbourne's Agency.

Poirot's reply was prompt:

"Useless to inquire at agency they will never have heard of her find out what vehicle took her up to hunters lodge when she first arrived there."

Though mystified, I was obedient. The means of transport in Elmer's Dale were limited. The local garage had two battered Ford cars, and there were two station flies. None of these had been requisitioned on the date in question. Questioned, Mrs. Havering explained that she had given the woman the money for her fare down to Derbyshire and sufficient to hire a car of fly to take her up to Hunter's Lodge. There was usually one of the Fords at the station on the chance of its being required. Taking into consideration the further fact that nobody at the station had noticed the arrival of a stranger, blackbearded or otherwise, on the fatal evening, everything seemed to point to the conclusion that the murderer had come to the spot in a car, which had been waiting near at hand to aid his escape, and that the same car had brought the mysterious housekeeper to her new post. I may mention that inquiries at the Agency in London bore out Poirot's prognostication. No such woman as "Mrs. Middleton" had ever been on their books. They had received the Hon. Mrs. Havering's application for a housekeeper, and had sent her various applicants for the post. When she sent them the engagement fee, she omitted to mention which woman she had selected.

Somewhat crestfallen, I returned to London. I found Poirot established in an arm-chair by the fire in a garish silk dressing-gown. He greeted me with much affection.

"Mon ami Hastings! But how glad I am to see you. Veritably I have for you a great affection! And you have enjoyed yourself? You have run to and fro with the good Japp? You have interrogated and investigated to your heart's content?"

"Poirot," I cried, "the thing's a dark mystery! It will never be solved."

"It is true that we are not likely to cover ourselves with glory over it."

"No, indeed. It's a hard nut to crack."

"Oh, as far as that goes, I am very good at cracking the nuts! A veritable squirrel! It is not that which embarrasses me. I know well enough who killed Mr. Harrington Pace."

"You know? How did you find out?"

"Your illuminating answers to my wires supplied me with the truth. See here, Hastings, let us examine the facts methodically and in order. Mr. Harrington Pace is a man with a considerable fortune which at his death will doubtless pass to his nephew. Point No. 1. His nephew is known to be desperately hard up. Point No. 2. His nephew is also known to be—shall we say a man of rather loose moral fiber? Point No. 3."

"But Roger Havering is proved to have journeyed straight up to London."

"Précisément—and therefore, as Mr. Havering left Elmer's Dale at 6.15, and since Mr. Pace cannot have been killed before he left, or the doctor would have spotted the time of the crime as being given wrongly

when he examined the body, we conclude quite rightly, that Mr. Havering did *not* shoot his uncle. But there is a Mrs. Havering, Hastings."

"Impossible! The housekeeper was with her when the shot was fired."

"Ah, yes, the housekeeper. But she has disappeared."

"She will be found."

"I think not. There is something peculiarly elusive about that housekeeper, don't you think so, Hastings? It struck me at once."

"She played her part, I suppose, and then got out in the nick of time."

"And what was her part?"

"Well, presumably to admit her confederate, the black-bearded man."

"Oh, no, that was not her part! Her part was what you have just mentioned, to provide an alibi for Mrs. Havering at the moment the shot was fired. And no one will ever find her, *mon ami,* because she does not exist! 'There's no sech person,' as your so great Shakespeare says."

"It was Dickens," I murmured, unable to suppress a smile. "But what do you mean, Poirot?"

"I mean that Zoe Havering was an actress before her marriage. that you and Japp only saw the housekeeper in a dark hall, a dim middle-aged figure in black with a faint subdued voice, and finally that neither you nor Japp, nor the local police whom the housekeeper fetched, ever saw Mrs. Middleton and her mistress at one and the same time. It was child's play for that clever and daring woman. On the pretext of summoning her mistress, she runs upstairs, slips on a bright jumper and a hat with black curls attached which she jams down over the gray transformation. A few deft touches and the makeup is removed, a slight dusting of rouge, and the brilliant Zoe Havering comes down with her clear ringing voice. Nobody looks particularly at the housekeeper. Why should they? There is nothing to connect her with the crime. She, too, has an alibi."

"But the revolver that was found at Ealing? Mrs. Havering could not have placed it there?"

"No, that was Roger Havering's job—but it was a mistake on their part. It put me on the right track. A man who has committed a murder with a revolver which he found on the spot would fling it away at once, he would not carry it up to London with him. No, the motive was clear, the criminals wished to focus the interest of the police on a spot far removed from Derbyshire; they were anxious to get the police away as soon as possible from the vicinity of Hunter's Lodge. Of course the revolver found at Ealing was not the one with which Mr. Pace was shot. Roger Havering discharged one shot from it, brought it up to London, went straight to his club to establish his alibi, then went quickly out to Ealing by the district, a matter of about twenty minutes only, placed the parcel where it was found and so back to town. That charming creature, his wife, quietly shoots Mr. Pace after dinner—you remember he was shot from behind? Another significant point, that!—reloads the revolver and puts it back in its place, and then starts off with her desperate little comedy."

"It's incredible," I murmured, fascinated, "and yet——"

"And yet it is true. *Bien sur,* my friend, it is true. But to bring that precious pair to justice, that is another matter. Well, Japp must do what he can—I have written him fully—but I very much fear, Hastings, that we shall be obliged to leave them to Fate, or *le bon Dieu,* whichever you prefer."

"The wicked flourish like a green bay tree," I reminded him.

"But at a price, Hastings, always at a price, *croyez-moi!*"

Poirot's forebodings were confirmed. Japp, though convinced of the truth of his theory, was unable to get together the necessary evidence to ensure a conviction.

Mr. Pace's huge fortune passed into the hands of his murderers. Nevertheless, Nemesis did overtake them, and when I read in the paper that the Hon. Roger and Mrs. Havering were amongst those killed in the crashing of the Air Mail to Paris I knew that Justice was satisfied.

V
THE MILLION DOLLAR
BOND ROBBERY

"What a number of bond robberies there have been lately!" I observed one morning, laying aside the newspaper. "Poirot, let us forsake the science of detection, and take to crime instead!"

"You are on the—how do you say it?—get-rich-quick tack, eh, *mon ami?*"

"Well, look at this last *coup,* the million dollars' worth of Liberty Bonds which the London and Scottish Bank were sending to New York, and which disappeared in such a remarkable manner on board the *Olympia.*"

"If it were not for the *mal de mer,* and the difficulty of practicing the so excellent method of Laverguier for a longer time than the few hours of crossing the channel I should delight to voyage myself on one of these big liners," murmured Poirot dreamily.

"Yes, indeed," I said enthusiastically. "Some of them must be perfect palaces; the swimming-baths, the lounges, the restaurant, the palm courts—really, it must be hard to believe that one is on the sea."

"Me, I always know when I am on the sea," said Poirot sadly. "And all those bagatelles that you enumerate, they say nothing to me; but, my friend, consider for a moment the geniuses that travel as it were incognito! On board these floating palaces, as you so justly call them, one would meet the élite, the *haute noblesse* of the criminal world!"

I laughed.

"So that's the way your enthusiasm runs! You would have liked to cross swords with the man who sneaked the Liberty Bonds?"

The landlady interrupted us.

"A young lady as wants to see you, Mr. Poirot. Here's her card."

The card bore the inscription: Miss Esmée Farquhar, and Poirot, after diving under the table to retrieve a stray crumb, and putting it carefully in the waste-paper-basket, nodded to the landlady to admit her.

In another minute one of the most charming girls I have ever seen was ushered into the room. She was perhaps about five-and-twenty, with big brown eyes and a perfect figure. She was well-dressed and perfectly composed in manner.

"Sit down, I beg of you, mademoiselle. This is my friend, Captain Hastings, who aids me in my little problems."

"I am afraid it is a big problem I have brought you to-day, Monsieur Poirot," said the girl, giving me a pleasant bow as she seated herself. "I dare say you have read about it in the papers. I am referring to the theft of Liberty Bonds on the *Olympia*." Some astonishment must have shown itself in Poirot's face, for she continued quickly: "You are doubtless asking yourself what I have to do with a grave institution like the London and Scottish Bank. In one sense nothing, in another sense everything. You see, Monsieur Poirot, I am engaged to Mr. Philip Ridgeway."

"Aha! and Mr. Philip Ridgeway——"

"Was in charge of the bonds when they were stolen. Of course no actual blame can attach to him, it was not his fault in any way. Nevertheless, he is half distraught over the matter, and his uncle, I know, insists that he must carelessly have mentioned having them in his possession. It is a terrible set-back in his career."

"Who is his uncle?"

"Mr. Vavasour, joint general manager of the London and Scottish Bank."

"Suppose, Miss Farquhar, that you recount to me the whole story?"

"Very well. As you know, the Bank wished to extend their credits in America, and for this purpose decided to send over a million dollars in Liberty Bonds. Mr. Vavasour selected his nephew, who had occupied a position of trust in the Bank for many years and who was conversant with all the details of the Bank's dealings in New York, to make the trip. The *Olympia* sailed from Liverpool on the 23rd, and the bonds were handed over to Philip on the morning of that day by Mr. Vavasour and Mr. Shaw, the two joint general managers of the London and Scottish Bank. They were counted, enclosed in a package, and sealed in his presence, and he then locked the package at once in his portmanteau."

"A portmanteau with an ordinary lock?"

"No, Mr. Shaw insisted on a special lock being fitted to it by Hubbs's. Philip, as I say, placed the package at the bottom of the trunk. It was stolen just a few hours before reaching New York. A rigorous search of the whole ship was made, but without result. The bonds seemed literally to have vanished into thin air."

Poirot made a grimace.

"But they did not vanish absolutely, since I gather that they were sold in small parcels within half an hour of the docking of the *Olympia!* Well, undoubtedly the next thing is for me to see Mr. Ridgeway."

"I was about to suggest that you should lunch with me at the 'Cheshire Cheese.' Philip will be there. He is meeting me, but does not yet know that I have been consulting you on his behalf."

We agreed to this suggestion readily enough, and drove there in a taxi.

Mr. Philip Ridgeway was there before us, and looked somewhat surprised to see his fiancée arriving with two complete strangers. He was a nice-looking young fellow, tall and spruce, with a touch of graying hair at the temples, though he could not have been much over thirty.

Miss Farquhar went up to him and laid her hand on his arm.

"You must forgive my acting without consulting you, Philip," she said. "Let me introduce you to Monsieur Hercule Poirot, of whom you must often have heard, and his friend, Captain Hastings."

Ridgeway looked very astonished.

"Of course I have heard of you, Monsieur Poirot," he said, as he shook hands. "But I had no idea that Esmée was thinking of consulting you about my—our trouble."

"I was afraid you would not let me do it, Philip," said Miss Farquhar meekly.

"So you took care to be on the safe side," he observed, with a smile. "I hope Monsieur Poirot will be able to throw some light on this extraordinary puzzle, for I confess frankly that I am nearly out of my mind with worry and anxiety about it."

Indeed, his face looked drawn and haggard and showed only too clearly the strain under which he was laboring.

"Well, well," said Poirot. "Let us lunch, and over lunch we will put our heads together and see what can be done. I want to hear Mr. Ridgeway's story from his own lips."

Whilst we discussed the excellent steak and kidney pudding of the establishment, Philip Ridgeway narrated the circumstances leading to the disappearance of the bonds. His story agreed with that of Miss Farquhar in every particular. When he had finished, Poirot took up the thread with a question.

"What exactly led you to discover that the bonds had been stolen, Mr. Ridgeway?"

He laughed rather bitterly.

"The thing stared me in the face, Monsieur Poirot. I couldn't have missed it. My cabin trunk was half out from under the bunk and all scratched and cut about where they'd tried to force the lock."

"But I understood that it had been opened with a key?"

"That's so. They tried to force it, but couldn't. And, in the end, they must have got it unlocked somehow or other."

"Curious," said Poirot, his eyes beginning to flicker with the green light I knew so well. "Very curious! They waste much, much time trying to prise it open, and then— *sapristi!* they find that they have the key all the time— for each of Hubbs's locks are unique."

"That's just why they couldn't have had the key. It never left me day or night."

"You are sure of that?"

"I can swear to it, and besides, if they had had the key

or a duplicate, why should they waste time trying to force an obviously unforceable lock?"

"Ah! there is exactly the question we are asking ourselves! I venture to prophesy that the solution, if we ever find it, will hinge on that curious fact. I beg of you not to assault me if I ask you one more question: *Are you perfectly certain you did not leave the trunk unlocked?*"

Philip Ridgeway merely looked at him, and Poirot gesticulated apologetically.

"Ah, but these things can happen, I assure you! Very well, the bonds were stolen from the trunk. What did the thief do with them? How did he manage to get ashore with them?"

"Ah!" cried Ridgeway. "That's just it. How? Word was passed to the Customs authorities, and every soul that left the ship was gone over with a toothcomb!"

"And the bonds, I gather, made a bulky package?"

"Certainly they did. They could hardly have been hidden on board—and anyway we know they weren't because they were offered for sale within half an hour of the *Olympia*'s arrival, long before I got the cables going and the numbers sent out. One broker swears he bought some of them even before the *Olympia* got in. But you can't send bonds by wireless."

"Not by wireless, but did any tug come alongside?"

"Only the official ones, and that was after the alarm was given when every one was on the look-out. I was watching out myself for their being passed over to some one that way. My God, Monsieur Poirot, this thing will drive me mad! People are beginning to say I stole them myself."

"But you also were searched on landing, weren't you?" asked Poirot gently.

"Yes."

The young man stared at him in a puzzled manner.

"You do not catch my meaning, I see," said Poirot, smiling enigmatically. "Now I should like to make a few inquiries at the Bank."

Ridgeway produced a card and scribbled a few words on it.

"Send this in and my uncle will see you at once."

Poirot thanked him, bade farewell to Miss Farquhar, and together we started out for Threadneedle Street and the head office of the London and Scottish Bank. On production of Ridgeway's card, we were led through the labyrinth of counters and desks, skirting paying-in clerks and paying-out clerks and up to a small office on the first floor where the joint general managers received us. They were two grave gentlemen, who had grown gray in the service of the Bank. Mr. Vavasour had a short white beard, Mr. Shaw was clean shaven.

"I understand you are strictly a private inquiry agent?" said Mr. Vavasour. "Quite so, quite so. We have, of course, placed ourselves in the hands of Scotland Yard. Inspector McNeil has charge of the case. A very able officer, I believe."

"I am sure of it," said Poirot politely. "You will permit a few questions, on your nephew's behalf? About this lock, who ordered it from Hubbs's?"

"I ordered it myself," said Mr. Shaw. "I would not trust to any clerk in the matter. As to the keys, Mr. Ridgeway had one, and the other two are held by my colleague and myself."

"And no clerk has had access to them?"

Mr. Shaw turned inquiringly to Mr. Vavasour.

"I think I am correct in saying that they have remained in the safe where we placed them on the 23rd," said Mr. Vavasour. "My colleague was unfortunately taken ill a fortnight ago—in fact on the very day that Philip left us. He has only just recovered."

"Severe bronchitis is no joke to a man of my age," said Mr. Shaw ruefully. "But I am afraid Mr. Vavasour has suffered from the hard work entailed by my absence, especially with this unexpected worry coming on top of everything."

Poirot asked a few more questions. I judged that he was endeavoring to gauge the exact amount of intimacy between uncle and nephew. Mr. Vavasour's answers were brief and punctilious. His nephew was a trusted official of the Bank, and had no debts or money difficulties that he knew of. He had been entrusted with similar missions in the past. Finally we were politely bowed out.

"I am disappointed," said Poirot, as we emerged into the street.

"You hoped to discover more? They are such stodgy old men."

"It is not their stodginess which disappoints me, *mon ami*. I do not expect to find in a Bank manager a 'keen financier with an eagle glance' as your favorite works of fiction put it. No, I am disappointed in the case—it is too easy!"

"Easy?"

"Yes, do you not find it almost childishly simple?"

"You know who stole the bonds?"

"I do."

"But then—we must—why——"

"Do not confuse and fluster yourself, Hastings. We are not going to do anything at present."

"But why? What are you waiting for?"

"For the *Olympia*. She is due on her return trip from New York on Tuesday."

"But if you know who stole the bonds, why wait? He may escape."

"To a South Sea island where there is no extradition? No, *mon ami,* he would find life very uncongenial there. As to why I wait—*eh bien,* to the intelligence of Hercule Poirot the case is perfectly clear, but for the benefit of others, not so greatly gifted by the good God—the Inspector McNeil, for instance—it would be as well to make a few inquiries to establish the facts. One must have consideration for those less gifted than oneself."

"Good Lord, Poirot! Do you know, I'd give a considerable sum of money to see you make a thorough ass of yourself—just for once. You're so confoundedly conceited!"

"Do not enrage yourself, Hastings. In verity, I observe that there are times when you almost detest me! Alas, I suffer the penalties of greatness!"

The little man puffed out his chest, and sighed so comically that I was forced to laugh.

Tuesday saw us speeding to Liverpool in a first-class carriage of the L. & N. W. R. Poirot had obstinately refused to enlighten me as to his suspicions—or certainties. He contented himself with expressing surprise that I, too, was not equally *au fait* with the situation. I disdained to argue, and intrenched my curiosity behind a rampart of pretended indifference.

Once arrived at the quay alongside which lay the big transatlantic liner, Poirot became brisk and alert. Our proceedings consisted in interviewing four successive stewards and inquiring after a friend of Poirot's who had crossed to New York on the 23rd.

"An elderly gentleman, wearing glasses. A great invalid, hardly moved out of his cabin."

The description appeared to tally with one Mr. Ventnor who had occupied the cabin C 24 which was next to that of Philip Ridgeway. Although unable to see how Poirot had deduced Mr. Ventnor's existence and personal appearance, I was keenly excited.

"Tell me," I cried, "was this gentleman one of the first to land when you got to New York?"

The steward shook his head.

"No, indeed, sir, he was one of the last off the boat."

I retired crestfallen, and observed Poirot grinning at me. He thanked the steward, a note changed hands, and we took our departure.

"It's all very well," I remarked heatedly, "but that last answer must have damped your precious theory, grin as you please!"

"As usual, you see nothing, Hastings. That last answer is, on the contrary, the coping-stone of my theory."

I flung up my hands in despair.

"I give it up."

When we were in the train, speeding towards London, Poirot wrote busily for a few minutes, sealing up the result in an envelope.

"This is for the good Inspector McNeil. We will leave it at Scotland Yard in passing, and then to the Rendezvous Restaurant, where I have asked Miss Esmée Farquhar to do us the honor of dining with us."

"What about Ridgeway?"

"What about him?" asked Poirot with a twinkle.

"Why, you surely don't think—you can't——"

"The habit of incoherence is growing upon you, Hastings. As a matter of fact I *did* think. If Ridgeway had been the thief—which was perfectly possible—the case would have been charming; a piece of neat methodical work."

"But not so charming for Miss Farquhar."

"Possibly you are right. Therefore all is for the best. Now, Hastings, let us review the case. I can see that you are dying to do so. The sealed package is removed from the trunk and vanishes, as Miss Farquhar puts it, into thin air. We will dismiss the thin air theory, which is not practicable at the present stage of science, and consider what is likely to have become of it. Every one asserts the incredibility of its being smuggled ashore——"

"Yes, but we know——"

"You may know, Hastings. I do not. I take the view that, since it seemed incredible, it *was* incredible. Two possibilities remain: it was hidden on board—also rather difficult—or it was thrown overboard."

"With a cork on it, do you mean?"

"Without a cork."

I stared.

"But if the bonds were thrown overboard, they couldn't have been sold in New York."

"I admire your logical mind, Hastings. The bonds were sold in New York, therefore they were not thrown overboard. You see where that leads us?"

"Where we were when we started."

"Jamais de la vie! If the package was thrown overboard, and the bonds were sold in New York, the package could not have contained the bonds. Is there any evidence that the package *did* contain the bonds? Remember, Mr. Ridgeway never opened it from the time it was placed in his hands in London."

"Yes, but then——"

Poirot waved an impatient hand.

"Permit me to continue. The last moment that the bonds are seen as bonds is in the office of the London and Scottish Bank on the morning of the 23rd. They reappear in New York half an hour after the *Olympia* gets in, and according to one man, whom nobody listens to, actually *before* she gets in. Supposing, then, that they have never been on the *Olympia* at all? Is there any other way they could get to New York? Yes. The *Gigantic* leaves Southampton on the same day as the *Olympia,* and she holds the record for the Atlantic. Mailed by the *Gigantic,* the bonds would be in New York the day before the *Olympia* arrived. All is clear, the case begins to explain itself. The sealed packet is only a dummy, and the moment of its substitution must be in the office in the Bank. It would be an easy matter for any of the three men present to have prepared a duplicate package which could be substituted for the genuine one. *Très bien,* the bonds are mailed to a confederate in New York, with instructions to sell as soon as the *Olympia* is in, but some one must travel on the *Olympia* to engineer the supposed moment of the robbery."

"But why?"

"Because if Ridgeway merely opens the packet and finds it a dummy, suspicion flies at once to London. No, the man on board in the cabin next door does his work, pretends to force the lock in an obvious manner so as to draw immediate attention to the theft, really unlocks the trunk with a duplicate key, throws the package overboard and waits until the last to leave the boat. Naturally he wears glasses to conceal his eyes, and is an invalid since he does not want to run the risk of meeting Ridgeway. He steps ashore in New York and returns by the first boat available."

"But who—which was he?"

"The man who had a duplicate key, the man who ordered the lock, the man who has *not* been severely ill with bronchitis at his home in the country—*enfin,* that 'stodgy' old man, Mr. Shaw! There are criminals in high places sometimes, my friend. Ah, here we are. Mademoiselle, I have succeeded! You permit?"

And, beaming, Poirot kissed the astonished girl lightly on either cheek!

VI
THE ADVENTURE OF
THE EGYPTIAN TOMB

I have always considered that one of the most thrilling and dramatic of the many adventures I have shared with Poirot was that of our investigation into the strange series of deaths which followed upon the discovery and opening of the Tomb of King Men-her-Ra.

Hard upon the discovery of the Tomb of Tut-ankh-Amen by Lord Carnarvon, Sir John Willard and Mr. Bleibner of New York, pursuing their excavations not far from Cairo, in the vicinity of the Pyramids of Gizeh, came unexpectedly on a series of funeral chambers. The greatest interest was aroused by their discovery. The Tomb appeared to be that of King Men-her-Ra, one of those shadowy kings of the Eighth Dynasty, when the Old Kingdom was falling to decay. Little was known about this period, and the discoveries were fully reported in the newspapers.

An event soon occurred which took a profound hold on the public mind. Sir John Willard died quite suddenly of heart failure.

The more sensational newspapers immediately took the opportunity of reviving all the old superstitious stories connected with the ill luck of certain Egyptian treasures. The unlucky Mummy at the British Museum, that hoary old chestnut, was dragged out with fresh zest, was quietly denied by the Museum, but nevertheless enjoyed all its usual vogue.

A fortnight later Mr. Bleibner died of acute blood poisoning, and a few days afterwards a nephew of his shot himself in New York. The "Curse of Men-her-Ra" was the talk of the day, and the magic power of dead and gone Egypt was exalted to a fetish point.

It was then that Poirot received a brief note from Lady Willard, widow of the dead archaeologist, asking him to go and see her at her house in Kensington Square. I accompanied him.

Lady Willard was a tall, thin woman, dressed in deep mourning. Her haggard face bore eloquent testimony to her recent grief.

"It is kind of you to have come so promptly, Monsieur Poirot."

"I am at your service, Lady Willard. You wished to consult me?"

"You are, I am aware, a detective, but it is not only as a detective that I wish to consult you. You are a man of original views, I know, you have imagination, experience of the world—tell me, Monsieur Poirot, what are your views on the supernatural?"

Poirot hesitated for a moment before he replied. He seemed to be considering. Finally he said:

"Let us not misunderstand each other, Lady Willard. It is not a general question that you are asking me there. It has a personal application, has it not? You are referring obliquely to the death of your late husband?"

"That is so," she admitted.

"You want me to investigate the circumstances of his death?"

"I want you to ascertain for me exactly how much is newspaper chatter, and how much may be said to be founded on fact. Three deaths, Monsieur Poirot—each one explicable taken by itself, but taken together surely an almost unbelievable coincidence, and all within a month of the opening of the tomb! It may be mere superstition, it may be some potent curse from the past that operates in ways undreamed of by modern science. The fact remains—three deaths! And I am afraid, Monsieur Poirot, horribly afraid. It may not yet be the end."

"For whom do you fear?"

"For my son. When the news of my husband's death came I was ill. My son, who has just come down from Oxford, went out there. He brought the—the body home, but now he has gone out again, in spite of my prayers and entreaties. He is so fascinated by the work that he intends to take his father's place and carry on the system of excavations. You may think me a foolish, credulous woman, but, Monsieur Poirot, I am afraid. Supposing that the spirit of the dead King is not yet appeased? Perhaps to you I seem to be talking nonsense——"

"No, indeed, Lady Willard," said Poirot quickly. "I, too, believe in the force of superstition, one of the greatest forces the world has ever known."

I looked at him in surprise. I should never have credited Poirot with being superstitious. But the little man was obviously in earnest.

"What you really demand is that I shall protect your son? I will do my utmost to keep him from harm."

"Yes, in the ordinary way, but against an occult influence?"

"In volumes of the Middle Ages, Lady Willard, you will find many ways of counteracting black magic. Perhaps they knew more than we moderns with all our boasted science. Now let us come to facts, that I may have guidance. Your husband had always been a devoted Egyptologist, hadn't he?"

"Yes, from his youth upwards. He was one of the greatest living authorities upon the subject."

"But Mr. Bleibner, I understand, was more or less of an amateur?"

"Oh, quite. He was a very wealthy man who dabbled freely in any subject that happened to take his fancy. My husband managed to interest him in Egyptology, and it was his money that was so useful in financing the expedition."

"And the nephew? What do you know of his tastes? Was he with the party at all?"

"I do not think so. In fact I never knew of his existence till I read of his death in the paper. I do not think he and Mr. Bleibner can have been at all intimate. He never spoke of having any relations."

"Who are the other members of the party?"

"Well, there is Dr. Tosswill, minor official connected with the British Museum; Mr. Schneider of the Metropolitan Museum in New York; a young American secretary; Dr. Ames, who accompanies the expedition in his professional capacity; and Hassan, my husband's devoted native servant."

"Do you remember the name of the American secretary?"

"Harper, I think, but I cannot be sure. He had not been with Mr. Bleibner very long, I know. He was a very pleasant young fellow."

"Thank you, Lady Willard."

"If there is anything else——?"

"For the moment, nothing. Leave it now in my hands, and be assured that I will do all that is humanly possible to protect your son."

They were not exactly reassuring words, and I observed Lady Willard wince as he uttered them. Yet, at the same time, the fact that he had not pooh-poohed her fears seemed in itself to be a relief to her.

For my part I had never before suspected that Poirot had so deep a vein of superstition in his nature. I tackled him on the subject as we went homewards. His manner was grave and earnest.

"But yes, Hastings. I believe in these things. You must not underrate the force of superstition."

"What are we going to do about it?"

"*Toujours pratique,* the good Hastings! *Eh bien,* to begin with we are going to cable to New York for fuller details of young Mr. Bleibner's death."

He duly sent off his cable. The reply was full and precise. Young Rupert Bleibner had been in low water for several years. He had been a beach-comber and a remittance man in several South Sea islands, but had returned to New York two years ago, where he had rapidly sunk lower and lower. The most significant thing, to my mind, was that he had recently managed to borrow enough money to take him to Egypt. "I've a good friend there I can borrow from," he had declared. Here, however, his plans had gone awry. He had returned to New York cursing his skinflint of an uncle who cared more for the bones of dead and gone kings than his own flesh and blood. It was during his sojourn in Egypt that the death of Sir John Willard occurred. Rupert had plunged once more into his life of dissipation in New York, and then, without warning, he had committed suicide, leaving-behind him a letter which contained some curious phrases. It seemed written in a sudden fit of remorse. He referred to himself as a leper and an outcast, and the letter ended by declaring that such as he were better dead.

A shadowy theory leapt into my brain. I had never really believed in the vengeance of a long dead Egyptian king. I saw here a more modern crime. Supposing this young man had decided to do away with his uncle —preferably by poison. By mistake, Sir John Willard receives the fatal dose. The young man returns to New York, haunted by his crime. The news of his uncle's death reaches him. He realizes how unnecessary his crime has been, and stricken with remorse takes his own life.

I outlined my solutions to Poirot. He was interested.

"It is ingenious what you have thought of there—decidedly it is ingenious. It may even be true. But you leave out of count the fatal influence of the Tomb."

I shrugged my shoulders.

"You still think that has something to do with it?"

"So much so, *mon ami,* that we start for Egypt tomorrow."

"What?" I cried, astonished.

"I have said it." An expression of conscious heroism spread over Poirot's face. Then he groaned. "But, oh," he lamented, "the sea! The hateful sea!"

It was a week later. Beneath our feet was the golden sand of the desert. The hot sun poured down overhead. Poirot, the picture of misery, wilted by my side. The little man was not a good traveler. Our four days' voyage from Marseilles had been one long agony to him. He had landed at Alexandria the wraith of his former self, even his usual neatness had deserted him. We had arrived in Cairo and had driven out at once to the Mena House Hotel, right in the shadow of the Pyramids.

The charm of Egypt had laid hold of me. Not so Poirot. Dressed precisely the same as in London, he carried a small clothes-brush in his pocket and waged an unceasing war on the dust which accumulated on his dark apparel.

"And my boots," he wailed. "Regard them, Hastings.

My boots, of the neat patent leather, usually so smart and shining. See, the sand is inside them, which is painful, and outside them, which outrages the eyesight. Also the heat, it causes my mustaches to become limp—but limp!"

"Look at the Sphinx," I urged. "Even I can feel the mystery and the charm it exhales."

Poirot looked at it discontentedly.

"It has not the air happy," he declared. "How could it, half-buried in sand in that untidy fashion. Ah, this cursed sand!"

"Come, now, there's a lot of sand in Belgium," I reminded him, mindful of a holiday spent at Knocke-sur-mer in the midst of *"les dunes impeccables"* as the guide-book had phrased it.

"Not in Brussels," declared Poirot. He gazed at the Pyramids thoughtfully. "It is true that they, at least, are of a shape solid and geometrical, but their surface is of an unevenness most unpleasing. And the palm-trees I like them not. Not even do they plant them in rows!"

I cut short his lamentations, by suggesting that we should start for the camp. We were to ride there on camels, and the beasts were patiently kneeling, waiting for us to mount, in charge of several picturesque boys headed by a voluble dragoman.

I pass over the spectacle of Poirot on a camel. He started by groans and lamentations and ended by shrieks, gesticulations and invocations to the Virgin Mary and every Saint in the calendar. In the end, he descended ignominiously and finished the journey on a diminutive donkey. I must admit that a trotting camel is no joke for the amateur. I was stiff for several days.

At last we neared the scene of the excavations. A sun-burnt man with a gray beard, in white clothes, and wearing a helmet, came to meet us.

"Monsieur Poirot and Captain Hastings? We received your cable. I'm sorry that there was no one to meet you in Cairo. An unforeseen event occurred which completely disorganized our plans."

Poirot paled. His hand, which had stolen to his clothes-brush, stayed its course.

"Not another death?" he breathed.

"Yes."

"Sir Guy Willard?" I cried.

"No, Captain Hastings. My American colleague, Mr. Schneider."

"And the cause?" demanded Poirot.

"Tetanus."

I blanched. All around me I seemed to feel an atmosphere of evil, subtle and menacing. A horrible thought flashed across me. Supposing I were the next?

"Mon Dieu," said Poirot, in a very low voice, "I do not understand this. It is horrible. Tell me, monsieur, there is no doubt that it was tetanus?"

"I believe not. But Dr. Ames will tell you more than I can do."

"Ah, of course, you are not the doctor."

"My name is Tosswill."

This, then, was the British expert described by Lady Willard as being a minor official at the British Museum. There was something at once grave and steadfast about him that took my fancy.

"If you will come with me," continued Dr. Tosswill, "I will take you to Sir Guy Willard. He was most anxious to be informed as soon as you should arrive."

We were taken across the camp to a large tent. Dr. Tosswill lifted up the flap and we entered. Three men were sitting inside.

"Monsieur Poirot and Captain Hastings have arrived, Sir Guy," said Tosswill.

The youngest of the three men jumped up and came forward to greet us. There was a certain impulsiveness in his manner which reminded me of his mother. He was not nearly so sunburnt as the others, and that fact, coupled with a certain haggardness round the eyes, made him look older than his twenty-two years. He was clearly endeavoring to bear up under a severe mental strain.

He introduced his two companions, Dr. Ames, a capable looking man of thirty odd, with a touch of graying hair at the temples, and Mr. Harper, the secretary, a pleasant lean young man wearing the national insignia of horn-rimmed spectacles.

After a few minutes' desultory conversation the latter

went out, and Dr. Tosswill followed him. We were left alone with Sir Guy and Dr. Ames.

"Please ask any questions you want to ask, Monsieur Poirot," said Willard. "We are utterly dumfounded at this strange series of disasters, but it isn't—it can't be, anything but coincidence."

There was a nervousness about his manner which rather belied the words. I saw that Poirot was studying him keenly.

"Your heart is really in this work, Sir Guy?"

"Rather. No matter what happens, or what comes of it, the work is going on. Make up your mind to that."

Poirot wheeled round on the other.

"What have you to say to that, *monsieur le docteur?*"

"Well," drawled the doctor, "I'm not for quitting myself."

Poirot made one of those expressive grimaces of his.

"Then, *évidemment,* we must find out just how we stand. When did Mr. Schneider's death take place?"

"Three days ago."

"You are sure it was tetanus?"

"Dead sure."

"It couldn't have been a case of strychnine poisoning, for instance?"

"No, Monsieur Poirot. I see what you're getting at. But it was a clear case of tetanus."

"Did you not inject anti-serum?"

"Certainly we did," said the doctor dryly. "Every conceivable thing that could be done was tried."

"Had you the anti-serum with you?"

"No. We procured it from Cairo."

"Have there been any other cases of tetanus in the camp?"

"No, not one."

"Are you certain that the death of Mr. Bleibner was not due to tetanus?"

"Absolutely plumb certain. He had a scratch upon his thumb which became poisoned, and septicæmia set in. It sounds pretty much the same to a layman, I dare say, but the two things are entirely different."

"Then we have four deaths—all totally dissimilar, one heart failure, one blood poisoning, one suicide and one tetanus."

"Exactly, Monsieur Poirot."

"Are you certain that there is nothing which might link the four together?"

"I don't quite understand you?"

"I will put it plainly. Was any act committed by those four men which might seem to denote disrespect to the spirit of Men-her-Ra?"

The doctor gazed at Poirot in astonishment.

"You're talking through your hat, Monsieur Poirot. Surely you've not been guyed into believing all that fool talk?"

"Absolute nonsense," muttered Willard angrily.

Poirot remained placidly immovable, blinking a little out of his green cat's eyes.

"So you do not believe it, *monsieur le docteur?*"

"No, sir, I do not," declared the doctor emphatically. "I am a scientific man, and I believe only what science teaches."

"Was there no science then in Ancient Egypt?" asked Poirot softly. He did not wait for a reply, and indeed Dr. Ames seemed rather at a loss for the moment. "No, no, do not answer me, but tell me this. What do the native workmen think?"

"I guess," said Dr. Ames, "that, where white folk lose their heads, natives aren't going to be far behind. I'll admit that they're getting what you might call scared—but they've no cause to be."

"I wonder," said Poirot non-committally.

Sir Guy leant forward.

"Surely," he cried incredulously, "you cannot believe in—oh, but the thing's absurd! You can know nothing of Ancient Egypt if you think that."

For answer Poirot produced a little book from his pocket—an ancient tattered volume. As he held it out I saw its title, *The Magic of the Egyptians and Chaldeans.* Then, wheeling round, he strode out of the tent. The doctor stared at me.

"What is his little idea?"

The phrase, so familiar on Poirot's lips, made me smile as it came from another.

"I don't know exactly," I confessed. "He's got some plan of exorcizing the evil spirits, I believe."

I went in search of Poirot, and found him talking to the lean-faced young man who had been the late Mr. Bleibner's secretary.

"No," Mr. Harper was saying, "I've only been six months with the expedition. Yes, I knew Mr. Bleibner's affairs pretty well."

"Can you recount to me anything concerning his nephew?"

"He turned up here one day, not a bad-looking fellow. I'd never met him before, but some of the others had—Ames, I think, and Schneider. The old man wasn't at all pleased to see him. They were at it in no time, hammer and tongs. 'Not a cent,' the old man shouted. 'Not one cent now or when I'm dead. I intend to leave my money to the furtherance of my life's work. I've been talking it over with Mr. Schneider to-day.' And a bit more of the same. Young Bleibner lit out for Cairo right away."

"Was he in perfectly good health at the time?"

"The old man?"

"No, the young one."

"I believe he did mention there was something wrong with him. But it couldn't have been anything serious, or I should have remembered."

"One thing more, has Mr. Bleibner left a will?"

"So far as we know, he has not."

"Are you remaining with the expedition, Mr. Harper?"

"No, sir, I am not. I'm for New York as soon as I can square up things here. You may laugh if you like, but I'm not going to be this blasted old Men-her-Ra's next victim. He'll get me if I stop here."

The young man wiped the perspiration from his brow.

Poirot turned away. Over his shoulder he said with a peculiar smile:

"Remember, he got one of his victims in New York."

"Oh, hell!" said Mr. Harper forcibly.

"That young man is nervous," said Poirot thoughtfully. "He is on the edge, but absolutely on the edge."

I glanced at Poirot curiously, but his enigmatical smile told me nothing. In company with Sir Guy Willard and Dr. Tosswill we were taken round the excavations. The principal finds had been removed to Cairo, but some of the tomb furniture was extremely interesting. The enthusiasm of the young baronet was obvious, but I fancied that I detected a shade of nervousness in his manner as though he could not quite escape from the feeling of menace in the air. As we entered the tent which had been assigned to us, for a wash before joining the evening meal, a tall dark figure in white robes stood aside to let us pass with a graceful gesture and a murmured greeting in Arabic. Poirot stopped.

"You are Hassan, the late Sir John Willard's servant?"

"I served my Lord Sir John, now I serve his son." He took a step nearer to us and lowered his voice. "You are a wise one, they say, learned in dealing with evil spirits. Let the young master depart from here. There is evil in the air around us."

And with an abrupt gesture, not waiting for a reply, he strode away.

"Evil in the air," muttered Poirot. "Yes, I feel it."

Our meal was hardly a cheerful one. The floor was left to Dr. Tosswill, who discoursed at length upon Egyptian antiquities. Just as we were preparing to retire to rest, Sir Guy caught Poirot by the arm and pointed. A shadowy figure was moving amidst the tents. It was no human one: I recognized distinctly the dog-headed figure I had seen carved on the walls of the tomb.

My blood literally froze at the sight.

"Mon Dieu!" murmured Poirot, crossing himself vigorously. "Anubis, the jackal-headed, the god of departing souls."

"Some one is hoaxing us," cried Dr. Tosswill, rising indignantly to his feet.

"It went into your tent, Harper," muttered Sir Guy, his face dreadfully pale.

"No," said Poirot, shaking his head, "into that of the Dr. Ames."

The doctor stared at him incredulously; then, repeating Dr. Tosswill's words, he cried:

"Some one is hoaxing us. Come, we'll soon catch the fellow."

He dashed energetically in pursuit of the shadowy apparition. I followed him, but, search as we would, we could find no trace of any living thing having passed that way. We returned, somewhat disturbed in mind, to find Poirot taking energetic measures, in his own way, to ensure his personal safety. He was busily surrounding our tent with various diagrams and inscriptions which he was drawing in the sand. I recognized the five-pointed star or Pentagon many times repeated. As was his wont, Poirot was at the same time delivering an impromptu lecture on witchcraft and magic in general, White Magic as opposed to Black, with various references to the Ka and the Book of the Dead thrown in.

It appeared to excite the liveliest contempt in Dr. Tosswill, who drew me aside, literally snorting with rage.

"Balderdash, sir," he exclaimed angrily. "Pure balderdash. The man's an impostor. He doesn't know the difference between the superstitions of the Middle Ages and the beliefs of Ancient Egypt. Never have I heard such a hotch-potch of ignorance and credulity."

I calmed the excited expert, and joined Poirot in the tent. My little friend was beaming cheerfully.

"We can now sleep in peace," he declared happily. "And I can do with some sleep. My head, it aches abominably. Ah, for a good *tisane!*"

As though in answer to prayer, the flap of the tent was lifted and Hassan appeared, bearing a steaming cup which he offered to Poirot. It proved to be camomile tea, a beverage of which he is inordinately fond. Having thanked Hassan and refused his offer of another cup for myself, we were left alone once more. I stood at the door of the tent some time after undressing, looking out over the desert.

"A wonderful place," I said aloud, "and a wonderful work. I can feel the fascination. This desert life, this probing into the heart of a vanished civilization. Surely, Poirot, you, too, must feel the charm?"

I got no answer, and I turned, a little annoyed. My annoyance was quickly changed to concern. Poirot was lying back across the rude couch, his face horribly convulsed. Beside him was the empty cup. I rushed to his side, then dashed out and across the camp to Dr. Ames's tent.

"Dr. Ames!" I cried. "Come at once."

"What's the matter?" said the doctor, appearing in pyjamas.

"My friend. He's ill. Dying. The camomile tea. Don't let Hassan leave the camp."

Like a flash the doctor ran to our tent. Poirot was lying as I left him.

"Extraordinary," cried Ames. "Looks like a seizure—or—what did you say about something he drank?" He picked up the empty cup.

"Only I did not drink it!" said a placid voice.

We turned in amazement. Poirot was sitting up on the bed. He was smiling.

"No," he said gently. "I did not drink it. While my good friend Hastings was apostrophizing the night, I took the opportunity of pouring it, not down my throat, but into a little bottle. That little bottle will go to the analytical chemist. No"—as the doctor made a sudden movement—"as a sensible man, you will understand that violence will be of no avail. During Hastings' brief absence to fetch you, I have had time to put the bottle in safe keeping. Ah, quick, Hastings, hold him!"

I misunderstood Poirot's anxiety. Eager to save my friend, I flung myself in front of him. But the doctor's swift movement had another meaning. His hand went to his mouth, a smell of bitter almonds filled the air, and he swayed forward and fell.

"Another victim," said Poirot gravely, "but the last. Perhaps it is the best way. He has three deaths on his head."

"Dr. Ames?" I cried, stupefied. "But I thought you believed in some occult influence?"

"You misunderstood me, Hastings. What I meant was that I believe in the terrific force of superstition. Once get it firmly established that a series of deaths are super-

natural, and you might almost stab a man in broad daylight, and it would still be put down to the curse, so
strongly is the instinct of the supernatural implanted in
the human race. I suspected from the first that a man
was taking advantage of that instinct. The idea came to
him, I imagine, with the death of Sir John Willard. A
fury of superstition arose at once. As far as I could see,
nobody could derive any particular profit from Sir John's
death. Mr. Bleibner was a different case. He was a man
of great wealth. The information I received from New
York contained several suggestive points. To begin with,
young Bleibner was reported to have said he had a good
friend in Egypt from whom he could borrow. It was
tacitly understood that he meant his uncle, but it seemed
to me that in that case he would have said so outright.
The words suggest some boon companion of his own.
Another thing, he scraped up enough money to take him
to Egypt, his uncle refused outright to advance him a
penny, yet he was able to pay the return passage to New
York. Some one must have lent him the money."

"All that was very thin," I objected.

"But there was more. Hastings, there occur often enough
words spoken metaphorically which are taken literally.
The opposite can happen too. In this case, words which
were meant literally were taken metaphorically. Young
Bleibner wrote plainly enough: 'I am a leper,' but nobody
realized that he shot himself because he believed that he
had contracted the dread disease of leprosy."

"What?" I ejaculated.

"It was the clever invention of a diabolical mind. Young
Bleibner was suffering from some minor skin trouble, he
had lived in the South Sea Islands, where the disease is
common enough. Ames was a former friend of his, and
a well-known medical man, he would never have dreamed
of doubting his word. When I arrived here, my suspicions
were divided between Harper and Dr. Ames, but I soon
realized that only the doctor could have perpetrated and
concealed the crimes, and I learnt from Harper that he
was previously acquainted with young Bleibner. Doubtless
the latter at some time or another had made a will or
had insured his life in favor of the doctor. The latter saw

his chance of acquiring wealth. It was easy for him to in-
oculate Mr. Bleibner with the deadly germs. Then the
nephew, overcome with despair at the dread news his
friend had conveyed to him, shot himself. Mr. Bleibner,
whatever his intentions, had made no will. His fortune
would pass to his nephew and from him to the doctor."

"And Mr. Schneider?"

"We cannot be sure. He knew young Bleibner too, remember, and may have suspected something, or, again,
the doctor may have thought that a further death motive-
less and purposeless would strengthen the coils of superstition. Furthermore, I will tell you an interesting psy-
chological fact, Hastings. A murderer has always a strong
desire to repeat his successful crime, the performance of
it grows upon him. Hence my fears for young Willard.
The figure of Anubis you saw to-night was Hassan,
dressed up by my orders. I wanted to see if I could fright-
en the doctor. But it would take more than the supernatural to frighten him. I could see that he was not entirely taken in by my pretenses of belief in the occult. The
little comedy I played for him did not deceive him. I
suspected that he would endeavor to make me the next
victim. Ah, but in spite of *la mer maudite,* the heat abom-
inable, and the annoyances of the sand, the little gray
cells still functioned!"

Poirot proved to be perfectly right in his premises.
Young Bleibner, some years ago, in a fit of drunken merri-
ment, had made a jocular will, leaving "my cigarette case
you admire so much and everything else of which I die
possessed which will be principally debts to my good
friend Robert Ames who once saved my life from drown-
ing."

The case was hushed up as far as possible, and, to
this day, people talk of the remarkable series of deaths
in connection with the Tomb of Men-her-Ra as a trimph-
al proof of the vengeance of a bygone king upon the
desecrators of his tomb—a belief which, as Poirot pointed
out to me, is contrary to all Egyptian belief and thought.

VII
THE JEWEL ROBBERY
AT THE GRAND METROPOLITAN

"Poirot," I said, "a change of air would do you good."

"You think so, *mon ami?*"

"I am sure of it."

"Eh—eh?" said my friend, smiling. "It is all arranged, then?"

"You will come?"

"Where do you propose to take me?"

"Brighton. As a matter of fact, a friend of mine in the City put me on to a very good thing, and—well, I have money to burn, as the saying goes. I think a week-end at the *Grand Metropolitan* would do us all the good in the world."

"Thank you, I accept most gratefully. You have the good heart to think of an old man. And the good heart, it is in the end worth all the little gray cells. Yes, yes, I who speak to you am in danger of forgetting that sometimes."

I did not quite relish the implication. I fancy that Poirot is sometimes a little inclined to underestimate my mental capacities. But his pleasure was so evident that I put my slight annoyance aside.

"Then, that's all right," I said hastily.

Saturday evening saw us dining at the *Grand Metropolitan* in the midst of a gay throng. All the world and his wife seemed to be at Brighton. The dresses were marvellous, and the jewels—worn sometimes with more love of display than good taste—were something magnificent.

"*Hein,* it is a sight this!" murmured Poirot. "This is the home of the Profiteer, is it not so, Hastings?"

"Supposed to be," I replied. "But we'll hope they aren't all tarred with the profiteering brush."

Poirot gazed round him placidly.

"The sight of so many jewels makes me wish I had turned my brains to crime, instead of to its detection. What a magnificent opportunity for some thief of distinction! Regard, Hastings, that stout woman by the pillar. She is, as you would say, plastered with gems."

I followed his eyes.

"Why," I exclaimed, "it's Mrs. Opalsen."

"You know her?"

"Slightly. Her husband is a rich stockbroker who made a fortune in the recent Oil boom."

After dinner we ran across the Opalsens in the lounge, and I introduced Poirot to them. We chatted for a few minutes, and ended by having our coffee together.

Poirot said a few words in praise of some of the costlier gems displayed on the lady's ample bosom, and she brightened up at once.

"It's a perfect hobby of mine, Mr. Poirot. I just *love* jewelry. Ed knows my weakness, and every time things go well he brings me something new. You are interested in precious stones?"

"I have had a good deal to do with them one time and another, madame. My profession has brought me into contact with some of the most famous jewels in the world."

He went on to narrate, with discreet pseudonyms, the story of the historic jewels of a reigning house, and Mrs. Opalsen listened with bated breath.

"There now!" she exclaimed, as he ended. "If it isn't just like a play! You know, I've got some pearls of my own that have a history attached to them. I believe it's supposed to be one of the finest necklaces in the world—pearls so beautifully matched and so perfect in color. I declare I really must run up and get it!"

"Oh, madame," protested Poirot, "you are too amiable. Pray do not derange yourself!"

"Oh, but I'd like to show it to you."

The buxom dame waddled across to the lift briskly enough. Her husband, who had been talking to me, looked at Poirot inquiringly.

"Madame your wife is so amiable as to insist on showing me her pearl necklace," explained the latter.

"Oh, the pearls!" Opalsen smiled in a satisfied fashion. "Well, they are worth seeing. Cost a pretty penny too! Still, the money's there all right; I could get what I paid for them any day—perhaps more. May have to, too, if things go on as they are now. Money's confoundedly tight in the City. All this infernal E.P.D." He rambled on, launching into technicalities where I could not follow him.

He was interrupted by a small page-boy who approached and murmured something in his ear.

"Eh—what? I'll come at once. Not taken ill, is she? Excuse me, gentlemen."

He left us abruptly. Poirot leaned back and lit one of his tiny Russian cigarettes. Then, carefully and meticulously, he arranged the empty coffee-cups in a neat row, and beamed happily on the result.

The minutes passed. The Opalsens did not return.

"Curious," I remarked, at length. "I wonder when they will come back."

Poirot watched the ascending spirals of smoke, and then said thoughtfully:

"They will not come back."

"Why?"

"Because, my friend, something has happened."

"What sort of thing? How do you know?" I asked curiously.

Poirot smiled.

"A few moments ago the manager came hurriedly out of his office and ran upstairs. He was much agitated. The lift-boy is deep in talk with one of the pages. The lift-bell has rung three times, but he heeds it not. Thirdly, even the waiters are *distrait;* and to make a waiter *distrait*—" Poirot shook his head with an air of finality. "The affair must indeed be of the first magnitude. Ah, it is as I thought! Here come the police."

Two men had just entered the hotel—one in uniform, the other in plain clothes. They spoke to a page, and were immediately ushered upstairs. A few minutes later, the same boy descended and came up to where we were sitting.

"Mr. Opalsen's compliments, and would you step upstairs."

Poirot sprang nimbly to his feet. One would have said that he awaited the summons. I followed with no less alacrity.

The Opalsens' apartments were situated on the first floor. After knocking on the door, the page-boy retired, and we answered the summons, "Come in!" A strange scene met our eyes. The room was Mrs. Opalsen's bedroom, and in the center of it, lying back in an armchair, was the lady herself, weeping violently. She presented an extraordinary spectacle, with tears making great furrows in the powder with which her complexion was liberally coated. Mr. Opalsen was striding up and down angrily. The two police officials stood in the middle of the room, one with a notebook in hand. An hotel chambermaid, looking frightened to death, stood by the fireplace; and on the other side of the room a Frenchwoman, obviously Mrs. Opalsen's maid, was weeping and wringing her hands, with an intensity of grief that rivaled that of her mistress.

Into this pandemonium stepped Poirot, neat and smiling. Immediately, with an energy surprising in one of her bulk, Mrs. Opalsen sprang from her chair towards him.

"There now; Ed may say what he likes, but I believe in luck. I do. It was fated I should meet you the way I did this evening, and I've a feeling that if you can't get my pearls back for me nobody can."

"Calm yourself, I pray of you, madame." Poirot patted her hand soothingly. "Reassure yourself. All will be well. Hercule Poirot will aid you!"

Mr. Opalsen turned to the police inspector.

"There will be no objection to my—er—calling in this gentleman, I suppose?"

"None at all, sir," replied the man civilly, but with complete indifference. "Perhaps now your lady's feeling better she'll just let us have the facts?"

Mrs. Opalsen looked helplessly at Poirot. He led her back to her chair.

"Seat yourself, madame, and recount to us the whole history without agitating yourself."

Thus abjured, Mrs. Opalsen dried her eyes gingerly, and began.

"I came upstairs after dinner to fetch my pearls for Mr. Poirot here to see. The chambermaid and Célestine were both in the room as usual——"

"Excuse me, madame, but what do you mean by 'as usual'?"

Mr. Opalsen explained.

"I make it a rule that no one is to come into this room unless Célestine, the maid, is there also. The chambermaid does the room in the morning while Célestine is present, and comes in after dinner to turn down the beds under the same conditions; otherwise she never enters the room."

"Well, as I was saying," continued Mrs. Opalsen, "I came up. I went to the drawer here,"—she indicated the bottom right-hand drawer of the kneehole dressing-table —"took out my jewel-case and unlocked it. It seemed quite as usual—but the pearls were not there!"

The inspector had been busy with his notebook. "When had you last seen them?" he asked.

"They were there when I went down to dinner."

"You are sure?"

"Quite sure. I was uncertain whether to wear them or not, but in the end I decided on the emeralds, and put them back in the jewel-case."

"Who locked up the jewel-case?"

"I did. I wear the key on a chain round my neck." She held it up as she spoke.

The inspector examined it, and shrugged his shoulders.

"The thief must have had a duplicate key. No difficult matter. The lock is quite a simple one. What did you do after you'd locked the jewel-case?"

"I put it back in the bottom drawer where I always keep it."

"You didn't lock the drawer?"

"No, I never do. My maid remains in the room till I come up, so there's no need."

The inspector's face grew graver.

"Am I to understand that the jewels were there when you went down to dinner, and that since then *the maid has not left the room?*"

Suddenly, as though the horror of her own situation for the first time burst upon her, Célestine uttered a piercing shriek, and, flinging herself upon Poirot, poured out a torrent of incoherent French.

The suggestion was infamous! That she should be suspected of robbing Madame! The police were well known to be of a stupidity incredible! But Monsieur, who was a Frenchman——

"A Belgian," interjected Poirot, but Célestine paid no attention to the correction.

Monsieur would not stand by and see her falsely accused, while that infamous chambermaid was allowed to go scot-free. She had never liked her—a bold, red-faced thing—a born thief. She had said from the first that she was not honest. And had kept a sharp watch over her too, when she was doing Madame's room! Let those idiots of policemen search her, and if they did not find Madame's pearls on her it would be very surprising!

Although this harangue was uttered in rapid and virulent French, Célestine had interlarded it with a wealth of gesture, and the chambermaid realized at least a part of her meaning. She reddened angrily.

"If that foreign woman's saying I took the pearls, it's a lie!" she declared heatedly. "I never so much as saw them."

"Search her!" screamed the other. "You will find it as I say."

"You're a liar—do you hear?" said the chambermaid, advancing upon her. "Stole 'em yourself, and want to put it on me. Why, I was only in the room about three minutes before the lady come up, and then you were sitting here the whole time, as you always do, like a cat watching a mouse."

The inspector looked across inquiringly at Célestine. "Is that true? Didn't you leave the room at all?"

"I did not actually leave her alone," admitted Célestine reluctantly, "but I went into my own room through the door here twice—once to fetch a reel of cotton, and once for my scissors. She must have done it then."

"You wasn't gone a minute," retorted the chambermaid angrily. "Just popped out and in again. I'd be glad if the police *would* search me. *I've* nothing to be afraid of."

At this moment there was a tap at the door. The inspector went to it. His face brightened when he saw who it was.

"Ah!" he said. "That's rather fortunate. I sent for one of our female searchers, and she's just arrived. Perhaps if you wouldn't mind going into the room next door."

He looked at the chambermaid, who stepped across the threshold with a toss of her head, the searcher following her closely.

The French girl had sunk sobbing into a chair. Poirot was looking round the room, the main features of which I have made clear by a sketch.

"Where does that door lead?" he inquired, nodding his head towards the one by the window.

"Into the next apartment, I believe," said the inspector. "It's bolted, anyway, on this side."

Poirot walked across to it, tried it, then drew back the bolt and tried it again.

"And on the other side as well," he remarked. "Well, that seems to rule out that."

He walked over to the windows, examining each of them in turn.

"And again—nothing. Not even a balcony outside."

"Even if there were," said the inspector impatiently, "I don't see how that would help us, if the maid never left the room."

"*Évidemment*," said Poirot, not disconcerted. "As Mademoiselle is positive she did not leave the room———"

He was interrupted by the reappearance of the chambermaid and the police searcher.

"Nothing," said the latter laconically.

"I should hope not, indeed," said the chambermaid virtuously. "And that French hussy ought to be ashamed of herself taking away an honest girl's character!"

"There, there, my girl; that's all right," said the inspector, opening the door. "Nobody suspects you. You go along and get on with your work."

The chambermaid went unwillingly.

"Going to search *her?*" she demanded, pointing at Célestine.

"Yes, yes!" He shut the door on her and turned the key.

Célestine accompanied the searcher into the small room in her turn. A few minutes later she also returned. Nothing had been found on her.

The inspector's face grew graver.

"I'm afraid I'll have to ask you to come along with me all the same, miss." He turned to Mrs. Opalsen. "I'm sorry, madam, but all the evidence points that way. If she's not got them on her, they're hidden somewhere about the room."

Célestine uttered a piercing shriek, and clung to Poirot's arm. The latter bent and whispered something in the girl's ear. She looked up at him doubtfully.

"*Si, si, mon enfant*—I assure you it is better not to resist." Then he turned to the inspector. "You permit, monsieur? A little experiment—purely for my own satisfaction."

"Depends on what it is," replied the police officer noncommittally.

Poirot addressed Célestine once more.

"You have told us that you went into your room to fetch a reel of cotton. Whereabouts was it?"

"On the top of the chest of drawers, monsieur."

"And the scissors?"

"They also."

"Would it be troubling you too much, mademoiselle, to ask you to repeat those two actions? You were sitting here with your work, you say?"

Célestine sat down, and then, at a sign from Poirot, rose, passing into the adjoining room, took up an object from the chest of drawers, and returned.

Poirot divided his attention between her movements and a large turnip of a watch which he held in the palm of his hand.

"Again, if you please, mademoiselle."

At the conclusion of the second performance, he made a note in his pocket-book, and returned the watch to his pocket.

"Thank you, mademoiselle. And you, monsieur,"—he bowed to the inspector—"for your courtesy."

The inspector seemed somewhat entertained by this excessive politeness. Célestine departed in a flood of tears, accompanied by the woman and the plain-clothes official.

Then, with a brief apology to Mrs. Opalsen, the inspector set to work to ransack the room. He pulled out drawers, opened cupboards, completely unmade the bed, and tapped the floor. Mr. Opalsen looked on skeptically.

"You really think you will find them?"

"Yes, sir. It stands to reason. She hadn't time to take them out of the room. The lady's discovering the robbery so soon upset her plans. No, they're here right enough. One of the two must have hidden them—and it's very unlikely for the chambermaid to have done so."

"More than unlikely—impossible!" said Poirot quietly.

"Eh?" The inspector stared.

Poirot smiled modestly.

"I will demonstrate. Hastings, my good friend, take my watch in your hand—with care. It is a family heirloom! Just now I timed Mademoiselle's movements—her first absence from the room was of twelve seconds, her second of fifteen. Now observe my actions. Madame will have the kindness to give me the key of the jewel-case. I thank you. My friend Hastings will have the kindness to say 'Go!' "

"Go!" I said.

With almost incredible swiftness, Poirot wrenched open the drawer of the dressing-table, extracted the jewel-case, fitted the key in the lock, opened the case, selected a piece of jewelry, shut and locked the case, and returned it to the drawer, which he pushed to again. His movements were like lightning.

"Well, *mon ami?*" he demanded of me breathlessly.

"Forty-six seconds," I replied.

"You see?" He looked round. "There would not have been time for the chambermaid even to take the necklace out, far less hide it."

"Then that settles it on the maid," said the inspector with satisfaction, and returned to his search. He passed into the maid's bedroom next door.

Poirot was frowning thoughtfully. Suddenly he shot a question at Mr. Opalsen.

"This necklace—it was, without doubt, insured?"

Mr. Opalsen looked a trifle surprised at the question.

"Yes," he said hesitatingly, "that is so."

"But what does that matter?" broke in Mrs. Opalsen tearfully. "It's my necklace I want. It was unique. No money could be the same."

"I comprehend, madame," said Poirot soothingly. "I comprehend perfectly. To *la femme* sentiment is everything—is it not so? But monsieur, who has not the so fine susceptibility, will doubtless find some slight consolation in the fact."

"Of course, of course," said Mr. Opalsen rather uncertainly. "Still——"

He was interrupted by a shout of triumph from the inspector. He came in dangling something from his fingers.

With a cry, Mrs. Opalsen heaved herself up from her chair. She was a changed woman.

"Oh, oh, my necklace!"

She clasped it to her breast with both hands. We crowded around.

"Where was it?" demanded Opalsen.

"Maid's bed. In among the springs of the wire mattress. She must have stolen it and hidden it there before the chambermaid arrived on the scene."

"You permit, madame?" said Poirot gently. He took the necklace from her and examined it closely; then handed it back with a bow.

"I'm afraid, madam, you'll have to hand it over to us for the time being," said the inspector. "We shall want it for the charge. But it shall be returned to you as soon as possible."

Mr. Opalsen frowned.

"Is that necessary?"

"I'm afraid so, sir. Just a formality."

"Oh, let him take it, Ed!" cried his wife. "I'd feel safer if he did. I shouldn't sleep a wink thinking someone else might try and get hold of it. That wretched girl! And I would never have believed it of her."

"There, there, my dear, don't take on so." I felt a gentle pressure on my arm. It was Poirot.

"Shall we slip away, my friend? I think our services are no longer needed."

Once outside, however, he hesitated, and then, much to my surprise, he remarked:

"I should rather like to see the room next door."

The door was not locked, and we entered. The room, which was a large double one, was unoccupied. Dust lay about rather noticeably, and my sensitive friend gave a characteristic grimace as he ran his finger round a rectangular mark on a table near the window.

"The *service* leaves to be desired," he observed dryly.

He was staring thoughtfully out of the window, and seemed to have fallen into a brown study.

"Well?" I demanded impatiently. "What did we come in here for?"

He stared.

"*Je vous demande pardon, mon ami.* I wished to see if the door was really bolted on this side also."

"Well," I said, glancing at the door which communicated with the room we had just left, "it *is* bolted."

Poirot nodded. He still seemed to be thinking.

"And, anyway," I continued, "what does it matter?

The case is over. I wish you'd had more chance of distinguishing yourself. But it was the kind of case that even a stiff-backed idiot like that inspector couldn't go wrong over."

Poirot shook his head.

"The case is not over, my friend. It will not be over until we find out who stole the pearls."

"But the maid did!"

"Why do you say that?"

"Why," I stammered, "they were found—actually in her mattress."

"Ta, ta, ta!" said Poirot impatiently. "Those were not the pearls."

"What?"

"Imitation, *mon ami.*"

The statement took my breath away. Poirot was smiling placidly.

"The good inspector obviously knows nothing of jewels. But presently there will be a fine hullabaloo!"

"Come!" I cried, dragging at his arm.

"Where?"

"We must tell the Opalsens at once."

"I think not."

"But that poor woman——"

"*Eh bien;* that poor woman, as you call her, will have a much better night believing the jewels to be safe."

"But the thief may escape with them!"

"As usual, my friend, you speak without reflection. How do you know that the pearls Mrs. Opalsen locked up so carefully to-night were not the false ones, and that the real robbery did not take place at a much earlier date?"

"Oh!" I said bewildered.

"Exactly," said Poirot, beaming. "We start again."

He led the way out of the room, paused a moment as though considering, and then walked down to the end of the corridor, stopping outside the small den where the chambermaids and valets of the respective floors congregated. Our particular chambermaid appeared to be holding a small court there, and to be retailing her late experiences to an appreciative audience. She stopped in the middle of a sentence. Poirot bowed with his usual politeness.

"Excuse that I derange you, but I shall be obliged if you will unlock for me the door of Mr. Opalsen's room."

The woman rose willingly, and we accompanied her down the passage again. Mr. Opalsen's room was on the other side of the corridor, its door facing that of his wife's room. The chambermaid unlocked it with her passkey, and we entered.

As she was about to depart Poirot detained her.

"One moment; have you ever seen among the effects of Mr. Opalsen a card like this?"

He held out a plain white card, rather highly glazed and uncommon in appearance. The maid took it and scrutinized it carefully.

"No, sir, I can't say I have. But, anyway, the valet has most to do with the gentlemen's rooms."

"I see. Thank you."

Poirot took back the card. The woman departed. Poirot appeared to reflect a little. Then he gave a short, sharp nod of the head.

"Ring the bell, I pray of you, Hastings. Three times, for the valet."

I obeyed, devoured with curiosity. Meanwhile Poirot had emptied the waste-paper basket on the floor, and was swiftly going through its contents.

In a few moments the valet answered the bell. To him Poirot put the same question, and handed him the card to examine. But the response was the same. The valet had never seen a card of that particular quality among Mr. Opalsen's belongings. Poirot thanked him, and he withdrew, somewhat unwillingly, with an inquisitive glance at the overturned waste-paper basket and the litter on the floor. He could hardly have helped overhearing Poirot's thoughtful remark as he bundled the torn papers back again:

"And the necklace was heavily insured. . . ."

"Poirot," I cried, "I see——"

"You see nothing, my friend," he replied quickly, "as

usual, nothing at all! It is incredible—but there it is. Let us return to our own apartments."

We did so in silence. Once there, to my intense surprise, Poirot effected a rapid change of clothing.

"I go to London to-night," he explained. "It is imperative."

"What?"

"Absolutely. The real work, that of the brain (ah, those brave little gray cells), it is done. I go to seek the confirmation. I shall find it! Impossible to deceive Hercule Poirot!"

"You'll come a cropper one of these days," I observed, rather disgusted by his vanity.

"Do not be enraged, I beg of you, *mon ami*. I count on you to do me a service—of your friendship."

"Of course," I said eagerly, rather ashamed of my moroseness. "What is it?"

"The sleeve of my coat that I have taken off—will you brush it? See you, a little white powder has clung to it. You without doubt observed me run my finger round the drawer of the dressing-table?"

"No, I didn't."

"You should observe my actions, my friend. Thus I obtained the powder on my finger, and, being a little overexcited, I rubbed it on my sleeve; an action without method which I deplore—false to all my principles."

"But what was the powder?" I asked, not particularly interested in Poirot's principles.

"Not the poison of the Borgias," replied Poirot, with a twinkle. "I see your imagination mounting. I should say it was French chalk."

"French chalk?"

"Yes, cabinet-makers use it to make drawers run smoothly."

I laughed.

"You old sinner! I thought you were working up to something exciting."

"Au revoir, my friend. I save myself. I fly!"

The door shut behind him. With a smile, half of derision, half of affection, I picked up the coat, and stretched out my hand for the clothes brush.

The next morning, hearing nothing from Poirot, I went out for a stroll, met some old friends, and lunched with them at their hotel. In the afternoon we went for a spin. A punctured tire delayed us, and it was past eight when I got back to the *Grand Metropolitan.*

The first sight that met my eyes was Poirot, looking even more diminutive than usual, sandwiched between the Opalsens, beaming in a state of placid satisfaction.

"Mon ami Hastings!" he cried, and sprang to meet me. "Embrace me, my friend; all has marched to a marvel!"

Luckily, the embrace was merely figurative—not a thing one is always sure of with Poirot.

"Do you mean—" I began.

"Just wonderful, I call it!" said Mrs. Opalsen, smiling all over her fat face. "Didn't I tell you, Ed, that if he couldn't get back my pearls nobody would?"

"You did, my dear, you did. And you were right."

I looked helplessly at Poirot, and he answered the glance.

"My friend Hastings is, as you say in England, all at the seaside. Seat yourself, and I will recount to you all the affair that has so happily ended."

"Ended?"

"But yes. They are arrested."

"Who are arrested?"

"The chambermaid and the valet, *parbleu!* You did not suspect? Not with my parting hint about the French chalk?"

"You said cabinet-makers used it."

"Certainly they do—to make drawers slide easily. Somebody wanted that drawer to slide in and out without any noise. Who could that be? Obviously, only the chambermaid. The plan was so ingenious that it did not at once leap to the eye—not even to the eye of Hercule Poirot.

"Listen, this was how it was done. The valet was in the empty room next door, waiting. The French maid leaves the room. Quick as a flash the chambermaid whips open the drawer, takes out the jewel-case, and, slipping back the bolt, passes it through the door. The valet opens it at his leisure with the duplicate key with which he has provided himself, extracts the necklace, and waits his time. Célestine leaves the room again, and—pst!—in a flash the case is passed back again and replaced in the drawer.

"Madame arrives, the theft is discovered. The chambermaid demands to be searched, with a good deal of righteous indignation, and leaves the room without a stain on her character. The imitation necklace with which they have provided themselves has been concealed in the French girl's bed that morning by the chambermaid—a master stroke, *ça!*"

"But what did you go to London for?"

"You remember the card?"

"Certainly. It puzzled me—and puzzles me still. I thought——"

I hesitated delicately, glancing at Mr. Opalsen.

Poirot laughed heartily.

"*Une blague!* For the benefit of the valet. The card was one with a specially prepared surface—for finger-prints. I went straight to Scotland Yard, asked for our old friend Inspector Japp, and laid the facts before him. As I had suspected, the finger-prints proved to be those of two well-known jewel thieves who have been 'wanted' for some time. Japp came down with me, the thieves were arrested, and the necklace was discovered in the valet's possession. A clever pair, but they failed in *method*. Have I not told you, Hastings, at least thirty-six times, that without method——"

"At least thirty-six thousand times!" I interrupted. "But where did their 'method' break down?"

"*Mon ami,* it is a good plan to take a place as chambermaid or valet—but you must not shirk your work. They left an empty room undusted; and therefore, when the man put down the jewel-case on the little table near the communicating door, it left a square mark——"

"I remember," I cried.

"Before, I was undecided. Then—I *knew!*"

There was a moment's silence.

"And I've got my pearls," said Mrs. Opalsen as a sort of Greek chorus.

"Well," I said, "I'd better have some dinner."

Poirot accompanied me.

"This ought to mean kudos for you," I observed.

"*Pas du tout*," replied Poirot tranquilly. "Japp and the local inspector will divide the credit between them. But"—he tapped his pocket—"I have a check here, from Mr. Opalsen, and, how say you, my friend? This week-end has not gone according to plan. Shall we return here next week-end—at my expense this time?"

VIII
THE KIDNAPPED PRIME MINISTER

Now that war and the problems of war are things of the past, I think I may safely venture to reveal to the world the part which my friend Poirot played in a moment of national crisis. The secret has been well guarded. Not a whisper of it reached the Press. But, now that the need for secrecy has gone by, I feel it is only just that England should know the debt it owes to my quaint little friend, whose marvelous brain so ably averted a great catastrophe.

One evening after dinner—I will not particularize the date; it suffices to say that it was at the time when "Peace by negotiation" was the parrot-cry of England's enemies —my friend and I were sitting in his rooms. After being invalided out of the Army I had been given a recruiting job, and it had become my custom to drop in on Poirot in the evenings after dinner and talk with him of any cases of interest that he might have on hand.

I was attempting to discuss with him the sensational news of that day—no less than an attempted assassination of Mr. David MacAdam, England's Prime Minister. The account in the papers had evidently been carefully censored. No details were given, save that the Prime Minister had had a marvelous escape, the bullet just grazing his cheek.

I considered that our police must have been shamefully careless for such an outrage to be possible. I could well understand that the German agents in England would be willing to risk much for such an achievement. "Fighting Mac," as his own party had nicknamed him, had strenuously and unequivocally combated the Pacifist influence which was becoming so prevalent.

107

He was more than England's Prime Minister—he *was* England; and to have removed him from his sphere of influence would have been a crushing and paralyzing blow to Britain.

Poirot was busy mopping a gray suit with a minute sponge. Never was there a dandy such as Hercule Poirot. Neatness and order were his passion. Now, with the odor of benzine filling the air, he was quite unable to give me his full attention.

"In a little minute I am with you, my friend. I have all but finished. The spot of grease—he is not good—I remove him—so!" He waved his sponge.

I smiled as I lit another cigarette.

"Anything interesting on?" I inquired, after a minute or two.

"I assist a—how do you call it?—'charlady' to find her husband. A difficult affair, needing the tact. For I have a little idea that when he is found he will not be pleased. What would you? For my part, I sympathize with him. He was a man of discrimination to lose himself."

I laughed.

"At last! The spot of grease, he is gone! I am at your disposal."

"I was asking you what you thought of this attempt to assassinate MacAdam?"

"Enfantillage!" replied Poirot promptly. "One can hardly take it seriously. To fire with the rifle—never does it succeed. It is a device of the past."

"It was very near succeeding this time," I reminded him.

Poirot shook his head impatiently. He was about to reply when the landlady thrust her head round the door and informed him that there were two gentlemen below who wanted to see him.

"They won't give their names, sir, but they says as it's very important."

"Let them mount," said Poirot, carefully folding his gray trousers.

In a few minutes the two visitors were ushered in, and my heart gave a leap as in the foremost I recognized no less a personage than Lord Estair, Leader of the House of Commons; whilst his companion, Mr. Bernard Dodge, was also a member of the War Cabinet, and, as I knew, a close personal friend of the Prime Minister.

"Monsieur Poirot?" said Lord Estair interrogatively. My friend bowed. The great man looked at me and hesitated. "My business is private."

"You may speak freely before Captain Hastings," said my friend, nodding to me to remain. "He has not all the gifts, no! But I answer for his discretion."

Lord Estair still hesitated, but Mr. Dodge broke in abruptly!

"Oh, come on—don't let's beat about the bush! As far as I can see, the whole of England will know the hole we're in soon enough! Time's everything."

"Pray be seated, messieurs," said Poirot politely. "Will you take the big chair, *milord?*"

Lord Estair started slightly. "You know me?"

Poirot smiled. "Certainly. I read the little papers with the pictures. How should I not know you?"

"Monsieur Poirot, I have come to consult you upon a matter of the most vital urgency. I must ask for absolute secrecy."

"You have the word of Hercule Poirot—I can say no more!" said my friend grandiloquently.

"It concerns the Prime Minister. We are in grave trouble."

"We're up a tree!" interposed Mr. Dodge.

"The injury is serious, then?" I asked.

"What injury?"

"The bullet wound."

"Oh, that!" cried Mr. Dodge contemptuously. "That's old history."

"As my colleague says," continued Lord Estair, "that affair is over and done with. Luckily, it failed. I wished I could say as much for the second attempt."

"There has been a second attempt, then?"

"Yes, though not of the same nature. Monsieur Poirot, the Prime Minister has disappeared."

"What?"

"He has been kidnapped!"

"Impossible!" I cried, stupefied.

Poirot threw a withering glance at me, which I knew enjoined me to keep my mouth shut.

"Unfortunately, impossible as it seems, it is only too true," continued his lordship.

Poirot looked at Mr. Dodge. "You said just now, monsieur, that time was everything. What did you mean by that?"

The two men exchanged glances, and then Lord Estair said:

"You have heard, Monsieur Poirot, of the approaching Allied Conference?"

My friend nodded.

"For obvious reasons, no details have been given of when and where it is to take place. But, although it has been kept out of the newspapers, the date is, of course, widely known in diplomatic circles. The Conference is to be held to-morrow—Thursday—evening at Versailles. Now you perceive the terrible gravity of the situation. I will not conceal from you that the Prime Minister's presence at the Conference is a vital necessity. The Pacifist propaganda, started and maintained by the German agents in our midst, has been very active. It is the universal opinion that the turning point of the Conference will be the strong personality of the Prime Minister. His absence may have the most serious results—possibly a premature and disastrous peace. And we have no one who can be sent in his place. He alone can represent England."

Poirot's face had grown very grave. "Then you regard the kidnapping of the Prime Minister as a direct attempt to prevent his being present at the Conference?"

"Most certainly I do. He was actually on his way to France at the time."

"And the Conference is to be held?"

"At nine o'clock to-morrow night."

Poirot drew an enormous watch from his pocket.

"It is now a quarter to nine."

"Twenty-four hours," said Mr. Dodge thoughtfully.

"And a quarter," amended Poirot. "Do not forget the quarter, monsieur—it may come in useful. Now for the details—the abduction, did it take place in England or in France?"

"In France. Mr. MacAdam crossed to France this morning. He was to stay to-night as the guest of the Commander-in-Chief, proceeding to-morrow to Paris. He was conveyed across the Channel by destroyer. At Boulogne he was met by a car from General Headquarters and one of the Commander-in-Chief's A.D.C.s."

"Eh bien?"

"Well, they started from Boulogne—but they never arrived."

"What?"

"Monsieur Poirot, it was a bogus car and a bogus A.D.C. The real car was found in a side road, with the chauffeur and the A.D.C. neatly gagged and bound."

"And the bogus car?"

"Is still at large."

Poirot made a gesture of impatience. "Incredible! Surely it cannot escape attention for long?"

"So we thought. It seemed merely a question of searching thoroughly. That part of France is under Military Law. We were convinced that the car could not go long unnoticed. The French police and our own Scotland Yard men, and the military are straining every nerve. It is, as you say, incredible—but nothing has been discovered!"

At that moment a tap came at the door, and a young officer entered with a heavily sealed envelope which he handed to Lord Estair.

"Just through from France, sir. I brought it on here, as you directed."

The minister tore it open eagerly, and uttered an exclamation. The officer withdrew.

"Here is news at last! This telegram has just been decoded. They have found the second car, also the secretary, Daniels, chloroformed, gagged, and bound, in an abandoned farm near C——. He remembers nothing, except something being pressed against his mouth and nose from behind, and struggling to free himself. The police are satisfied as to the genuineness of his statement."

"And they have found nothing else?"

"No."

"Not the Prime Minister's dead body? Then, there is hope. But it is strange. Why, after trying to shoot him this morning, are they now taking so much trouble to keep him alive?"

Dodge shook his head. "One thing's quite certain. They're determined at all costs to prevent his attending the Conference."

"If it is humanly possible, the Prime Minister shall be there. God grant it is not too late. Now, messieurs, recount to me everything—from the beginning. I must know about this shooting affair as well."

"Last night, the Prime Minister, accompanied by one of his secretaries, Captain Daniels——"

"The same who accompanied him to France?"

"Yes. As I was saying, they motored down to Windsor, where the Prime Minister was granted an Audience. Early this morning, he returned to town, and it was on the way that the attempted assassination took place."

"One moment, if you please. Who is this Captain Daniels? You have his dossier?"

Lord Estair smiled. "I thought you would ask me that. We do not know very much of him. He is of no particular family. He has served in the English Army, and is an extremely able secretary, being an exceptionally fine linguist. I believe he speaks seven languages. It is for that reason that the Prime Minister chose him to accompany him to France."

"Has he any relatives in England?"

"Two aunts. A Mrs. Everard, who lives at Hampstead, and a Miss Daniels, who lives near Ascot."

"Ascot? That is near to Windsor, is it not?"

"That point has not been overlooked. But it has led to nothing."

"You regard the Capitaine Daniels, then, as above suspicion?"

A shade of bitterness crept into Lord Estair's voice, as he replied:

"No, Monsieur Poirot. In these days, I should hesitate before I pronounced *anyone* above suspicion."

"*Très bien.* Now I understand, *milord,* that the Prime Minister would, as a matter of course, be under vigilant police protection, which ought to render any assault upon him an impossibility?"

Introducing the first and only complete hardcover collection of Agatha Christie's mysteries

Now you can enjoy the greatest mysteries ever written in a magnificent Home Library Edition.

Discover Agatha Christie's world of mystery, adventure and intrigue

Agatha Christie's timeless tales of mystery and suspense offer something for every reader—mystery fan or not—young and old alike. And now, you can build a complete hardcover library of her world-famous mysteries by subscribing to <u>The Agatha Christie Mystery Collection.</u>

This exciting Collection is your passport to a world where mystery reigns supreme. Volume after volume, you and your family will enjoy mystery reading at its very best.

You'll meet Agatha Christie's world-famous detectives like Hercule Poirot, Jane Marple, and the likeable Tommy and Tuppence Beresford.

In your readings, you'll visit Egypt, Paris, England and other exciting destinations where murder is always on the itinerary. And wherever you travel, you'll become deeply involved in some of the most

ingenious and diabolical plots ever invented ... "cliff-hangers" that only Dame Agatha could create!

It all adds up to mystery reading that's so good ... it's almost criminal. And it's yours every month with <u>The Agatha Christie Mystery Collection.</u>

Solve the greatest mysteries of all time. The Collection contains all of Agatha Christie's classic works including *Murder on the Orient Express, Death on the Nile, And Then There Were None, The ABC Murders* and her ever-popular whodunit, *The Murder of Roger Ackroyd.*

Each handsome hardcover volume is Smythe sewn and printed on high quality acid-free paper so it can withstand even the most murderous treatment. Bound in Sussex-blue simulated leather with gold titling, <u>The Agatha Christie Mystery Collection</u> will make a tasteful addition to your living room, or den.

Ride the Orient Express for 10 days without obligation.
To introduce you to the Collection, we're inviting you to examine the classic mystery, *Murder on the Orient Express*, without risk or obligation. If you're not completely satisfied, just return it within 10 days and owe nothing.

However, if you're like the millions of other readers who love Agatha Christie's thrilling tales of mystery and suspense, keep *Murder on the Orient Express* and pay just $9.95 plus postage and handling.

You will then automatically receive future volumes once a month as they are published on a fully returnable, 10-day free-examination basis. No minimum purchase is required, and you may cancel your subscription at any time.

This unique collection is not sold in stores. It's available only through this special offer. So don't miss out, begin your subscription now. Just mail this card today.

☐ Yes! Please send me *Murder on the Orient Express* for a 10-day free-examination and enter my subscription to <u>The Agatha Christie Mystery Collection</u>. If I keep *Murder on the Orient Express*, I will pay just $9.95 plus postage and handling and receive one additional volume each month on a fully returnable 10-day free-examination basis. There is no minimum number of volumes to buy, and I may cancel my subscription at any time.　　　　70110

Name_____

Address_____

City_____ State_____ Zip_____

QA12
Send No Money...
But Act Today!

NO POSTAGE
NECESSARY
IF MAILED
IN THE
UNITED STATES

BUSINESS REPLY MAIL

FIRST CLASS   PERMIT NO. 2154   HICKSVILLE, N.Y.

Postage will be paid by addressee:

The Agatha Christie
Mystery Collection
Bantam Books
P.O. Box 956
Hicksville, N.Y. 11802

Lord Estair bowed his head. "That is so. The Prime Minister's car was closely followed by another car containing detectives in plain clothes. Mr. MacAdam knew nothing of these precautions. He is personally a most fearless man, and would be inclined to sweep them away arbitrarily. But, naturally, the police make their own arrangements. In fact, the Premier's chauffeur, O'Murphy, is a C.I.D. man."

"O'Murphy? That is a name of Ireland, is it not so?"

"Yes, he is an Irishman."

"From what part of Ireland?"

"County Clare, I believe."

"*Tiens!* But proceed, *milord.*"

"The Premier started for London. The car was a closed one. He and Captain Daniels sat inside. The second car followed as usual. But, unluckily, for some unknown reason, the Prime Minister's car deviated from the main road——"

"At a point where the road curves?" interrupted Poirot.

"Yes—but how did you know?"

"Oh, *c'est évident!* Continue!"

"For some unknown reason," continued Lord Estair, "the Premier's car left the main road. The police car, unaware of the deviation, continued to keep to the high road. At a short distance down the unfrequented lane, the Prime Minister's car was suddenly held up by a band of masked men. The chauffeur——"

"That brave O'Murphy!" murmured Poirot thoughtfully.

"The chauffeur, momentarily taken aback, jammed on the brakes. The Prime Minister put his head out of the window. Instantly a shot rang out—then another. The first one grazed his cheek, the second, fortunately, went wide. The chauffeur, now realizing the danger, instantly forged straight ahead, scattering the band of men."

"A near escape," I ejaculated, with a shiver.

"Mr. MacAdam refused to make any fuss over the slight wound he had received. He declared it was only a scratch. He stopped at a local cottage hospital, where it was dressed and bound up—he did not, of course, reveal his identity. He then drove, as per schedule, straight to

Charing Cross, where a special train for Dover was awaiting him, and, after a brief account of what had happened
had been given to the anxious police by Captain Daniels,
he duly departed for France. At Dover, he went on board
the waiting destroyer. At Boulogne, as you know, the
bogus car was waiting for him, carrying the Union Jack,
and correct in every detail."

"That is all you have to tell me?"

"Yes."

"There is no other circumstance that you have omitted,
milord?"

"Well, there is one rather peculiar thing."

"Yes?"

"The Prime Minister's car did not return home after
leaving the Prime Minister at Charing Cross. The police
were anxious to interview O'Murphy, so a search was in-
stituted at once. The car was discovered standing outside
a certain unsavoury little restaurant in Soho, which is
well known as a meeting-place of German agents."

"And the chauffeur?"

"The chauffeur was nowhere to be found. He, too, had
disappeared."

"So," said Poirot thoughtfully, "there are two disappearances: the Prime Minister in France, and O'Murphy
in London."

He looked keenly at Lord Estair, who made a gesture
of despair.

"I can only tell you, Monsieur Poirot, that, if anyone
had suggested to me yesterday that O'Murphy was a
traitor, I should have laughed in his face."

"And to-day?"

"To-day I do not know what to think."

Poirot nodded gravely. He looked at his turnip of a
watch again.

"I understand that I have carte blanche, messieurs—
in every way, I mean? I must be able to go where I
choose, and how I choose."

"Perfectly. There is a special train leaving for Dover
in an hour's time, with a further contingent from Scotland
Yard. You shall be accompanied by a Military officer and

a C.I.D. man, who will hold themselves at your disposal in every way. Is that satisfactory?"

"Quite. One more question before you leave, messieurs. What made you come to me? I am unknown, obscure, in this great London of yours."

"We sought you out on the express recommendation and wish of a very great man of your own country."

"*Comment?* My old friend the *Préfet*——?"

Lord Estair shook his head.

"Once higher than the *Préfet*. One whose word was once law in Belgium—and shall be again! That England has sworn!"

Poirot's hand flew swiftly to a dramatic salute. "Amen to that! Ah, but my Master does not forget. . . . Messieurs, I, Hercule Poirot, will serve you faithfully. Heaven only send that it will be in time. But this is dark—dark. . . . I cannot see."

"Well, Poirot," I cried impatiently, as the door closed behind the Ministers, "what do you think?"

My friend was busy packing a minute suitcase, with quick, deft movements. He shook his head thoughtfully.

"I do not know what to think. My brains desert me."

"Why, as you said, kidnap him, when a knock on the head would do as well?" I mused.

"Pardon me, *mon ami*, but I did not quite say that. It is undoubtedly far more their affair to kidnap him."

"But why?"

"Because uncertainty creates panic. That is one reason. Were the Prime Minister dead, it would be a terrible calamity, but the situation would have to be faced. But now you have paralysis. Will the Prime Minister reappear, or will he not? Is he dead or alive? Nobody knows, and until they know nothing definite can be done. And, as I tell you, uncertainty breeds panic, which is what *les Boches* are playing for. Then, again, if the kidnappers are holding him secretly somewhere, they have the advantage of being able to make terms with both sides. The German Government is not a liberal paymaster, as a rule, but no doubt they can be made to disgorge substantial remittances in such a case as this. Thirdly, they run no risk of the hangman's rope. Oh, decidedly, kidnapping is their affair."

"Then, if that is so, why should they first try to shoot him?"

Poirot made a gesture of anger. "Ah, that is just what I do not understand! It is inexplicable—stupid! They have all their arrangements made (and very good arrangements too!) for the abduction, and yet they imperil the whole affair by a melodramatic attack, worthy of a cinema, and quite as unreal. It is almost impossible to believe in it, with its band of masked men, not twenty miles from London!"

"Perhaps they were two quite separate attempts which happened irrespective of each other," I suggested.

"Ah, no, that would be too much of a coincidence! Then, further—who is the traitor? There must have been a traitor—in the first affair, anyway. But who was it—Daniels or O'Murphy? It must have been one of the two, or why did the car leave the main road? We cannot suppose that the Prime Minister connived at his own assassination! Did O'Murphy take that turning of his own accord, or was it Daniels who told him to do so?"

"Surely it must have been O'Murphy's doing."

"Yes, because if it was Daniels' the Prime Minister would have heard the order, and would have asked the reason. But there are altogether too many 'whys' in this affair, and they contradict each other. If O'Murphy is an honest man, *why* did he leave the main road? But if he was a dishonest man, *why* did he start the car again when only two shots had been fired—thereby, in all probability, saving the Prime Minister's life? And, again, if he was honest, why did he, immediately on leaving Charing Cross, drive to a well-known rendezvous of German spies?"

"It looks bad," I said.

"Let us look at the case with method. What have we for and against these two men? Take O'Murphy first. Against: that his conduct in leaving the main road was suspicious; that he is an Irishman from County Clare; that he has disappeared in a highly suggestive manner. For: that his promptness in restarting the car saved the

Premier's life; that he is a Scotland Yard man, and, obviously, from the post allotted to him, a trusted detective. Now for Daniels. There is not much against him, except the fact that nothing is known of his antecedents, and that he speaks too many languages for a good Englishman! (Pardon me, *mon ami,* but, as linguists, you are deplorable!) Now *for* him, we have the fact that he was found gagged, bound, and chloroformed—which does not look as though he had anything to do with the matter."

"He might have gagged and bound himself, to divert suspicion."

Poirot shook his head. "The French police would make no mistake of that kind. Besides, once he had attained his object, and the Prime Minister was safely abducted, there would not be much point in his remaining behind. His accomplices *could* have gagged and chloroformed him, of course, but I fail to see what object they hoped to accomplish by it. He can be of little use to them now, for, until the circumstances concerning the Prime Minister have been cleared up, he is bound to be closely watched."

"Perhaps he hoped to start the police on a false scent?"

"Then why did he not do so? He merely says that something was pressed over his nose and mouth, and that he remembers nothing more. There is no false scent there. It sounds remarkably like the truth."

"Well," I said, glancing at the clock, "I suppose we'd better start for the station. You may find more clues in France."

"Possibly, *mon ami,* but I doubt it. It is still incredible to me that the Prime Minister has not been discovered in that limited area, where the difficulty of concealing him must be tremendous. If the military and the police of two countries have not found him, how shall I?"

At Charing Cross we were met by Mr. Dodge.

"This is Detective Barnes, of Scotland Yard, and Major Norman. They will hold themselves entirely at your disposal. Good luck to you. It's a bad business, but I've not given up hope. Must be off now." And the Minister strode rapidly away.

We chatted in a desultory fashion with Major Norman.

In the center of the little group of men on the platform I recognized a little ferret-faced fellow talking to a tall, fair man. He was an old acquaintance of Poirot's—Detective-Inspector Japp, supposed to be one of the smartest of Scotland Yard's officers. He came over and greeted my friend cheerfully.

"I heard you were on this job too. Smart bit of work. So far they've got away with the goods all right. But I can't believe they can keep him hidden long. Our people are going through France with a toothcomb. So are the French. I can't help feeling it's only a matter of hours now."

"That is, if he's still alive," remarked the tall detective gloomily.

Japp's face fell. "Yes. . . . But somehow I've got the feeling he's alive all right."

Poirot nodded. "Yes, yes; he's alive. But can he be found in time? I, like you, did not believe he could be hidden so long."

The whistle blew, and we all trooped up into the Pullman car. Then, with a slow, unwilling jerk, the train drew out of the station.

It was a curious journey. The Scotland Yard men crowded together. Maps of Northern France were spread out, and eager forefingers traced the lines of roads and villages. Each man had his own pet theory. Poirot showed none of his usual loquacity, but sat staring in front of him, with an expression on his face that reminded me of a puzzled child. I talked to Norman, whom I found quite an amusing fellow. On arriving at Dover Poirot's behavior moved me to intense amusement. The little man, as he went on board the boat, clutched desperately at my arm. The wind was blowing lustily.

Mon Dieu!" he murmured. "This is terrible!"

"Have courage, Poirot," I cried. "You will succeed. You will find him. I am sure of it."

"Ah, *mon ami,* you mistake my emotion. It is this villainous sea that troubles me! The *mal de mer*—it is horrible suffering!"

"Oh!" I said, rather taken aback.

The first throb of the engines was felt, and Poirot groaned and closed his eyes.

"Major Norman has a map of Northern France if you would like to study it?"

Poirot shook his head impatiently.

"But no, but no! Leave me, my friend. See you, to think, the stomach and the brain must be in harmony. Laverguier has a method most excellent for averting the *mal de mer*. You breathe in—and out—slowly, so—turning the head from left to right and counting six between each breath."

I left him to his gymnastic endeavors, and went on deck.

As we came slowly into Boulogne Harbor Poirot appeared, neat and smiling, and announced to me in a whisper that Laverguier's system had succeeded "to a marvel!"

Japp's forefinger was still tracing imaginary routes on his map. "Nonsense! The car started from Boulogne—here they branched off. Now, my idea is that they transferred the Prime Minister to another car. See?"

"Well," said the tall detective, "I shall make for the seaports. Ten to one, they've smuggled him on board a ship."

Japp shook his head. "Too obvious. The order went out at once to close all the ports."

The day was just breaking as we landed. Major Norman touched Poirot on the arm. "There's a military car here waiting for you, sir."

"Thank you, monsieur. But, for the moment, I do not propose to leave Boulogne."

"What?"

"No, we will enter this hotel here, by the quay."

He suited the action to the word, demanded and was accorded a private room. We three followed him, puzzled and uncomprehending.

He shot a quick glance at us. "It is not so that the good detective should act, eh? I perceived your thought. He must be full of energy. He must rush to and fro. He should prostrate himself on the dusty road and seek the marks of tires through a little glass. He must gather up the cigarette-end, the fallen match? That is your idea, is it not?"

His eyes challenged us. "But I—Hercule Poirot—tell you that it is not so! The true clues are within—*here!*" He tapped his forehead. "See you, I need not have left London. It would have been sufficient for me to sit quietly in my rooms there. All that matters is the little gray cells within. Secretly and silently they do their part, until suddenly I call for a map, and I lay my finger on a spot— so—and I say: the Prime Minister is *there!* And it is so! With method and logic one can accomplish anything! This frantic rushing to France was a mistake—it is playing a child's game of hide-and-seek. But now, though it may be too late, I will set to work the right way, from within. Silence, my friends, I beg of you."

And for five long hours the little man sat motionless, blinking his eyelids like a cat, his green eyes flickering and becoming steadily greener and greener. The Scotland Yard man was obviously contemptuous, Major Norman was bored and impatient, and I myself found the time pass with wearisome slowness.

Finally, I got up, and strolled as noiselessly as I could to the window. The matter was becoming a farce. I was secretly concerned for my friend. If he failed, I would have preferred him to fail in a less ridiculous manner. Out of the window I idly watched the daily leave boat, belching forth columns of smoke, as she lay alongside the quay.

Suddenly I was aroused by Poirot's voice close to my elbow.

"Mes amis, let us start!"

I turned. An extraordinary transformation had come over my friend. His eyes were flickering with excitement, his chest was swelled to the uttermost.

"I have been an imbecile, my friends! But I see day-light at last."

Major Norman moved hastily to the door. "I'll order the car."

"There is no need. I shall not use it. Thank Heaven the wind has fallen."

"Do you mean you are going to walk, sir?"

"No, my young friend. I am no St. Peter. I prefer to cross the sea by boat."

"To cross the *sea?*"

"Yes. To work with method, one must begin from the beginning. And the beginning of this affair was in England. Therefore, we return to England."

At three o'clock, we stood once more upon Charing Cross platform. To all our expostulations, Poirot turned a deaf ear, and reiterated again and again that to start at the beginning was not a waste of time, but the only way. On the way over, he had conferred with Norman in a low voice, and the latter had dispatched a sheaf of telegrams from Dover.

Owing to the special passes held by Norman, we got through everywhere in record time. In London, a large police car was waiting for us, with some plain-clothes men, one of whom handed a typewritten sheet of paper to my friend. He answered my inquiring glance.

"A list of the cottage hospitals within a certain radius west of London. I wired for it from Dover."

We were whirled rapidly through the London streets. We were on the Bath Road. On we went, through Hammersmith, Chiswick and Brentford. I began to see our objective. Through Windsor and on to Ascot. My heart gave a leap. Ascot was where Daniels had an aunt living. We were after *him,* then, not O'Murphy.

We duly stopped at the gate of a trim villa. Poirot jumped out and rang the bell. I saw a perplexed frown dimming the radiance of his face. Plainly, he was not satisfied. The bell was answered. He was ushered inside. In a few moments he reappeared, and climbed into the car with a short, sharp shake of his head. My hopes began to die down. It was past four now. Even if he found certain evidence incriminating Daniels, what would be the good of it, unless he could wring from some one the exact spot in France where they were holding the Prime Minister?

Our return progress towards London was an interrupted one. We deviated from the main road more than once, and occasionally stopped at a small building, which

I had no difficulty in recognizing as a cottage hospital. Poirot only spent a few minutes at each, but at every halt his radiant assurance was more and more restored.

He whispered something to Norman, to which the latter replied:

"Yes, if you turn off to the left, you will find them waiting by the bridge."

We turned up a side road, and in the failing light I discerned a second car, waiting by the side of the road. It contained two men in plain clothes. Poirot got down and spoke to them, and then we started off in a northerly direction, the other car following close behind.

We drove for some time, our objective being obviously one of the northern suburbs of London. Finally, we drove up to the front door of a tall house, standing a little back from the road in its own grounds.

Norman and I were left with the car. Poirot and one of the detectives went up to the door and rang. A neat parlormaid opened it. The detective spoke.

"I am a police officer, and I have a warrant to search this house."

The girl gave a little scream, and a tall, handsome woman of middle age appeared behind her in the hall.

"Shut the door, Edith. They are burglars, I expect."

But Poirot swiftly inserted his foot in the door, and at the same moment blew a whistle. Instantly the other detectives ran up, and poured into the house, shutting the door behind them.

Norman and I spent about five minutes cursing our forced inactivity. Finally the door reopened, and the men emerged, escorting three prisoners—a woman and two men. The woman, and one of the men, were taken to the second car. The other man was placed in our car by Poirot himself.

"I must go with the others, my friend. But have great care of this gentleman. You do not know him, no? *Eh bien*, let me present to you, Monsieur O'Murphy!"

O'Murphy! I *gaped* at him open-mouthed as we started again. He was not handcuffed, but I did not fancy he would try to escape. He sat there staring in front of him as though dazed. Anyway, Norman and I would be more than a match for him.

To my surprise, we still kept a northerly route. We were not returning to London, then! I was much puzzled. Suddenly, as the car slowed down, I recognized that we were close to Hendon Aerodrome. Immediately I grasped Poirot's idea. He proposed to reach France by aeroplane.

It was a sporting idea, but, on the face of it, impracticable. A telegram would be far quicker. Time was everything. He must leave the personal glory of rescuing the Prime Minister to others.

As we drew up, Major Norman jumped out, and a plain-clothes man took his place. He conferred with Poirot for a few minutes, and then went off briskly.

I, too, jumped out, and caught Poirot by the arm.

"I congratulate you, old fellow! They have told you the hiding-place? But, look here, you must wire to France at once. You'll be too late if you go yourself."

Poirot looked at me curiously for a minute or two.

"Unfortunately, my friend, there are some things that cannot be sent by telegram."

At that moment Major Norman returned, accompanied by a young officer in the uniform of the Flying Corps.

"This is Captain Lyall, who will fly you over to France. He can start at once."

"Wrap up warmly, sir," said the young pilot. "I can lend you a coat, if you like."

Poirot was consulting his enormous watch. He murmured to himself: "Yes, there is time—just time." Then he looked up, and bowed politely to the young officer. "I thank you, monsieur. But it is not I who am your passenger. It is this gentleman here."

He moved a little aside as he spoke, and a figure came forward out of the darkness. It was the second male prisoner who had gone in the other car, and as the light fell on his face, I gave a gasp of surprise.

It was the Prime Minister!

"For heaven's sake, tell me all about it," I cried impatiently, as Poirot, Norman, and I motored back to London. "How in the world did they manage to smuggle him back to England?"

"There was no need to smuggle him back," replied Poirot dryly. "The Prime Minister has never left England. He was kidnapped on his way from Windsor to London."

"*What?*"

"I will make all clear. The Prime Minister was in his car, his secretary beside him. Suddenly a pad of chloroform is clapped on his face——"

"But by whom?"

"By the clever linguistic Captain Daniels. As soon as the Prime Minister is unconscious, Daniels picks up the speaking-tube, and directs O'Murphy to turn to the right, which the chauffeur, quite unsuspicious, does. A few yards down that unfrequented road, a large car is standing, apparently broken down. Its driver signals to O'Murphy to stop. O'Murphy slows up. The stranger approaches. Daniels leans out of the window, and, probably with the aid of an instantaneous anæsthetic, such as ethylchloride, the chloroform trick is repeated. In a few seconds, the two helpless men are dragged out and transferred to the other car, and a pair of substitutes take their places."

"Impossible!"

"*Pas du tout!* Have you not seen music-hall turns imitating celebrities with marvelous accuracy? Nothing is easier than to personate a public character. The Prime Minister of England is far easier to understudy than Mr. John Smith of Clapham, say. As for O'Murphy's 'double,' no one was going to take much notice of him until after the departure of the Prime Minister, and by then he would have made himself scarce. He drives straight from Charing Cross to the meeting-place of his friends. He goes in as O'Murphy, he emerges as some one quite different. O'Murphy has disappeared, leaving a conveniently suspicious trail behind him."

"But the man who personated the Prime Minister was seen by everyone!"

"He was not seen by anyone who knew him privately or intimately. And Daniels shielded him from contact

with anyone as much as possible. Moreover, his face was
bandaged up, and anything unusual in his manner would
be put down to the fact that he was suffering from shock
as a result of the attempt upon his life. Mr. MacAdam
has a weak throat, and always spares his voice as much
as possible before any great speech. The deception was
perfectly easy to keep up as far as France. There it
would be impracticable and impossible—so the Prime
Minister disappears. The police of this country hurry
across the Channel, and no one bothers to go into the
details of the first attack. To sustain the illusion that the
abduction has taken place in France, Daniels is gagged
and chloroformed in a convincing manner."

"And the man who has enacted the part of the Prime
Minister?"

"Rids himself of his disguise. He and the bogus chauffeur may be arrested as suspicous characters, but no
one will dream of suspecting their real part in the drama,
and they will eventually be released for lack of evidence."

"And the real Prime Minister?"

"He and O'Murphy were driven straight to the house
of 'Mrs. Everard,' at Hampstead, Daniels' so-called
'aunt.' In reality, she is Frau Bertha Ebenthal, and the
police have been looking for her for some time. It is a
valuable little present that I have made to them—to say
nothing of Daniels! Ah, it was a clever plan, but he did
not reckon on the cleverness of Hercule Poirot!"

I think my friend might well be excused his moment
of vanity.

"When did you first begin to suspect the truth of the
matter?"

"When I began to work the right way—from *within!* I
could not make that shooting affair fit in—but when I
saw that the net result of it was that *the Prime Minister
went to France with his face bound up,* I began to comprehend! And when I visited all the cottage hospitals between Windsor and London, and found that no one answering to my description had had his face bound up and
dressed that morning, I was sure! After that, it was
child's-play for a mind like mine!"

The following morning, Poirot showed me a telegram he had just received. It had no place of origin, and was unsigned. It ran:

"In time."

Later in the day the evening papers published an account of the Allied Conference. They laid particular stress on the magnificent ovation accorded to Mr. David MacAdam, whose inspiring speech had produced a deep and lasting impression.

IX
THE DISAPPEARANCE OF
MR. DAVENHEIM

Poirot and I were expecting our old friend Inspector Japp of Scotland Yard to tea. We were sitting round the tea-table awaiting his arrival. Poirot had just finished carefully straightening the cups and saucers which our landlady was in the habit of throwing, rather than placing, on the table. He had also breathed heavily on the metal teapot, and polished it with a silk handkerchief. The kettle was on the boil, and a small enamel saucepan beside it contained some thick, sweet chocolate which was more to Poirot's palate than what he described as "your English poison."

A sharp "rat-tat" sounded below, and a few minutes afterwards Japp entered briskly.

"Hope I'm not late," he said as he greeted us. "To tell the truth, I was yarning with Miller, the man who's in charge of the Davenheim case."

I pricked up my ears. For the last three days the papers had been full of the strange disappearance of Mr. Davenheim, senior partner of Davenheim and Salmon, the well-known bankers and financiers. On Saturday last he had walked out of his house, and had never been seen since. I looked forward to extracting some interesting details from Japp.

"I should have thought," I remarked, "that it would be almost impossible for anyone to 'disappear' nowadays."

Poirot moved a plate of bread and butter the eighth of an inch, and said sharply:

"Be exact, my friend. What do you mean by 'disappear'? To which class of disappearance are you referring?"

127

"Are disappearances classified and labeled, then?" I laughed.

Japp smiled also. Poirot frowned at us both.

"But certainly they are! They fall into three categories: First, and most common, the voluntary disappearance. Second, the much abused 'loss of memory' case—rare, but occasionally genuine. Third, murder, and a more or less successful disposal of the body. Do you refer to all three as impossible of execution?"

"Very nearly so, I should think. You might lose your own memory, but some one would be sure to recognize you—especially in the case of a well-known man like Davenheim. Then 'bodies' can't be made to vanish into thin air. Sooner or later they turn up, concealed in lonely places, or in trunks. Murder will out. In the same way, the absconding clerk, or the domestic defaulter, is bound to be run down in these days of wireless telegraphy. He can be headed off from foreign countries; ports and railway stations are watched; and, as for concealment in this country, his features and appearance will be known to everyone who reads a daily newspaper. He's up against civilization."

"Mon ami," said Poirot, "you make one error. You do not allow for the fact that a man who had decided to make away with another man—or with himself in a figurative sense—might be that rare machine, a man of method. He might bring intelligence, talent, a careful calculation of detail to the task; and then I do not see why he should not be successful in baffling the police force."

"But not you, I suppose?" said Japp good-humoredly, winking at me. "He couldn't baffle you, eh, Monsieur Poirot?"

Poirot endeavored, with a marked lack of success, to look modest. "Me, also! Why not? It is true that I approach such problems with an exact science, a mathematical precision, which seems, alas, only too rare in the new generation of detectives!"

Japp grinned more widely.

"I don't know," he said. "Miller, the man who's on this case, is a smart chap. You may be very sure he won't overlook a footprint, or a cigar-ash, or a crumb even. He's got eyes that see everything."

"So, *mon ami*," said Poirot, "has the London sparrow. But all the same, I should not ask the little brown bird to solve the problem of Mr. Davenheim."

"Come now, monsieur, you're not going to run down the value of details as clues?"

"By no means. These things are all good in their way. The danger is they may assume undue importance. Most details are insignificant; one or two are vital. It is the brain, the little gray cells"—he tapped his forehead—"on which one must rely. The senses mislead. One must seek the truth within—not without."

"You don't mean to say, Monsieur Poirot, that you would undertake to solve a case without moving from your chair, do you?"

"That is exactly what I do mean—granted the facts were placed before me. I regard myself as a consulting specialist."

Japp slapped his knee. "Hanged if I don't take you at your word. Bet you a fiver that you can't lay your hand—or rather tell me where to lay my hand—on Mr. Davenheim, dead or alive, before a week is out."

Poirot considered. *"Eh bien, mon ami,* I accept. *Le sport,* it is the passion of you English. Now—the facts."

"On Saturday last, as is his usual custom, Mr. Davenheim took the 12.40 train from Victoria to Chingside, where his palatial country place, The Cedars, is situated. After lunch, he strolled round the grounds, and gave various directions to the gardeners. Everybody agrees that his manner was absolutely normal and as usual. After tea he put his head into his wife's boudoir, saying that he was going to stroll down to the village and post some letters. He added that he was expecting a Mr. Lowen, on business. If Lowen should come before he himself returned, he was to be shown into the study and asked to wait. Mr. Davenheim then left the house by the front door, passed leisurely down the drive, and out at the gate, and—was never seen again. From that hour, he vanished completely."

"Pretty—very pretty—altogether a charming little problem," murmured Poirot. "Proceed, my good friend."

"About a quarter of an hour later a tall, dark man with a thick black mustache rang the front-door bell, and explained that he had an appointment with Mr. Davenheim. He gave the name of Lowen, and in accordance with the banker's instructions was shown into the study. Nearly an hour passed. Mr. Davenheim did not return. Finally Mr. Lowen rang the bell, and explained that he was unable to wait any longer, as he must catch his train back to town. Mrs. Davenheim apologized for her husband's absence, which seemed unaccountable, as she knew him to have been expecting the visitor. Mr. Lowen reiterated his regrets and took his departure.

"Well, as everyone knows, Mr. Davenheim did *not* return. Early on Sunday morning the police were communicated with, but could make neither head nor tail of the matter. Mr. Davenheim seemed literally to have vanished into thin air. He had not been to the post office; nor had he been seen passing through the village. At the station they were positive he had not departed by any train. His own motor had not left the garage. If he had hired a car to meet him in some lonely spot, it seems almost certain that by this time, in view of the large reward offered for information, the driver of it would have come forward to tell what he knew. True, there was a small race-meeting at Entfield, five miles away, and if he had walked to that station he might have passed unnoticed in the crowd. But since then his photograph and a full description of him have been circulated in every newspaper, and nobody has been able to give any news of him. We have, of course, received many letters from all over England, but each clue, so far, has ended in disappointment.

"On Monday morning a further sensational discovery came to light. Behind a *portière* in Mr. Davenheim's study stands a safe, and that safe had been broken into and rifled. The windows were fastened securely on the inside, which seems to put an ordinary burglary out of court, unless, of course, an accomplice within the house fastened them again afterwards. On the other hand, Sunday having intervened, and the household being in a state of chaos, it is likely that the burglary was committed on the Saturday, and remained undetected until Monday."

"*Précisément*," said Poirot dryly. "Well, is he arrested, *ce pauvre* M. Lowen?"

Japp grinned. "Not yet. But he's under pretty close supervision."

Poirot nodded. "What was taken from the safe? Have you any idea?"

"We've been going into that with the junior partner of the firm and Mrs. Davenheim. Apparently there was a considerable amount in bearer bonds, and a very large sum in notes, owing to some large transaction having been just carried through. There was also a small fortune in jewelry. All Mrs. Davenheim's jewels were kept in the safe. The purchasing of them had become a passion with her husband of late years, and hardly a month passed that he did not make her a present of some rare and costly gem."

"Altogether a good haul," said Poirot thoughtfully. "Now, what about Lowen? Is it known what his business was with Davenheim that evening?"

"Well, the two men were apparently not on very good terms. Lowen is a speculator in quite a small way. Nevertheless, he has been able once or twice to score a *coup* off Davenheim in the market, though it seems, they seldom or never actually met. It was a matter concerning some South American shares which led the banker to make his appointment."

"Had Davenheim interests in South America, then?"

"I believe so. Mrs. Davenheim happened to mention that he spent all last autumn in Buenos Aires."

"Any trouble in his home life? Were the husband and wife on good terms?"

"I should say his domestic life was quite peaceful and uneventful. Mrs. Davenheim is a pleasant, rather unintelligent woman. Quite a nonentity, I think."

"Then we must not look for the solution of the mystery there. Had he any enemies?"

"He had plenty of financial rivals, and no doubt there are many people whom he has got the better of who bear him no particular good will. But there was no one likely to make away with him—and, if they had, where is the body?"

"Exactly. As Hastings says, bodies have a habit of coming to light with fatal persistency."

"By the way, one of the gardeners says he saw a figure going round to the side of the house toward the rose-garden. The long French window of the study opens on to the rose-garden, and Mr. Davenheim frequently entered and left the house that way. But the man was a good way off, at work on some cucumber frames, and cannot even say whether it was the figure of his master or not. Also, he cannot fix the time with any accuracy. It must have been before six, as the gardeners cease work at that time."

"And Mr. Davenheim left the house?"

"About half-past five or thereabouts."

"What lies beyond the rose-garden?"

"A lake."

"With a boathouse?"

"Yes, a couple of punts are kept there. I suppose you're thinking of suicide, Monsieur Poirot? Well, I don't mind telling you that Miller's going down to-morrow expressly to see that piece of water dragged. That's the kind of man he is!"

Poirot smiled faintly, and turned to me. "Hastings, I pray you, hand me that copy of the *Daily Megaphone*. If I remember rightly, there is an unusually clear photograph there of the missing man."

I rose, and found the sheet required. Poirot studied the features attentively.

"H'm!" he murmured. "Wears his hair rather long and wavy, full mustache and pointed beard, bushy eyebrows. Eyes dark?"

"Yes."

"Hair and beard turning gray?"

The detective nodded. "Well, Monsieur Poirot, what have you got to say to it all? Clear as daylight, eh?"

"On the contrary, most obscure."

The Scotland Yard man looked pleased.

"Which gives me great hopes of solving it," finished Poirot placidly.

"Eh?"

"I find it a good sign when a case is obscure. If a thing is clear as daylight—*eh bien,* mistrust it! Someone has made it so."

Japp shook his head almost pityingly. "Well, each to their fancy. But it's not a bad thing to see your way clear ahead."

"I do not see," murmured Poirot. "I shut my eyes—and think."

Japp sighed. "Well, you've got a clear week to think in."

"And you will bring me any fresh developments that arise—the result of the labors of the hard-working and lynx-eyed Inspector Miller, for instance?"

"Certainly. That's in the bargain."

"Seems a shame, doesn't it?" said Japp to me as I accompanied him to the door. "Like robbing a child!"

I could not help agreeing with a smile. I was still smiling as I re-entered the room.

"Eh bien!" said Poirot immediately. "You make fun of Papa Poirot, is it not so?" He shook his finger at me. "You do not trust his gray cells? Ah, do not be confused! Let us discuss this little problem—incomplete as yet, I admit, but already showing one or two points of interest."

"The lake!" I said significantly.

"And even more than the lake, the boathouse!"

I looked sidewise at Poirot. He was smiling in his most inscrutable fashion. I felt that, for the moment, it would be quite useless to question him further.

We heard nothing of Japp until the following evening, when he walked in about nine o'clock. I saw at once by his expression that he was bursting with news of some kind.

"Eh bien, my friend," remarked Poirot. "All goes well? But do not tell me that you have discovered the body of Mr. Davenheim in your lake, because I shall not believe you."

"We haven't found the body, but we did find his *clothes*—the identical clothes he was wearing that day. What do you say to that?"

"Any other clothes missing from the house?"

"No, his valet is quite positive on that point. The rest of his wardrobe is intact. There's more. We've arrested Lowen. One of the maids, whose business it is to fasten the bedroom windows, declares that she saw Lowen coming *towards* the study through the rose-garden about a quarter past six. That would be about ten minutes before he left the house."

"What does he himself say to that?"

"Denied first of all that he had ever left the study. But the maid was positive, and he pretended afterwards that he had forgotten just stepping out of the window to examine an unusual species of rose. Rather a weak story! And there's fresh evidence against him come to light. Mr. Davenheim always wore a thick gold ring set with a solitaire diamond on the little finger of his right hand. Well, that ring was pawned in London on Saturday night by a man called Billy Kellett! He's already known to the police—did three months last autumn for lifting an old gentleman's watch. It seems he tried to pawn the ring at no less than five different places, succeeded at the last one, got gloriously drunk on the proceeds, assaulted a policeman, and was run in in consequence. I went to Bow Street with Miller and saw him. He's sober enough now, and I don't mind admitting we pretty well frightened the life out of him, hinting he might be charged with murder. This is his yarn, and a very queer one it is.

"He was at Entfield races on Saturday, though I dare say scarfpins was his line of business, rather than betting. Anyway, he had a bad day, and was down on his luck. He was tramping along the road to Chingside, and sat down in a ditch to rest just before he got into the village. A few minutes later he noticed a man coming along the road to the village, 'dark-complexioned gent, with a big mustache, one of them city toffs,' is his description of the man.

"Kellett was half concealed from the road by a heap of stones. Just before he got abreast of him, the man looked quickly up and down the road, and seeing it apparently deserted he took a small object from his pocket and threw it over the hedge. Then he went on towards the station.

Now, the object he had thrown over the hedge had fallen with a slight 'chink' which aroused the curiosity of the human derelict in the ditch. He investigated and, after a short search, discovered the ring! That is Kellett's story. It's only fair to say that Lowen denies it utterly, and of course the word of a man like Kellett can't be relied upon in the slightest. It's within the bounds of possibility that he met Davenheim in the lane and robbed and murdered him."

Poirot shook his head.

"Very improbable, *mon ami*. He had no means of disposing of the body. It would have been found by now. Secondly, the open way in which he pawned the ring makes it unlikely that he did murder to get it. Thirdly, your sneak-thief is rarely a murderer. Fourthly, as he has been in prison since Saturday, it would be too much of a coincidence that he is able to give so accurate a description of Lowen."

Japp nodded. "I don't say you're not right. But all the same, you won't get a jury to take much note of a jail-bird's evidence. What seems odd to me is that Lowen couldn't find a cleverer way of disposing of the ring."

Poirot shrugged his shoulders. "Well, after all, if it were found in the neighborhood, it might be argued that Davenheim himself had dropped it."

"But why remove it from the body at all?" I cried.

"There might be a reason for that," said Japp. "Do you know that just beyond the lake, a little gate leads out on to the hill, and not three minutes' walk brings you to—what do you think?—a *lime kiln*."

"Good heavens!" I cried. "You mean that the lime which destroyed the body would be powerless to affect the metal of the ring?"

"Exactly."

"It seems to me," I said, "that that explains everything. What a horrible crime!"

By common consent we both turned and looked at Poirot. He seemed lost in reflection, his brow knitted, as though with some supreme mental effort. I felt that at last his keen intellect was asserting itself. What would his first words be? We were not long left in doubt. With a

sigh, the tension of his attitude relaxed, and turning to
Japp, he asked:

"Have you any idea, my friend, whether Mr. and Mrs.
Davenheim occupied the same bedroom?"

The question seemed so ludicrously inappropriate that
for a moment we both stared in silence. Then Japp burst
into a laugh. "Good Lord, Monsieur Poirot, I thought
you were coming out with something startling. As to your
question, I'm sure I don't know."

"You could find out?" asked Poirot with curious per-
sistence.

"Oh, certainly—if you *really* want to know."

"*Merci, mon ami.* I should be obliged if you would
make a point of it."

Japp stared at him a few minutes longer, but Poirot
seemed to have forgotten us both. The detective shook
his head sadly at me, and murmuring, "Poor old fellow!
War's been too much for him!" gently withdrew from the
room.

As Poirot still seemed sunk in a daydream, I took a
sheet of paper, and amused myself by scribbling notes
upon it. My friend's voice aroused me. He had come out
of his reverie, and was looking brisk and alert.

"*Que faites vous là, mon ami?*"

"I was jotting down what occurred to me as the main
points of interest in this affair."

"You become methodical—at last!" said Poirot approvingly.

I concealed my pleasure. "Shall I read them to you?"

"By all means."

I cleared my throat.

" 'One: All the evidence points to Lowen having been
the man who forced the safe.

" 'Two: He had a grudge against Davenheim.

" 'Three: He lied in his first statement that he had
never left the study.

" 'Four: If you accept Billy Kellett's story as true,
Lowen is unmistakably implicated.' "

I paused. "Well?" I asked, for I felt that I had put my
finger on all the vital facts.

Poirot looked at me pityingly, shaking his head very

gently. *"Mon pauvre ami!* But it is that you have not the gift! The important detail, you appreciate him never! Also, your reasoning is false."

"How?"

"Let me take your four points.

"One: Mr. Lowen could not possibly know that he would have the chance to open the safe. He came for a business interview. He could not know beforehand that Mr. Davenheim would be absent posting a letter, and that he would consequently be alone in the study!"

"He might have seized his opportunity," I suggested.

"And the tools? City gentlemen do not carry round housebreaker's tools on the off chance! And one could not cut into that safe with a penknife, *bien entendu!*"

"Well, what about Number Two?"

"You say Lowen had a grudge against Mr. Davenheim. What you mean is that he had once or twice got the better of him. And presumably those transactions were entered into with the view of benefiting himself. In any case you do not as a rule bear a grudge against a man you have got the better of—it is more likely to be the other way about. Whatever grudge there might have been would have been on Mr. Davenheim's side."

"Well, you can't deny that he lied about never having left the study?"

"No. But he may have been frightened. Remember, the missing man's clothes had just been discovered in the lake. Of course, as usual, he would have done better to speak the truth."

"And the fourth point?"

"I grant you that. If Kellett's story is true, Lowen is undeniably implicated. That is what makes the affair so very interesting."

"Then I did appreciate *one* vital fact?"

"Perhaps—but you have entirely overlooked the two most important points, the ones which undoubtedly hold the clue to the whole matter."

"And pray, what are they?"

"One, the passion which has grown upon Mr. Davenheim in the last few years for buying jewelry. Two, his trip to Buenos Aires last autumn."

"Poirot, you are joking!"

"I am most serious. Ah, sacred thunder, but I hope Japp will not forget my little commission."

But the detective, entering into the spirit of the joke, had remembered it so well that a telegram was handed to Poirot about eleven o'clock the next day. At his request I opened it and read it out:

"'Husband and wife have occupied separate rooms since last winter.'"

"Aha!" cried Poirot. "And now we are in mid-June! All is solved!"

I stared at him.

"You have no moneys in the bank of Davenheim and Salmon, *mon ami?*"

"No," I said, wondering. "Why?"

"Because I should advise you to withdraw it—before it is too late."

"Why, what do you expect?"

"I expect a big smash in a few days—perhaps sooner. Which reminds me, we will return the compliment of a *dépêche* to Japp. A pencil, I pray you, and a form. *Voilà!* 'Advise you to withdraw any money deposited with firm in question.' That will intrigue him, the good Japp! His eyes will open wide—wide! He will not comprehend in the slightest—until to-morrow, or the next day!"

I remained skeptical, but the morrow forced me to render tribute to my friend's remarkable powers. In every paper was a huge headline telling of the sensational failure of the Davenheim bank. The disappearance of the famous financier took on a totally different aspect in the light of the revelation of the financial affairs of the bank.

Before we were half-way through breakfast, the door flew open and Japp rushed in. In his left hand was a paper; in his right was Poirot's telegram, which he banged down on the table in front of my friend.

"How did you know, Monsieur Poirot? How the blazes could you know?"

Poirot smiled placidly at him. "Ah, *mon ami,* after your wire, it was a certainty! From the commencement, see you, it struck me that the safe burglary was somewhat remarkable. Jewels, ready money, bearer bonds—all so conveniently arranged for—whom? Well, the good Monsieur Davenheim was of those who 'look after Number One' as your saying goes! It seemed almost certain that it was arranged for—himself! Then his passion of late years for buying jewelry! How simple! The funds he embezzled, he converted into jewels, very likely replacing them in turn with paste duplicates, and so he put away in a safe place, under another name, a considerable fortune to be enjoyed all in good time when everyone has been thrown off the track. His arrangements completed, he makes an appointment with Mr. Lowen (who has been imprudent enough in the past to cross the great man once or twice), drills a hole in the safe, leaves orders that the guest is to be shown into the study, and walks out of the house— where?" Poirot stopped, and stretched out his hand for another boiled egg. He frowned. "It is really insupportable," he murmured, "that every hen lays an egg of a different size! What symmetry can there be on the breakfast table? At least they should sort them in dozens at the shop!"

"Never mind the eggs," said Japp impatiently. "Let 'em lay 'em square if they like. Tell us where our customer went to when he left The Cedars—that is, if you know!"

"*Eh bien,* he went to his hiding-place. Ah, this Monsieur Davenheim, there may be some malformation in his gray cells, but they are of the first quality!"

"Do you know where he is hiding?"

"Certainly! It is most ingenious."

"For the Lord's sake, tell us, then!"

Poirot gently collected every fragment of shell from his plate, placed them in the egg-cup, and reversed the empty egg-shell on top of them. This little operation concluded, he smiled at the neat effect, and then beamed affectionately on us both.

"Come, my friends, you are men of intelligence. Ask

yourselves the question which I asked myself. 'If I were this man, where should *I* hide?' Hastings, what do you say?"

"Well," I said, "I'm rather inclined to think I'd not do a bolt at all. I'd stay in London—in the heart of things, travel by tubes and buses; ten to one I'd never be recognized. There's safety in a crowd."

Poirot turned inquiringly to Japp.

"I don't agree. Get clear away at once—that's the only chance. I would have had plenty of time to prepare things beforehand. I'd have a yacht waiting, with steam up, and I'd be off to one of the most out-of-the-way corners of the world before the hue and cry began!"

We both looked at Poirot. "What do *you* say, monsieur?"

For a moment he remained silent. Then a very curious smile flitted across his face.

"My friends, if *I* were hiding from the police, do you know *where* I should hide? *In a prison!*"

"*What?*"

"You are seeking Monsieur Davenheim in order to put him in prison, so you never dream of looking to see if he may not be already there!"

"What do you mean?"

"You tell me Madame Davenheim is not a very intelligent woman. Nevertheless I think that if you took her to Bow Street and confronted her with the man Billy Kellett, she would recognize him! In spite of the fact that he has shaved his beard and mustache and those bushy eyebrows, and has cropped his hair close. A woman nearly always knows her husband, though the rest of the world may be deceived!"

"Billy Kellett? But he's known to the police!"

"Did I not tell you Davenheim was a clever man? He prepared his alibi long beforehand. He was not in Buenos Aires last autumn—he was creating the character of Billy Kellett, 'doing three months,' so that the police should have no suspicions when the time came. He was playing, remember, for a large fortune, as well as liberty. It was worth while doing the thing thoroughly. Only——"

"Yes?"

"*Eh bien,* afterwards he had to wear a false beard and wig, had to *make up as himself* again, and to sleep with a false beard is not easy—it invites detection! He cannot risk continuing to share the chamber of madame his wife. You found out for me that for the last six months, or ever since his supposed return from Buenos Aires, he and Mrs. Davenheim occupied separate rooms. Then I was sure! Everything fitted in. The gardener who fancied he saw his master going round to the side of the house was quite right. He went to the boathouse, donned his 'tramp' clothes, which you may be sure had been safely hidden from the eyes of his valet, dropped the others in the lake, and proceeded to carry out his plan by pawning the ring in an obvious manner, and then assaulting a policeman, getting himself safely into the haven of Bow Street, where nobody would ever dream of looking for him!"

"It's impossible," murmured Japp.

"Ask Madame," said my friend, smiling.

The next day a registered letter lay beside Poirot's plate. He opened it, and a five-pound note fluttered out. My friend's brow puckered.

"*Ah, sacré!* But what shall I do with it? I have much remorse! *Ce pauvre Japp!* Ah, an idea! We will have a little dinner, we three! That consoles me. It was really too easy. I am ashamed. I, who would not rob a child—*mille tonnerres! Mon ami,* what have you, that you laugh so heartily?"

X
THE ADVENTURE OF
THE ITALIAN NOBLEMAN

Poirot and I had many friends and acquaintances of a rather informal nature. Amongst these was to be numbered Dr. Hawker, a near neighbor of ours, and a member of the medical profession. It was the genial doctor's habit to drop in sometimes of an evening and have a chat with Poirot, of whose genius he was an ardent admirer. The doctor himself, frank and unsuspicious to the last degree, admired the talents so far removed from his own.

On one particular evening in early June, he arrived about half-past eight and settled down to a comfortable discussion on the cheery topic of the prevalence of arsenical poisoning in crimes. It must have been about a quarter of an hour later when the door of our sitting-room flew open, and a distracted female precipitated herself into the room.

"Oh, doctor, you're wanted! Such a terrible voice. It gave me a turn, it did indeed."

I recognized in our new visitor Dr. Hawker's housekeeper, Miss Rider. The doctor was a bachelor, and lived in a gloomy old house a few streets away. The usually placid Miss Rider was now in a state bordering on incoherence.

"What terrible voice? Who is it, and what's the trouble?"

"It was the telephone, doctor. I answered it—and a voice spoke. 'Help,' it said. 'Doctor—help. They've killed me!' Then it sort of trailed away. 'Who's speaking?' I said. 'Who's speaking?' Then I got a reply, just a whisper, it seemed, 'Foscatine'—something like that—'Regent's Court.'"

The doctor uttered an exclamation.

"Count Foscatini. He has a flat in Regent's Court. I must go at once. What can have happened?"

"A patient of yours?" asked Poirot.

"I attended him for some slight ailment a few weeks ago. An Italian, but he speaks English perfectly. Well, I must wish you good night, Monsieur Poirot, unless—" He hesitated.

"I perceive the thought in your mind," said Poirot, smiling. "I shall be delighted to accompany you. Hastings, run down and get hold of a taxi."

Taxis always make themselves sought for when one is particulary pressed for time, but I captured one at last, and we were soon bowling along in the direction of Regent's Park. Regent's Court was a new block of flats, situated just off St. John's Wood Road. They had only recently been built, and contained the latest service devices.

There was no one in the hall. The doctor pressed the lift-bell impatiently, and when the lift arrived questioned the uniformed attendant sharply.

"Flat 11. Count Foscatini. There's been an accident there, I understand."

The man stared at him.

"First I've heard of it. Mr. Graves—that's Count Foscatini's man—went out about half an hour ago, and he said nothing."

"Is the Count alone in the flat?"

"No, sir, he's got two gentlemen dining with him."

"What are they like?" I asked eagerly.

We were in the lift now, ascending rapidly to the second floor, on which Flat 11 was situated.

"I didn't see them myself, sir, but I understand that they were foreign gentlemen."

He pulled back the iron door, and we stepped out on the landing. No. 11 was opposite to us. The doctor rang the bell. There was no reply, and we could hear no sound from within. The doctor rang again and again; we could hear the bell trilling within, but no sign of life rewarded us.

"This is getting serious," muttered the doctor. He turned to the lift attendant.

"Is there any pass-key to this door?"

"There is one in the porter's office downstairs."

"Get it, then, and, look here, I think you'd better send for the police."

Poirot approved with a nod of the head.

The man returned shortly; with him came the manager.

"Will you tell me, gentlemen, what is the meaning of all this?"

"Certainly. I received a telephone message from Count Foscatini stating that he had been attacked and was dying. You can understand that we must lose no time— if we are not already too late."

The manager produced the key without more ado, and we all entered the flat.

We passed first into a small square lounge hall. A door on the right of it was half open. The manager indicated it with a nod.

"The dining-room."

Dr. Hawker led the way. We followed close on his heels. As we entered the room I gave a gasp. The round table in the center bore the remains of a meal; three chairs were pushed back, as though their occupants had just risen. In the corner, to the right of the fire-place, was a big writing-table, and sitting at it was a man—or what had been a man. His right hand still grasped the base of the telephone, but he had fallen forward, struck down by a terrific blow on the head from behind. The weapon was not far to seek. A marble statuette stood where it had been hurriedly put down, the base of it stained with blood.

The doctor's examination did not take a minute. "Stone dead. Must have been almost instantaneous. I wonder he even managed to telephone. It will be better not to move him until the police arrive."

On the manager's suggestion we searched the flat, but the result was a foregone conclusion. It was not likely that the murderers would be concealed there when all they had to do was to walk out.

We came back to the dining-room. Poirot had not accompanied us in our tour. I found him studying the center table with close attention. I joined him. It was a well-polished round mahogany table. A bowl of roses decorated the center, and white lace mats reposed on the gleaming surface. There was a dish of fruit, but the three dessert plates were untouched. There were three coffee-cups with remains of coffee in them—two black, one with milk. All three men had taken port, and the decanter, half-full, stood before the center plate. One of the men had smoked a cigar, the other two cigarettes. A tortoise shell-and-silver box, holding cigars and cigarettes, stood open upon the table.

I enumerated all these facts to myself, but I was forced to admit that they did not shed any brilliant light on the situation. I wondered what Poirot saw in them to make him so intent. I asked him.

"Mon ami," he replied, "you miss the point. I am looking for something that I do *not* see."

"What is that?"

"A mistake—even a little mistake—on the part of the murderer."

He stepped swiftly to the small adjoining kitchen, looked in, and shook his head.

"Monsieur," he said to the manager, "explain to me, I pray, your system of serving meals here."

The manager stepped to a small hatch in the wall.

"This is the service lift," he explained. "It runs to the kitchens at the top of the building. You order through this telephone, and the dishes are sent down in the lift, one course at a time. The dirty plates and dishes are sent up in the same manner. No domestic worries, you understand, and at the same time you avoid the wearying publicity of always dining in a restaurant."

Poirot nodded.

"Then the plates and dishes that were used tonight are on high in the kitchen. You permit that I mount there?"

"Oh, certainly, if you like! Roberts, the lift man, will take you up and introduce you; but I'm afraid you won't find anything that's of any use. They're handling hundreds of plates and dishes, and they'll be all lumped together."

Poirot remained firm, however, and together we visited

the kitchens and questioned the man who had taken the order from Flat 11.

"The order was given from the *à la carte menu*—for three," he explained. "Soup julienne, filet de sole normande, tournedos of beef, and a rice soufflé. What time? Just about eight o'clock, I should say. No, I'm afraid the plates and dishes have been all washed up by now. Unfortunate. You were thinking of finger-prints, I suppose?"

"Not exactly," said Poirot, with an enigmatical smile. "I am more interested in Count Foscatini's appetite. Did he partake of every dish?"

"Yes; but of course I can't say how much of each he ate. The plates were all soiled, and the dishes empty— that is to say, with the exception of the rice soufflé. There was a fair amount of that left."

"Ah!" said Poirot, and seemed satisfied with the fact.

As we descended to the flat again he remarked in a low tone:

"We have decidedly to do with a man of method."

"Do you mean the murderer, or Count Foscatini?"

"The latter was undoubtedly an orderly gentleman. After imploring help and announcing his approaching demise, he carefully hung up the telephone receiver."

I stared at Poirot. His words now and his recent inquiries gave me the glimmering of an idea.

"You suspect poison?" I breathed. "The blow on the head was a blind."

Poirot merely smiled.

We re-entered the flat to find the local inspector of police had arrived with two constables. He was inclined to resent our appearance, but Poirot calmed him with the mention of our Scotland Yard friend, Inspector Japp, and we were accorded a grudging permission to remain. It was a lucky thing we were, for we had not been back five minutes before an agitated middle-aged man came rushing into the room with every appearance of grief and agitation.

This was Graves, valet-butler to the late Count Foscatini. The story he had to tell was a sensational one.

On the previous morning, two gentlemen had called to see his master. They were Italians, and the elder of the two, a man of about forty, gave his name as Signor Ascanio. The younger was a well-dressed lad of about twenty-four.

Count Foscatini was evidently prepared for their visit and immediately sent Graves out upon some trivial errand. Here the man paused and hesitated in his story. In the end, however, he admitted that, curious as to the purport of the interview, he had not obeyed immediately, but had lingered about endeavoring to hear something of what was going on.

The conversation was carried on in so low a tone that he was not as successful as he had hoped; but he gathered enough to make it clear that some kind of monetary proposition was being discussed, and that the basis of it was a threat. The discussion was anything but amicable. In the end, Count Foscatini raised his voice slightly, and the listener heard these words clearly:

"I have no time to argue further now, gentlemen. If you will dine with me to-morrow night at eight o'clock, we will resume the discussion."

Afraid of being discovered listening, Graves had then hurried out to do his master's errand. This evening the two men had arrived punctually at eight. During dinner they had talked of indifferent matters—politics, the weather, and the theatrical world. When Graves had placed the port upon the table and brought in the coffee his master told him that he might have the evening off.

"Was that a usual proceeding of his when he had guests?" asked the inspector.

"No, sir; it wasn't. That's what made me think it must be some business of a very unusual kind that he was going to discuss with these gentlemen."

That finished Graves's story. He had gone out about 8.30, and, meeting a friend, had accompanied him to the Metropolitan Music Hall in Edgware Road.

Nobody had seen the two men leave, but the time of the murder was fixed clearly enough at 8.47. A small clock on the writing-table had been swept off by Foscatini's arm, and had stopped at that hour, which agreed with Miss Rider's telephone summons.

The police surgeon had made his examination of the

body, and it was now lying on the couch. I saw the face for the first time—the olive complexion, the long nose, the luxuriant black mustache, and the full red lips drawn back from the dazzlingly white teeth. Not altogether a pleasant face.

"Well," said the inspector, refastening his notebook. "The case seems clear enough. The only difficulty will be to lay our hands on this Signor Ascanio. I suppose his address is not in the dead man's pocket-book by any chance?"

As Poirot had said, the late Foscatini was an orderly man. Neatly written in small, precise handwriting was the inscription, "Signor Paolo Ascanio, Grosvenor Hotel."

The inspector busied himself with the telephone, then turned to us with a grin.

"Just in time. Our fine gentleman was off to catch the boat train to the Continong. Well, gentlemen, that's about all we can do here. It's a bad business, but straightforward enough. One of these Italian vendetta things, as likely as not."

Thus airily dismissed, we found our way downstairs. Dr. Hawker was full of excitement.

"Like the beginning of a novel, eh? Real exciting stuff. Wouldn't believe it if you read about it."

Poirot did not speak. He was very thoughtful. All the evening he had hardly opened his lips.

"What says the master detective, eh?" asked Hawker, clapping him on the back. "Nothing to work your gray cells over this time."

"You think not?"

"What could there be?"

"Well, for example, there is the window."

"The window? But it was fastened. Nobody could have got out or in that way. I noticed it specially."

"And why were you able to notice it?"

The doctor looked puzzled. Poirot hastened to explain.

"It is to the curtains I refer. They were not drawn. A little odd, that. And then there was the coffee. It was very black coffee."

"Well, what of it?"

"Very black," repeated Poirot. "In conjunction with

that let us remember that very little of the rice soufflé was eaten, and we get—what?"

"Moonshine," laughed the doctor. "You're pulling my leg."

"Never do I pull the leg. Hastings here knows that I am perfectly serious."

"I don't know what you are getting at, all the same," I confessed. "You don't suspect the manservant, do you? He might have been in with the gang, and put some dope in the coffee. I suppose they'll test his alibi?"

"Without doubt, my friend; but it is the alibi of Signor Ascanio that interests me."

"You think he has an alibi?"

"That is just what worries me. I have no doubt that we shall soon be enlightened on that point."

The *Daily Newsmonger* enabled us to become conversant with succeeding events.

Signor Ascanio was arrested and charged with the murder of Count Foscatini. When arrested, he denied knowing the Count, and declared he had never been near Regent's Court either on the evening of the crime or on the previous morning. The younger man had disappeared entirely. Signor Ascanio had arrived alone at the Grosvenor Hotel from the Continent two days before the murder. All efforts to trace the second man failed.

Ascanio, however, was not sent for trial. No less a personage than the Italian Ambassador himself came forward and testified at the police-court proceedings that Ascanio had been with him at the Embassy from eight till nine that evening. The prisoner was discharged. Naturally, a lot of people thought that the crime was a political one, and was being deliberately hushed up.

Poirot had taken a keen interest in all these points. Nevertheless, I was somewhat surprised when he suddenly informed me one morning that he was expecting a visitor at eleven o'clock, and that that visitor was none other than Ascanio himself.

"He wishes to consult you?"

"*Du tout*, Hastings. I wish to consult him."

"What about?"

"The Regent's Court murder."

"You are going to prove that he did it?"

"A man cannot be tried twice for murder, Hastings. Endeavor to have the common sense. Ah, that is our friend's ring."

A few minutes later Signor Ascanio was ushered in— a small, thin man with a secretive and furtive glance in his eyes. He remained standing, darting suspicious glances from one to the other of us.

"Monsieur Poirot?"

My little friend tapped himself gently on the chest.

"Be seated, signor. You received my note. I am determined to get to the bottom of this mystery. In some small measure you can aid me. Let us commence. You—in company with a friend—visited the late Count Foscatini on the morning of Tuesday the 9th——"

The Italian made an angry gesture.

"I did nothing of the sort. I have sworn in court——"

"*Précisément*—and I have a little idea that you have sworn falsely."

"You threaten me? Bah! I have nothing to fear from you. I have been acquitted."

"Exactly; and as I am not an imbecile, it is not with the gallows I threaten you—but with publicity. Publicity! I see that you do not like the word. I had an idea that you would not. My little ideas, you know, they are very valuable to me. Come, signor, your only chance is to be frank with me. I do not ask to know whose indiscretions brought you to England. I know this much, you came for the especial purpose of seeing Count Foscatini."

"He was not a count," growled the Italian.

"I have already noted the fact that his name does not appear in the *Almanach de Gotha*. Never mind, the title of count is often useful in the profession of blackmailing."

"I suppose I might as well be frank. You seem to know a great deal."

"I have employed my gray cells to some advantage. Come, Signor Ascanio, you visited the dead man on the Tuesday morning—that is so, is it not?"

"Yes; but I never went there on the following evening. There was no need. I will tell you all. Certain information concerning a man of great position in Italy had come into this scoundrel's possession. He demanded a big sum of money in return for the papers. I came over to England to arrange the matter. I called upon him by appointment that morning. One of the young secretaries of the Embassy was with me. The Count was more reasonable than I had hoped, although even then the sum of money I paid him was a huge one."

"Pardon, how was it paid?"

"In Italian notes of comparatively small denomination. I paid over the money then and there. He handed me the incriminating papers. I never saw him again."

"Why did you not say all this when you were arrested?"

"In my delicate position I was forced to deny any association with the man."

"And how do you account for the events of the evening, then?"

"I can only think that some one must have deliberately impersonated me. I understand that no money was found in the flat."

Poirot looked at him and shook his head.

"Strange," he murmured. "We all have the little gray cells. And so few of us know how to use them. Good morning, Signor Ascanio. I believe your story. It is very much as I had imagined. But I had to make sure."

After bowing his guest out, Poirot returned to his armchair and smiled at me.

"Let us hear M. le Capitaine Hastings on the case?"

"Well, I suppose Ascanio is right—somebody impersonated him."

"Never, never will you use the brains the good God has given you. Recall to yourself some words I uttered after leaving the flat that night. I referred to the window-curtains not being drawn. We are in the month of June. It is still light at eight o'clock. The light is failing by half-past. *Ça vous dit quelque chose?* I perceive a struggling impression that you will arrive some day. Now let us continue. The coffee was, as I said, very black. Count Foscatini's teeth were magnificently white. Coffee stains the teeth. We reason from that that Count Foscatini did not drink any coffee. Yet there was coffee in all three cups. Why should anyone pretend Count Foscatini had drunk coffee when he had not done so?"

I shook my head, utterly bewildered.

"Come, I will help you. What evidence have we that Ascanio and his friend, or two men posing as them, ever came to the flat that night? Nobody saw them go in; nobody saw them go out. We have the evidence of one man and of a host of inanimate objects."

"You mean?"

"I mean knives and forks and plates and empty dishes. Ah, but it was a clever idea! Graves is a thief and a scoundrel, but what a man of method! He overhears a portion of the conversation in the morning, enough to realize that Ascanio will be in an awkward position to defend himself. The following evening, about eight o'clock, he tells his master he is wanted at the telephone. Foscatini sits down, stretches out his hand to the telephone, and from behind Graves strikes him down with the marble figure. Then quickly to the service telephone—dinner for three! It comes, he lays the table, dirties the plates, knives, and forks, etc. But he has to get rid of the food too. Not only is he a man of brain; he has a resolute and capacious stomach! But after eating three tournedos, the rice soufflé is too much for him! He even smokes a cigar and two cigarettes to carry out the illusion. Ah, but it was magnificently thorough! Then, having moved on the hands of the clock to 8.47, he smashes it and stops it. The one thing he does not do is to draw the curtains. But if there had been a real dinner party the curtains would have been drawn as soon as the light began to fail. Then he hurries out, mentioning the guests to the lift man in passing. He hurries to a telephone box, and as near as possible to 8.47 rings up the doctor with his master's dying cry. So successful is his idea that no one ever inquires if a call was put through from Flat 11 at that time."

"Except Hercule Poirot, I suppose?" I said sarcastically.

"Not even Hercule Poirot," said my friend, with a smile. "I am about to inquire now. I had to prove my point to you first. But you will see, I shall be right; and then Japp, to whom I have already given a hint, will be able to arrest the respectable Graves. I wonder how much of the money he has spent."

Poirot *was* right. He always is, confound him!

XI
THE CASE OF
THE MISSING WILL

The problem presented to us by Miss Violet Marsh made rather a pleasant change from our usual routine work. Poirot had received a brisk and business-like note from the lady asking for an appointment, and he had replied asking her to call upon him at eleven o'clock the following day.

She arrived punctually—a tall, handsome young woman, plainly but neatly dressed, with an assured and business-like manner. Clearly a young woman who meant to get on in the world. I am not a great admirer of the so-called New Woman myself, and, in spite of her good looks, I was not particularly prepossessed in her favor.

"My business is of a somewhat unusual nature, Monsieur Poirot," she began, after she had accepted a chair. "I had better begin at the beginning and tell you the whole story."

"If you please, mademoiselle."

"I am an orphan. My father was one of two brothers, sons of a small yeoman farmer in Devonshire. The farm was a poor one, and the elder brother, Andrew, emigrated to Australia, where he did very well indeed, and by means of successful speculation in land became a very rich man. The younger brother, Roger (my father), had no leanings towards the agricultural life. He managed to educate himself a little, and obtained a post as a clerk with a small firm. He married slightly above him; my mother was the daughter of a poor artist. My father died when I was six years old. When I was fourteen, my mother followed him to the grave. My only living relation then was my Uncle Andrew, who had recently returned from Australia and bought a small place, Crabtree Manor, in his native county. He was exceedingly kind to his brother's orphan child, took me to live with him, and treated me in every way as though I was his own daughter.

"Crabtree Manor, in spite of its name, is really only an old farmhouse. Farming was in my uncle's blood, and he was intensely interested in various modern farming experiments. Although kindness itself to me, he had certain peculiar and deeply-rooted ideas as to the up-bringing of women. Himself a man of little or no education, though possessing remarkable shrewdness, he placed little value on what he called 'book knowledge.' He was especially opposed to the education of women. In his opinion, girls should learn practical housework and a dairy-work, be useful about the home, and have as little to do with book learning as possible. He proposed to bring me up on these lines, to my bitter disappointment and annoyance. I rebelled frankly. I knew that I possessed a good brain, and had absolutely no talent for domestic duties. My uncle and I had many bitter arguments on the subject, for, though much attached to each other, we were both self-willed. I was lucky enough to win a scholarship, and up to a certain point was successful in getting my own way. The crisis arose when I resolved to go to Girton. I had a little money of my own, left me by my mother, and I was quite determined to make the best use of the gifts God had given me. I had one long, final argument with my uncle. He put the facts plainly before me. He had no other relations, and he had intended me to be his sole heiress. As I have told you, he was a very rich man. If I persisted in these 'new-fangled notions' of mine, however, I need look for nothing from him. I remained polite, but firm. I should always be deeply attached to him, I told him, but I must lead my own life. We parted on that note. 'You fancy your brain, my girl,' were his last words. 'I've no book learning, but for all that, I'll pit mine against yours any day. We'll see what we shall see.'

"That was nine years ago. I have stayed with him for a week-end occasionally, and our relations were perfectly amicable, though his views remained unaltered. He never referred to my having matriculated, nor to my B.Sc. For the last three years his health had been failing, and a month ago he died.

"I am now coming to the point of my visit. My uncle left a most extraordinary will. By its terms, Crabtree Manor and its contents are to be at my disposal for a year from his death—'during which time my clever niece may prove her wits,' the actual words run. At the end of that period, 'my wits having proved better than hers,' the house and all my uncle's large fortune pass to various charitable institutions."

"That is a little hard on you, mademoiselle, seeing that you were Mr. Marsh's only blood relation."

"I do not look on it in that way. Uncle Andrew warned me fairly, and I chose my own path. Since I would not fall in with his wishes, he was at perfect liberty to leave his money to whom he pleased."

"Was the will drawn up by a lawyer?"

"No; it was written on a printed will-form and witnessed by the man and his wife who live in the house and do for my uncle."

"There might be a possibility of upsetting such a will?"

"I would not even attempt to do such a thing."

"You regard it, then, as a sporting challenge on the part of your uncle?"

"That is exactly how I look upon it."

"It bears that interpretation, certainly," said Poirot thoughtfully. "Somewhere in this rambling old manor-house your uncle has concealed either a sum of money in notes or possibly a second will, and has given you a year in which to exercise your ingenuity to find it."

"Exactly, Monsieur Poirot; and I am paying you the compliment of assuming that your ingenuity will be greater than mine."

"Eh, eh! but that is very charming of you. My gray cells are at your disposal. You have made no search yourself?"

"Only a cursory one; but I have too much respect for my uncle's undoubted abilities to fancy that the task will be an easy one."

"Have you the will or a copy of it with you?"

Miss Marsh handed a document across the table. Poirot ran through it, nodding to himself.

"Made three years ago. Dated March 25; and the time is given also—11 A.M.—that is very suggestive. It narrows the field of search. Assuredly it is another will we have to seek for. A will made even half-an-hour later would upset this. *Eh bien,* mademoiselle, it is a problem charming and ingenious that you have presented to me here. I shall have all the pleasure in the world in solving it for you. Granted that your uncle was a man of ability, his gray cells cannot have been of the quality of Hercule Poirot's!"

(Really, Poirot's vanity is blatant!)

"Fortunately, I have nothing of moment on hand at the minute. Hastings and I will go down to Crabtree Manor to-night. The man and wife who attended on your uncle are still there, I presume?"

"Yes, their name is Baker."

The following morning saw us started on the hunt proper. We had arrived late the night before. Mr. and Mrs. Baker, having received a telegram from Miss Marsh, were expecting us. They were a pleasant couple, the man gnarled and pink-cheeked, like a shriveled pippin, and his wife a woman of vast proportions and true Devonshire calm.

Tired with our journey and the eight-mile drive from the station, we had retired at once to bed after a supper of roast chicken, apple pie, and Devonshire cream. We had now disposed of an excellent breakfast, and were sitting in a small paneled room which had been the late Mr. Marsh's study and living-room. A roll-top desk stuffed with papers, all neatly docketed, stood against the wall, and a big leather armchair showed plainly that it had been its owner's constant resting-place. A big chintz-covered settee ran along the opposite wall, and the deep low window seats were covered with the same faded chintz of an old-fashioned pattern.

"*Eh bien, mon ami,*" said Poirot, lighting one of his tiny cigarettes, "we must map out our plan of campaign. Already I have made a rough survey of the house, but

I am of opinion that any clue will be found in this room. We shall have to go through the documents in the desk with meticulous care. Naturally, I do not expect to find the will amongst them; but it is likely that some apparently innocent paper may conceal the clue to its hiding-place. But first we must have a little information. Ring the bell, I pray of you."

I did so. While we were waiting for it to be answered, Poirot walked up and down, looking about him approvingly.

"A man of method this Mr. Marsh. See how neatly the packets of papers are docketed; then the key to each drawer has its ivory label—so has the key of the china cabinet on the wall; and see with what precision the china within is arranged. It rejoices the heart. Nothing here offends the eye——"

He came to an abrupt pause, as his eye was caught by the key of the desk itself, to which a dirty envelope was affixed. Poirot frowned at it and withdrew it from the lock. On it were scrawled the words: "Key of Roll Top Desk," in a crabbed handwriting, quite unlike the neat superscriptions on the other keys.

"An alien note," said Poirot, frowning. "I could swear that here we have no longer the personality of Mr. Marsh. But who else has been in the house? Only Miss Marsh, and she, if I mistake not, is also a young lady of method and order."

Baker came in answer to the bell.

"Will you fetch madame your wife, and answer a few questions?"

Baker departed, and in a few moments returned with Mrs. Baker, wiping her hands on her apron and beaming all over her face.

In a few clear words Poirot set forth the object of his mission. The Bakers were immediately sympathetic.

"Us don't want to see Miss Violet done out of what's hers," declared the woman. "Cruel hard 'twould be for hospitals to get it all."

Poirot proceeded with his questions. Yes, Mr. and Mrs. Baker remembered perfectly witnessing the will. Baker had previously been sent in to the neighboring town to get two printed will-forms.

"Two?" said Poirot sharply.

"Yes, sir, for safety like, I suppose, in case he should spoil one—and sure enough, so he did do. Us had signed one——"

"What time of day was that?"

Baker scratched his head, but his wife was quicker.

"Why, to be sure, I'd just put the milk on for the cocoa at eleven. Don't ee remember? It had all boiled over on the stove when us got back to kitchen."

"And afterwards?"

" 'Twould be about an hour later. Us had to go in again. 'I've made a mistake,' says old master, 'had to tear the whole thing up. I'll trouble you to sign again,' and us did. And afterwards master give us a tidy sum of money each. 'I've left you nothing in my will,' says he, 'but each year I live you'll have this to be a nest-egg when I'm gone'; and sure enough, so he did."

Poirot reflected.

"After you had signed the second time, what did Mr. Marsh do? Do you know?"

"Went out to the village to pay tradesmen's books."

That did not seem very promising. Poirot tried another tack. He held out the key of the desk.

"Is that your master's writing?"

I may have imagined it, but I fancied that a moment or two elapsed before Baker replied: "Yes, sir, it is."

"He's lying," I thought. "But why?"

"Has your master let the house?—have there been any strangers in it during the last three years?"

"No, sir."

"No visitors?"

"Only Miss Violet."

"No strangers of any kind been inside this room?"

"No, sir."

"You forget the workmen, Jim," his wife reminded him.

"Workmen?" Poirot wheeled round on her. "What workmen?"

The woman explained that about two years and a half ago workmen had been in the house to do certain repairs. She was quite vague as to what the repairs were. Her view seemed to be that the whole thing was a fad of her master's and quite unnecessary. Part of the time the workmen had been in the study; but what they had done there she could not say, as her master had not let either of them into the room whilst the work was in progress. Unfortunately, they could not remember the name of the firm employed, beyond the fact that it was a Plymouth one.

"We progress, Hastings," said Poirot, rubbing his hands as the Bakers left the room. "Clearly he made a second will and then had workmen from Plymouth in to make a suitable hiding-place. Instead of wasting time taking up the floor and tapping the walls, we will go to Plymouth."

With a little trouble, we were able to get the information we wanted. After one or two essays, we found the firm employed by Mr. Marsh.

Their employees had all been with them many years, and it was easy to find the two men who had worked under Mr. Marsh's orders. They remembered the job perfectly. Amongst various other minor jobs, they had taken up one of the bricks of the old-fashioned fireplace, made a cavity beneath, and so cut the brick that it was impossible to see the join. By pressing on the second brick from the end, the whole thing was raised. It had been quite a complicated piece of work, and the old gentleman had been very fussy about it. Our informant was a man called Coghan, a big, gaunt man with a grizzled mustache. He seemed an intelligent fellow.

We returned to Crabtree Manor in high spirits, and, locking the study door, proceeded to put our newly acquired knowledge into effect. It was impossible to see any sign on the bricks, but when we pressed in the manner indicated, a deep cavity was at once disclosed.

Eagerly Poirot plunged in his hand. Suddenly his face fell from complacent elation to consternation. All he held was a charred fragment of stiff paper. But for it, the cavity was empty.

"*Sacré!*" cried Poirot angrily. "Some one has been before us."

We examined the scrap of paper anxiously. Clearly it was a fragment of what we sought. A portion of Baker's signature remained, but no indication of what the terms of the will had been.

Poirot sat back on his heels. His expression would have been comical if we had not been so overcome.

"I understand it not," he growled. "Who destroyed this? And what was their object?"

"The Bakers?" I suggested.

"*Pourquoi?* Neither will makes any provision for them, and they are more likely to be kept on with Miss Marsh than if the place became the property of a hospital. How could it be to anyone's advantage to destroy the will? The hospitals benefit—yes; but one cannot suspect institutions."

"Perhaps the old man changed his mind and destroyed it himself," I suggested.

Poirot rose to his feet, dusting his knees with his usual care.

"That may be," he admitted. "One of your more sensible observations, Hastings. Well, we can do no more here. We have done all that mortal man can do. We have successfully pitted our wits against the late Andrew Marsh's; but, unfortunately, his niece is no better off for our success."

By driving to the station at once, we were just able to catch a train to London, though not the principal express. Poirot was sad and dissatisfied. For my part, I was tired and dozed in a corner. Suddenly, as we were just moving out of Taunton, Poirot uttered a piercing squeal.

"*Vite*, Hastings! Awake and jump! But jump I say!"

Before I knew where I was we were standing on the platform, bareheaded and minus our valises, whilst the train disappeared into the night. I was furious. But Poirot paid no attention.

"Imbecile that I have been!" he cried. "Triple imbecile! Not again will I vaunt my little gray cells!"

"That's a good job at any rate," I said grumpily. "But what is this all about?"

As usual, when following out his own ideas, Poirot paid absolutely no attention to me.

"The tradesmen's books—I have left them entirely out of account! Yes, but where? Where? Never mind, I cannot be mistaken. We must return at once."

Easier said than done. We managed to get a slow train to Exeter, and there Poirot hired a car. We arrived back at Crabtree Manor in the small hours of the morning. I pass over the bewilderment of the Bakers when we had at last aroused them. Paying no attention to anybody, Poirot strode at once to the study.

"I have been, not a triple imbecile, but thirty-six times one, my friend," he deigned to remark. "Now, behold!"

Going straight to the desk, he drew out the key, and detached the envelope from it. I stared at him stupidly. How could he possibly hope to find a big will-form in that tiny envelope? With great care he cut open the envelope, laying it out flat. Then he lighted the fire and held the plain inside surface of the envelope to the flame. In a few minutes faint characters began to appear.

"Look, *mon ami!*" cried Poirot in triumph.

I looked. There were just a few lines of faint writing stating briefly that he left everything to his niece, Violet Marsh. It was dated March 25, 12.30 P.M., and witnessed by Albert Pike, confectioner, and Jessie Pike, married woman.

"But is it legal?" I gasped.

"As far as I know, there is no law against writing your will in a blend of disappearing and sympathetic ink. The intention of the testator is clear, and the beneficiary is his only living relation. But the cleverness of him! He foresaw every step that a searcher would take—that I, miserable imbecile, took. He gets two will-forms, makes the servants sign twice, then sallies out with his will written on the inside of a dirty envelope and a fountain-pen containing his little ink mixture. On some excuse he gets the confectioner and his wife to sign their names under his own signature, then he ties it to the key of his desk and chuckles to himself. If his niece sees through his little ruse, she will have justified her choice of life and elaborate education, and be thoroughly welcome to his money."

"She didn't see through it, did she?" I said slowly. "It seems rather unfair. The old man really won."

"But no, Hastings. It is *your* wits that go astray. Miss Marsh proved the astuteness of her wits and the value of the higher education for women by at once putting the matter in *my* hands. Always employ the expert. She has amply proved her right to the money."

I wonder—I very much wonder—what old Andrew Marsh would have thought!

XII
THE VEILED LADY

I had noticed that for some time Poirot had been growing increasingly dissatisfied and restless. We had had no interesting cases of late, nothing on which my little friend could exercise his keen wits and remarkable powers of deduction. This morning he flung down the newspaper with an impatient *"Tchah!"*—a favorite exclamation of his which sounded exactly like a cat sneezing.

"They fear me, Hastings; the criminals of your England they fear me! When the cat is there, the little mice, they come no more to the cheese!"

"I don't suppose the greater part of them even know of your existence," I said, laughing.

Poirot looked at me reproachfully. He always imagines that the whole world is thinking and talking of Hercule Poirot. He had certainly made a name for himself in London, but I could hardly believe that his existence struck terror into the criminal world.

"What about that daylight robbery of jewels in Bond Street the other day?" I asked.

"A neat *coup*," said Poirot approvingly, "though not in my line. *Pas de finesse, seulment de l'audace!* A man with a loaded cane smashes the plate-glass window of a jeweler's shop and grabs a number of precious stones. Worthy citizens immediately seize him; a policeman arrives. He is caught red-handed with the jewels on him. He is marched off to the police station, and then it is discovered that the stones are paste. He has passed the real ones to a confederate—one of the aforementioned worthy citizens. He will go to prison—true; but when he comes out, there will be a nice little fortune awaiting him. Yes, not badly imagined. But I could do better than that. Sometimes,

Hastings, I regret that I am of such a moral disposition. To work against the law, it would be pleasing, for a change."

"Cheer up, Poirot; you know you are unique in your own line."

"But what is there on hand in my own line?"

I picked up the paper.

"Here's an Englishman mysteriously done to death in Holland," I said.

"They always say that—and later they find that he ate the tinned fish and that his death is perfectly natural."

"Well, if you're determined to grouse!"

"*Tiens!*" said Poirot, who had strolled across to the window. "Here in the street is what they call in novels a 'heavily veiled lady.' She mounts the steps; she rings the bell—she comes to consult us. Here is a possibility of something interesting. When one is as young and pretty as that one, one does not veil the face except for a big affair."

A minute later our visitor was ushered in. As Poirot had said, she was indeed heavily veiled. It was impossible to distinguish her features until she raised her veil of black Spanish lace. Then I saw that Poirot's intuition had been right; the lady was extremely pretty, with fair hair and large blue eyes. From the costly simplicity of her attire, I deduced at once that she belonged to the upper strata of society.

"Monsieur Poirot," said the lady in a soft, musical voice, "I am in great trouble. I can hardly believe that you can help me, but I have heard such wonderful things of you that I come literally as a last hope to beg you to do the impossible."

"The impossible, it pleases me always," said Poirot. "Continue, I beg of you, mademoiselle."

Our fair guest hesitated.

"But you must be frank," added Poirot. "You must not leave me in the dark on any point."

"I will trust you," said the girl suddenly. "You have heard of Lady Millicent Castle Vaughan?"

I looked up with keen interest. The announcement of Lady Millicent's engagement to the young Duke of Southshire had appeared a few days previously. She was, I knew, the fifth daughter of an impecunious Irish peer, and the Duke of Southshire was one of the best matches in England.

"I am Lady Millicent," continued the girl. "You may have read of my engagement. I should be one of the happiest girls alive; but oh, M. Poirot, I am in terrible trouble! There is a man, a horrible man—his name is Lavington; and he—I hardly know how to tell you. There was a letter I wrote—I was only sixteen at the time; and he—he——"

"A letter that you wrote to this Mr. Lavington?"

"Oh, no—not to him! To a young soldier—I was very fond of him—he was killed in the war."

"I understand," said Poirot kindly.

"It was a foolish letter, an indiscreet letter, but indeed, M. Poirot, nothing more. But there are phrases in it which—which might bear a different interpretation."

"I see," said Poirot. "And this letter has come into the possession of Mr. Lavington?"

"Yes, and he threatens, unless I pay him an enormous sum of money, a sum that it is quite impossible for me to raise, to send it to the Duke."

"The dirty swine!" I ejaculated. "I beg your pardon, Lady Millicent."

"Would it not be wiser to confess all to your future husband?"

"I dare not, M. Poirot. The Duke is a rather peculiar character, jealous and suspicious and prone to believe the worst. I might as well break off my engagement at once."

"Dear, dear," said Poirot with an expressive grimace. "And what do you want me to do, milady?"

"I thought perhaps that I might ask Mr. Lavington to call upon you. I would tell him that you were empowered by me to discuss the matter. Perhaps you could reduce his demands."

"What sum does he mention?"

"Twenty thousand pounds—an impossibility. I doubt if I could raise a thousand, even."

"You might perhaps borrow the money on the prospect of your approaching marriage—but I doubt if you could get hold of half that sum. Besides—*eh bien,* it is repugnant to me that you should pay! No, the ingenuity of Hercule Poirot shall defeat your enemies! Send me this Mr. Lavington. Is he likely to bring the letter with him?"

The girl shook her head.

"I do not think so. He is very cautious."

"I suppose there is no doubt that he really has it?"

"He showed it to me when I went to his house."

"You went to his house? That was very imprudent, milady."

"Was it? I was so desperate. I hoped my entreaties might move him."

"Oh, *là là!* The Lavingtons of this world are not moved by entreaties! He would welcome them as showing how much importance you attached to the document. Where does he live, this fine gentleman?"

"At Buona Vista, Wimbledon. I went there after dark—" Poirot groaned. "I declared that I would inform the police in the end, but he only laughed in a horrid, sneering manner. 'By all means, my dear Lady Millicent, do so if you wish,' he said."

"Yes, it is hardly an affair for the police," murmured Poirot.

" 'But I think you will be wiser than that,' he continued. 'See, here is your letter—in this little Chinese puzzle box!' He held it so that I could see. I tried to snatch at it, but he was too quick for me. With a horrid smile he folded it up and replaced it in the little wooden box. 'It will be quite safe here, I assure you,' he said; 'and the box itself lives in such a clever place that you would never find it.' My eyes turned to the small wall-safe, and he shook his head and laughed. 'I have a better safe than that,' he said. Oh, he was odious! M. Poirot, do you think that you can help me?"

"Have faith in Papa Poirot. I will find a way."

These reassurances were all very well, I thought, as Poirot gallantly ushered his fair client down the stairs, but it seemed to me that we had a tough nut to crack. I said as much to Poirot when he returned. He nodded ruefully.

"Yes—the solution does not leap to the eye. He has

the whip hand, this M. Lavington. For the moment I do
not see how we are to circumvent him."

Mr. Lavington duly called upon us that afternoon.
Lady Millicent had spoken truly when she described him
as an odious man. I felt a positive tingling in the end of
my boot, so keen was I to kick him down the stairs. He
was blustering and overbearing in manner, laughed Poirot's gentle suggestions to scorn, and generally showed
himself as master of the situation. I could not help feeling
that Poirot was hardly appearing at his best. He looked
discouraged and crestfallen.

"Well, gentlemen," said Lavington, as he took up his
hat, "we don't seem to be getting much farther. The case
stands like this: I'll let the Lady Millicent off cheap, as
she is such a charming young lady," he leered odiously.
"We'll say eighteen thousand. I'm off to Paris to-day—a
little piece of business to attend to over there. I shall be
back on Tuesday. Unless the money is paid by Tuesday
evening, the letter goes to the Duke. Don't tell me Lady
Millicent can't raise the money. Some of her gentlemen
friends would be only too willing to oblige such a pretty
woman with a loan—if she goes the right way about it."

My face flushed, and I took a step forward, but Lavington had wheeled out of the room as he finished his
sentence.

"My God!" I cried. "Something has got to be done.
You seem to be taking this lying down, Poirot."

"You have an excellent heart, my friend—but your
gray cells are in a deplorable condition. I have no wish to
impress Mr. Lavington with my capabilities. The more
pusillanimous he thinks me, the better."

"Why?"

"It is curious," murmured Poirot reminiscently, "that
I should have uttered a wish to work against the law just
before Lady Millicent arrived!"

"You are going to burgle his house while he is away?"
I gasped.

"Sometimes, Hastings, your mental processes are
amazingly quick."

"Suppose he takes the letter with him?"

Poirot shook his head.

"That is very unlikely. He has evidently a hiding-place in his house that he fancies to be pretty impregnable."

"When do we—er—do the deed?"

"To-morrow night. We will start from here about eleven o'clock."

At the time appointed I was ready to set off. I had donned a dark suit, and a soft dark hat. Poirot beamed kindly on me.

"You have dressed the part, I see," he observed. "Come let us take the underground to Wimbledon."

"Aren't we going to take anything with us? Tools to break in with?"

"My dear Hastings, Hercule Poirot does not adopt such crude methods."

I retired, snubbed, but my curiosity was alert.

It was just on midnight that we entered the small suburban garden of Buona Vista. The house was dark and silent. Poirot went straight to a window at the back of the house, raised the sash noiselessly and bade me enter.

"How did you know this window would be open?" I whispered, for really it seemed uncanny.

"Because I sawed through the catch this morning."

"What?"

"But yes, it was the most simple. I called, presented a fictitious card and one of Inspector Japp's official ones. I said I had been sent, recommended by Scotland Yard, to attend to some burglar-proof fastenings that Mr. Lavington wanted fixed while he was away. The housekeeper welcomed me with enthusiasm. It seems they have had two attempted burglaries here lately—evidently our little idea has occurred to other clients of Mr. Lavington's—with nothing of value taken. I examined all the windows, made my little arrangement, forbade the servants to touch the windows until to-morrow, as they were electrically connected up, and withdrew gracefully."

"Really, Poirot, you are wonderful."

"*Mon ami,* it was of the simplest. Now, to work! The servants sleep at the top of the house, so we will run little risk of disturbing them."

"I presume the safe is built into the wall somewhere?"

"Safe? Fiddlesticks! There is no safe. Mr. Lavington is an intelligent man. You will see, he will have devised a hiding-place much more intelligent than a safe. A safe is the first thing everyone looks for."

Whereupon we began a systematic search of the entire place. But after several hours' ransacking of the house, our search had been unavailing. I saw symptoms of anger gathering on Poirot's face.

"*Ah, sapristi,* is Hercule Poirot to be beaten? Never! Let us be calm. Let us reflect. Let us reason. Let us— *enfin!*—employ our little gray cells!"

He paused for some moments, bending his brows in concentration; then the green light I knew so well stole into his eyes.

"I have been an imbecile! The kitchen!"

"The kitchen," I cried. "But that's impossible. The servants!"

"Exactly. Just what ninety-nine people out of a hundred would say! And for that very reason the kitchen is the ideal place to choose. It is full of various homely objects. *En avant,* to the kitchen!"

I followed him, completely skeptical, and watched whilst he dived into bread-bins, tapped saucepans, and put his head into the gas-oven. In the end, tired of watching him, I strolled back to the study. I was convinced that there, and there only, would we find the *cache.* I made a further minute search, noted that it was now a quarter past four and that therefore it would soon be growing light, and then went back to the kitchen regions.

To my utter amazement, Poirot was now standing right inside the coal-bin, to the utter ruin of his neat light suit. He made a grimace.

"But yes, my friend, it is against all my instincts so to ruin my appearance, but what will you?"

"But Lavington can't have buried it under the coal?"

"If you would use your eyes, you would see that it is not the coal that I examine."

I then saw that on a shelf behind the coal-bunker some logs of wood were piled. Poirot was dexterously taking them down one by one. Suddenly he uttered a low exclamation.

"Your knife, Hastings!"

I handed it to him. He appeared to insert it in the wood, and suddenly the log split in two. It had been neatly sawn in half and a cavity hollowed out in the center. From this cavity Poirot took a little wooden box of Chinese make.

"Well done!" I cried, carried out of myself.

"Gently, Hastings! Do not raise your voice too much. Come, let us be off, before the daylight is upon us."

Slipping the box into his pocket, he leaped lightly out of the coal-bunker, brushed himself down as well as he could, and leaving the house by the same way as we had come, we walked rapidly in the direction of London.

"But what an extraordinary place!" I expostulated. "Anyone might have used the log."

"In July, Hastings? And it was at the bottom of the pile—a very ingenious hiding-place. Ah, here is a taxi! Now for home, a wash, and a refreshing sleep."

After the excitement of the night, I slept late. When I finally strolled into our sitting-room just before one o'clock, I was surprised to see Poirot, leaning back in an armchair, the Chinese box open beside him, calmly reading the letter he had taken from it.

He smiled at me affectionately, and tapped the sheet he held.

"She was right, the Lady Millicent; never would the Duke have pardoned this letter! It contains some of the most extravagant terms of affection I have ever come across."

"Really, Poirot," I said, rather disgustedly, "I don't think you should have read the letter. That's the sort of thing that isn't done."

"It is done by Hercule Poirot," replied my friend imperturbably.

"And another thing," I said. "I don't think using Japp's official card yesterday was quite playing the game."

"But I was not playing a game, Hastings. I was conducting a case."

I shrugged my shoulders. One can't argue with a point of view.

"A step on the stairs," said Poirot. "That will be Lady Millicent."

Our fair client came in with an anxious expression on her face which changed to one of delight on seeing the letter and box which Poirot held up.

"Oh M. Poirot. How wonderful of you! How did you do it?"

"By rather reprehensible methods, milady. But Mr. Lavington will not prosecute. This is your letter, is it not?"

She glanced through it.

"Yes. Oh, how can I ever thank you! You are a wonderful, wonderful man. Where was it hidden?"

Poirot told her.

"How very clever of you!" She took up the small box from the table. "I shall keep this as a souvenir."

"I had hoped, milady, that you would permit me to keep it—also as a souvenir."

"I hope to send you a better souvenir than that—on my wedding-day. You shall not find me ungrateful, M. Poirot."

"The pleasure of doing you a service will be more to me than a check—so you permit that I retain the box."

"Oh, no, M. Poirot, I simply must have that," she cried laughingly.

She stretched out her hand, but Poirot was before her. His hand closed over it.

"I think not." His voice had changed.

"What do you mean?" Her voice seemed to have grown sharper.

"At any rate, permit me to abstract its further contents. You observe that the original cavity has been reduced by half. In the top half, the compromising letter; in the bottom——"

He made a nimble gesture, then held out his hand. On

the palm were four large glittering stones, and two big milky white pearls.

"The jewels stolen in Bond Street the other day, I rather fancy," murmured Poirot. "Japp will tell us."

To my utter amazement, Japp himself stepped out from Poirot's bedroom.

"An old friend of yours, I believe," said Poirot politely to Lady Millicent.

"Nabbed, by the Lord!" said Lady Millicent, with a complete change of manner. "You nippy old devil!" She looked at Poirot with almost affectionate awe.

"Well, Gertie, my dear," said Japp, "the game's up this time, I fancy. Fancy seeing you again so soon! We've got your pal, too, the gentleman who called here the other day calling himself Lavington. As for Lavington himself, alias Croker, alias Reed, I wonder which of the gang it was who stuck a knife into him the other day in Holland? Thought he'd got the goods with him, didn't you? And he hadn't. He double-crossed you properly—hid 'em in his own house. You had two fellows looking for them, and then you tackled M. Poirot here, and by a piece of amazing luck he found them."

"You do like talking, don't you?" said the late Lady Millicent. "Easy there, now. I'll go quietly. You can't say that I'm not the perfect lady. *Ta-ta*, all!"

"The shoes were wrong," said Poirot dreamily, while I was still too stupefied to speak. "I have made my little observations of your English nation, and a lady, a born lady, is always particular about her shoes. She may have shabby clothes, but she will be well shod. Now, this Lady Millicent had smart, expensive clothes, and cheap shoes. It was not likely that either you or I should have seen the real Lady Millicent; she has been very little in London, and this girl had a certain superficial resemblance which would pass well enough. As I say, the shoes first awakened my suspicions, and then her story—and her veil— were a little melodramatic, eh? The Chinese box with a bogus compromising letter in the top must have been known to all the gang, but the log of wood was the late Mr. Lavington's own idea. *Eh, par exemple,* Hastings, I hope you will not again wound my feelings as you did yesterday by saying that I am unknown to the criminal classes. *Ma foi,* they even employ me when they themselves fail!"

XIII
THE LOST MINE

I laid down my bank-book with a sigh.

"It is a curious thing," I observed, "but my overdraft never seems to grow any less."

"And it perturbs you not? Me, if I had an overdraft, never should I close my eyes all night," declared Poirot.

"You deal in comfortable balances, I suppose!" I retorted.

"Four hundred and forty-four pounds, four and fourpence," said Poirot with some complacency. "A neat figure, is it not?"

"It must be tact on the part of your bank manager. He is evidently acquainted with your passion for symmetrical details. What about investing, say three hundred of it, in the Porcupine oil-fields? Their prospectus, which is advertised in the papers to-day says that they will pay one hundred per cent in dividends next year."

"Not for me," said Poirot, shaking his head. "I like not the sensational. For me the safe, the prudent investment—*les rentes,* the consols, the—how do you call it?—the conversion."

"Have you never made a speculative investment?"

"No, *mon ami,*" replied Poirot severely. "I have not. And the only shares I own which have not what you call the gilded edge are fourteen thousand shares in the Burma Mines, Ltd."

Poirot paused with an air of waiting to be encouraged to go on.

"Yes?" I prompted.

"And for them I paid no cash—no, they were the reward of the exercise of my little gray cells. You would like to hear the story? Yes?"

"Of course I would."

"These mines are situated in the interior of Burma about two hundred miles inland from Rangoon. They were discovered by the Chinese in the fifteenth century and worked down to the time of the Mohammedan Rebellion, being finally abandoned in the year 1868. The Chinese extracted the rich lead-silver ore from the upper part of the ore body, smelting it for the silver alone, and leaving large quantities of rich lead-bearing slag. This, of course, was soon discovered when prospecting work was carried out in Burma, but owing to the fact that the old workings had become full of loose filling and water, all attempts to find the source of the ore proved fruitless. Many parties were sent out by syndicates, and they dug over a large area, but this rich prize still eluded them. But a representative of one of the syndicates got on the track of a Chinese family who were supposed to have still kept a record of the situation of the mine. The present head of the family was one Wu Ling."

"What a fascinating page of commercial romance!" I exclaimed.

"Is it not? Ah, *mon ami*, one can have romance without golden-haired girls of matchless beauty—no, I am wrong; it is auburn hair that so excites you always. You remember——"

"Go on with the story," I said hastily.

"*Eh bien*, my friend, this Wu Ling was approached. He was an estimable merchant, much respected in the province where he lived. He admitted at once that he owned the documents in question, and was perfectly prepared to negotiate for this sale, but he objected to dealing with any other than principals. Finally it was arranged that he should journey to England and meet the directors of an important company.

"Wu Ling made the journey to England in the S.S. *Assunta*, and the *Assunta* docked at Southampton on a cold, foggy morning in November. One of the directors, Mr. Pearson, went down to Southampton to meet the boat, but owing to the fog, the train down was very much delayed, and by the time he arrived, Wu Ling had disembarked and left by special train for London. Mr. Pearson returned to town somewhat annoyed, as he had no idea where the Chinaman proposed to stay. Later in the day, however, the offices of the Company were rung up on the telephone. Wu Ling was staying at the Russell Square Hotel. He was feeling somewhat unwell after the voyage, but declared himself perfectly able to attend the Board meeting on the following day.

"The meeting of the Board took place at eleven o'clock. When half-past eleven came, and Wu Ling had not put in an appearance, the secretary rang up the Russell Hotel. In answer to his inquiries, he was told that the Chinaman had gone out with a friend about half-past ten. It seemed clear that he had started out with the intention of coming to the meeting, but the morning wore away, and he did not appear. It was, of course, possible that he had lost his way, being unacquainted with London, but at a late hour that night, he had not returned to the hotel. Thoroughly alarmed now, Mr. Pearson put matters in the hands of the police. On the following day, there was still no trace of the missing man, but towards evening of the day after that again, a body was found in the Thames which proved to be that of the ill-fated Chinaman. Neither on the body, nor in the luggage at the hotel, was there any trace of the papers relating to the mine.

"At this juncture, *mon ami,* I was brought into the affair. Mr. Pearson called upon me. While profoundly shocked by the death of Wu Ling, his chief anxiety was to recover the papers which were the object of the Chinaman's visit to England. The main anxiety of the police, of course, would be to track down the murderer—the recovery of the papers would be a secondary consideration. What he wanted me to do was to coöperate with the police while acting in the interests of the Company.

"I consented readily enough. It was clear that there were two fields of search open to me. On the one hand, I might look among the employees of the Company who knew of the Chinaman's coming; on the other, among the passengers on the boat who might have been acquainted with his mission. I started with the second, as being a narrower field of search. In this I coincided with

Inspector Miller, who was in charge of the case—a man altogether different to our friend Japp, conceited, ill-mannered and quite insufferable. Together we interviewed the officers of the ship. They had little to tell us. Wu Ling had kept much to himself on the voyage. He had been intimate with but two of the other passengers—one a broken-down European named Dyer who appeared to bear a somewhat unsavory reputation, the other a young bank-clerk named Charles Lester, who was returning from Hongkong. We were lucky enough to obtain snapshots of both these men. At the moment there seemed little doubt that if either of the two was implicated, Dyer was the man. He was known to be mixed up with a gang of Chinese crooks, and was altogether a most likely suspect.

"Our next step was to visit the Russell Square Hotel. Shown a snapshot of Wu Ling, they recognized him at once. We then showed them the snapshot of Dyer, but to our disappointment, the hall porter declared positively that that was not the man who had come to the hotel on the fatal morning. Almost as an afterthought, I produced the photograph of Lester, and to my surprise the man at once recognized it.

" 'Yes sir,' he asserted, 'that's the gentleman who came in at half-past ten and asked for Mr. Wu Ling, and afterwards went out with him.'

"The affair was progressing. Our next move was to interview Mr. Charles Lester. He met us with the utmost frankness, was desolated to hear of the Chinaman's untimely death, and put himself at our disposal in every way. His story was as follows: By arrangement with Wu Ling, he called for him at the hotel at ten-thirty. Wu Ling, however, did not appear. Instead, his servant came, explained that his master had had to go out, and offered to conduct the young man to where his master now was. Suspecting nothing, Lester agreed, and the Chinaman procured a taxi. They drove for some time in the direction of the docks. Suddenly becoming mistrustful, Lester stopped the taxi and got out, disregarding the servant's protests. That, he assured us, was all he knew.

"Apparently satisfied, we thanked him and took our leave. His story was soon proved to be a somewhat inaccurate one. To begin with, Wu Ling had had no servant with him, either on the boat or at the hotel. In the second place, the taxi-driver who had driven the two men on that morning came forward. Far from Lester's having left the taxi en route, he and the Chinese gentleman had driven to a certain unsavory dwelling-place in Limehouse, right in the heart of Chinatown. The place in question was more or less well known as an opium-den of the lowest description. The two gentlemen had gone in—about an hour later the English gentleman, whom he identified from the photograph, came out alone. He looked very pale and ill, and directed the taxi-man to take him to the nearest underground station.

"Inquiries were made about Charles Lester's standing, and it was found that, though bearing an excellent character, he was heavily in debt, and had a secret passion for gambling. Dyer, of course, was not lost sight of. It seemed just faintly possible that he might have impersonated the other man, but that idea was proved utterly groundless. His alibi for the whole of the day in question was absolutely unimpeachable. Of course, the proprietor of the opium-den denied everything with Oriental stolidity. He had never seen Wu Ling; he had never seen Charles Lester. No two gentlemen had been to the place that morning. In any case, the police were wrong: no opium was ever smoked there.

"His denials, however well meant, did little to help Charles Lester. He was arrested for the murder of Wu Ling. A search of his effects was made, but no papers relating to the mine were discovered. The proprietor of the opium-den was also taken into custody, but a cursory raid of his premises yielded nothing. Not even a stick of opium rewarded the zeal of the police.

"In the meantime my friend Mr. Pearson was in a great state of agitation. He strode up and down my room, uttering great lamentations.

" 'But you must have some ideas, M. Poirot!' he kept urging. 'Surely you must have some ideas?'

" 'Certainly I have ideas,' I replied cautiously. 'That is the trouble—one has too many; therefore they all lead in different directions.'

" 'For instance?' he suggested.

" 'For instance—the taxi-driver. We have only his word for it that he drove the two men to that house. That is one idea. Then—was it really that house they went to? Supposing that they left the taxi there, passed through the house and out by another entrance and went elsewhere?'

"Mr. Pearson seemed struck by that.

" 'But you do nothing but sit and think? Can't we *do* something?'

"He was of an impatient temperament, you comprehend.

" 'Monsieur,' I said with dignity, 'it is not for Hercule Poirot to run up and down the evil-smelling streets of Limehouse like a little dog of no breeding. Be calm. My agents are at work.'

"On the following day I had news for him. The two men had indeed passed through the house in question, but their real objective was a small eating-house close to the river. They were seen to pass in there, and Lester came out alone.

"And then, figure to yourself, Hastings, an idea of the most unreasonable seized this Mr. Pearson! Nothing would suit him but that we should go ourselves to this eating-house and make investigations. I argued and prayed, but he would not listen. He talked of disguising himself—he even suggested that I—*I* should—I hesitate to say it—should shave off my mustache! Yes, *rien que ça!* I pointed out to him that that was an idea ridiculous and absurd. One destroys not a thing of beauty wantonly. Besides, shall not a Belgian gentleman with a mustache desire to see life and smoke the opium just as readily as one without a mustache?

"*Eh bien,* he gave in on that, but he still insisted on his project. He turned up that evening—*Mon Dieu,* what a figure! He wore what he called the 'pea-jacket,' his chin, it was dirty and unshaved; he had a scarf of the vilest that offended the nose. And figure to yourself, he was enjoying himself! Truly, the English are mad! He made some changes in my own appearance. I permitted it. Can one argue with a maniac? We started out—after all, could I let him go alone, a child dressed up to act the charades?"

"Of course you couldn't," I replied.

"To continue—we arrived. Mr. Pearson talked English of the strangest. He represented himself to be a man of the sea. He talked of 'lubbers' and 'focselles' and I know not what. It was a low little room with many Chinese in it. We ate of peculiar dishes. *Ah, Dieu, mon estomac!*" Poirot clasped that portion of his anatomy tenderly before continuing. "Then there came to us the proprietor, a Chinaman with a face of evil smiles.

" 'You gentlemen no likee food here,' he said. 'You come for what you likee better. Piecee pipe, eh?'

"Mr. Pearson, he gave me the great kick under the table. (He had on the boots of the sea, too!) And he said: 'I don't mind if I do, John. Lead ahead.'

"The Chinaman smiled, and he took us through a door and to a cellar and through a trapdoor, and down some steps and up again into a room all full of divans and cushions of the most comfortable. We lay down and a Chinese boy took off our boots. It was the best moment of the evening. Then they brought us the opium-pipes and cooked the opium pills, and we pretended to smoke and then to sleep and dream. But when we were alone, Mr. Pearson called softly to me, and immediately he began crawling along the floor. We went into another room where other people were asleep, and so on, until we heard two men talking. We stayed behind a curtain and listened. They were speaking of Wu Ling.

" 'What about the papers?' said one.

" 'Mr. Lester, he takee those,' answered the other, who was a Chinaman. 'He say, puttee them allee in safee place—where pleeceman no lookee.'

" 'Ah, but he's nabbed,' said the first one.

" 'He gettee free. Pleeceman not sure he done it.'

"There was more of the same kind of thing, then apparently the two men were coming our way, and we scuttled back to our beds.

" 'We'd better get out of here,' said Pearson, after a few minutes had elapsed. 'This place isn't healthy.'

" 'You are right, monsieur,' I agreed. 'We have played the farce long enough.'

"We succeeded in getting away, all right, paying handsomely for our smoke. Once clear of Limehouse, Pearson drew a long breath.

" 'I'm glad to get out of that,' he said. 'But it's something to be sure.'

" 'It is indeed,' I agreed. 'And I fancy that we shall not have much difficulty in finding what we want—after this evening's masquerade.'

"And there was no difficulty whatsoever," finished Poirot suddenly.

This abrupt ending seemed so extraordinary that I stared at him.

"But—but where were they?" I asked.

"In his pocket—*tout simplement.*"

"But in whose pocket?"

"Mr. Pearson's, *parbleu!*" Then, observing my look of bewilderment, he continued gently! "You do not yet see it? Mr. Pearson, like Charles Lester, was in debt. Mr. Pearson, like Charles Lester, was fond of gambling. And he conceived the idea of stealing the papers from the Chinaman. He met him all right at Southampton, came up to London with him, and took him straight to Limehouse. It was foggy that day; the Chinaman would not notice where he was going. I fancy Mr. Pearson smoked the opium fairly often down there and had some peculiar friends in consequence. I do not think he meant murder. His idea was that one of the Chinamen should impersonate Wu Ling and receive the money for the sale of the document. So far, so good! But, to the Oriental mind, it was infinitely simpler to kill Wu Ling and throw his body into the river, and Pearson's Chinese accomplices followed their own methods without consulting him. Imagine, then, what you would call the 'funk *bleu*' of M. Pearson. Some one may have seen him in the train with Wu Ling—murder is a very different thing to simple abduction.

"His salvation lies with the Chinaman who is personating Wu Ling at the Russell Square Hotel. If only the body is not discovered too soon! Probably Wu Ling had told him of the arrangement between him and Charles Lester whereby the latter was to call for him at the hotel. Pearson sees there an excellent way of diverting suspicion from himself. Charles Lester shall be the last person to be seen in company with Wu Ling. The impersonator has orders to represent himself to Lester as the servant of Wu Ling, and to bring him as speedily as possible to Limehouse. There, very likely, he was offered a drink. The drink would be suitably drugged, and when Lester emerged an hour later, he would have a very hazy impression of what had happened. So much was this the case, that as soon as Lester learned of Wu Ling's death, he loses his nerve, and denies that he ever reached Limehouse.

"By that, of course, he plays right into Pearson's hands. But is Pearson content? No—my manner disquiets him, and he determines to complete the case against Lester. So he arranges an elaborate masquerade. Me, I am to be gulled completely. Did I not say just now that he was as a child acting the charades? *Eh bien,* I play my part. He goes home rejoicing. But in the morning, Inspector Miller arrives on his doorstep. The papers are found on him; the game is up. Bitterly he regrets permitting himself to play the farce with Hercule Poirot! There was only one real difficulty in the affair."

"What was that?" I demanded curiously.

"Convincing Inspector Miller! What an animal, that! Both obstinate and imbecile. And in the end he took all the credit!"

"Too bad," I cried.

"Ah, well, I had my compensations. The other directors of the Burma Mines, Ltd., awarded me fourteen thousand shares as a small recompense for my services. Not so bad, eh? But when investing money, keep, I beg of you, Hastings, strictly to the conservative. The things you read in the paper, they may not be true. The directors of the Porcupine—they may be so many Mr. Pearsons!"

XIV
THE CHOCOLATE BOX

It was a wild night. Outside, the wind howled malevolently, and the rain beat against the windows in great gusts.

Poirot and I sat facing the hearth, our legs stretched out to the cheerful blaze. Between us was a small table. On my side of it stood some carefully brewed hot toddy; on Poirot's was a cup of thick, rich chocolate which I would not have drunk for a hundred pounds! Poirot sipped the thick brown mess in the pink china cup, and sighed with contentment.

"Quelle belle vie!" he murmured.

"Yes, it's a good old world," I agreed. "Here am I with a job, and a good job too! And here are you, famous———"

"Oh, *mon ami!*" protested Poirot.

"But you are. And rightly so! When I think back on your long line of successes, I am positively amazed. I don't believe you know what failure is!"

"He would be a droll kind of original who could say that!"

"No, but seriously, *have* you ever failed?"

"Innumerable times, my friend. What would you? *La bonne chance,* it cannot always be on your side. I have been called in too late. Very often another, working toward the same goal, has arrived there first. Twice have I been stricken down with illness just as I was on the point of success. One must take the downs with the ups, my friend."

"I didn't quite mean that," I said. "I meant, had you ever been completely down and out over a case through your own fault?"

"Ah, I comprehend! You ask if I have ever made the complete prize ass of myself, as you say over here? Once, my friend—" A slow, reflective smile hovered over his face. "Yes, once I made a fool of myself."

He sat up suddenly in his chair.

"See here, my friend, you have, I know, kept a record of my little successes. You shall add one more story to the collection, the story of a failure!"

He leaned forward and placed a log on the fire. Then, after carefully wiping his hands on a little duster that hung on a nail by the fireplace, he leaned back and commenced his story.

That of which I tell you, (said M. Poirot), took place in Belgium many years ago. It was at the time of the terrible struggle in France between church and state. M. Paul Déroulard was a French deputy of note. It was an open secret that the portfolio of a Minister awaited him. He was among the bitterest of the anti-Catholic party, and it was certain that on his accession to power, he would have to face violent enmity. He was in many ways a peculiar man. Though he neither drank nor smoked, he was nevertheless not so scrupulous in other ways. You comprehend, Hastings, *c' etait des femmes—toujours des femmes!*

He had married some years earlier a young lady from Brussels who had brought him a substantial dot. Undoubtedly the money was useful to him in his career, as his family was not rich, though on the other hand he was entitled to call himself M. le Baron if he chose. There were no children of the marriage, and his wife died after two years—the result of a fall downstairs. Among the property which she bequeathed to him was a house on the Avenue Louise in Brussels.

It was in this house that his sudden death took place, the event coinciding with the resignation of the Minister whose portfolio he was to inherit. All the papers printed long notices of his career. His death, which had taken place quite suddenly in the evening after dinner, was attributed to heart-failure.

At that time, *mon ami,* I was, as you know, a member of the Belgian detective force. The death of M. Paul

Déroulard was not particularly interesting to me. I am, as you also know, *bon catholique,* and his demise seemed to me fortunate.

It was some three days afterward, when my vacation had just begun, that I received a visitor at my own apartments—a lady, heavily veiled, but evidently quite young; and I perceived at once that she was a *jeune fille tout à fait comme il faut.*

"You are Monsieur Hercule Poirot?" she asked in a low sweet voice.

I bowed.

"Of the detective service?"

Again I bowed. "Be seated, I pray of you, mademoiselle," I said.

She accepted a chair and drew aside her veil. Her face was charming, though marred with tears, and haunted as though with some poignant anxiety.

"Monsieur," she said, "I understand that you are now taking a vacation. Therefore you will be free to take up a private case. You understand that I do not wish to call in the police."

I shook my head. "I fear what you ask is impossible, mademoiselle. Even though on vacation, I am still of the police."

She leaned forward. *"Ecoutez, monsieur.* All that I ask of you is to investigate. The result of your investigations you are at perfect liberty to report to the police. If what I believe to be true *is* true, we shall need all the machinery of the law."

That placed a somewhat different complexion on the matter, and I placed myself at her service without more ado.

A slight color rose in her cheeks. "I thank you, monsieur. It is the death of M. Paul Déroulard that I ask you to investigate."

"Comment?" I exclaimed, surprised.

"Monsieur, I have nothing to go upon—nothing but my woman's instinct, but I am convinced—*convinced,* I tell you—that M. Déroulard did not die a natural death!"

"But surely the doctors——"

"Doctors may be mistaken. He was so robust, so

strong. Ah, Monsieur Poirot, I beseech of you to help me——"

The poor child was almost beside herself. She would have knelt to me. I soothed her as best I could.

"I will help you, mademoiselle. I feel almost sure that your fears are unfounded, but we will see. First, I will ask you to describe to me the inmates of the house."

"There are the domestics, of course, Jeannette, Félicie, and Denise the cook. She has been there many years; the others are simple country girls. Also there is François, but he too is an old servant. Then there is Monsieur Déroulard's mother who lived with him, and myself. My name is Virginie Mesnard. I am a poor cousin of the late Madame Déroulard, M. Paul's wife, and I have been a member of their ménage for over three years. I have now described to you the household. There were also two guests staying in the house."

"And they were?"

"M. de Saint Alard, a neighbor of M. Déroulard's in France. Also an English friend, Mr. John Wilson."

"Are they still with you?"

"Mr. Wilson, yes, but M. de Saint Alard departed yesterday."

"And what is your plan, Mademoiselle Mesnard?"

"If you will present yourself at the house in half an hour's time, I will have arranged some story to account for your presence. I had better represent you to be connected with journalism in some way. I shall say you have come from Paris, and that you have brought a card of introduction from M. de Saint Alard. Madame Déroulard is very feeble in health, and will pay little attention to details."

On mademoiselle's ingenious pretext I was admitted to the house, and after a brief interview with the dead deputy's mother, who was a wonderfully imposing and aristocratic figure though obviously in failing health, I was made free of the premises.

I wonder, my friend (continued Poirot), whether you can possibly figure to yourself the difficulties of my task? Here was a man whose death had taken place three days previously. If there *had* been foul play, only one possibility was admittable—*poison!* And I had had no chance of seeing the body, and there was no possibility of examining, or analyzing, any medium in which the poison could have been administered. There were no clues, false or otherwise, to consider. Had the man been poisoned? Had he died a natural death? I, Hercule Poirot, with nothing to help me, had to decide.

First, I interviewed the domestics, and with their aid, I recapitulated the evening. I paid especial notice to the food at dinner, and the method of serving it. The soup had been served by M. Déroulard himself from a tureen. Next a dish of cutlets, then a chicken. Finally a compote of fruits. And all placed on the table, and served by Monsieur himself. The coffee was brought in a big pot to the dinner-table. Nothing there, *mon ami*—impossible to poison one without poisoning all!

After dinner Madame Déroulard had retired to her own apartments and Mademoiselle Virginie had accompanied her. The three men had adjourned to M. Déroulard's study. Here they had chatted amicably for some time, when suddenly, without any warning, the deputy had fallen heavily to the ground. M. de Saint Alard had rushed out and told François to fetch a doctor immediately. He said it was without doubt an apoplexy, explained the man. But when the doctor arrived, the patient was past help.

Mr. John Wilson, to whom I was presented by Mademoiselle Virginie, was what was known in those days as a regular John Bull Englishman, middle-aged and burly. His account, delivered in very British French, was substantially the same.

"Déroulard went very red in the face, and down he fell."

There was nothing further to be found out there. Next I went to the scene of the tragedy, the study, and was left alone there at my own request. So far there was nothing to support Mademoiselle Mesnard's theory. I could not but believe that it was a delusion on her part. Evidently she had entertained a romantic passion for the dead man which had not permitted her to take a normal view of the case. Nevertheless, I searched the study with meticulous care. It was just possible that a hypodermic needle might have been introduced into the dead man's chair in such a way as to allow of a fatal injection. The minute puncture it would cause was likely to remain unnoticed. But I could discover no sign to support that theory. I flung myself down in the chair with a gesture of despair.

"*Enfin*, I abandon it!" I said aloud. "There is not a clue anywhere! Everything is perfectly normal."

As I said the words, my eyes fell on a large box of chocolates standing on a table near by, and my heart gave a leap. It might not be a clue to M. Déroulard's death, but here at least was something that was *not* normal. I lifted the lid. The box was full, untouched; not a chocolate was missing—but that only made the peculiarity that had caught my eye more striking. For, see you, Hastings, while the box itself was pink, the lid was *blue*. Now, one often sees a blue ribbon on a pink box, and vice versa, but a box of one color, and a lid of another— no, decidedly—*ça ne se voit jamais!*

I did not as yet see that this little incident was of any use to me, yet I determined to investigate it as being out of the ordinary. I rang the bell for François, and asked him if his late master had been fond of sweets. A faint melancholy smile came to his lips.

"Passionately fond of them, monsieur. He would always have a box of chocolates in the house. He did not drink wine of any kind, you see."

"Yet this box has not been touched?" I lifted the lid to show him.

"Pardon, monsieur, but that was a new box purchased on the day of his death, the other being nearly finished."

"Then the other box was finished on the day of his death," I said slowly.

"Yes, monsieur, I found it empty in the morning and threw it away."

"Did M. Déroulard eat sweets at all hours of the day?"

"Usually after dinner, monsieur."

I began to see light.

"François," I said, "you can be discreet?"

"If there is need, monsieur."

"*Bon!* Know, then, that I am of the police. Can you find me that other box?"

"Without doubt, monsieur. It will be in the dustbin."

He departed, and returned in a few minutes with a dust-covered object. It was the duplicate of the box I held, save for the fact that this time the box was *blue* and the lid was *pink*. I thanked François, recommended him once more to be discreet, and left the house in the Avenue Louise without more ado.

Next I called upon the doctor who had attended M. Déroulard. With him I had a difficult task. He entrenched himself prettily behind a wall of learned phraseology, but I fancied that he was not quite as sure about the case as he would like to be.

"There have been many curious occurrences of the kind," he observed, when I had managed to disarm him somewhat. "A sudden fit of anger, a violent emotion,— after a heavy dinner, *c'est entendu,*—then, with an access of rage, the blood flies to the head, and *pst!*—there you are!"

"But M. Déroulard had had no violent emotion."

"No? I made sure that he had been having a stormy altercation with M. de Saint Alard."

"Why should he?"

"*C'est évident!*" The doctor shrugged his shoulders. "Was not M. de Saint Alard a Catholic of the most fanatical? Their friendship was being ruined by this question of church and state. Not a day passed without discussions. To M. de Saint Alard, Déroulard appeared almost as Antichrist."

This was unexpected, and gave me food for thought.

"One more question, Doctor: would it be possible to introduce a fatal dose of poison into a chocolate?"

"It would be possible, I suppose," said the doctor slowly. "Pure prussic acid would meet the case if there were no chance of evaporation, and a tiny globule of anything might be swallowed unnoticed—but it does not seem a very likely supposition. A chocolate full of morphine or strychnine—" He made a wry face. "You comprehend, M. Poirot—one bite would be enough! The unwary one would not stand upon ceremony."

"Thank you, M. le Docteur."

I withdrew. Next I made inquiries of the chemists, especially those in the neighborhood of the Avenue Louise. It is good to be of the police. I got the information I wanted without any trouble. Only in one case could I hear of any poison having been supplied to the house in question. This was some eye drops of atropine sulphate for Madame Déroulard. Atropine is a potent poison, and for the moment I was elated, but the symptoms of atropine poisoning are closely allied to those of ptomaine, and bear no resemblance to those I was studying. Besides, the prescription was an old one. Madame Déroulard had suffered from cataract in both eyes for many years.

I was turning away discouraged when the chemist's voice called me back.

"Un moment, M. Poirot. I remember, the girl who brought that prescription, she said something about having to go on to the *English* chemist. You might try there."

I did. Once more enforcing my official status, I got the information I wanted. On the day before M. Déroulard's death they had made up a prescription for Mr. John Wilson. Not that there was any making up about it. They were simply little tablets of trinitrin. I asked if I might see some. He showed me them, and my heart beat faster —for the tiny tablets were of *chocolate.*

"It is a poison?" I asked.

"No, monsieur."

"Can you describe to me its effect?"

"It lowers the blood-pressure. It is given for some forms of heart trouble—angina pectoris for instance. It relieves the arterial tension. In arteriosclerosis——"

I interrupted him. *"Ma foi!* This rigmarole says nothing to me. Does it cause the face to flush?"

"Certainly it does."

"And supposing I ate ten—twenty of your little tablets, what then?"

"I should not advise you to attempt it," he replied dryly.

"And yet you say it is not poison?"

"There are many things not called poison which can kill a man," he replied as before.

I left the shop elated. At last, things had begun to march!

I now knew that John Wilson held the means for the crime—but what about the motive? He had come to Belgium on business, and had asked M. Déroulard, whom he knew slightly, to put him up. There was apparently no way in which Déroulard's death could benefit him. Moreover, I discovered by inquiries in England that he had suffered for some years from that painful form of heart disease known as angina. Therefore he had a genuine right to have those tablets in his possession. Nevertheless, I was convinced that someone had gone to the chocolate box, opening the full one first by mistake, and had abstracted the contents of the last chocolate, cramming in instead as many little trinitrin tablets as it would hold. The chocolates were large ones. Between twenty or thirty tablets, I felt sure, could have been inserted. But who had done this?

There were two guests in the house. John Wilson had the means. Saint Alard had the motive. Remember, he was a fanatic, and there is no fanatic like a religious fanatic. Could he, by any means, have got hold of John Wilson's trinitrin?

Another little idea came to me. Ah! You smile at my little ideas! Why had Wilson run out of trinitrin? Surely he would bring an adequate supply from England. I called once more at the house in the Avenue Louise. Wilson was out, but I saw the girl who did his room, Félicie. I demanded of her immediately whether it was not true that M. Wilson had lost a bottle from his washstand some little time ago. The girl responded eagerly. It was quite true. She, Félicie, had been blamed for it. The English gentleman had evidently thought that she had broken it, and did not like to say so. Whereas she had never even touched it. Without doubt it was Jeannette—always nosing round where she had no business to be——

I calmed the flow of words, and took my leave. I knew now all that I wanted to know. It remained for me to prove my case. That, I felt, would not be easy. *I* might be sure that Saint Alard had removed the bottle of trinitrin from John Wilson's washstand, but to convince others, I would have to produce evidence. And I had none to produce!

Never mind. I *knew*—that was the great thing. You remember our difficulty in the Styles case, Hastings? There again, I *knew*—but it took me a long time to find the last link which made my chain of evidence against the murderer complete.

I asked for an interview with Mademoiselle Mesnard. She came at once. I demanded of her the address of M. de Saint Alard. A look of trouble came over her face.

"Why do you want it, monsieur?"

"Mademoiselle, it is necessary."

She seemed doubtful—troubled.

"He can tell you nothing. He is a man whose thoughts are not in this world. He hardly notices what goes on around him."

"Possibly, mademoiselle. Nevertheless, he was an old friend of M. Déroulard's. There may be things he can tell me—things of the past—old grudges—old love-affairs."

The girl flushed and bit her lip. "As you please—but —but—I feel sure now that I have been mistaken. It was good of you to accede to my demand, but I was upset— almost distraught at the time. I see now that there is no mystery to solve. Leave it, I beg of you, monsieur."

I eyed her closely.

"Mademoiselle," I said, "it is sometimes difficult for a dog to find a scent, but once he *has* found it, nothing on earth will make him leave it! That is if he is a good dog! And I, mademoiselle, I, Hercule Poirot, am a very good dog."

Without a word she turned away. A few minutes later she returned with the address written on a sheet of paper. I left the house. François was waiting for me outside. He looked at me anxiously.

"There is no news, monsieur?"

"None as yet, my friend."

"Ah! *Pauvre* Monsieur Déroulard!" he sighed. "I too was of his way of thinking. I do not care for priests. Not that I would say so in the house. The women are all devout—a good thing perhaps. *Madame est très pieuse—et Mademoiselle Virginie aussi."*

Mademoiselle Virginie? Was she *"très pieuse?"* Thinking of the tear-stained passionate face I had seen that first day, I wondered.

Having obtained the address of M. de Saint Alard, I wasted no time. I arrived in the neighborhood of his château in the Ardennes but it was some days before I could find a pretext for gaining admission to the house. In the end I did—how do you think—as a plumber, *mon ami!* It was the affair of a moment to arrange a neat little gas leak in his bedroom. I departed for my tools, and took care to return with them at an hour when I knew I should have the field pretty well to myself. What I was searching for, I hardly knew. The one thing needful, I could not believe there was any chance of finding. He would never have run the risk of keeping it.

Still when I found a little cupboard above the washstand locked, I could not resist the temptation of seeing what was inside it. The lock was quite a simple one to pick. The door swung open. It was full of old bottles. I took them up one by one with a trembling hand. Suddenly, I uttered a cry. Figure to yourself, my friend, I held in my hand a little phial with an English chemist's label. On it were the words: *"Trinitrin Tablets. One to be taken when required. Mr. John Wilson."*

I controlled my emotion, closed the little cupboard, slipped the bottle into my pocket, and continued to repair the gas leak! One must be methodical. Then I left the château, and took train for my own country as soon as possible. I arrived in Brussels late that night. I was writing out a report for the préfet in the morning, when a note was brought to me. It was from old Madame Déroulard, and it summoned me to the house in the Avenue Louise without delay.

François opened the door to me.

"Madame la Boronne is awaiting you."

He conducted me to her apartments. She sat in state in a large armchair. There was no sign of Mademoiselle Virginie.

"M. Poirot," said the old lady. "I have just learned that you are not what you pretend to be. You are a police officer."

"That is so, madame."

"You came here to inquire into the circumstances of my son's death?"

Again I replied: "That is so, madame."

"I should be glad if you would tell me what progress you have made."

I hesitated.

"First I would like to know how you have learned all this, madame."

"From one who is no longer of this world."

Her words, and the brooding way she uttered them, sent a chill to my heart. I was incapable of speech.

"Therefore, monsieur, I would beg of you most urgently to tell me exactly what progress you have made in your investigation."

"Madame, my investigation is finished."

"My son?"

"Was killed deliberately."

"You know by whom?"

"Yes, madame."

"Who, then?"

"M. de Saint Alard."

The old lady shook her head.

"You are wrong. M. de Saint Alard is incapable of such a crime."

"The proofs are in my hands."

"I beg of you once more to tell me all."

This time I obeyed, going over each step that had led me to the discovery of the truth. She listened attentively. At the end she nodded her head.

"Yes, yes, it is all as you say, all but one thing. It was not M. de Saint Alard who killed my son. It was I, his mother."

I stared at her. She continued to nod her head gently.

"It is well that I sent for you. It is the providence of the good God that Virginie told me before she departed for the convent, what she had done. Listen, M. Poirot! My son was an evil man. He persecuted the church. He led a life of mortal sin. He dragged down other souls beside his own. But there was worse than that. As I came out of my room in this house one morning, I saw my daughter-in-law standing at the head of the stairs. She was reading a letter. I saw my son steal up behind her. One swift push, and she fell, striking her head on the marble steps. When they picked her up she was dead. My son was a murderer, and only I, his mother, knew it."

She closed her eyes for a moment. "You cannot conceive, monsieur, of my agony, my despair. What was I to do? Denounce him to the police? I could not bring myself to do it. It was my duty, but my flesh was weak. Besides, would they believe me? My eyesight had been failing for some time—they would say I was mistaken. I kept silence. But my conscience gave me no peace. By keeping silence I too was a murderer. My son inherited his wife's money. He flourished as the green bay tree. And now he was to have a Minister's portfolio. His persecution of the church would be redoubled. And there was Virginie. She, poor child, beautiful, naturally pious, was fascinated by him. He had a strange and terrible power over women. I saw it coming. I was powerless to prevent it. He had no intention of marrying her. The time came when she was ready to yield everything to him.

"Then I saw my path clear. He was my son. I had given him life. I was responsible for him. He had killed one woman's body, now he would kill another's soul! I went to Mr. Wilson's room, and took the bottle of tablets. He had once said laughingly that there were enough in it to kill a man! I went into the study and opened the big box of chocolates that always stood on the table. I opened a new box by mistake. The other was on the table also. There was just one chocolate left in it. That simplified things. No one ate chocolates except my son and Virginie. I would keep her with me that night. All went as I had planned——"

She paused, closing her eyes a minute then opened them again.

"M. Poirot, I am in your hands. They tell me I have

not many days to live. I am willing to answer for my action before the good God. Must I answer for it on earth also?"

I hesitated. "But the empty bottle, madame," I said to gain time. "How came that into M. de Saint Alard's possession?"

"When he came to say good-by to me, monsieur, I slipped it into his pocket. I did not know how to get rid of it. I am so infirm that I cannot move about much without help, and finding it empty in my rooms might have caused suspicion. You understand, monsieur,"—she drew herself up to her full height,—"it was with no idea of casting suspicion on M. de Saint Alard! I never dreamed of such a thing. I thought his valet would find an empty bottle and throw it away without question."

I bowed my head. "I comprehend, madame," I said.

"And your decision, monsieur?"

Her voice was firm and unfaltering, her head held as high as ever.

I rose to my feet.

"Madame," I said, "I have the honor to wish you good day. I have made my investigations—and failed! The matter is closed."

He was silent for a moment, then said quietly: "She died just a week later. Mademoiselle Virginie passed through her novitiate, and duly took the veil. That, my friend, is the story. I must admit that I do not make a fine figure in it."

"But that was hardly a failure," I expostulated. "What else could you have thought under the circumstances?"

"Ah, sacré, mon ami," cried Poirot, becoming suddenly animated. "Is it that you do not see? But I was thirty-six times an idiot! My gray cells, they functioned not at all. The whole time I had the true clue in my hands."

"What clue?"

"The chocolate box! Do you not see? Would anyone in possession of their full eyesight make such a mistake? I knew Madame Déroulard had cataract—the atropine drops told me that. There was only one person in the household whose eyesight was such that she could not see which lid to replace. It was the chocolate box that started me on the track, and yet up to the end I failed consistently to perceive its real significance!

"Also my psychology was at fault. Had M. de Saint Alard been the criminal, he would never have kept an incriminating bottle. Finding it was a proof of his innocence. I had learned already from Mademoiselle Virginie that he was absent-minded. Altogether it was a miserable affair that I have recounted to you there! Only to you have I told the story. You comprehend, I do not figure well in it! An old lady commits a crime in such a simple and clever fashion that I, Hercule Poirot, am completely deceived. *Sapristi!* it does not bear thinking of! Forget it. Or no—remember it, and if you think at any time that I am growing conceited—it is not likely, but it might arise."

I concealed a smile.

"*Eh bien,* my friend, you shall say to me, 'Chocolate box.' Is it agreed?"

"It's a bargain!"

"After all," said Poirot reflectively, "it was an experience! I, who have undoubtedly the finest brain in Europe at present, can afford to be magnanimous!"

"Chocolate box," I murmured gently.

"*Pardon, mon ami?*"

I looked at Poirot's innocent face, as he bent forward inquiringly, and my heart smote me. I had suffered often at his hands, but I, too, though not possessing the finest brain in Europe, could afford to be magnanimous!

"Nothing," I lied, and lit another pipe, smiling to myself.

ABOUT THE AUTHOR

AGATHA CHRISTIE, the great mystery writer, was born in
England. After the publication of her first mystery in
1920, she wrote over sixty books. She was one of the few
writers of detective and mystery fiction whose books
consistently appeared on bestseller lists. In addition to her
fiction, she also wrote successful plays, including *The
Mousetrap* and *Witness for the Prosecution*. Many of her
books and plays have been made into movies.

THE MYSTERIOUS WORLD OF AGATHA CHRISTIE

Acknowledged as the world's most popular mystery writer of all time, Dame Agatha Christie's books have thrilled millions of readers for generations. With her care and attention to characters, the intriguing situations and the breathtaking final deduction, it's no wonder that Agatha Christie is the world's best-selling mystery writer.

☐	25678	SLEEPING MURDER	$3.50
☐	26795	A HOLIDAY FOR MURDER	$3.50
☐	23908	POIROT INVESTIGATES	$2.95
☐	26477	THE SECRET ADVERSARY	$3.50
☐	26138	DEATH ON THE NILE	$3.50
☐	26547	THE MYSTERIOUS AFFAIR AT STYLES	
☐	25493	THE POSTERN OF FATE	$3.50
☐	23905	THE SEVEN DIALS MYSTERY	$2.95

Prices and availability subject to change without notice.

Buy them at your local bookstore or use this convenient coupon for ordering:

Bantam Books, Inc., Dept. AC, 414 East Golf Road, Des Plaines, Ill. 60016

Please send me the books I have checked above. I am enclosing $_____ (please add $1.50 to cover postage and handling). Send check or money order —no cash or C.O.D.s please.

Mr/Ms _____

Address _____

City/State _____ Zip _____

AC—1/88

Please allow four to six weeks for delivery. This offer expires 7/88.

The Genuine & Original

GREENBOOK

Guide To

BEANIE BABIES

Third Edition

SO-AQM-899

This Book Belongs To:

Claire

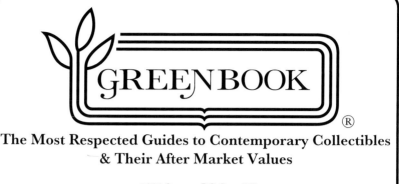

GREENBOOK

The Most Respected Guides to Contemporary Collectibles & Their After Market Values

2000 Sunset, PO Box 645
Pacific Grove, California 93950
408.656.9000
FAX 408.656.9004
www.greenbooks.com

ISBN 0-923628-58-4

Printed in Canada.

GREENBOOK TRUMARKET™ PRICES are compiled from trades and information provided by retailers, dealers and collectors. Manufacturers are not consulted or involved in any way in determining our TRUMARKET™ Secondary Market Prices.

Copyrights in the pieces depicted in photographs and illustrations are reserved by their owner. The creators and owners of these copyrights are in no way affiliated with GREENBOOK. These subjects are depicted for the sole purpose of identification and GREENBOOK in no way claims any rights in the copyrights.

Ty and Beanie Babies are registered Trademarks of Ty Inc. ©1998 Ty Inc.
All Beanie Babies names are a registered Trademark of Ty Inc.
The Teenie Beanie Babies are trademarks of Ty Inc.
McDonald's & Happy Meal ©1998 McDonald's Corporation

©1998 GREENBOOK. ALL RIGHTS RESERVED.
All names and illustrations contained herein are copyrighted.
Their reproduction or use elsewhere, in any form whatsoever,
without the written permission of the copyright owners is strictly FORBIDDEN.
NO PART OF THIS BOOK MAY BE REPRODUCED OR UTILIZED IN ANY WAY
including but not limited to electronic, mechanical, photographic, information storage and
retrieval methods–WITHOUT THE WRITTEN PERMISSION OF THE GREENBOOK.

So, are we still having fun?

I've been involved in contemporary collectibles for almost 20 years now and the whole Beanie Babies Phenomenon has caused me to stop and think about some of the basics I think I'd forgotten.

First and foremost, collecting should be about having FUN.

If you agree with that premise, then why are Beanie Babies so much fun?

Two things are at the top of my list.

Number 1 is the $5.00 Suggested Retail Price.

Number 2 is best described by the phrase *the fun is in the hunt and the find*. I'll explain in a minute.

I can't tell you how many grandparents we've heard from who are thrilled they can buy one of each of something for multiple grandchildren. Not only that, Beanie Babies are value—both style and quality for the price—in my opinion, almost unbelievably so. The key? Collectors aren't spending more than they can afford. When you spend more than is comfortable, it becomes a source of stress in your life instead of an outlet.

My Dad used to say collecting is about having something that not everyone can have. If it's just about money, and whoever has the most money wins, it's not fun. I have acquaintances who could easily afford the secondary market prices some are charging for Princess and Erin who want to tell me about the one they stood in line for or stumbled upon for $5. And so, *the fun is in the hunt and the find*. As a colleague of mine wrote in another title we publish, all too often a call from the retailer is "your pieces are in and already charged to your credit card ... please pick them up when you can." There is no hunt. They're too easily found.

We explain it in the "How To," but I'd like to repeat it here: In this Guide, all current Beanie Babies have a GREENBOOK TruMarket Value equal to their Suggested Retail Price of $5. While we're very much aware that many stores charge anywhere from $5 to $8 for current Beanies, and in many cases more for the hard-to-find Beanies, we do not print secondary market prices for current items. There are many retailers who are fair and just in their sale of Beanies. Find one.

In addition, may I caution you to think a long time before you part with more of your hard earned dollars for things like a piece having PVC instead of PE pellets. And to be unhappy because you have the hard-to-find piece, but with the wrong pellets? Looks ridiculous in writing, doesn't it?

Each new batch of Beanies is cuter than the previous one. I've heard for two years now it's not going to last. In the meantime, Beanies have given hours of pleasure to millions of people.

Louise Langenfeld
Editor & Publisher

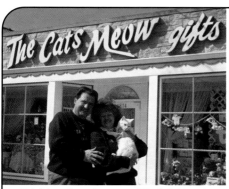

Rich & Lana Gernady, owners of The Cat's Meow & Jack Frost, resident cat.

With thanks to... The Cat's Meow

Once upon a time, there was a favorite saying which parents — in fact, adults in general — used with great frequency. That well-worn saying was, "Children should be seen, and not heard." Ask Rich and Lana Gernady, owners of The Cat's Meow gift shop in Glenview, Illinois about that old saying, and they will readily admit that they are glad they DID listen to the children who visited their shop.

It is certain that Rich and Lana do listen, and will continue to listen to their young customers' requests and questions. These youngsters were the ones who brought TY Beanie Babies to Rich and Lana's attention. When the children first started asking for Beanie Babies, the Gernadys had no idea what they were talking about. What was a "Beanie Baby?"

Curiosity aroused, Rich went shopping for information. Lucky the ladybug was the first Beanie Baby he purchased. He gave it to Lana, commenting that he hoped it would bring them luck!

Since the arrival of that first Beanie Baby at The Cat's Meow, Rich and Lana have welcomed visitors – adults and children alike – from all parts of the country, who come to see their complete collection of every Beanie Baby ever made. Other than in photographs, many of their visitors have never seen some of the styles and variations in the Beanie Babies line. Many a "wish list" is conveyed to parents and grandparents when excited children see a Humphrey the camel or a Peace the bear for the first time.

Lucky the ladybug seems to have done her job in bringing luck to the Gernadys, who began carrying Beanie Babies soon after the arrival of Lucky. "Beanies are magical," says Lana. "These adorable bean-filled animals are popular with everyone from babies to grandmas and grandpas. Kids use their allowance money to buy them. Parents and grandparents buy them to use as gifts and rewards. Teachers use them in many educational ways. No matter what age the "kids" are, people just seem to love them."

It took a bit of time and effort on the part of the Gernadys to convince their customers that these charming animals were "collectible." Their first efforts in this direction were to compile a list of all the Beanie Babies — whether retired, out of production or current. Soon children were making their first ventures into becoming collectors. With the checklist in hand, they were able to keep track of the Beanie Babies they had, and let family and friends know the ones they wanted for their collections. The children quickly discovered the fun of the search and the thrill of the find!

From this idea, the Gernadys took Beanie Babies to a craft fair, still working to build the idea of collectability. Their next step was to take them to a collectibles show, where dealers and collectibles experts laughed at what the Gernadys were predicting was going to happen with Beanie Babies. It wasn't long before these experts were no longer laughing, as Beanie Babies quickly became the drawing card for collectibles shows — and soon, collectibles shows exclusively for Beanie Babies popped up across the country.

Rich and Lana's store has been called the "first true Beanie Babies Museum in the country." In a July, 1995 People magazine interview, Rich was quoted as saying of Beanie Babies, "I love them. There must be one which appeals to everyone, whether it is because of the style, color, or birthdate. It is impossible not to like one, and then you are hooked!" His excitement for Beanie Babies is contagious, and many have caught the bug. Customers who began collecting Beanies at The Cat's Meow occasionally remind him of how he tried to get them started collecting Beanies earlier and reflect on how sorry they are that they didn't listen.

Rich and Lana invite you to stop in for a visit if you're ever in the North Chicago area. Many of the Beanie Babies photographed for this book were photographed from their collection at The Cat's Meow.

And if you do drop by, make sure you meet Jack Frost, The Cat's Meow's resident cat. Legend has it that Jack Frost was the model for Flip.

The Cat's Meow, 1814 Glenview Road, Glenview, IL 60025 Phone: (847)657-6369 Fax: (847)657-9368

TABLE OF CONTENTS

GREENBOOK—WHAT WE DO & HOW WE DO IT

HOW TO READ A LISTING

The GREENBOOK ARTCHARTS & LISTINGS developed for the BEANIE BABIES Collection feature color photographs, factual information and GREENBOOK TRUMARKET PRICES. The ARTCHARTS & LISTINGS are in alphabetical order by Beanie Baby Name.

The specific factual information includes Name, Item Number, Date Issued, Ty Swing Tags Available, Status, Description, Birthday and Poem.

GREENBOOK TRUMARKET PRICE   % CHANGE IN GBTRU   NAME   ITEM #   STATUS   YEAR OF ISSUE   TY SWING TAGS AVAILABLE

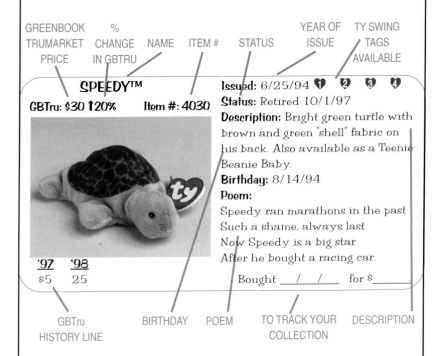

SPEEDY™

GBTru: $30 ↑20%   Item #: 4030

Issued: 6/25/94

Status: Retired 10/1/97

Description: Bright green turtle with brown and green "shell" fabric on his back. Also available as a Teenie Beanie Baby.

Birthday: 8/14/94

Poem:
Speedy ran marathons in the past
Such a shame, always last
Now Speedy is a big star
After he bought a racing car.

Bought ___ / ___ / ___ for $_____

'97   '98
$5   25

GBTru HISTORY LINE   BIRTHDAY   POEM   TO TRACK YOUR COLLECTION   DESCRIPTION

6

GREENBOOK TRUMARKET PRICES (GBTru)

All current Beanies are listed with a GBTru equal to their Suggested Retail Price of $5. While we are very much aware that many stores charge anywhere from $5 to $8 for current Beanie Babies, and in many cases more for the hard-to-find Beanies, we do not print secondary market prices for current items. The availability of any current Beanie changes on a day-to-day basis. What may be considered hard-to-find today may be available in abundance tomorrow. Patience is often rewarded.

Secondary Market Prices are reported to us by retailers and collectors. The data is compiled, checked for accuracy, and a **GREENBOOK TRUMARKET PRICE** established as a benchmark as a result of this research. There are many factors which determine the price a collector will pay for a piece and most acquisitions are a matter of personal judgment. The price will fluctuate with the time of year, section of the country and type of sale. **GREENBOOK** takes all of these factors into consideration when determining **TRUMARKET** Prices. **GREENBOOK TRUMARKET Prices are never an absolute number.** Use them as a basis for comparison, as a point of information when considering an acquisition and as a guide when insuring for replacement value.

The "% Change in **GBTru**" is the percent change up or down (↑ ↓) in **GBTru** as compared to the last edition of the Guide (February 1998). No change indicates just that. All **GREENBOOK TRUMARKET PRICES** are for items in mint condition.

TY SWING TAGS

This Guide includes information indicating which Swing Tags (#1 - #5) are/were available on each Beanie.

Remember, all tags (#1 - #5) are/were not necessarily available on every Beanie. Before purchasing an expensive Beanie Baby, make sure that a correct Swing Tag is attached.

THE TY SWING TAGS

TY SWING TAG #1
· Single heart swing tag.

TY SWING TAG #2 ❷
· Mid 1994
· Double-sided heart swing tag opens like a book.

TY SWING TAG #3 ❸
· Mid 1995
· Double-sided heart swing tag opens like a book.
· Larger type "ty."

TY SWING TAG #4 ❹
· Mid 1996
· Double-sided heart swing tag opens like a book.
· Larger type "ty."
· "BEANIE ORIGINAL BABY" yellow star on front.
· First tag with birthday and poem.

TY SWING TAG #5 ❺
· 1998
· Double-sided heart swing tag opens like a book.
· Larger type "ty."
· "BEANIE ORIGINAL BABY" font change.

· Black and White.

· Red and White without the Beanie Baby's name.

· Red and White with the Beanie Baby's name.

· Red and White with the Beanie Baby's name.
· Clear sticker star.

· Red and White with the Beanie Baby's name.
· Printed star.

GREENBOOK

Introduces

GREENWARE™

The Collectors' Personal Inventory Software For

Ty® Beanie Babies™

GREENBOOK
GREENWARE™
Collectors' Personal Inventory Software

Companion to GREENBOOK'S

VERSION
1.0
FOR
WINDOWS®
3.X, '95, NT

Original Guide to Ty® Beanie Babies™

Ty® Beanie Babies™
©1998 Greenbook
Design & Source Code
©1994-1998 Storer Software
©1998 Ty, Inc.
ALL RIGHTS RESERVED

This complete, easy-to-use software program is designed to help collectors and dealers track their **Beanie Babies** inventory. Our unique CD-ROM is created from the collector's standpoint, utilizing all the information found in this bestselling GREENBOOK Guide to Ty® **Beanie Babies**™

Our program incorporates:
· Pre-entered factual information & data on every single cute, cuddly, collectible critter
· Secondary Market History of each piece
· Current Secondary Market Values
· Beautiful full color photographs of everything

Only $39.95 USA!

With this software you'll track your personal collection in a spreadsheet format that lays it all out for you. You can enter every detail of your collection, including quantity, condition, purchase price & date, dealer & collector contacts. You can customize & then print high quality reports tailored to your specific need: Insurance, Swapping & Selling... Our program features power and flexibility married to ease-of-use. Updates will be available annually. Make tracking your collection a pleasure instead of a pain. This GREENBOOK CD-ROM is just what you've been looking for!

Tech Support & Sample Screens: http://www.greenbooksoftware.com

For more information:
www.greenbooks.com

Minimum System Requirements: · PC Compatible Computer w/Microsoft Windows 3.x, '95 or NT · 486DX processor · 8 MB RAM · 12 MB hard drive space · CD-ROM drive · SVGA display (256 colors)

How To Join The BBOC And Obtain "Clubby™"

The **BBOC** (Beanie Babies Official Club) was announced by Ty in January of 1998. Membership kits are $10.00 from a participating retailer. The kit comes in 2 parts: a shrink-wrapped packet which includes an accordion style handled box filled with goodies, & a separately wrapped poster. Inside the membership kit is an Official Membership Card, an application/return postcard for your Official Club Certificate, color stickers for placing on your poster, & the first Official Newsletter for Beanie Babies. Also inside the box is a gold "Official Membership Card." The cards in each kit have an individual number to identify you as a member of the **BBOC**. In order to register as an official member you MUST complete the registration card and mail it back to Ty.

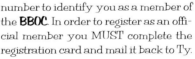

"Clubby™" was announced on Ty's website (www.ty.com) on May 1, 1998. The suggested retail price for Clubby™ is $5.99.

QUIKREFERENCE-RETIRED

RETIRED

Name	Item#	Ret.
❏ 1997 Holiday Teddy™	4200	'97
❏ Ally™ the alligator	4032	'97
❏ Baldy™ the eagle	4074	'98
❏ Bessie™ the cow	4009	'97
❏ Blizzard™ the snow tiger	4163	'98
❏ Bones™ the dog	4001	'98
❏ Bronty™ the brontosaurus	4085	'96
❏ Brownie™ the brown bear	4010	'97
❏ Bubbles™ the fish	4078	'97
❏ Bucky™ the beaver	4016	'97
❏ Bumble™ the bee	4045	'96
❏ Caw™ the crow	4071	'96
❏ Chilly™ the polar bear	4012	'96
❏ Chops™ the lamb	4019	'97
❏ Coral™ the fish	4079	'97
❏ Cubbie™ the brown bear	4010	'97
❏ Digger™ the crab ver. 1	4027	'97
❏ Digger™ the crab ver. 2	4027	'97
❏ Ears™ the brown rabbit	4018	'98
❏ Echo™ the dolphin	4180	'98
❏ Flash™ the dolphin	4021	'97
❏ Flip™ the white cat	4012	'97
❏ Floppity™ the lilac bunny	4118	'98
❏ Flutter™ the butterfly	4043	'96
❏ Garcia™ the bear	4051	'97
❏ Goldie™ the goldfish	4023	'97
❏ Gracie™ the swan	4126	'98
❏ Grunt™ the razorback	4092	'97
❏ Happy™ the hippo ver. 1	4061	'98
❏ Happy™ the hippo ver. 2	4061	'98
❏ Hippity™ the mint bunny	4119	'98
❏ Hoot™ the owl	4073	'97
❏ Hoppity™ the rose bunny	4117	'98
❏ Humphrey™ the camel	4060	'95
❏ Inch™ the inchworm ver. 1	4044	'98
❏ Inch™ the inchworm ver. 2	4044	'98
❏ Inky™ the octopus ver. 1	4028	'98
❏ Inky™ the octopus ver. 2	4028	'98
❏ Inky™ the octopus ver. 3	4028	'98
❏ Jolly™ the walrus	4082	'98
❏ Kiwi™ the toucan	4070	'97
❏ Lefty™ the donkey	4085	'97
❏ Legs™ the frog	4020	'97

RETIRED

Name	Item#	Ret.
❏ Libearty™ the bear	4057	'97
❏ Lizzy™ the lizard ver. 1	4033	'97
❏ Lizzy™ the lizard ver. 2	4033	'97
❏ Lucky™ the ladybug ver. 1	4040	'98
❏ Lucky™ the ladybug ver. 2	4040	'98
❏ Lucky™ the ladybug ver. 3	4040	'98
❏ Magic™ the dragon ver. 1	4088	'97
❏ Magic™ the dragon ver. 2	4088	'97
❏ Manny™ the manatee	4081	'97
❏ Nip™ the cat ver. 1	4003	'97
❏ Nip™ the cat ver. 2	4003	'97
❏ Nip™ the cat ver. 3	4003	'97
❏ Patti™ the platypus ver. 1	4025	'98
❏ Patti™ the platypus ver. 2	4025	'98
❏ Peanut™ the elephant ver. 1	4062	'98
❏ Peanut™ the elephant ver. 2	4062	'98
❏ Peking™ the panda	4013	'96
❏ Pinchers™ the lobster	4026	'98
❏ Punchers™ the lobster	4026	'98
❏ Quacker™ the duck ver. 1	4024	'98
❏ Quackers™ the duck ver. 2	4024	'98
❏ Radar™ the bat	4091	'97
❏ Rex™ the tyrannosaurus	4086	'96
❏ Righty™ the elephant	4086	'97
❏ Rover™ the dog	4101	'98
❏ Scottie™ the Scottish terrier	4102	'98
❏ Seamore™ the seal	4029	'97
❏ Slither™ the snake	4031	'95
❏ Snowball™ the snowman	4201	'97
❏ Sparky™ the Dalmatian	4100	'97
❏ Speedy™ the turtle	4030	'97
❏ Splash™ the whale	4022	'97
❏ Spook™ the ghost	4090	'97
❏ Spooky™ the ghost	4090	'97
❏ Spot™ the dog ver. 1	4000	'97
❏ Spot™ the dog ver. 2	4000	'97
❏ Squealer™ the pig	4005	'98
❏ Steg™ the Stegosaurus	4087	'96
❏ Sting™ the stingray	4077	'97
❏ Stripes™ the tiger ver. 1	4065	'98
❏ Stripes™ the tiger ver. 2	4065	'98
❏ Stripes™ the tiger ver. 3	4065	'98
❏ Tabasco™ the bull	4002	'97

continued

12

RETIRED (cont.)

Name	Item#	Ret.
☐ Tank™ the armadillo ver. 1	4031	'97
☐ Tank™ the armadillo ver. 2	4031	'97
☐ Tank™ the armadillo ver. 3	4031	'97
☐ Teddy™ brown old face	4050	'97
☐ Teddy™ brown new face	4050	'97
☐ Teddy™ cranberry old face	4052	'96
☐ Teddy™ cranberry new face	4052	'96
☐ Teddy™ jade old face	4057	'96
☐ Teddy™ jade new face	4057	'96
☐ Teddy™ magenta old face	4056	'96
☐ Teddy™ magenta new face	4056	'96
☐ Teddy™ teal old face	4051	'96
☐ Teddy™ teal new face	4051	'96
☐ Teddy™ violet old face	4055	'96
☐ Teddy™ violet new face	4055	'96
☐ Trap™ the mouse	4042	'95
☐ Tusk™ the walrus	4076	'97
☐ Twigs™ the giraffe	4068	'98
☐ Velvet™ the panther	4064	'97
☐ Waddle™ the penguin	4075	'98
☐ Waves™ the whale	4084	'98
☐ Web™ the spider	4041	'96
☐ Weenie™ the dachshund	4013	'98
☐ Ziggy™ the zebra	4063	'98
☐ Zip™ the cat ver. 1	4004	'98
☐ Zip™ the cat ver. 2	4004	'98
☐ Zip™ the cat ver. 3	4004	'98

OUT OF PRODUCTION

Name	Item#
☐ Derby™ the horse ver. 1	4008
☐ Derby™ the horse ver. 2	4008
☐ Doodle™ the rooster	4171
☐ Iggy™ the iguana ver. 1	4038
☐ Mystic™ the unicorn ver. 1	4007
☐ Mystic™ the unicorn ver. 2	4007
☐ Nana™ the monkey	4067
☐ Sly™ the fox ver. 1	4115
☐ Smoochy™ the frog ver. 1	4039

THE ORIGINAL 9*

Name	Item#
Brownie™/Cubbie™ the bear	4010
Chocolate™ the moose	4015
Flash™ the dolphin	4021
Legs™ the frog	4020
Patti™ the platypus	4025
Punchers™/Pinchers™ the lobster	4026
Splash™ the whale	4022
Spot™ the dog	4000
Squealer™ the pig	4005

NON-USA EXCLUSIVES

Britannia™	Great Britain
Maple™/Pride™	Canada

TEENIE BEANIES
Group 1

Name	Item#
Patti™ the platypus	1
Pinky™ the flamingo	2
Chops™ the lamb	3
Chocolate™ the moose	4
Goldie™ the goldfish	5
Speedy™ the turtle	6
Seamore™ the seal	7
Snort™ the bull	8
Quacks™ the duck	9
Lizz™ the lizard	10

TEENIE BEANIES
Group 2

Name	Item#
Doby™	1
Bongo™	2
Twigs™	3
Inch™	4
Pinchers™	5
Happy™	6
Mel™	7
Scoop™	8
Bones™	9
Zip™	10
Waddle™	11
Peanut™	12

QUIKREFERENCE-BEANIES BY SUBJECT

Alligator:
❑ Ally™

Anteater:
❑ Ants™

Armadillo:
❑ Tank™

Bats:
❑ Batty™
❑ Radar™

Bears:
❑ 1997 Holiday Teddy™
❑ Blackie™
❑ Britannia™
❑ Brownie™
❑ Chilly™
❑ Clubby™
❑ Cubbie™
❑ Curly™
❑ Erin™
❑ Garcia™
❑ Glory™
❑ Libearty™
❑ Maple™
❑ Peace™
❑ Princess™
❑ Teddy™ Brown
❑ Teddy™ Cranberry
❑ Teddy™ Jade
❑ Teddy™ Magenta
❑ Teddy™ Teal
❑ Teddy™ Violet
❑ Valentino™

Beaver:
❑ Bucky™

Bee :
❑ Bumble™

Birds:
❑ Baldy™
❑ Caw™
❑ Doodle™
❑ Early™
❑ Gobbles™
❑ Gracie™
❑ Hoot™
❑ Jabber™
❑ Jake™
❑ Kiwi™
❑ KuKu™
❑ Pinky™
❑ Puffer™
❑ Quacker™
❑ Quackers™
❑ Quacks™
❑ Rocket™
❑ Scoop™
❑ Stretch™
❑ Strut™
❑ Waddle™
❑ Wise™

Bulls:
❑ Snort™
❑ Tabasco™

Bunnies:
❑ Ears™
❑ Floppity™
❑ Hippity™
❑ Hoppity™

Butterfly:
❑ Flutter™

Camel:
❑ Humphrey™

Cats (Domestic):
❑ Chip™
❑ Flip™
❑ Nip™
❑ Pounce™
❑ Prance™
❑ Snip™
❑ Zip™

Cats (Wild):
❑ Blizzard™
❑ Freckles™
❑ Roary™
❑ Stripes™
❑ Velvet™

Cows:
❑ Bessie™
❑ Daisy™

Crabs:
❑ Claude™
❑ Digger™

Dinosaurs:
❑ Bronty™
❑ Rex™
❑ Steg™

Dogs:
❑ Bernie™
❑ Bones™
❑ Bruno™
❑ Doby™
❑ Dotty™
❑ Fetch™
❑ GiGi™
❑ Nanook™
❑ Pugsly™
❑ Rover™
❑ Scottie™
❑ Sparky™
❑ Spot™
❑ Spunky™
❑ Tracker™
❑ Tuffy™
❑ Weenie™
❑ Wrinkles™

Dolphins:
❑ Echo™
❑ Flash™

Donkey:
❑ Lefty™

Dragon:
❑ Magic™

Elephants:
❑ Peanut™
❑ Righty™

Fawn:
❑ Whisper™

Fish:
❑ Bubbles™
❑ Coral™
❑ Crunch™
❑ Goldie™

Fox:
❑ Sly™

Frogs:
❑ Legs™
❑ Smoochy™

Ghosts:
❑ Spook™
❑ Spooky™

Giraffe:
❑ Twigs™

Gorilla:
❑ Congo™

Hippo:
❑ Happy™

Horse:
❑ Derby™

Inchworm:
❑ Inch™

Kangaroo:
❑ Pouch™

Koala:
❑ Mel™

Ladybug:
❑ Lucky™

Lambs:
❑ Chops™
❑ Fleece™

QUIKREFERENCE—BEANIES BY SUBJECT

Lizards:
- ☐ Iggy™
- ☐ Lizz™
- ☐ Lizzy™
- ☐ Rainbow™

Lobsters:
- ☐ Pinchers™
- ☐ Punchers™

Manatee:
- ☐ Manny™

Monkeys:
- ☐ Bongo™
- ☐ Nana™

Moose:
- ☐ Chocolate™

Mouse:
- ☐ Trap™

Octopus:
- ☐ Inky™

Otter:
- ☐ Seaweed™

Pandas:
- ☐ Fortune™
- ☐ Peking™

Pig:
- ☐ Squealer™

Platypus:
- ☐ Patti™

Raccoon:
- ☐ Ringo™

Razorback Pig:
- ☐ Grunt™

Rhino:
- ☐ Spike™

Scorpion:
- ☐ Stinger™

Seal:
- ☐ Seamore™

Skunk:
- ☐ Stinky™

Snakes:
- ☐ Hissy™
- ☐ Slither™

Snowman:
- ☐ Snowball™

Spiders:
- ☐ Spinner™
- ☐ Web™

Squirrel:
- ☐ Nuts™

Stingray:
- ☐ Sting™

Turtle:
- ☐ Speedy™

Unicorn:
- ☐ Mystic™

Walruses:
- ☐ Jolly™
- ☐ Tusk™

Whales:
- ☐ Splash™
- ☐ Waves™

Zebra:
- ☐ Ziggy™

Rainbow & Iggy Update

Mr. Warner has been quoted many times, including in our 2nd Edition Guide, as saying one of his goals with Beanie Babies was to introduce children to a huge sampling of the world's animals.

Well, the adults at GREENBOOK now know more about iguanas and chameleons than we ever thought possible!

There is still a great deal of confusion over the Beanies Iggy and Rainbow. It's so confusing collectors are referring to the pieces as Iggy/Rainbow and Rainbow/Iggy. We have decided to identify the pieces consistent with the Ty Swing Tags and tush tags they are shipping with because it is what the lizards should look like—iguanas with a spine, chameleons a collar. However, this is contrary to the Ty 1998 catalog and website.

In trying to figure out what happened with the Rainbow & Iggy mixup, GREENBOOK came to the conclusion, in the previous Edition, that they were mistakenly crafted with each other's fabric and then identified by fabric for placement in the Ty catalog and website.

Dear company,

My name is Amanda and i got a Question on your 2 version of the Green Book. In it is Iggy and Rain bow. And in the book is the Blue chameleon and its name in the Book is Rainbow. Why does the poem say Red, green, Blue, and yellow! I thought that Iggy was the Blue one and Rainbow is the Rainbow one. Did you make a mastake or is it right?

♥ Love
Amanda

P.S: If you can phase right back or tell me some how.

P.SS. I Love Your Book!!! its cool !!
☺

Amanda wrote us with an additional observation—most likely Rainbow would be the name of a chameleon and Rainbow's poem reads: "Red, green, blue and yellow."

15

QUIKREFERENCE-BEANIE BABIES' BIRTHDAYS

JANUARY

Jan. 3, 1993	Spot™
Jan. 5, 1997	KuKu™
Jan. 6, 1993	Patti™
Jan. 13, 1996	Crunch™
Jan. 14, 1997	Spunky™
Jan. 15, 1996	Mel™
Jan. 18, 1994	Bones™
Jan. 21, 1996	Nuts™
Jan. 25, 1995	Peanut™
Jan. 26, 1996	Chip™

FEBRUARY

Feb. 1, 1996	Peace™
Feb. 4, 1997	Fetch™
Feb. 13, 1995	Stinky™
Feb. 13, 1995	Pinky™
Feb. 14, 1994	Valentino™
Feb. 17, 1996	Baldy™
Feb. 20, 1996	Roary™
Feb. 20, 1997	Early™
Feb. 22, 1995	Tank™
Feb. 25, 1994	Happy™
Feb. 27, 1996	Sparky™
Feb. 28, 1995	Flip™

MARCH

Mar. 2, 1995	Coral™
Mar. 6, 1994	Nip™
Mar. 8, 1996	Doodle™
Mar. 8, 1996	Strut™
Mar. 12, 1997	Rocket™
Mar. 14, 1994	Ally™
Mar. 17, 1997	Erin™
Mar. 19, 1996	Seaweed™
Mar. 21, 1996	Fleece™
Mar. 28, 1994	Zip™

APRIL

Apr. 3, 1996	Hoppity™
Apr. 4, 1997	Hissy™
Apr. 5, 1997	Whisper™
Apr. 7, 1997	GiGi™
Apr. 12, 1996	Curly™
Apr. 16, 1997	Jake™
Apr. 18, 1995	Ears™
Apr. 19, 1994	Quackers™
Apr. 23, 1993	Squealer™
Apr. 25, 1993	Legs™
Apr. 27, 1993	Chocolate™

MAY

May 1, 1995	Lucky™
May 1, 1996	Wrinkles™
May 2, 1996	Pugsly™
May 3, 1996	Chops™
May 10, 1994	Daisy™
May 11, 1995	Lizzy™
May 13, 1993	Flash™
May 15, 1995	Tabasco™
May 15, 1995	Snort™
May 19, 1995	Twigs™
May 21, 1994	Mystic™
May 28, 1996	Floppity™
May 30, 1996	Rover™
May 31, 1997	Wise™

JUNE

Jun. 1, 1996	Hippity™
Jun. 3, 1996	Freckles™
Jun. 5, 1997	Tracker™
Jun. 8, 1995	Bucky™
Jun. 8, 1995	Manny™
Jun. 11, 1995	Stripes™
Jun. 15, 1996	Scottie™
Jun. 17, 1996	Gracie™
Jun. 19, 1993	Pinchers™
Jun. 27, 1995	Bessie™

JULY

Jul. 1, 1996	Scoop™
Jul. 1, 1996	Maple™
Jul. 2, 1995	Bubbles™
Jul. 4, 1997	Glory™
Jul. 4, 1996	Lefty™
Jul. 4, 1996	Righty™
Jul. 8, 1993	Splash™
Jul. 14, 1995	Ringo™
Jul. 15, 1994	Blackie™
Jul. 19, 1995	Grunt™
Jul. 20, 1995	Weenie™

AUGUST

Aug. 1, 1995	Garcia™
Aug. 9, 1995	Hoot™
Aug. 12, 1997	Iggy™
Aug. 13, 1996	Spike™
Aug. 14, 1994	Speedy™
Aug. 17, 1995	Bongo™
Aug. 23, 1995	Digger™
Aug. 27, 1995	Sting™
Aug. 28, 1997	Pounce™

SEPTEMBER

Sep. 3, 1995	Inch™
Sep. 3, 1996	Claude™
Sep. 5, 1995	Magic™
Sep. 9, 1997	Bruno™
Sep. 12, 1996	Sly™
Sep. 16, 1995	Kiwi™
Sep. 16, 1995	Derby™
Sep. 18, 1995	Tusk™
Sep. 21, 1997	Stretch™
Sep. 29, 1997	Stinger™

OCTOBER

Oct. 1, 1997	Smoochy™
Oct. 3, 1996	Bernie™
Oct. 9, 1996	Doby™
Oct. 10, 1997	Jabber™
Oct. 12, 1996	Tuffy™
Oct. 14, 1997	Rainbow™
Oct. 16, 1995	Bumble™
Oct. 17, 1996	Dotty™
Oct. 22, 1996	Snip™
Oct. 28, 1996	Spinner™
Oct. 29, 1996	Batty™
Oct. 30, 1995	Radar™
Oct. 31, 1995	Spooky™

NOVEMBER

Nov. 3, 1997	Puffer™
Nov. 6, 1996	Pouch™
Nov. 7, 1997	Ants™
Nov. 9, 1996	Congo™
Nov. 14, 1993	Cubbie™
Nov. 14, 1994	Goldie™
Nov. 20, 1997	Prance™
Nov. 21, 1996	Nanook™
Nov. 27, 1996	Gobbles™
Nov. 28, 1995	Teddy™ Brown
Nov. 29, 1994	Inky™

DECEMBER

Dec. 2, 1996	Jolly™
Dec. 6, 1997	Fortune™
Dec. 8, 1996	Waves™
Dec. 12, 1996	Blizzard™
Dec. 14, 1996	Seamore™
Dec. 15, 1997	Britannia™
Dec. 16, 1995	Velvet™
Dec. 19, 1995	Waddle™
Dec. 21, 1996	Echo™
Dec. 22, 1996	Snowball™
Dec. 24, 1995	Ziggy™
Dec. 25, 1996	1997 Teddy™

16

1 is for 1997...

Issued: 10/1/97 🛡 🛡

Status: Retired 12/31/97

Description: Brown plush teddy wears red and white Santa cap and matching scarf.

Birthday: 12/25/96

Poem:

Beanie Babies are special no doubt
All filled with love—inside and out
Wishes for fun times filled with joy
Ty's holiday teddy is a magical toy!

Bought ___/___/___ for $_____.

1997 HOLIDAY TEDDY™

GBTru: $75 ↑ 50%   Item #: 4200

'98
$50

Issued: 6/25/94 🛡 🛡 🛡 🛡

Status: Retired 10/1/97

Description: Moss green alligator with brown and green tie-dyed fabric along spine and over head.

Birthday: 3/14/94

Poem:

When Ally gets out of classes
He wears a hat and dark glasses
He plays bass in a street band
He's the coolest gator in the land!

Bought ___/___/___ for $_____.

ALLY™

GBTru: $50 ↑ 100%   Item #: 4032

'97   **'98**
$5   25

Issued: 5/30/98 🛡

Status: Current

Description: Anteater. Grey fabric with grey felt ears, two white stripes separated by black stripe.

Birthday: 11/7/97

Poem:

Most anteaters love to eat bugs
But this little fellow gives big hugs
He'd rather dine on apple pie
Than eat an ant or harm a fly!

Bought ___/___/___ for $_____.

ANTS™

GBTru: $5   Item #: 4195

17

B is for Baldy...

BALDY™

GBTru: $25 ↑ 400%   Item #: 4074

'97	'98
$5	5

Issued: 5/11/97 🛡 🛡

Status: Retired 5/1/98

Description: Black eagle with white head, gold beak and feet.

Birthday: 2/17/96

Poem:
Hair on his head is quite scant
We suggest Baldy get a transplant
Watching over the land of the free
Hair in his eyes would make it hard to see!

Bought ___/___/___ for $_____.

BATTY™

GBTru: $5 no change   Item #: 4035

'98
$5

Issued: 10/1/97 🛡 🛡

Status: Current

Description: Rose-beige bat with velcro tabs on lower wing tips so wings will fold.

Birthday: 10/29/96

Poem:
Bats may make some people jitter
Please don't be scared of this critter
If you're lonely or have nothing to do
This Beanie Baby would love to hug you!

Bought ___/___/___ for $_____.

BERNIE™

GBTru: $5 no change   Item #: 4109

'97	'98
$5	5

Issued: 1/1/97 🛡 🛡

Status: Current

Description: Tan, cream and brown tricolor St. Bernard dog.

Birthday: 10/3/96

Poem:
This little dog can't wait to grow
To rescue people lost in snow
Don't let him out—keep him on your shelf
He doesn't know how to rescue himself!

Bought ___/___/___ for $_____.

B is for Bessie...

BESSIE™

Issued: 6/3/95 ♥ ♥

GBTru: $70 ↑ 100%   Item #: 4009

Status: Retired 10/1/97

Description: Brown cow with white face and hooves.

Birthday: 6/27/95

Poem:

Bessie the cow likes to dance and sing
Because music is her favorite thing
Every night when you're counting sheep
She'll sing you a song to put you to sleep.

'97	'98
$5	35

Bought ___/___/___ for $_____.

BLACKIE™

Issued: 6/25/94 ♥ ♥ ♥ ♥ ♥

GBTru: $5 no change   Item #: 4011

Status: Current

Description: Black bear with brown snout.

Birthday: 7/15/94

Poem:

Living in a national park
He only played after dark
Then he met his friend Cubbie
Now they play when it's sunny!

'97	'98
$5	5

Bought ___/___/___ for $_____.

BLIZZARD™

Issued: 5/11/97 ♥ ♥

GBTru: $20 ↑ 300%   Item #: 4163

Status: Retired 5/1/98

Description: White snow tiger with thin black stripes, pink nose and blue eyes.

Birthday: 12/12/96

Poem:

In the mountains, where it's snowy and cold
Lives a beautiful tiger, I've been told
Black and white, she's hard to compare
Of all the tigers, she is most rare.

'97	'98
$5	5

Bought ___/___/___ for $_____.

19

B is for Bones...

BONES™

GBTru: $15 ↑ 200%   Item #: 4001

'97	'98
$5	5

Issued: 6/25/94 ❷ ❸ ❹ ❺

Status: Retired 5/1/98

Description: Brown dog with dark brown ears. Also available as a Teenie Beanie Baby.

Birthday: 1/18/94

Poem:

Bones is a dog that loves to chew
Chairs and a table and a smelly old shoe
"You're so destructive" all would shout
But that all stopped, when his teeth fell out!

Bought ____ / ____ / ____ for $_____.

BONGO™

GBTru: $5 no change   Item #: 4067

'97	'98
$5	5

Issued: 2/6/96 ❸ ❹ ❺

Status: Current

Description: Brown monkey with tan paws and face. Tail color has changed back and forth between tan and brown. "Nana" was the original Bongo. See page 51. Also available as a Teenie Beanie Baby.

Birthday: 8/17/95

Poem: Bongo the monkey lives in a tree
He's the happiest monkey that you'll ever see
In his spare time he plays the guitar
One of these days he will be a big star!

Bought ____ / ____ / ____ for $_____.

BRITANNIA™

GBTru: $500   Item #: 4601

'98
NE

= Not Established

Issued: 12/31/97 ❺

Status: Great Britain Exclusive

Description: Brown teddy bear with red ribbon around neck wearing British flag. Flags have appeared both as embroidered directly on the fabric, and as sewn-on patches.

Birthday: 12/15/97

Poem: Britannia the bear will sail the sea,
So that she can be with you and me,
She's always sure to catch the tide,
And wear the Union Flag with pride.

Bought ____ / ____ / ____ for $_____.

B is for Bronty...

BRONTY™

Issued: 6/3/95 🛡

GBTru: $800 ↑ 60%   Item #: 4085

Status: Retired 6/15/96

Description: Dinosaur. Blue tie-dyed Brontosaurus.

Birthday: unknown

Poem: None.

'97	'98
$375	500

Bought ___/___/___ for $_____.

BROWNIE™

Issued: 1/8/94 ♥

GBTru: $4300 ↑ 139%   Item #: 4010

Status: Retired 12/31/97

Description: Brown bear with slightly lighter brown snout. One of the "Original 9." Available under this name for very short time. Name changed to Cubbie in 1994. See Cubbie on page 26. IMPORTANT: All Brownies have the single Ty Heart Swing Tag #1 with the name "Brownie."

Birthday: unknown

Poem: None.

'97	'98
$200	1800

Bought ___/___/___ for $_____.

BRUNO™

Issued: 12/31/97 🛡

GBTru: $5 no change   Item #: 4183

Status: Current

Description: Terrier. Brown blanket color pattern with white muzzle, paws and underside.

Birthday: 9/9/97

Poem:

Bruno the dog thinks he's a brute
But all the other Beanies think he's cute
He growls at his tail and runs in a ring
And everyone says, "Oh, how darling!"

'98
$5

Bought ___/___/___ for $_____.

B is for Bubbles...

BUBBLES™

GBTru: $175 ↑ 150%   Item #: 4078

'97	'98
$35	70

Issued: 6/3/95 🛡 🛡
Status: Retired 5/11/97
Description: Black and yellow fish.
Birthday: 7/2/95
Poem:

All day long Bubbles likes to swim
She never gets tired of flapping her fins
Bubbles lived in a sea of blue
Now she is ready to come home with
you!

Bought ___/___/___ for $_____.

BUCKY™

GBTru: $35 ↑ 40%   Item #: 4016

'97	'98
$5	25

Issued: 1/7/96 🛡 🛡 🛡
Status: Retired 12/31/97
Description: Dark brown beaver
with black whiskers and protruding
white front teeth.
Birthday: 6/8/95
Poem:

His teeth are as shiny as can be
Often used for cutting trees
He hides in his dam night and day
Maybe for you he will come out and
play!

Bought ___/___/___ for $_____.

BUMBLE™

GBTru: $600 ↑ 85%   Item #: 4045

'97	'98
$150	325

Issued: 6/3/95 🛡 🛡
Status: Retired 6/15/96
Description: Black bee w/yellow
highlights. Ty Swing Tag #4 with the poem
and birthday is harder to find than older
#3 Swing Tag. Add $100 for the #4 Swing
Tag.
Birthday: 10/16/95
Poem:

Bumble the bee will not sting you
It is only love that this bee will bring you
So don't be afraid to give this bee a hug
Because Bumble the bee is a love-bug.

Bought ___/___/___ for $_____.

C is for Caw...

Issued: 6/3/95 🛡

Status: Retired 6/15/96

Description: Black crow with orange beak and feet.

Birthday: unknown

Poem: None.

CAW™

GBTru: **$700** ↑ 100%   Item #: **4071**

'97	'98
$150	350

Bought ___/___/___ for $_____.

Issued: 6/25/94 🛡 🛡 🛡

Status: Retired 1/7/96

Description: White polar bear.

Birthday: unknown

Poem: None.

CHILLY™

GBTru: **$2100** ↑ 121%   Item #: **4012**

'97	'98
$750	950

Bought ___/___/___ for $_____.

Issued: 5/11/97 🛡 🛡

Status: Current

Description: Brown, black and white Calico cat with pink nose.

Birthday: 1/26/96

Poem:
Black and gold, brown and white
The shades of her coat are quite a sight
At mixing her colors she was a master
On anyone else it would be a disaster!

CHIP™

GBTru: **$5** no change   Item #: **4121**

'97	'98
$5	5

Bought ___/___/___ for $_____.

C is for Chocolate...

CHOCOLATE™

GBTru: $5 no change   Item #: 4015

'97	'98
$5	5

Issued: 1/8/94

Status: Current

Description: Brown moose w/orange antlers. One of the "Original 9." Also available as a Teenie Beanie Baby.

Birthday: 4/27/93

Poem:

Licorice, gum and peppermint candy
This moose always has these handy
But there is one more thing he likes to eat
Can you guess his favorite sweet?

Bought ___ / ___ / ___ for $_____.

CHOPS™

GBTru: $185 ↑ 95%   Item #: 4019

'97	'98
$75	95

Issued: 1/7/96

Status: Retired 1/1/97

Description: Cream lamb with black face and inner ears. Also available as a Teenie Beanie Baby.

Birthday: 5/3/96

Poem:

Chops is a little lamb
This lamb you'll surely know
Because every path that you may take
This lamb is sure to go!

Bought ___ / ___ / ___ for $_____.

CLAUDE™

GBTru: $5 no change   Item #: 4083

'97	'98
$5	5

Issued: 5/11/97

Status: Current

Description: Tie-dyed crab in multi-colors of browns, blues and oranges.

Birthday: 9/3/96

Poem:

Claude the crab paints by the sea
A famous artist he hopes to be
But the tide came in and his paints fell
Now his art is on his shell!

Bought ___ / ___ / ___ for $_____.

C is for Clubby...

CLUBBY™

Issued: 5/1/98
Status: BBOC Members Only Exclusive
Birthday: 7/7/98
Poem:
Wearing his club pin for all to see
He's a proud member like you and me
Made especially with you in mind
Clubby the bear is one of a kind.

GBTru: $5.99   Item #: N/A

Bought ___/___/___ for $_____.

CONGO™

Issued: 6/15/96 🛡 🛡
Status: Current
Description: Black gorilla with brown ears, face and paws.
Birthday: 11/9/96
Poem:
Black as night and fierce is he
On the ground or in a tree
Strong and mighty as the Congo
He's related to our friend Bongo!

GBTru: $5 no change   Item #: 4160

'97	'98
$5	5

Bought ___/___/___ for $_____.

CORAL™

Issued: 6/3/95 🛡 🛡
Status: Retired 1/1/97
Description: Tie-dyed fish in a wide variety of tropical colors.
Birthday: 3/2/95
Poem:
Coral is beautiful, as you know
Made of colors in the rainbow
Whether it's pink, yellow or blue
These colors were chosen just for you!

GBTru: $200 ↑ 167%   Item #: 4079

'97	'98
$50	75

Bought ___/___/___ for $_____.

C is for Crunch...

CRUNCH™

GBTru: $5 no change   Item #: 4130

'97	'98
$5	5

Issued: 1/1/97 🛡 🛡

Status: Current

Description: Shark with blue-grey body and white belly.

Birthday: 1/13/96

Poem:
What's for breakfast? What's for lunch?
Yum? Delicious! Munch, munch, munch!
He's eating everything by the bunch
That's the reason we named him Crunch!

Bought ___ / ___ / ___ for $_____.

CUBBIE™

GBTru: $25 ↓ 50%   Item #: 4010

'97	'98
$5	50

Issued: 1/8/94 🛡 🛡 🛡 🛡 🛡

Status: Retired 12/31/97

Description: Brown bear with slightly lighter brown snout. One of the "Original 9." Original name "Brownie." See page 21. Name changed to Cubbie in 1994.

Birthday: 11/14/93

Poem:
Cubbie used to eat crackers and honey
And what happened to him was funny
He was stung by fourteen bees
Now Cubbie eats broccoli and cheese.

Bought ___ / ___ / ___ for $_____.

CURLY™

GBTru: $5 no change   Item #: 4052

'97	'98
$5	5

Issued: 6/15/96 🛡 🛡

Status: Current

Description: Brown teddy bear with curly-textured fabric and burgundy ribbon.

Birthday: 4/12/96

Poem:
A bear so cute with hair that's curly
You will love and want him surely
To this bear always be true
He will be a friend to you!

Bought ___ / ___ / ___ for $_____.

D is for Daisy...

Issued: 6/25/94 ❤ ❤ ❤ ❤ ❤

Status: Current

Description: Black and white Holstein cow.

Birthday: 5/10/94

Poem:
Daisy drinks milk each night
So her coat is shiny and bright
Milk is good for your hair and skin
What a way for your day to begin!

Bought ___/___/___ for $_____.

GBTru: $5 no change   Item #: 4006

'97	'98
$5	5

OTHER GUIDES FROM GREENBOOK

GREENBOOK Guide to
   The Enesco Precious Moments Collection

GREENBOOK Guide to
   Department 56® Villages including
   The Original Snow Village and
   The Heritage Village Collections

GREENBOOK Guide to
   Department 56® Snowbabies™

GREENBOOK Guide to
   Hallmark Keepsake Ornaments

GREENBOOK Guide to
   Hallmark Kiddie Car Classics

GREENBOOK Guide to
   The Walt Disney Classics Collection

GREENBOOK Guide to
   Cherished Teddies by Enesco

GREENBOOK Guide to
   Precious Moments Company Dolls

GREENBOOK Guide to
   Harbour Lights

GREENBOOK Guide to
   Boyds Bears

GREENBOOK Guide to
   Charming Tails

D is for Derby...

DERBY™ VERSION 1

GBTru: $4200 ↑ 367% Item #: 4008

'97	'98
$150	900

Issued: 6/3/95 🛡️
Status: Out Of Production 1995
Description: All brown horse with dark brown mane and tail. Version 1: <u>Soft fine yarn</u> for mane and tail.
Birthday: unknown
Poem: None.

Bought ___/___/___ for $_____.

DERBY™ VERSION 2

GBTru: $25 ↑ 67%   Item #: 4008

'97	'98
$5	15

Issued: 6/3/95 🛡️ 🛡️
Status: Out Of Production 12/15/97
Description: All brown horse with dark brown mane and tail. Version 2: <u>Coarse yarn</u> for mane and tail. Change to Version 3 on 12/15/97.
Birthday: 9/16/95
Poem:
All the other horses used to tattle
Because Derby never wore his saddle
He left the stables, and the horses too
Just so Derby can be with you!

Bought ___/___/___ for $_____.

DERBY™ VERSION 3

GBTru: $5 no change   Item #: 4008

'98
$5

Issued: 12/15/97 🛡️
Status: Current
Description: Horse. Version 3: Brown with <u>white star</u>.
Birthday: 9/16/95
Poem:
All the other horses used to tattle
Because Derby never wore his saddle
He left the stables, and the horses too
Just so Derby can be with you!

Bought ___/___/___ for $_____.

D is for Digger...

DIGGER™ VERSION 1

Issued: 6/25/94 🛡 🛡

Status: Retired 5/11/97

Description: Crab. Version 1: <u>Orange</u> crab. Change to Version 2 on 6/3/95.

Birthday: 8/23/95

Poem: None.

GBTru: $750 ↑ 100%   Item #: 4027

'97	'98
$300	375

Bought ___/___/___ for $_____.

DIGGER™ VERSION 2

Issued: 6/3/95 🛡 🛡

Status: Retired 5/11/97

Description: Crab. Version 2: <u>Red</u> crab.

Birthday: 8/23/95

Poem:

Digging in the sand and walking sideways
That's how Digger spends her days
Hard on the outside but sweet deep inside
Basking in the sun, riding the tide!

GBTru: $130 ↑ 160%   Item #: 4027

'97	'98
$30	50

Bought ___/___/___ for $_____.

DOBY™

Issued: 1/1/97 🛡 🛡

Status: Current

Description: Brown and black Doberman dog. Also available as a Teenie Beanie Baby.

Birthday: 10/9/96

Poem:

This dog is little but he has might
Keep him close when you sleep at night
He lays around with nothing to do
Until he sees it's time to protect you!

GBTru: $5 no change   Item #: 4110

'97	'98
$5	5

Bought ___/___/___ for $_____.

29

D is for Doodle...

DOODLE™

GBTru: $50 ↑ 25%   Item #: 4171

'97	'98
$5	40

Issued: 5/11/97 🟣

Status: Out Of Production 7/12/97

Description: Rooster. Red crest, wings and tail on multicolored reds, pinks and yellows tie-dyed body. Name changed to Strut in 7/97. See page 73.

Birthday: 3/8/96

Poem:
Listen closely to "Cock-a-doodle-doo"
What's the rooster saying to you?
Hurry, wake up sleepy head
We have lots to do, get out of bed!

Bought ___/___/___ for $_____.

DOTTY™

GBTru: $5 no change   Item #: 4100

'97	'98
$5	5

Issued: 5/11/97 🟣 🔵

Status: Current

Description: Dalmatian. Black ears on spotted dog.

Birthday: 10/17/96

Poem:
The Beanies all thought it was a big joke
While writing her tag, their ink pen broke
She got in the way, and got all spotty
So now the Beanies call her Dotty!

Bought ___/___/___ for $_____.

EARLY™

GBTru: $5   Item #: 4190

Issued: 5/30/98 🔵

Status: Current

Description: Brown robin with red breast, yellow bill and orange feet.

Birthday: 2/20/97

Poem:
Early is a red breasted robin
For a worm he'll soon be bobbin'
Always known as a sign of spring
This happy robin loves to sing!

Bought ___/___/___ for $_____.

EARS™

Issued: 1/7/96

Status: Retired 5/1/98

Description: Brown rabbit with white face and inner ears.

Birthday: 4/18/95

Poem:

He's been eating carrots so long
Didn't understand what was wrong
Couldn't see the board during classes
Until the doctor gave him glasses!

GBTru: $15 ↑ 200%   Item #: 4018

'97   '98
$5   5

Bought ___/___/___ for $_____.

ECHO™

Issued: 5/11/97

Status: Retired 5/1/98

Description: Blue-grey dolphin with white belly. Echo and Waves were originally shipped with each others swing tag and tush tag. GBTru for Echo with Waves tag is $35.00.

Birthday: 12/21/96

Poem:

Echo the dolphin lives in the sea
Playing with her friends, like you and me
Through the waves she echoes the sound
"I'm so glad to have you around!"

GBTru: $15 ↑ 200%   Item #: 4180

'97   '98
$5   5

Bought ___/___/___ for $_____.

ERIN™

Issued: 1/31/98

Status: Current

Description: Green bear with white shamrock on chest.

Birthday: 3/17/97

Poem:

Named after the beautiful Emerald Isle
This Beanie Baby will make you smile.
A bit of luck, a pot of gold,
Light up the faces, both young and old!

GBTru: $5   Item #: 4186

Bought ___/___/___ for $_____.

31

FETCH™

GBTru: $5   **Item #:** 4189

Issued: 5/30/98 🛡

Status: Current

Description: Golden Retriever. Solid gold plush fabric.

Birthday: 2/4/97

Poem:

Fetch is alert at the crack of dawn
Walking through dew drops on the lawn
Always golden, loyal and true
This little puppy is the one for you!

Bought ____/____/____ for $_____.

FLASH™

GBTru: $125 ↑ 92%   **Item #:** 4021

'97	'98
$35	65

Issued: 1/8/94 🛡 🛡 🛡 🛡

Status: Retired 5/11/97

Description: Grey dolphin with white belly. One of the "Original 9."

Birthday: 5/13/93

Poem:

You know dolphins are the smartest breed
Well Flash the dolphin knows how to read
She's teaching her friend Splash to read too
So maybe one day they can both read to you.

Alternate Poem:

You know dolphins are a smart breed
Our friend Flash knows how to read
Splash the whale is the one who taught her
Although reading is difficult under the water!

Bought ____/____/____ for $_____.

FLEECE™

Issued: 1/1/97

Status: Current

Description: White lamb with curly-textured fabric and light tan face.

Birthday: 3/21/96

Poem:
Fleece would like to sing a lullaby
Please be patient, she's really shy
When you sleep, keep her by your ear
Her song will leave you nothing to fear.

Bought ___/___/___ for $_____.

GBTru: $5 no change   **Item #: 4125**

'97	'98
$5	5

FLIP™

Issued: 1/7/96

Status: Retired 10/1/97

Description: White cat with pink whiskers, nose and inner ears, blue eyes.

Birthday: 2/28/95

Poem:
Flip the cat is an acrobat
She loves playing on her mat
This cat flips with such grace and flair
She can somersault in midair.

Bought ___/___/___ for $_____.

GBTru: $50 ↑ 11%   **Item #: 4012**

'97	'98
$5	45

FLOPPITY™

Issued: 1/1/97

Status: Retired 5/1/98

Description: Lavender toy bunny with floppy ears and lavender ribbon.

Birthday: 5/28/96

Poem:
Floppity hops from here to there
Searching for eggs without a care
Lavender coat from head to toe
All dressed up and nowhere to go!

Bought ___/___/___ for $_____.

GBTru: $20 ↑ 300%   **Item #: 4118**

'97	'98
$5	5

F is for Flutter...

FLUTTER™

GBTru: $950 ↑ 90%   Item #: 4043

'97   **'98**
$350 500

Issued: 6/3/95 🛡️ 🛡️
Status: Retired 6/15/96
Description: Butterfly with black body, multicolored tie-dyed wings.
Birthday: unknown
Poem: None.

Bought ___/___/___ for $_____.

FORTUNE™

GBTru: $5   Item #: 4196

Issued: 5/30/98 🛡️
Status: Current
Description: Black and white sitting panda wearing red ribbon bow.
Birthday: 12/6/97
Poem:
Nibbling on a bamboo tree
This little panda is hard to see
You're so lucky with this one you found
Only a few are still around!

Bought ___/___/___ for $_____.

FRECKLES™

GBTru: $5 no change   Item #: 4066

'97   **'98**
$5   5

Issued: 6/15/96 🛡️ 🛡️
Status: Current
Description: Brown, gold and white spotted leopard. Alternate birthday is 7/28/96.
Birthday: 6/3/96
Poem:
From the trees he hunts his prey
In the night and in the day
He's the king of camouflage
Look real close, he's no mirage!

Bought ___/___/___ for $_____.

GARCIA™

Issued: 1/7/96 🛡 ⛆

Status: Retired 5/11/97

Description: Multicolored tie-dyed teddy bear.

Birthday: 8/1/95

Poem:

The Beanies use to follow him around
Because Garcia traveled from town to town
He's pretty popular as you can see
Some even say he's legendary.

GBTru: **$175** ↑ 75%   Item #: 4051

'97	'98
$50	100

Bought ___/___/___ for $_____.

GIGI™

Issued: 5/30/98 🛡

Status: Current

Description: Black poodle. Curly textured fabric, red bows decorate ears.

Birthday: 4/7/97

Poem:

Prancing and dancing all down the street
Thinking her hairdo is oh so neat
Always so careful in the wind and rain
She's a dog that is anything but plain!

GBTru: **$5**   Item #: 4191

Bought ___/___/___ for $_____.

GLORY™

Issued: 5/30/98 🛡

Status: Current

Description: White teddy bear dotted with red and blue stars, wearing U.S. flag.

Birthday: 7/4/97

Poem:

Wearing the flag for all to see
Symbol of freedom for you and me
Red white and blue—Independence Day
Happy Birthday USA!

GBTru: **$5**   Item #: 4188

Bought ___/___/___ for $_____.

G is for Gobbles...

GOBBLES™

GBTru: $5 no change   Item #: 4034

'98
$5

Issued: 10/1/97 🛡 🛡

Status: Current

Description: Turkey. Brown body with brown and red wings. The bill and feet are yellow and the head is red. The tail is circles of brown, red and white.

Birthday: 11/27/96

Poem:
Gobbles the turkey loves to eat
Once a year she has a feast
I have a secret I'd like to divulge
If she eats too much her tummy will bulge!

   Bought ___/___/___ for $_____.

GOLDIE™

GBTru: $50 no change   Item #: 4023

'97   '98
$5   50

Issued: 6/25/94 🛡 🛡 🛡 🛡 🛡

Status: Retired 12/31/97

Description: Goldfish. Also available as a Teenie Beanie Baby.

Birthday: 11/14/94

Poem:
She's got the rhythm, she's got the soul
What more could you want in a fish bowl?
Through sound waves Goldie swam
Because this goldfish likes to jam.

   Bought ___/___/___ for $_____.

GRACIE™

GBTru: $15 ↑ 200%   Item #: 4126

'97   '98
$5   5

Issued: 1/1/97 🛡 🛡

Status: Retired 5/1/98

Description: White swan with fluorescent orange feet and bill.

Birthday: 6/17/96

Poem:
As a duckling, she was confused,
Birds on the lake were quite amused.
Poking fun until she would cry,
Now the most beautiful swan at Ty!

   Bought ___/___/___ for $_____.

GRUNT™

Issued: 1/7/96

Status: Retired 5/11/97

Description: Red razorback pig.

Birthday: 7/19/95

Poem:

Some Beanies think Grunt is tough

No surprise, he's scary enough

But if you take him home you'll see

Grunt is the sweetest Beanie Baby!

GBTru: $185 ↑ 48%   **Item #: 4092**

'97	'98
$35	125

Bought ___/___/___ for $_____.

HAPPY™ VERSION 1

Issued: 6/25/94

Status: Retired 5/1/98

Description: Hippopotamus. Version 1: Light <u>grey</u>. Change to Version 2 in 6/95.

Birthday: unknown

Poem: None.

GBTru: $785 ↑ 124%   **Item #: 4061**

'97	'98
$300	350

Bought ___/___/___ for $_____.

HAPPY™ VERSION 2

Issued: 6/3/95

Status: Retired 5/1/98

Description: Hippopotamus. Version 2: <u>Lavender</u>. Also available as a Teenie Beanie Baby.

Birthday: 2/25/94

Poem:

Happy the hippo loves to wade

In the river and in the shade

When Happy shoots water out of his snout

You'll know he's happy without a doubt!

GBTru: $20 ↑ 300%   **Item #: 4061**

'97	'98
$5	5

Bought ___/___/___ for $_____.

H is for Hippity...

HIPPITY™

GBTru: $20 ↑ 300%   Item #: 4119

'97	'98
$5	5

Issued: 1/1/97 🛡 🛡
Status: Retired 5/1/98
Description: Mint green toy bunny with floppy ears and green ribbon.
Birthday: 6/1/96
Poem:
Hippity is a cute little bunny
Dressed in green, he looks quite funny
Twitching his nose in the air
Sniffing a flower here and there!

Bought ___/___/___ for $_____.

HISSY™

GBTru: $5 no change   Item #: 4185

'98
$5

Issued: 12/31/97 🛡
Status: Current
Description: Coiled snake with lemon yellow undersides and blue-green tie-dyed upper body.
Birthday: 4/4/97
Poem:
Curled and coiled and ready to play
He waits for you patiently every day
He'll keep his best friend, but not his skin
And stay with you through thick and thin!

Bought ___/___/___ for $_____.

HOOT™

GBTru: $50 ↑ 43%   Item #: 4073

'97	'98
$5	35

Issued: 1/7/96 🛡 🛡
Status: Retired 10/1/97
Description: Brown owl with light brown face, belly and under wings.
Birthday: 8/9/95
Poem:
Late to bed, late to rise
Nevertheless, Hoot's quite wise
Studies by candlelight, nothing new
Like a president, do you know who?

Bought ___/___/___ for $_____.

HOPPITY™

Issued: 1/1/97

Status: Retired 5/1/98

Description: Pink toy bunny with floppy ears and pink ribbon.

Birthday: 4/3/96

Poem:

Hopscotch is what she likes to play
If you don't join in, she'll hop away
So play a game if you have the time,
She likes to play, rain or shine.

Bought ___/___/___ for $_____.

GBTru: $20 ↑ 300%   Item #: 4117

'97	'98
$5	5

HUMPHREY™

Issued: 6/25/94

Status: Retired 6/15/95

Description: Brown camel.

Birthday: unknown

Poem: None.

Bought ___/___/___ for $_____.

GBTru: $2000 ↑ 82%   Item #: 4060

'97	'98
$600	1100

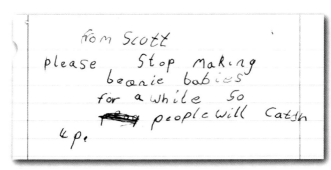

from Scott

please stop making beanie babies for a while so ~~peop~~ people will catch up.

Scott of Sugar Hill, GA probably speaks for a lot of collectors.

I is for Iggy...

IGGY™ VERSION 1

GBTru: $5 no change   Item #: 4038

'98
$5

Issued: 12/31/97 🦃

Status: Out of Production 6/98

Description: Multicolored tie-dyed iguana with prominent eyes and razorback spine. Version 1: <u>No tongue</u>. Change to Version 2 in 6/98. See page 15.

Birthday: 8/12/97

Poem:

Sitting on a rock, basking in the sun
Is this Iguana's idea of fun
Towel and glasses, book and beach chair
His life is so perfect without a care!

    Bought ___/___/___ for $_____.

IGGY™ VERSION 2

GBTru: $5   Item #: 4038

Issued: 6/98 🦃

Status: Current

Description: Multicolored tie-dyed iguana with prominent eyes and razorback spine. Version 2: <u>Pink tongue</u> added. See page 15.

Birthday: 8/12/97

Poem:

Sitting on a rock, basking in the sun
Is this Iguana's idea of fun
Towel and glasses, book and beach chair
His life is so perfect without a care!

    Bought ___/___/___ for $_____.

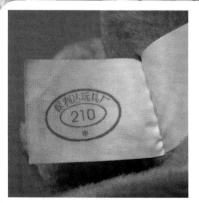

In June 1998 stamps like this started to appear on the inside of the tush tag. The symbols and number appear to be different for each Beanie Baby.

I is for Inch...

INCH™ VERSION 1

Issued: 6/3/95 🛡 🛡

Status: Retired 5/1/98

Description: Rainbow-colored inchworm with black antennae. Version 1: Black <u>felt</u> antenna. Change to Version 2 on 10/15/97.

Birthday: 9/3/95

Poem:

Inch the worm is a friend of mine
He goes so slow all the time
Inching around from here to there
Traveling the world without a care.

Bought ___/___/___ for $_____.

GBTru: $195 ↑ 95%   **Item #: 4044**

'97	'98
$100	100

INCH™ VERSION 2

Issued: 10/15/97 🛡 🛡

Status: Retired 5/1/98

Description: Rainbow-colored inchworm with black antennae. Version 2: Black <u>yarn</u> antenna. Also available as a Teenie Beanie Baby.

Birthday: 9/3/95

Poem:

Inch the worm is a friend of mine
He goes so slow all the time
Inching around from here to there
Traveling the world without a care.

Bought ___/___/___ for $_____.

GBTru: $20 ↑ 300%   **Item #: 4044**

'97	'98
$5	5

ying (the bear)

tie-die

all tie-die (I didn't have time to color this in)

Girl - birthday December 4th

"Tie-die" coloring is time consuming.

Illustration by Patsy of Spokane, WA.

I is for Inky...

INKY™ VERSION 1

GBTru: $800 ↑ 129%   Item #: 4028

'97   '98
$225   350

Issued: 6/25/94 💙 ❷
Status: Retired 5/1/98
Description: <u>Tan</u> octopus. Version 1:
<u>Without a mouth</u>. Change to
Version 2 on 9/12/94.
Birthday: unknown
Poem: None.

Bought ___/___/___ for $_____.

INKY™ VERSION 2

GBTru: $750 ↑ 114%   Item #: 4028

'97   '98
$225   350

Issued: 9/12/94 ❷ ❸
Status: Retired 5/1/98
Description: <u>Tan</u> octopus. Version 2:
<u>With a mouth</u>. Change to Version 3
on 6/3/95.
Birthday: unknown
Poem: None.

Bought ___/___/___ for $_____.

INKY™ VERSION 3

GBTru: $20 ↑ 300%   Item #: 4028

'97   '98
$5   5

Issued: 6/3/95 ❸ ❹ ❺
Status: Retired 5/1/98
Description: Octopus. Version 3:
<u>Pink</u>. Has been found either missing
legs or with more than eight legs!
Birthday: 11/29/94
Poem:
Inky's head is big and round
As he swims he makes no sound
If you need a hand, don't hesitate
Inky can help because he has eight!

Bought ___/___/___ for $_____.

J is for Jabber...

JABBER™

Issued: 5/30/98 🛡
Status: Current

GBTru: $5   Item #: 4197

Description: Parrot with red body, yellow beak, feet, under wings; blue wing and tail tips and top of head; white eye patches with black stripes.

Birthday: 10/10/97

Poem:

Teaching Jabber to move his beak
A large vocabulary he now can speak
Jabber will repeat what you say
Teach him a new word everyday!

Bought ___/___/___ for $_____.

JAKE™

Issued: 5/30/98 🛡
Status: Current

GBTru: $5   Item #: 4199

Description: Mallard duck. Teal green head and tail, brown and light grey body, dark gray and white wings, white ring around his neck.

Birthday: 4/16/97

Poem:

Jake the drake likes to splash in a puddle
Take him home and give him a cuddle
Quack, Quack, Quack, he will say
He's so glad you're here to play!

Bought ___/___/___ for $_____.

JOLLY™

Issued: 5/11/97 🛡 🛡
Status: Retired 5/1/98

GBTru: $20 ↑   300%   Item #: 4082

Description: Dark brown walrus with fuzzy fabric mustache and white tusks.

Birthday: 12/2/96

Poem:

Jolly the walrus is not very serious
He laughs and laughs until he's delirious
He often reminds me of my dad
Always happy, never sad!

'97	'98
$5	5

Bought ___/___/___ for $_____.

K is for Kiwi...

KIWI™

GBTru: **$225 ↑ 150%**   Item #: **4070**

'97	'98
$50	90

Issued: 6/3/95 🛡 🛡
Status: Retired 1/1/97
Description: Black, yellow blue and red toucan.
Birthday: 9/16/95
Poem:
Kiwi waits for the April showers
Watching a garden bloom with flowers
There trees grow with fruit that's sweet
I'm sure you'll guess his favorite treat!

Bought ___/___/___ for $_____.

KUKU™

GBTru: **$5**   Item #: **4192**

Issued: 5/30/98 🛡
Status: Current
Description: White cockatoo with grey beak and feet.
Birthday: 1/5/97
Poem:
This fancy bird loves to converse
He talks in poems, rhythms and verse
So take him home and give him some time
You'll be surprised how he can rhyme!

Bought ___/___/___ for $_____.

LEFTY™

GBTru: **$275 ↑ 104%**   Item #: **4085**

'97	'98
$50	135

Issued: 6/15/96 🛡
Status: Retired 1/1/97
Description: Blue donkey with American flag is symbol of the Democratic Party.
Birthday: 7/4/96
Poem:
Donkeys to the left, elephants to the right
Often seems like a crazy sight
This whole game seems very funny
Until you realize they're spending your money!

Bought ___/___/___ for $_____.

L is for Leg

LEGS™

Issued: 1/8/94 🛡 🛡 🛡 🛡

Status: Retired 10/1/97

Description: Green frog. One of the "Original 9."

Birthday: 4/25/93

Poem:

Legs lives in a hollow log
Legs likes to play leap frog
If you like to hang out at the lake
Legs will be the new friend you make!

GBTru: $25 no change   Item #

'97	'98
$5	25

Bought ___ / ___ / ___ for $_____.

LIBEARTY™

Issued: 6/15/96 🛡

Status: Retired 1/1/97

Description: White teddy bear with American flag on chest and red and blue ribbon around neck was introduced to commemorate the 1996 Olympics.

Birthday: Summer '96

Poem:

I am called Libearty
I wear the flag for all to see
Hope and freedom is my way
That's why I wear flag USA.

GBTru: $325 ↑ 117%   Item #: 4057

'97	'98
$50	150

Bought ___ / ___ / ___ for $_____.

feathers
March 10th 1998

This is my idea for a new Beanie baby. I would like you to make me nine dozen of these and send them to me.

Jenna

Most collectors who submit ideas for Beanies request pieces for friends and family!

is for Lizzy...

LIZZY™ VERSION 1

GBTru: $800 ↑ 60%   **Item #: 4033**

'97   **'98**
$350   500

Issued: 6/3/95 ❷ ❸
Status: Retired 12/31/97
Description: Lizard. Version 1:
Bright multicolored <u>tie-dyed</u>.
Change to Version 2 on 1/7/96.
Birthday: unknown
Poem: None.

Bought ___/___/___ for $_____.

LIZZY™ VERSION 2

GBTru: $25 ↓ 29%   **Item #: 4033**

'97   **'98**
$5   35

Issued: 1/7/96 ❸ ❹ ❺
Status: Retired 12/31/97
Description: Lizard. Version 2: <u>Blue</u>
back covered with black spots,
yellow belly. Also available as
Teenie Beanie Baby, "Lizz."
Birthday: 5/11/95
Poem:

Her best friend Legs was at her house
waiting
Today is the day they go roller blading
But Lizzy Lou had to stay home
So Legs had to roller blade alone.

Alternate Poem:

Lizzy loves Legs the frog
She hides with him under logs
Both of them search for flies
Underneath the clear blue skies!

Bought ___/___/___ for $_____.

L is for Lucky...

LUCKY™ VERSION 1

Issued: 6/25/94 ♥ ❷ ❸

Status: Retired 5/1/98

Description: Ladybug. Version 1: <u>Seven</u> black felt spots glued on. Change to Version 2 on 2/27/96.

Birthday: unknown

Poem: None.

GBTru: $200 ↑ 100%   Item #: 4040

'97	'98
$100	100

Bought ___/___/___ for $_____.

LUCKY™ VERSION 2

Issued: 2/27/96 ❹ ❺

Status: Retired 5/1/98

Description: Ladybug. Version 2: Approximately <u>11</u> black spots are printed on fabric. (Can be +/- 3 depending on how it's sewn.)

Birthday: 5/1/95

Poem: Lucky the lady bug loves the lotto "Someone must win" that's her motto But save your dimes and even a penny Don't spend on the lotto and You'll have many!

GBTru: $15 ↑ 200%   Item #: 4040

'97	'98
$5	5

Bought ___/___/___ for $_____.

LUCKY™ VERSION 3

Issued: 1996 ♥

Status: Retired 5/1/98

Description: Ladybug. Version 3: Approximately <u>21</u> small spots are printed on fabric. (Can be +/- 3 depending on how it's sewn.) Introduced late '96.

Birthday: 5/1/95

Poem: Lucky the lady bug loves the lotto "Someone must win" that's her motto But save your dimes and even a penny Don't spend on the lotto and You'll have many!

GBTru: $500 ↑ 25%   Item #: 4040

'97	'98
$5	400

Bought ___/___/___ for $_____.

M is for Magic...

MAGIC™ VERSION 1

GBTru: $75 ↑ 50%   Item #: 4088

'97 **'98**
$5   50

Issued: 6/3/95 🛡 🛡 🛡
Status: Retired 12/31/97
Description: White dragon with iridescent wings and scales down back. Version 1: Wing thread color was <u>pale pink</u>.
Birthday: 9/5/95
Poem:

Magic the dragon lives in a dream
The most beautiful that you have ever seen
Through magic lands she likes to fly
Look up and watch her, way up high!

Bought ___/___/___ for $_____.

MAGIC™ VERSION 2

GBTru: $200 ↑ 33%   Item #: 4088

'97 **'98**
$75   150

Issued: 1996 🛡
Status: Retired 12/31/97
Description: White dragon with iridescent wings and scales down back. Version 2: Wing thread color was <u>hot pink</u>.
Birthday: 9/5/95
Poem:

Magic the dragon lives in a dream
The most beautiful that you have ever seen
Through magic lands she likes to fly
Look up and watch her, way up high!

Bought ___/___/___ for $_____.

To Whom it may Concern,
    My name is Toni. I had a dog who
I had for 14 years, (my whole life)
Her name was Mandy, recently she got
Cancer, and two days ago we had
to put her to sleep.
    I am a fond collector of Beanie Babies,
and I think it would be the coolest
thing in the world, if (ty) would make a
West Highland white terrier, and
named her Mandy, (MANDI)
If there's any way this is possible or
if you have a way to contact (ty) and
I would be very grateful.
                            Toni

MANNY™

Issued: 1/7/96 🦋 🖤
Status: Retired 5/11/97
Description: Grey manatee.
Birthday: 6/8/95
Poem:

Manny is sometimes called a sea cow
She likes to twirl and likes to bow
Manny sure is glad you bought her
Because it's so lonely underwater!

GBTru: $175 ↑ 106%   Item #

'97	'98
$35	85

Bought ___/___/___ for $_____.

MAPLE™

Issued: 1/1/97 🖤 🖐
Status: Canadian Exclusive
Description: Teddy bear with Maple Leaf flag. Canadian exclusive, commemorates Confederation Day. First pieces issued with name "Pride" on tush tag. Maple with a Pride tush tag has a GBTru of $600.00
Birthday: 7/1/96
Poem: Maple the bear likes to ski
With his friends, he plays hockey.
He loves his pancakes and eats every crumb.
Can you guess which country he's from?

GBTru: $365 ↑ 265%   Item #: 4600

'97	'98
$5	100

Bought ___/___/___ for $_____.

MEL™

Issued: 1/1/97 🖤 🖐
Status: Current
Description: Grey koala with white inner ears and belly. Also available as a Teenie Beanie Baby.
Birthday: 1/15/96
Poem:

How do you name a Koala bear?
It's rather tough, I do declare!
It confuses me, I get in a funk
I'll name him Mel, after my favorite hunk!

GBTru: $5 no change   Item #: 4162

'97	'98
$5	5

MYSTIC™ VERSION 1

GBTru: $310 ↑ 107%   **Item #: 4007**

'97	**'98**
$100	150

Issued: 6/25/94

Status: Out Of Production 1995

Description: White unicorn with <u>tan horn</u>. Version 1: <u>Soft fine yarn</u> for mane and tail. Change to Version 2 in 1995.

Birthday: unknown

Poem: None.

Bought ___/___/___ for $_____.

MYSTIC™ VERSION 2

GBTru: $30 ↑ 100%   **Item #: 4007**

'97	**'98**
$5	15

Issued: 1995

Status: Out Of Production 10/23/97

Description: White unicorn with <u>tan horn</u>. Version 2: <u>Coarse yarn</u> for mane and tail. Change to Version 3 on 10/23/97.

Birthday: 5/21/94

Poem:
Once upon a time in a land far away
A baby unicorn was born one day in May
Keep Mystic with you she's a prize
You'll see the magic in her blue eyes.

Bought ___/___/___ for $_____.

MYSTIC™ VERSION 3

GBTru: $5. no change   **Item #: 4007**

'98
$5

Issued: 10/23/97

Status: Current

Description: White unicorn. Version 3: <u>Iridescent horn</u> with pink stitching.

Birthday: 5/21/94

Poem:
Once upon a time in a land far away
A baby unicorn was born one day in May
Keep Mystic with you she's a prize
You'll see the magic in her blue eyes.

Bought ___/___/___ for $_____.

N is for Nana...

NANA™

Issued: 6/3/95 🛡️

Status: Out Of Production 1995

Description: Brown monkey with lighter brown paws and face. The original Bongo. Nana has a #3 Swing Tag with a "Nana" sticker over the name "Bongo."

Birthday: unknown

Poem: None.

GBTru: $4100 ↑ 242%   **Item #:** 4067

'97	'98
$100	1200

Bought ___/___/___ for $_____.

NANOOK™

Issued: 5/11/97 🛡️ 🛡️

Status: Current

Description: Slate gray Husky dog with white face, paws, belly and tail.

Birthday: 11/21/96

Poem:

Nanook is a dog that loves cold weather
To him a sled is light as a feather
Over the snow and through the slush
He runs at hearing the cry of "mush!"

GBTru: $5 no change   **Item #:** 4104

'97	'98
$5	5

Bought ___/___/___ for $_____.

```
        Wishes
        1-27-98

Blow out the candles
But watch out their hot!!!
This bear will bring you wishes
Lots and lots!!
        www.ty.com
```

Brittany & Kaitlyn of Savage, MN wrote with "some good suggestions for new Beanie Babies that you [GREENBOOK] could possibly send to Ty."

N is for Nip...

NIP™ VERSION 1

GBTru: $450 ↑ 29%   **Item #:** 4003

'97   **'98**
$250 350

Issued: 1/7/95 🛡 🛡
Status: Retired 12/31/97
Description: Gold cat. Version 1: Larger gold body with white triangle on face and <u>white belly</u>. Pink ears, nose and whiskers. Change to Version 2 on 1/7/96.
Birthday: unknown
Poem: None.

Bought ___/___/___ for $_____.

NIP™ VERSION 2

GBTru: $800 ↑ 19%   **Item #:** 4003

'97   **'98**
$650 675

Issued: 1/7/96 🛡
Status: Retired 12/31/97
Description: Gold cat. Version 2: Smaller <u>all gold body</u>. Pink ears and whiskers. Change to Version 3 on 3/10/96.
Birthday: unknown
Poem: None.

Bought ___/___/___ for $_____.

NIP™ VERSION 3

GBTru: $30 ↑ 20%   **Item #:** 4003

'97   **'98**
$5   25

Issued: 3/10/96 🛡 🛡 🛡
Status: Retired 12/31/97
Description: Gold cat. Version 3: Smaller gold body with <u>white paws</u>. Pink nose, white ears and whiskers.
Birthday: 3/6/94
Poem:

His name is Nipper, but we call him Nip
His best friend is a black cat named Zip
Nip likes to run in races for fun
He runs so fast he's always number one!

Bought ___/___/___ for $_____.

N is for Nuts...

NUTS™

Issued: 1/1/97

Status: Current

Description: Brown squirrel with soft, bushy tail and white belly.

Birthday: 1/21/96

Poem:

With his bushy tail, he'll scamper up a tree

The most cheerful critter you'll ever see.

He's nuts about nuts, and he loves to chat

Have you ever seen a squirrel like that?

Bought ___/___/___ for $_____.

GBTru: $5 no change   Item #: 4114

'97	'98
$5	5

PATTI™ VERSION 1

Issued: 1/8/94

Status: Retired 5/1/98

Description: Platypus. One of the "Original 9." Version 1: <u>Maroon</u>. Change to Version 2 on 2/28/95.

Birthday: unknown

Poem: None.

Bought ___/___/___ for $_____.

GBTru: $800 ↑ 23%   Item #: 4025

'97	'98
$1500	650

PATTI™ VERSION 2

Issued: 2/28/95

Status: Retired 5/1/98

Description: Platypus. One of the "Original 9." Version 2: <u>Magenta</u> (Purple). Version 2 of Patti has the same fabric as Inch's tail. Also available as a Teenie Beanie Baby.

Birthday: 1/6/93

Poem:

Ran into Patti one day while walking

Believe me she wouldn't stop talking!

Listened and listened to her speak

That would explain her extra large beak!

Bought ___/___/___ for $_____.

GBTru: $20 ↑ 300%   Item #: 4025

'97	'98
$5	5

P is for Peace...

PEACE™

GBTru: $5 no change   Item #: 4053

'97	'98
$5	5

Issued: 5/11/97 🛡 🛡

Status: Current

Description: Multicolored tie-dyed teddy bear with peace symbol.

Birthday: 2/1/96

Poem:

All races, all colors, under the sun
Join hands together and have some fun
Dance to the music, rock and roll is the sound
Symbols of peace and love abound!

Bought ___/___/___ for $_____.

PEANUT™ VERSION 1

GBTru: $4400 ↑ 76%   Item #: 4062

'97	'98
$2000	2500

Issued: 6/3/95 🛡

Status: Retired 5/1/98

Description: Elephant. Version 1: <u>Royal blue</u> with pale pink inner ears. Change to Version 2 on 10/2/95.

Birthday: unknown

Poem: None.

Bought ___/___/___ for $_____.

PEANUT™ VERSION 2

GBTru: $25 ↑ 400%   Item #: 4062

'97	'98
$5	5

Issued: 10/2/95 🛡 🛡 🛡

Status: Retired 5/1/98

Description: Elephant. Version 2: <u>Light blue</u> with pink inner ears. Also available as a Teenie Beanie Baby.

Birthday: 1/25/95

Poem:

Peanut the elephant walks on tip-toes
Quietly sneaking wherever she goes
She'll sneak up on you and a hug you will get
Peanuts is a friend you won't soon forget.

Bought ___/___/___ for $_____.

P is for Peking...

PEKING™

Issued: 6/25/94

Status: Retired 1/7/96

Description: Black and white panda.

Birthday: unknown

Poem: None.

GBTru: $2200 ↑ 144%   Item #: 4013

'97	'98
$650	900

Bought ___/___/___ for $_____.

PINCHERS™

Issued: 1/8/94

Status: Retired 5/1/98

Description: Red lobster. Successor to "Punchers." See page 58. One of the "Original 9." Also available as a Teenie Beanie Baby.

Birthday: 6/19/93

Poem:

This lobster loves to pinch
Eating his food inch by inch
Balancing carefully with his tail
Moving forward slow as a snail!

GBTru: $15 ↑ 200%   Item #: 4026

'97	'98
$5	5

Bought ___/___/___ for $_____.

PINKY™

Issued: 6/3/95

Status: Current

Description: Bright pink flamingo with light pink dangling legs and orange beak. Also available as a Teenie Beanie Baby.

Birthday: 2/13/95

Poem:

Pinky loves the Everglades
From the hottest pink she's made
With floppy legs and big orange beak
She's the Beanie that you seek!

GBTru: $5 no change   Item #: 4072

'97	'98
$5	5

Bought ___/___/___ for $_____.

55

P is for Pouch...

POUCH™

GBTru: $5 no change   Item #: 4161

'97	'98
$5	5

Issued: 1/1/97

Status: Current

Description: Brown kangaroo with tiny baby stitched into its pouch.

Birthday: 11/6/96

Poem:
My little pouch is handy I've found
It helps me carry my baby around
I hop up and down without any fear
Knowing my baby is safe and near.

Bought ___/___/___ for $_____.

POUNCE™

GBTru: $5 no change   Item #: 4122

'98
$5

Issued: 12/31/97

Status: Current

Description: Dark brown tie-dyed cat with cream paws, inner ears and muzzle.

Birthday: 8/28/97

Poem:
Sneaking and slinking down the hall
To pounce upon a fluffy yarn ball
Under the tables, around the chairs
Through the rooms and down the stairs!

Bought ___/___/___ for $_____.

PRANCE™

GBTru: $5 no change   Item #: 4123

'98
$5

Issued: 12/31/97

Status: Current

Description: Striped grey tabby with white paws, inner ears and small triangle on face. Pink nose, whiskers and blue eyes.

Birthday: 11/20/97

Poem:
She darts around and swats the air
Then looks confused when nothing's there
Pick her up and pet her soft fur
Listen closely, and you'll hear her purr!

Bought ___/___/___ for $_____.

56

P is for Princess...

Issued: 10/29/97 🛡 🛡

PRINCESS™

Status: Current

GBTru: $5   Item #: 4300

Description: Royal purple teddy bear, violet
satin ribbon. White embroidered rose on chest.
First Swing Tag reads, "All profits of Ty from this
collectible will be donated to the DIANA,
PRINCESS OF WALES MEMORIAL FUND."

Birthday: none

Poem:

Like an angel, she came from heaven above
She shared her compassion, her pain, her love
She only stayed with us long enough to teach
The world to share, to give, to reach.

Bought ____/____/____ for $_____.

Issued: 12/31/97 🛡

PUFFER™

Status: Current

GBTru: $5 no change   Item #: 4181

Description: Puffin has a black and
white body and head with red feet
and colorful orange and red beak.

Birthday: 11/3/97

Poem:

What in the world does a puffin do?
We're sure that you would like to know too
We asked Puffer how she spends her days
Before she answered, she flew away!

'98
$5

Bought ____/____/____ for $_____.

Issued: 5/11/97 🛡 🛡

PUGSLY™

Status: Current

GBTru: $5 no change   Item #: 4106

Description: Cream pug dog with
black ears and muzzle.

Birthday: 5/2/96

Poem:

Pugsly is picky about what he will wear
Never a spot, a stain or a tear
Image is something of which he'll gloat
Until he noticed his wrinkled coat!

'97   '98
$5   5

Bought ____/____/____ for $_____.

P is for Punchers...

PUNCHERS™

GBTru: $4000 ↑ 233% Item #: 4026

'98
$1200

Issued: 1994 ♥

Status: Retired 5/1/98

Description: Red lobster. The original "Pinchers." See page 55. Aside from the name on the Swing Tag, the two lobsters are differentiated by the stitching on the tail. One of the "Original 9."

Birthday: unknown

Poem: None.

Bought ___/___/___ for $_____.

QUACKER™ VERSION 1

GBTru: $2000 ↑ 43% Item #: 4024

'97   **'98**
$1800   1400

Issued: 6/25/94 ♥   ♥

Status: Retired 5/1/98

Description: Yellow duck with orange bill and feet. Version 1: <u>No wings</u>. Change to Version 2 on 1/7/95.

Birthday: unknown

Poem: None.

Bought ___/___/___ for $_____.

QUACKERS™ VERSION 2

GBTru: $25 ↑ 400% Item #: 4024

'97   **'98**
$5   5

Issued: 1/7/95 ♥   ♥   ♥   ♥

Status: Retired 5/1/98

Description: Yellow duck with orange bill and feet. Version 2: <u>With wings.</u> Also available as Teenie Beanie Baby, "Quacks."

Birthday: 4/19/94

Poem:

There is a duck by the name of Quackers
Every night he eats animal crackers
He swims in a lake that's clear and blue
But he'll come to the shore to be with you!

Bought ___/___/___ for $_____.

R is for Radar...

RADAR™

Issued: 9/1/95

Status: Retired 5/11/97

Description: Black bat with red eyes.

Birthday: 10/30/95

Poem:
Radar the bat flies late at night
He can soar to an amazing height
If you see something as high as a star
Take a good look, it might be Radar!

GBTru: $200 ↑ 100%   Item #: 4091

'97	'98
$40	100

Bought ___/___/___ for $_____.

RAINBOW™

Issued: 12/31/97

Status: Current

Description: Dark blue tie-dyed chameleon; yellow eyes and mouth. See page 15.

Birthday: 10/14/97

Poem:
Red, green, blue and yellow
This chameleon is a colorful fellow
A blend of colors, his own unique hue
Rainbow was made especially for you!

GBTru: $5 no change   Item #: 4037

'98
$5

Bought ___/___/___ for $_____.

The second org in ty Ty Beanie Babies

Dear Company, (Greenbook),
I have on of your new 1998 Greenbook Ty beanie baby books and it's great!

This letter was my first to a company so I hope it gets in.

R is for Rex...

REX™

GBTru: **$875** ↑ **150%**   Item #: **4086**

'97   **'98**
$275   350

Issued: 6/3/95 🛡
Status: Retired 6/15/96
Description: Dinosaur. Red and purple tie-dyed Tyrannosaurus Rex.
Birthday: unknown
Poem: None.

Bought ___/___/___ for $_____.

RIGHTY™

GBTru: **$250** ↑ **67%**   Item #: **4086**

'97   **'98**
$50   150

Issued: 6/15/96 🛡
Status: Retired 1/1/97
Description: Grey elephant with American flag is symbol of the Republican Party.
Birthday: 7/4/96
Poem:
Donkeys to the left, elephants to the right
Often seems like a crazy sight
This whole game seems very funny
Until you realize they're spending your money!

Bought ___/___/___ for $_____.

RINGO™

GBTru: **$5** no change   Item #: **4014**

'97   **'98**
$5   5

Issued: 1/7/96 🛡 🛡 🛡
Status: Current
Description: Brown raccoon with black rings around tail and eyes, white inner ears and muzzle.
Birthday: 7/14/95
Poem:
Ringo hides behind his mask
He will come out, if you should ask
He loves to chitter, he loves to chatter
Just about anything, it doesn't matter!

Bought ___/___/___ for $_____.

ROARY™

Issued: 5/11/97 4️ 5️

Status: Current

Description: Brown lion with soft, fluffy mane and tail tuft.

Birthday: 2/20/96

Poem:

Deep in the jungle they crowned him king
But being brave is not his thing
A cowardly lion some may say
He hears his roar and runs away!

Bought ___/___/___ for $_____.

GBTru: $5 no change   Item #: 4069

'97	'98
$5	5

ROCKET™

Issued: 5/30/98 5️

Status: Current

Description: Blue jay. White and bright blue plush fabric with black feet and beak.

Birthday: 3/12/97

Poem:

Rocket is the fastest blue jay ever
He flies in all sorts of weather
Aerial tricks are his specialty
He's so entertaining for you and me!

Bought ___/___/___ for $_____.

GBTru: $5   Item #: 4202

ROVER™

Issued: 6/15/96 4️ 5️

Status: Retired 5/1/98

Description: Red dog with long, floppy ears.

Birthday: 5/30/96

Poem:

This dog is red and his name is Rover
If you call him he is sure to come over
He barks and plays with all his might
But worry not he won't bite!

Bought ___/___/___ for $_____.

GBTru: $15 ↑ 200%   Item #: 4101

'97	'98
$5	5

S is for Scoop...

SCOOP™

GBTru: $5 no change   Item #: 4107

'97	'98
$5	5

Issued: 6/15/96 🛡 🛡
Status: Current
Description: Grey pelican with bright orange bill and feet. Also available as a Teenie Beanie Baby.
Birthday: 7/1/96
Poem:
All day long he scoops up fish
To fill his bill, is his wish
Diving fast and diving low
Hoping those fish are very slow!

Bought ___/___/___ for $_____.

SCOTTIE™

GBTru: $30 ↑ 500%   Item #: 4102

'97	'98
$5	5

Issued: 6/15/96 🛡 🛡
Status: Retired 5/1/98
Description: Black terrier with curly-textured fabric. Alternate birthday is 6/3/96.
Birthday: 6/15/96
Poem:
Scottie is a friendly sort
Even though his legs are short
He is always happy as can be
His best friends are you and me!

Bought ___/___/___ for $_____.

SEAMORE™

GBTru: $195 ↑ 160%   Item #: 4029

'97	'98
$5	75

Issued: 6/25/94 🛡 🛡 🛡
Status: Retired 10/1/97
Description: White seal with black whiskers. Also available as a Teenie Beanie Baby.
Birthday: 12/14/96
Poem:
Seamore is a little white seal
Fish and clams are her favorite meal
Playing and laughing in the sand
She's the happiest seal in the land!

Bought ___/___/___ for $_____.

S is for Seaweed...

Issued: 1/7/96

Status: Current

Description: Brown otter holding green felt seaweed.

Birthday: 3/19/96

Poem:

Seaweed is what she likes to eat
It's supposed to be a delectable treat
Have you tried the treat from the water?
If you haven't maybe you "otter"!

Bought ___/___/___ for $_____.

SEAWEED™

GBTru: $5 no change   Item #: 4080

'97	'98
$5	5

Issued: 6/25/94

Status: Retired 6/15/95

Description: Snake, almost 2 feet long, dark two-tone mottled top to resemble scales, yellow underside.

Birthday: unknown

Poem: None.

Bought ___/___/___ for $_____.

SLITHER™

GBTru: $2100 ↑ 121%   Item #: 4031

'97	'98
$450	950

---

birthday: 12-13-98

status: current   Leon

poem: Leon the Lion is always sneezing and when he's not sick it's always pretending

descripition: Lion. Golden mane and body. Darker Golden feet and face, red smile and black eyes and brown tail

Not only did Chelsea "invent" a Beanie with her Mom's birthday— she completed the GREENBOOK listing.

S is for Sly...

SLY™ VERSION 1

GBTru: $200 ↑ 100%   **Item #: 4115**

'97	'98
$100	100

Issued: 6/15/96 🐾

Status: Out Of Production 8/6/96

Description: Fox. Version 1: <u>All brown</u> body. White inner ears and muzzle. Change to Version 2 on 8/6/96.

Birthday: 9/12/96

Poem:

Sly is a fox and tricky is he
Please don't chase him, let him be
If you want him, just say when
He'll peek out from his den!

Bought ___ / ___ / ___ for $_____.

SLY™ VERSION 2

GBTru: $5 no change   **Item #: 4115**

'97	'98
$5	5

Issued: 8/6/96 🐾 🐾

Status: Current

Description: Fox. Version 2: Brown body with <u>white belly</u>. White inner ears and muzzle.

Birthday: 9/12/96

Poem:

Sly is a fox and tricky is he
Please don't chase him, let him be
If you want him, just say when
He'll peek out from his den!

Bought ___ / ___ / ___ for $_____.

Smoochy Ver. 1 —
Embroidery thread
mouth.

Smoochy Ver. 2 —
Stitched-in red felt fabric
mouth.

S is for Smoochy...

SMOOCHY™ VERSION 1

Issued: 12/31/97 🛡

Status: Out Of Production 6/98

Description: Bright green frog with yellow belly and feet. Version 1: <u>Embroidery thread mouth.</u>

Birthday: 10/1/97

Poem:

Is he a frog or maybe a prince?
This confusion makes him wince
Find the answer, help him with this
Be the one to give him a kiss!

GBTru: $5 no change   Item #: 4039

'98
$5

Bought ___/___/___ for $_____.

SMOOCHY™ VERSION 2

Issued: 6/98 🛡

Status: Current

Description: Bright green frog with yellow belly and feet. Version 2: <u>Stitched-in red felt fabric mouth.</u>

Birthday: 10/1/97

Poem:

Is he a frog or maybe a prince?
This confusion makes him wince
Find the answer, help him with this
Be the one to give him a kiss!

GBTru: $5   Item #: 4039

Bought ___/___/___ for $_____.

SNIP™

Issued: 1/1/97 🛡 🛡

Status: Current

Description: Cream and brown Siamese cat.

Birthday: 10/22/96

Poem:

Snip the cat is Siamese
She'll be your friend if you please
So toss her a toy or a piece of string
Playing with you is her favorite thing.

GBTru: $5 no change   Item #: 4120

'97   '98
$5   5

Bought ___/___/___ for $_____.

S is for Snort...

SNORT™

GBTru: $5 no change   Item #: 4002

'97	'98
$5	5

Issued: 1/1/97 🛡 🛡

Status: Current

Description: Red bull with cream hooves, ears, and nose. Also available as a Teenie Beanie Baby. Snort is the revised Tobasco. See Tobasco on page 73.

Birthday: 5/15/95

Poem:
Although Snort is not so tall
He loves to play basketball
He is a star player in his dreams
Can you guess his favorite team?

Bought ___/___/___ for $_____.

SNOWBALL™

GBTru: $50 ↑ 25%   Item #: 4201

'98
$40

Issued: 10/1/97 🛡 🛡

Status: Retired 12/31/97

Description: Snowman w/orange nose, black hat & red scarf. Sewn on black mouth, shiny black eyes & shiny black buttons.

Birthday: 12/22/96

Poem:
There is a snowman, I've been told
That plays with Beanies out in the cold
What is better out in a winter wonderland
Than a Beanie Snowman in your hand!

Bought ___/___/___ for $_____.

SPARKY™

GBTru: $150 ↑ 173%   Item #: 4100

'97	'98
$35	55

Issued: 6/15/96 🛡

Status: Retired 5/11/97

Description: White and black Dalmatian.

Birthday: 2/27/96

Poem:
Sparky rides proud on the fire truck
Ringing the bell and pushing his luck
He gets underfoot when trying to help
He often gets stepped on and lets out a yelp!

Bought ___/___/___ for $_____.

S is for Speedy...

Issued: 6/25/94 ❶ ❷ ❸ ❹

SPEEDY™

GBTru: $30 ↑ 20%   Item #: 4030

Status: Retired 10/1/97

Description: Bright green turtle with brown and green "shell" fabric on his back. Also available as a Teenie Beanie Baby.

Birthday: 8/14/94

Poem:

Speedy ran marathons in the past
Such a shame, always last
Now Speedy is a big star
After he bought a racing car.

Bought ____/____/____ for $_____.

'97	'98
$5	25

Issued: 6/15/96 ❶ ❺

SPIKE™

GBTru: $5 no change   Item #: 4060

Status: Current

Description: Grey rhinoceros with dark brown horn.

Birthday: 8/13/96

Poem:

Spike the rhino loves to stampede
He's the bruiser that you need
Gentle to birds on his back and spike
You can be his friend if you like!

Bought ____/____/____ for $_____.

'97	'98
$5	5

Issued: 10/1/97 ❶ ❺

SPINNER™

GBTru: $5 no change   Item #: 4036

Status: Current

Description: Spider with black head and legs and gold and black striped body.

Birthday: 10/28/96

Poem:

Does this spider make you scared?
Among many people that feeling is shared
Remember spiders have feelings too
In fact, this spider really likes you!

Bought ____/____/____ for $_____.

'98
$5

S is for Splash...

SPLASH™

GBTru: $120 ↑ 85%   Item #: 4022

'97	'98
$30	65

Issued: 1/8/94 ♥ ❷ ❸ ❹
Status: Retired 5/11/97
Description: Black and white orca whale. One of the "Original 9."
Birthday: 7/8/93
Poem:

Maybe it's because she sprained a limb
But Splash never learned how to swim
I'm sure Splash is happy that you caught her
Just be carefully not to leave her under water.

Alternate Poem:

Splash loves to jump and dive
He's the fastest whale alive
He always wins the 100 yard dash
With a victory jump he'll make a splash!

Bought ___/___/___ for $_____.

SPOOK™

GBTru: $400 ↑ 167%   Item #: 4090

'98
$150

Issued: 1995 ❸
Status: Retired 12/31/97
Description: White ghost with orange ribbon, stitched on smile and glued on red mouth. The original "Spooky." Spook has a #3 Swing Tag with the name "Spook."
Birthday: unknown
Poem: None.

Bought ___/___/___ for $_____.

S is for Spooky...

SPOOKY™

Issued: 9/1/95 🛡️ 🛡️ 🛡️

Status: Retired 12/31/97

Description: White ghost with orange ribbon, stitched on smile and glued on red mouth. Successor to "Spook." Exists with 3 different mouth styles. Black thread smile in V-shape, full-smile and half-smile.

Birthday: 10/31/95

Poem: Ghosts can be a scary sight
But don't let Spooky bring you any fright
Because when you're alone, you will see
The best friend that Spooky can be!

Bought ___/___/___ for $_____.

GBTru: $50 ↑ 25%   Item #: 4090

'97	'98
$5	40

SPOT™ VERSION 1

Issued: 1/8/94 🛡️ 🛡️

Status: Retired 10/1/97

Description: White dog with black tail and ears. One of the "Original 9." Version 1: No spot on back. Change to Version 2 on 4/13/94.

Birthday: unknown

Poem: None.

Bought ___/___/___ for $_____.

GBTru: $2100 ↑ 50%   Item #: 4000

'97	'98
$1800	1400

SPOT™ VERSION 2

Issued: 4/13/94 🛡️ 🛡️ 🛡️

Status: Retired 10/1/97

Description: White dog with black tail and ears. One of the "Original 9." Version 2: Black spot on back.

Birthday: 1/3/93

Poem:
See Spot sprint, see Spot run
You and Spot can have lots of fun
Watch out now, because he's not slow
Just stand back and watch him go!

Bought ___/___/___ for $_____.

GBTru: $55 ↑ 57%   Item #: 4000

'97	'98
$5	35

S is for Spunky...

SPUNKY™

GBTru: $5 no change   Item #: 4184

'98
$5

Issued: 12/31/97 🛡

Status: Current

Description: Fawn colored Cocker Spaniel with long-haired faux fur ears.

Birthday: 1/14/97

Poem:

Bouncing around without much grace
To jump on your lap and lick your face
But watch him closely, he has no fears
He'll run so fast, he'll trip over his ears!

Bought ___/___/___ for $_____.

SQUEALER™

GBTru: $30 ↑ 500%   Item #: 4005

'97   '98
$5   5

Issued: 1/8/94 🛡 🛡 🛡 🛡 🛡

Status: Retired 5/1/98

Description: Pink pig with dark pink snout, ears and tail. One of the "Original 9."

Birthday: 4/23/93

Poem:

Squealer likes to joke around
He is known as class clown
Listen to his stories for a while
There is no doubt he will make you smile!

Bought ___/___/___ for $_____.

STEG™

GBTru: $900 ↑ 125%   Item #: 4087

'97   '98
$225   400

Issued: 6/3/95 🛡

Status: Retired 6/15/96

Description: Dinosaur. Brown tie-dyed Stegosaurus.

Birthday: unknown

Poem: None.

Bought ___/___/___ for $_____.

S is for Sting...

STING™

Issued: 6/3/95

Status: Retired 1/1/97

Description: Blue-grey tie-dyed manta ray.

Birthday: 8/27/95

Poem:
I'm a manta ray and my name is Sting
I'm quite unusual and this is the thing
Under the water I glide like a bird
Have you ever seen something so absurd?

GBTru: $175 ↑ 75%   Item #: 4077

'97	'98
$50	100

Bought ___/___/___ for $_____.

STINGER™

Issued: 5/30/98

Status: Current

Description: Shiny, velvety brown fabric scorpion with black button eyes and curly stinger/tail.

Birthday: 9/29/97

Poem:
Stinger the scorpion will run and dart
But this little fellow is really all heart
So if you see him don't run away
Say hello and ask him to play!

GBTru: $5   Item #: 4193

Bought ___/___/___ for $_____.

STINKY™

Issued: 6/3/95

Status: Current

Description: Black and white skunk.

Birthday: 2/13/95

Poem:
Deep in the woods he lived in a cave
Perfume and mints were the gifts he gave
He showered every night in the kitchen sink
Hoping one day he wouldn't stink!

GBTru: $5 no change   Item #: 4017

'97	'98
$5	5

Bought ___/___/___ for $_____.

S is for Stretch...

STRETCH™

GBTru: $5 no change   Item #: 4182

'98
$5

Issued: 12/31/97 🛡
Status: Current
Description: Ostrich has a ruff of feathery fabric at base of neck. Head and feet are beige and the body and wings are brown and ecru.
Birthday: 9/21/97
Poem:
She thinks when her head is underground
The rest of her body can't be found
The Beanie Babies think it's absurd
To play hide and seek with this bird!

Bought ___/___/___ for $_____.

STRIPES™ VERSION 1

GBTru: $1200 ↑ 167%   Item #: 4065

'97   '98
$400   450

Issued: 1/7/96 🛡
Status: Retired 5/1/98
Description: Gold and black tiger. Version 1: "Fuzzy Belly." Dark gold background and wide black stripes close together, different "fuzzier" fabric used on the underside. (Has B&W tush tag.)
Birthday: unknown
Poem: None.

Bought ___/___/___ for $_____.

STRIPES™ VERSION 2

GBTru: $500 ↑ 150%   Item #: 4065

'97   '98
$250   200

Issued: 1996 🛡
Status: Retired 5/1/98
Description: Gold and black tiger. Version 2: Dark gold background with wide black stripes placed farther apart. (Has R&W tush tag.) Change to Version 3 on 6/3/96.
Birthday: unknown
Poem: None.

Bought ___/___/___ for $_____.

S is for Stripes...

STRIPES™ VERSION 3

Issued: 6/3/96 🛡 🛡
Status: Retired 5/1/98
Description: Tiger. Version 3: Color change to light gold or yellow or tan fabric with fewer narrow black stripes.
Birthday: 6/11/95
Poem:

Stripes was never fierce nor strong
So with tigers, he didn't get along
Jungle life was hard to get by
So he came to his friends at Ty.

Bought ___/___/___ for $_____.

GBTru: $15 ↑ 200%   **Item #: 4065**

'97	'98
$5	5

STRUT™

Issued: 7/12/97 🛡 🛡
Status: Current
Description: Rooster. Red crest, wings and tail on multicolored reds, pinks and yellows tie-dyed body. Replacement for "Doodle." See page 30.
Birthday: 3/8/96
Poem:

Listen closely to "Cock-a-doodle-doo"
What's the rooster saying to you?
Hurry, wake up sleepy head
We have lots to do, get out of bed!

Bought ___/___/___ for $_____.

GBTru: $5 no change   **Item #: 4171**

'98
$5

TABASCO™

Issued: 6/3/95 🛡 🛡
Status: Retired 1/1/97
Description: Red bull with white nose. Reintroduced as Snort with small changes. See Snort on page 66.
Birthday: 5/15/95
Poem:

Although Tabasco is not so tall
He loves to play basketball
He is a star player in his dream
Can you guess his favorite team?

Bought ___/___/___ for $_____.

GBTru: $185 ↓ 5%   **Item #: 4002**

'97	'98
$200	195

T is for Tank...

TANK™ VERSION 1

GBTru: $260 ↑ 73%   **Item #: 4031**

'97   **'98**
$100   150

Issued: 1/7/95 🛡
Status: Retired 10/1/97
Description: Grey armadillo.
Version 1: Greater bean fill and 7
plated shell lines. No shell.
Birthday: unknown
Poem: None.

Bought ___/___/___ for $_____.

TANK™ VERSION 2

GBTru: $350 ↑ 19%   **Item #: 4031**

'97   **'98**
$150   295

Issued: 1996 🛡 🛡
Status: Retired 10/1/97
Description: Grey armadillo.
Version 2: Less bean fill and 9
plated shell lines. Still no shell.
Change to Version 3 on 1/7/96.
Birthday: 2/22/95
Poem:
This armadillo lives in the South
Shoving Tex-Mex in his mouth
He sure loves it south of the border
Keeping his friends in good order!

Bought ___/___/___ for $_____.

TANK™ VERSION 3

GBTru: $80 ↑ 60%   **Item #: 4031**

'97   **'98**
$5   50

Issued: 1/7/96 🛡
Status: Retired 10/1/97
Description: Grey armadillo.
Version 3: Smaller body with 7 or
9 plated shell lines and shell.
Birthday: 2/22/95
Poem:
This armadillo lives in the South
Shoving Tex-Mex in his mouth
He sure loves it south of the border
Keeping his friends in good order!

Bought ___/___/___ for $_____.

T is for Teddy...

Issued: 6/25/94

Status: Retired 10/1/97

Description: Brown teddy bear. Old pointed face, eyes set wide apart and small nose. Change to New Face on 1/7/95.

Birthday: unknown

Poem: None.

TEDDY™ BROWN OLD FACE

GBTru: $3075 ↑ 156%   Item #: 4050

'97	'98
$400	1200

Bought ___/___/___ for $_____.

Issued: 1/7/95

Status: Retired 10/1/97

Description: Brown teddy bear. New round face, with eyes set closer together, burgundy neck ribbon.

Birthday: 11/28/95

Poem:

Teddy wanted to go out today
All his friends went out to play
But he'd rather help whatever you do
After all, his best friend is you!

TEDDY™ BROWN NEW FACE

GBTru: $85 ↑ 70%   Item #: 4050

'97	'98
$5	50

Bought ___/___/___ for $_____.

Sometimes you have to put the unusual side-by-side with the normal to figure out what's different.

Photo courtesy of Lana from Warsaw, IN.

T is for Teddy...

TEDDY™ CRANBERRY
OLD FACE

GBTru: $2200 ↑ 144% Item #: 4052

'97   **'98**
$300   900

Issued: 6/25/94 🧡 ❷
Status: Retired 1/7/96
Description: Cranberry teddy bear.
Old pointed face, eyes set wide
apart and small nose. Change to
New Face on 1/7/95.
Birthday: unknown
Poem: None.

Bought ___/___/___ for $_____.

TEDDY™ CRANBERRY
NEW FACE

GBTru: $1960 ↑ 106% Item #: 4052

'97   **'98**
$400   950

Issued: 1/7/95 ❷ ❸
Status: Retired 1/7/96
Description: Cranberry teddy bear.
New round face, with eyes set
closer together, green neck ribbon.
Birthday: unknown
Poem: None.

Bought ___/___/___ for $_____.

TEDDY™ JADE
OLD FACE

GBTru: $2100 ↑ 147% Item #: 4057

'97   **'98**
$275   850

Issued: 6/25/94 🧡 ❷
Status: Retired 1/7/96
Description: Dark green teddy bear.
Old pointed face, eyes set wide
apart and small nose. Change to
New Face on 1/7/95.
Birthday: unknown
Poem: None.

Bought ___/___/___ for $_____.

T is for Teddy...

Issued: 1/7/95

Status: Retired 1/7/96

Description: Dark green teddy bear. New round face, with eyes set closer together, maroon neck ribbon.

Birthday: unknown

Poem: None.

TEDDY™ JADE
NEW FACE

GBTru: $1900 ↑ 111%   Item #: 4057

'97	'98
$325	900

Bought ___/___/___ for $_____.

Issued: 6/25/94

Status: Retired 1/7/96

Description: Magenta teddy bear. Old pointed face, eyes set wide apart and small nose. Change to New Face on 1/7/95.

Birthday: unknown

Poem: None.

TEDDY™ MAGENTA
OLD FACE

GBTru: $2075 ↑ 131%   Item #: 4056

'97	'98
$400	900

Bought ___/___/___ for $_____.

Issued: 1/7/95

Status: Retired 1/7/96

Description: Magenta teddy bear. New round face, with eyes set closer together, pink neck ribbon.

Birthday: unknown

Poem: None.

TEDDY™ MAGENTA
NEW FACE

GBTru: $1900 ↑ 100%   Item #: 4056

'97	'98
$600	950

Bought ___/___/___ for $_____.

T is for Teddy...

TEDDY™ TEAL
OLD FACE

GBTru: $2100 ↑ 133%   Item #: 4051

'97   '98
$400   900

Issued: 6/25/94 💔 💙
Status: Retired 1/7/96
Description: Green teddy bear. Old pointed face, eyes set wide apart and small nose. Change to New Face on 1/7/95.
Birthday: unknown
Poem: None.

Bought ___/___/___ for $_____.

TEDDY™ TEAL
NEW FACE

GBTru: $2100 ↑ 91%   Item #: 4051

'97   '98
$600   1100

Issued: 1/7/95 💙 💚
Status: Retired 1/7/96
Description: Green teddy bear. New round face, with eyes closer together, blue neck ribbon.
Birthday: unknown
Poem: None.

Bought ___/___/___ for $_____.

TEDDY™ VIOLET
OLD FACE

GBTru: $2100 ↑ 110%   Item #: 4055

'97   '98
$400   1000

Issued: 6/25/94 💔 💙
Status: Retired 1/7/96
Description: Violet teddy bear. Old pointed face, eyes set wide apart and small nose. Change to New Face on 1/7/95.
Birthday: unknown
Poem: None.

Bought ___/___/___ for $_____.

Issued: 1/7/95 ❷ ❸

Status: Retired 1/7/96

Description: Violet teddy bear. New round face, with eyes closer together, green neck ribbon.

Birthday: unknown

Poem: None.

TEDDY™ VIOLET NEW FACE

GBTru: $2100 ↑ 91%   Item #: 4055

'97   '98
$650 1100

Bought ___/___/___ for $_____.

Status: Exclusive

Description: Employee gift at Christmas party. New Face Violet Bear with either green or red satin ribbon. No Swing Tag. R&W tush tag with no name.

Birthday: unknown

Poem: None.

TEDDY™ VIOLET NEW FACE EMPLOYEE EDITION

GBTru: $2500/each no change

'98
$2500

Bought ___/___/___ for $_____.

Issued: 5/30/98 ❺

Status: Current

Description: Cream basset hound with brown ears, eye patches and back.

Birthday: 6/5/97

Poem:

Sniffing and tracking and following trails
Tracker the basset always wags his tail
It doesn't matter what you do
He's always happy when he's with you!

TRACKER™

GBTru: $5   Item #: 4198

Bought ___/___/___ for $_____.

T is for Trap...

TRAP™

GBTru: $1400 ↑ 100%   Item #: 4042

'97	'98
$350	700

Issued: 6/25/94 🛡️ 🛡️ 🛡️
Status: Retired 6/15/95
Description: Grey mouse with pink tail, feet, nose and inner ears. Eyes and whiskers are black.
Birthday: unknown
Poem: None.

Bought ___/___/___ for $_____.

TUFFY™

GBTru: $5 no change   Item #: 4108

'97	'98
$5	5

Issued: 5/11/97 🛡️ 🛡️
Status: Current
Description: Terrier. Dark and light brown pup. Curly-textured fabric.
Birthday: 10/12/96
Poem:
Taking off with a thunderous blast
Tuffy rides his motorcycle fast
The Beanies roll with laughs & squeals
He never took off his training wheels!

Bought ___/___/___ for $_____.

TUSK™

GBTru: $170 ↑ 240%   Item #: 4076

'97	'98
$50	50

Issued: 1/7/95 🛡️ 🛡️
Status: Retired 1/1/97
Description: Brown walrus with white tusks. Small quantity found with misprint 'Tuck' tush tag; GBTru is $175. Some early pieces had upturned tusks.
Birthday: 9/18/95
Poem:
Tusk brushes his teeth everyday
To keep them shiny, it's the only way
Teeth are special, so you must try
And they will sparkle when you say "Hi"!

Bought ___/___/___ for $_____.

TWIGS™

Issued: 1/7/96

Status: Retired 5/1/98

Description: Yellow and orange spotted giraffe with brown feet and mane. Also available as a Teenie Beanie Baby.

Birthday: 5/19/95

Poem:

Twigs has his head in the clouds
He stands tall, he stands proud
With legs so skinny they wobble and shake
What an unusual friend he will make!

Bought ___/___/___ for $_____.

GBTru: $15 ↑ 200%   Item #: 4068

'97	'98
$5	5

VALENTINO™

Issued: 1/7/95

Status: Current

Description: White teddy bear has red embroidered heart on chest. Note Valentine Birthday.

Birthday: 2/14/94

Poem:

His heart is red and full of love
He cares for you so give him a hug
Keep him close when feeling blue
Feel the love he has for you!

Bought ___/___/___ for $_____.

GBTru: $5 no change   Item #: 4058

'97	'98
$5	5

VELVET™

Issued: 6/3/95

Status: Retired 10/1/97

Description: Black panther.

Birthday: 12/16/95

Poem:

Velvet loves to sleep in the trees
Lulled to dreams by the bees
She snoozes all day and plays all night
Running and jumping in the moonlight!

Bought ___/___/___ for $_____.

GBTru: $30 ↑ 50%   Item #: 4064

'97	'98
$5	20

W is for Waddle...

WADDLE™

GBTru: $15 ↑ 200%   Item #: 4075

'97   **'98**
$5   5

Issued: 6/3/95 ③ ④ ⑤
Status: Retired 5/1/98
Description: Black and white penguin. Also available as a Teenie Beanie Baby.
Birthday: 12/19/95
Poem:
Waddle the penguin likes to dress up
Every night he wears his tux
When Waddle walks, it never fails
He always trips over his tails!

Bought ___/___/___ for $_____.

WAVES™

GBTru: $15 ↑ 200%   Item #: 4084

'97   **'98**
$5   5

Issued: 5/11/97 ④ ⑤
Status: Retired 5/1/98
Description: Whale. Black with white underbelly. Echo and Waves were originally shipped with each others swing tag and tush tag. GBTru for Waves with an Echo tag is $30.00.
Birthday: 12/8/96
Poem: Join him today on the Internet
Don't be afraid to get your feet wet
He taught all the Beanies how to surf
Our web page is his home turf!

Bought ___/___/___ for $_____.

WEB™

GBTru: $1525 ↑ 103%   Item #: 4041

'97   **'98**
$350   750

Issued: 6/25/94 ① ② ③
Status: Retired 1/7/96
Description: Black spider with red belly.
Birthday: unknown
Poem: None.

Bought ___/___/___ for $_____.

WEENIE™

Issued: 1/7/96 💙 💜 💚

Status: Retired 5/1/98

Description: Brown Dachshund.

Birthday: 7/20/95

Poem:

Weenie the dog is quite a sight
Long of body and short of height
He perches himself high on a log
And considers himself to be top dog!

GBTru: $20 ↑ 300%   Item

'97 '98
$5   5

Bought ____/____/____ for $_____.

WHISPER™

Issued: 5/30/98 💚

Status: Current

Description: Brown fawn with white spots; white belly and inner ears; dark brown hooves.

Birthday: 4/5/97

Poem:

She's very shy as you can see
When she hides behind a tree
With big brown eyes and soft to touch
This little fawn will love you so much!

GBTru: $5   Item #: 4194

Bought ____/____/____ for $_____.

WISE™

Issued: 5/30/98 💚

Status: Current

Description: Brown tie-dyed owl wearing mortarboard which reads "Class of '98."

Birthday: 5/31/97

Poem:

Wise is at the head of the class
With A's and B's he'll always pass
He's got his diploma and feels really great
Meet the newest graduate: Class of 98!

GBTru: $5   Item #: 4187

Bought ____/____/____ for $_____.

WRINKLES™

GBTru: $5 no change   Item #: 4103

'97   **'98**
$5   5

Issued: 6/15/96

Status: Current

Description: Tan and white Old English Bull dog.

Birthday: 5/1/96

Poem:

This little dog is named Wrinkles
His nose is soft and often crinkles
Likes to climb up on your lap
He's a cheery sort of chap!

Bought ___/___/___ for $_____.

ZIGGY™

GBTru: $17 ↑ 240%   Item #: 4063

'97   **'98**
$5   5

Issued: 6/3/95

Status: Retired 5/1/98

Description: Black and white zebra.

Birthday: 12/24/95

Poem:

Ziggy likes soccer—he's a referee
That way he watches the games for free
The other Beanies don't think it's fair
But Ziggy the zebra doesn't care.

Bought ___/___/___ for $_____.

Jabber by Ally

Inch by Jessie

Z is for Zip...

ZIP™ VERSION 1

Issued: 1/7/95 🛡️ 🛡️ 🛡️

Status: Retired 5/1/98

Description: Black cat. Version 1: Larger black body with white triangle on face and <u>white belly</u>. Pink ears, nose and whiskers. Change to Version 2 on 1/7/96.

Birthday: unknown

Poem: None.

GBTru: $535 ↑ 53%   Item #: 4004

'97	'98
$300	350

Bought ___/___/___ for $_____.

ZIP™ VERSION 2

Issued: 1/7/96 🛡️

Status: Retired 5/1/98

Description: Black cat. Version 2: Smaller, <u>all black body</u>. Pink ears and whiskers. Change to Version 3 on 3/10/96.

Birthday: unknown

Poem: None.

GBTru: $1875 ↑ 34%   Item #: 4004

'97	'98
$1400	1400

Bought ___/___/___ for $_____.

ZIP™ VERSION 3

Issued: 3/10/96 🛡️ 🛡️ 🛡️

Status: Retired 5/1/98

Description: Black cat. Version 3: Smaller black body with <u>white paws</u>. White ears and whiskers, pink nose. Also available as a Teenie Beanie Baby.

Birthday: 3/28/94

Poem:
Keep Zip by your side all the day through
Zip is good luck, you'll see it's true
When you have something you need to do
Zip will always believe in you!

GBTru: $50 ↑ 900%   Item #: 4004

'97	'98
$5	5

Bought ___/___/___ for $_____.

McDonald's Teenie Beanies

In April of 1997, McDonald's began what was to be a 5-week Happy Meal promotion with two different Teenie Beanie designs offered each week. Despite production of 100 million Teenie Beanies, demand far exceeded supply and, in many places around the country, restaurants sold out of the entire five week supply in just 3 days!

Group 1 (G1), April, 1997

Fast forward to May 22, 1998 for the return of McDonald's most successful promotion in history. This time twelve Teenies (up from ten last year) were to be given out, three per week, over a four week period, May 22 through June 18. As with the previous year, restaurants were depleted of their entire 4 week supply in a matter of days as Moms, Dads and Grandparents went from store to store keeping checklists of what locations were on which Beanie!

Group 2 (G2), May, 1998

Teenie Beanies are also referred to as "McBeanies" and "TBB's."

Teenie Beanies are about 1/3 the size of regular Beanies and have a single heart swing tag that does not open. Because the toys are for children of all ages, for safety, they have embroidered eyes, nose...

The Item # appears on the plastic bag they are packaged in, but not on the swing tag or tush tag. A Teenie Beanie Baby is considered mint only if it is in its original unopened bag.

BONES™ (TBB)

GBTru: $8   **Item #:** G2 - #09

Issued: 5/98
Status: McDonald's Promotion
Description: Brown dog with dark brown ears.
Birthday: unknown
Poem: None.

Bought ___ / ___ / ___ for $_____

BONGO™ (TBB)

Issued: 5/98

Status: McDonald's Promotion

Description: Brown monkey with tan paws and face.

Birthday: unknown

Poem: None.

GBTru: $15   Item #: G2 - #02

Bought ___/___/___   for $_____ .

CHOCOLATE™ (TBB)

Issued: 4/97

Status: Happy Meal Promotion

Description: Brown moose with orange antlers.

Birthday: unknown

Poem: None.

GBTru: $27 ↑ 125%   Item #: G1 - #4

'97	'98
$10	12

Bought ___/___/___   for $_____ .

CHOPS™ (TBB)

Issued: 4/97

Status: Happy Meal Promotion

Description: Cream lamb with black face and inner ears.

Birthday: unknown

Poem: None.

GBTru: $30 ↑ 100%   Item #: G1 - #3

'97	'98
$12	15

Bought ___/___/___   for $_____ .

Teenie Beanies...

DOBY™ (TBB)

GBTru: $15 Item #: G2 - #01

Issued: 5/98
Status: McDonald's Promotion
Description: Brown and black Doberman dog.
Birthday: unknown
Poem: None.

Bought ___/___/___ for $_____.

GOLDIE™ (TBB)

GBTru: $22 ↑ 175% Item #: G1 - #5

'97	'98
$8	8

Issued: 4/97
Status: Happy Meal Promotion
Description: Goldfish.
Birthday: unknown
Poem: None.

Bought ___/___/___ for $_____.

HAPPY™ (TBB)

GBTru: $6 Item #: G2 - #06

Issued: 5/98
Status: McDonald's Promotion
Description: Lavender hippo.
Birthday: unknown
Poem: None.

Bought ___/___/___ for $_____.

INCH™ (TBB)

GBTru: $10   **Item #:** G2 - #04

Issued: 5/98
Status: McDonald's Promotion
Description: Rainbow-colored inch-worm with black antennae.
Birthday: unknown
Poem: None.

Bought ___ / ___ / ___   for $_____.

LIZZ™ (TBB)

GBTru: $20 ↑ 67%   **Item #:** G1 - #10

Issued: 4/97
Status: Happy Meal Promotion
Description: Lizard with blue back covered with black spots, yellow belly.
Birthday: unknown
Poem: None.

'97	'98
$12	12

Bought ___ / ___ / ___   for $_____.

MEL™ (TBB)

GBTru: $6   **Item #:** G2 - #07

Issued: 5/98
Status: McDonald's Promotion
Description: Grey koala with white inner ears and belly.
Birthday: unknown
Poem: None.

Bought ___ / ___ / ___   for $_____.

Teenie Beanies...

PATTI™ (TBB)

GBTru: $35 ↑ 75%   Item #: G1 - #1

'97   **'98**
$14   20

Issued: 4/97
Status: Happy Meal Promotion
Description: Purple platypus.
Birthday: unknown
Poem: None.

Bought ___/___/___ for $_____.

PEANUT™ (TBB)

GBTru: $8   Item #: G2 - #12

Issued: 5/98
Status: McDonald's Promotion
Description: Light blue elephant
with pink inner ears.
Birthday: unknown
Poem: None.

Bought ___/___/___ for $_____.

PINCHERS™ (TBB)

GBTru: $6   Item #: G2 - #05

Issued: 5/98
Status: McDonald's Promotion
Description: Red lobster.
Birthday: unknown
Poem: None.

Bought ___/___/___ for $_____.

90

PINKY™ (TBB)

Issued: 4/97
Status: Happy Meal Promotion
Description: Bright pink flamingo with light pink dangling legs and orange beak.
Birthday: unknown
Poem: None.

GBTru: $35 ↑ 40%   Item #: G1 - #2

'97	'98
$16	25

Bought ___ / ___ / ___ for $_____.

QUACKS™ (TBB)

Issued: 4/97
Status: Happy Meal Promotion
Description: Yellow duck.
Birthday: unknown
Poem: None.

GBTru: $15 ↑ 88%   Item #: G1 - #9

'97	'98
$8	8

Bought ___ / ___ / ___ for $_____.

SCOOP™ (TBB)

Issued: 5/98
Status: McDonald's Promotion
Description: Grey pelican with bright orange bill and feet.
Birthday: unknown
Poem: None.

GBTru: $6   Item #: G2 - #08

Bought ___ / ___ / ___ for $_____.

SEAMORE™ (TBB)

GBTru: $25 ↑ 150%   **Item #: G1 - #7**

'97	'98
$8	10

Issued: 4/97
Status: Happy Meal Promotion
Description: White seal.
Birthday: unknown
Poem: None.

Bought ___ / ___ / ___   for $_____.

SNORT™ (TBB)

GBTru: $15 ↑ 25%   **Item #: G1 - #8**

'97	'98
$12	12

Issued: 4/97
Status: Happy Meal Promotion
Description: Red bull.
Birthday: unknown
Poem: None.

Bought ___ / ___ / ___   for $_____.

SPEEDY™ (TBB)

GBTru: $22 ↑ 175%   **Item #: G1 - #6**

'97	'98
$8	8

Issued: 4/97
Status: Happy Meal Promotion
Description: Bright green turtle with "shell" fabric on his back.
Birthday: unknown
Poem: None.

Bought ___ / ___ / ___   for $_____.

TWIGS™ (TBB)

Issued: 5/98
Status: McDonald's Promotion
Description: Yellow and orange spotted giraffe with brown feet and mane.
Birthday: unknown
Poem: None.

GBTru: $10   Item #: G2 - #03

Bought ___/___/___ for $_____.

WADDLE™ (TBB)

Issued: 5/98
Status: McDonald's Promotion
Description: Black and white penguin.
Birthday: unknown
Poem: None.

GBTru: $30   Item #: G2 - #11

Bought ___/___/___ for $_____.

ZIP™ (TBB)

Issued: 5/98
Status: McDonald's Promotion
Description: Black cat.
Birthday: unknown
Poem: None.

GBTru: $10   Item #: G2 - #10

Bought ___/___/___ for $_____.

Item# Index

94

Picture Gallery Index

95

Picture Gallery Index

Picture Gallery Index

97

Picture Gallery Index

98

Picture Gallery Index

Picture Gallery Index

Picture Gallery Index

101

Picture Gallery Index

Picture Gallery Index

103

Quite simply, our genuine

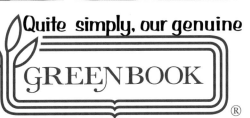

GREENBOOK

®

Collectible Guides & GREENWARE Software CDs stack up as the best secondary market information available. For more than a decade, we've been looking out for the collector's needs.

GREENBOOK® Inventory Software for Ty® Beanie Babies™

GREENBOOK® Inventory Software for Department 56® Villages

The Second Original GREENBOOK Guide to Ty® Beanie Babies™

7th Greenbook® Guide To Department 56® Villages

THE SECOND GREENBOOK GUIDE TO THE WALT DISNEY CLASSICS COLLECTION

The Second GREENBOOK Guide to Priscilla Hillman's CHERISHED TEDDIES® COLLECTION by Enesco

1998 GREENBOOK® GUIDE to Precious Moments® by Enesco

SIXTH GREENBOOK GUIDE TO DEPARTMENT 56® VILLAGES

Department Published Annually, Midsummer GREENBOOK

FIRST GREENBOOK GUIDE DEVOTED EXCLUSIVELY TO HALLMARK COLLECTIBLES

The Second Original GREENBOOK Guide to Ty® Beanie Babies™

GREENBOOK Guide To Ornaments Second Edition

The Third GREENBOOK GUIDE to Priscilla Hillman's CHERISHED TEDDIES® COLLECTION by Enesco

1997-1998 GREENBOOK GUIDE TO HALLMARK KEEPSAKE ORNAMENTS

PREMIERE GREENBOOK GUIDE TO DEPARTMENT 56 COLLECTIBLES
SNOWBABIES • SNOWBUNNIES • WINTER SILHOUETTE • ALL THROUGH THE HOUSE • UPSTAIRS DOWNSTAIRS BEARS
MERCURY GLASS ORNAMENTS • CCP'S • WATERGLOBES • VILLAGE RELATED ORNAMENTS AND MUCH, MUCH MORE!

Tenth Anniversary GREENBOOK GUIDE™ to The Enesco Precious Moments™ Collection

The Fifth GREENBOOK Guide to DEPARTMENT 56 VILLAGES GREENBOOK

COLLECTIONS WITHIN
THE ENESCO PRECIOUS MOMENTS COLLECTION GREENBOOK

GREENBOOK Guide To Department 56 First Edition

Available at fine gift and collectible stores nationwide. We invite you to visit our website

www.greenbooks.com

© 1998 GREENBOOK P.O. Box 645, Pacific Grove, CA 93950
(408)656-9000